ules' earliest known declaration that she planned to be a riter came at the age of ten.

Along the way she was diverted by the glamorous world f PR and worked on many luxury brands, taking journalists on press trips to awful places like Turin, Milan, Geneva, Paris, Brussels and Amsterdam and occasionally losing the odd member of the press in an airport. It gave her the opportunity to eat amazing food, drink free alcohol as well as providing opportunities to hone her writing skills on press releases and to research European cities for her books.

Eventually the voices in her head persuaded her it was time to sit down and write the novel she'd always talked about. Her debut novel, *Talk to Me* in 2014, was quickly followed by the best selling *From Italy With Love*, published by HarperImpulse which reached the top ten in the Amazon Kindle charts. This was followed by *From Paris With Love This Christmas* and more recently, the best-selling *Escape to the Riviera* published by Avon in June this year.

@juleswake
www.facebook.com/juleswake.co.uk
www.juleswake.co.uk

Also by Jules Wake

From Italy with Love
From Paris with Love This Christmas
Escape to the Riviera

Jules Wake

From Rome With Love

A division of HarperCollins*Publishers*
www.harpercollins.co.uk

Harper*Impulse* an imprint of
HarperCollins*Publishers*
1 London Bridge Street
London SE1 9GF

www.harpercollins.co.uk

A Paperback Original 2017
1

Jules Wake asserts the moral right to
be identified as the author of this work

A catalogue record for this book
is available from the British Library

ISBN: 9780008221959

Set in Birka by Palimpsest Book Production Limited,
Falkirk, Stirlingshire

Printed and bound in Great Britain

For Tina Mundy,
who understands the important things in life.

Acknowledgements

For all the lovely readers who were so keen to find out what happened to Will and Lisa and for those who wanted to see more of Laurie and Cam – this is for you.

Thanks go to my office besties, Gordana Sikora and Alison Head who are endlessly supportive, and put up with me muttering, from the desk at the back, about the imaginary people in my head, edits and deadlines.

The apartment where Lisa and Will stay is based on a wonderful house which really is built within the arch of an ancient aqueduct. It's situated in the grounds of the British Ambassador's residence, the Villa Wolkonsky, where I was lucky enough to stay as a guest of the wonderful Briscoe family, Neil, Olivia, Theo and Minna, who were posted there at the time. They were fabulous hosts and gave a real insight into life in the Eternal City, particularly the importance of not ordering Cappuccino after eleven!

And a special thank you to the brilliant team at HarperImpulse, especially editor extraordinaire, Charlotte Ledger, Special Agent, Broo Doherty and my Prosecco partner, writing buddy and ace friend, Donna Ashcroft. Last but not least, an enormous thank you to the lovely Lisa for letting me use her name.

Chapter 1

'Nan, what are you doing?'

Lisa stepped over a pile of tablecloths and linens covering the living-room floor of her Nan's tiny lounge. She lived a couple of streets away and Lisa popped around most days after work for a cup of tea – not that Nan ever seemed particularly grateful, although she was quick to complain if Lisa missed a day.

'What do you think I'm doing? Inviting the Queen to tea?' She bustled by, a miniature dynamo rustling a large black dustbin bag in her hand. At four-foot nothing, with a face concertinaed by time, she looked as if she'd shrunk, leaving her skin two sizes too big. 'I'm having a sort-out.'

'Again.' Lisa shook her head in dismay, looking at the piles of mismatched napkins, lace doilies and faded pillowcases, most of which she'd never seen before.

'When am I ever going to use this lot? Load of old rubbish, cluttering up the place, attracting a shedload of moths. There's a hole in my cardigan.' Nan didn't say the words but Lisa knew the thinking behind the latest clear-out. 'I'm not getting any younger.'

'Nan, there's years left in you.' Her grandmother was an indomitable force of nature. Pushing eighty-five and as sharp as they came. She had all her marbles, and then some.

'That's as maybe, but I don't need all this tat.' Her mouth wrinkled, prune-like, in derision. 'It'll save you the job when I'm dead and gone.'

'I hate it when you say things like that.'

'Don't be daft. Now give us a hand with that box over there.'

'You never brought that down from the loft on your own?' asked Lisa incredulously.

'Course I did. Who else? You think Superman popped by?' Her nan shook her head in amused disgust.

'Where do you want it?'

'I don't want it. I'm chucking it out. There's a load of your granddad's books in there. No good to anyone. But if you want them, help yourself.'

Lisa picked up the ancient cardboard box, resting her chin on the top to keep the uppermost layer of books from slithering precariously on to the floor as she moved it towards the dining table. As she was about to put it down, the bottom gave way and a flood of hard-backed books cascaded to the floor, brittle paper flapping as some of the books collapsed, the pages fluttering out like pigeons released and the hard corners knocking her shins as they landed.

'Now look what you've done,' Nan tsked, sucking on her teeth.

'Don't worry, I'll pick everything up. Don't want you putting your back out, do we?'

'There's nowt wrong with my back, Missy,' retorted Nan, as usual refusing to admit to any weakness or acknowledge her creaking joints. 'But I'll put the kettle on while you tidy up.' She shuffled off to the kitchen, leaving Lisa piling the books on the table. Most of them were ancient, the print so tiny and close together that they were difficult to read and the paper was yellowed and speckled with mildew. None of the titles or authors were any she'd heard of and in this state she couldn't imagine anyone would want them.

As she bent to pick up the last two books, they see-sawed in her hand, separated by a bulky brown envelope that had been sandwiched between them. Although her mother had died when she was seven, Lisa recognised her distinctive rounded handwriting on the front of the envelope immediately. *For Vittorio.* The words had faded, the final *o* almost invisible, but they were underlined with two vivid dark slashes, which Lisa instinctively felt turned them into an instruction.

She frowned and toyed with the envelope, feeling the weight of it in her hand. The name 'Vittorio' conjured up confusing elusive memories that danced away whenever she tried to catch them.

Why did Nan have it? Vittorio, her father – not that he deserved that title – had upped and left a few years before her mother had died. Was this envelope a deathbed request? Lisa didn't remember much about her mother, except that she'd been ill a lot. At the age of seven it was probably kinder not to explain the life-sucking treatments that left her mother wan and listless in a fight against cancer.

Sometimes she remembered, or maybe misremembered,

things about her father. Being carried on his shoulders, pushed high on a swing, riding a carousel pony and him running alongside the merry-go-round, waving all the way, but they didn't tally with what Nan had to say about him. She winced, her back teeth protesting at the sudden tensing of her jaw. What sort of father abandoned a daughter and didn't come back for her even after her mother had died? Well, that was his loss. Thank goodness she'd had Nan.

As she turned the envelope in her hand, the moral question of what right she had to open it became moot as the old gum on the seal yawned open. Two photographs slipped out, or perhaps she'd helped them with an illicit shake. A handsome man in sunglasses laughed up at her, his arm around Lisa's mother, who was heavily pregnant. Lisa studied the picture, a sudden lump blocking her throat. She had so few photos of her mother, because many of them had been lost when the bathroom in Nan's house flooded and the ceiling collapsed in the lounge. Few of the photos had been salvageable and Nan being Nan had chucked them all out. She didn't do sentiment.

And Lisa had no photos of her father at all. She turned it over, looking for confirmation. There it was, *Me and Vittorio, Rome.* She studied the picture, but it wasn't a great shot and with the sunglasses and his face in shadow it was difficult to get much of a feel for what he looked like. Her lip curled. She knew what he was like. Irresponsible. Selfish. Heartless.

In the second picture, blurred and out of focus, the same man was pictured on his own outside a building, which she guessed was somewhere in Italy. She turned it over.

Vittorio & the family home. 32 Via del Mattonato, Rome, 001

'What have you got there?'

Lisa started and almost shoved the envelope behind her back.

'I found this and the envelope.'

Nan peered at the picture.

'Is this…' Lisa stopped. Nan had always refused to talk about him, but maybe this time she would.

She huffed. 'Yes, that's your father. Buggered off and left your poor mum holding the baby. Not that he was missed. We did just fine without him.'

Lisa stared curiously at the picture. It was the first time she'd seen her father. She didn't want to be curious about him. She wanted to be indifferent, the way that he'd been indifferent to her, throughout those years when her six-year-old, eight-year-old, eleven-year-old self secretly believed that one day he would turn up and be her daddy.

'Loved the ladies, that one. A roaming Roman.' Nan sniffed.

'He was from Rome?'

'Of course he was from Rome. He was Roman.'

'And he's much taller than I thought he'd be.' She deliberately kept her voice cool.

'Not all jockeys are midgets. He was very skinny, like your mother. A pair of matchsticks they were.'

Lisa's mother had worked at a local racing stables for the owner, Sir Robert Harding, managing all the admin in the office relating to entering the horses in races, charging the owners stable fees and paying the jockeys, which was where she'd met Vittorio Vettese, one of the stable's full-time jockeys.

Going up to the stables had been a rare treat that Lisa had loved, although she wasn't allowed to very often. Sir Robert's wife had had an accident that had left her in a wheelchair and unable to have children. Lisa's visits tended to be timed for when Lady Mary was away.

'That's where you get those knobbly knees from.' Nan gave another one of her characteristic disdainful sniffs. She had them down to a fine art, conveying a mix of taciturn disapproval and regal superiority.

Lisa glanced down at her legs with a smile at Nan's typical bluntness.

'What's this, then?' Lisa pulled out a small jewellery box and Nan's mouth pursed mollusc-tight, her lips pressed together in a vacuum-like seal.

The black box sat in her palm with all the allure of Pandora's and gave Lisa a misty sense of premonition. Once opened, there was no going back.

Lisa looked at Nan, her thin, stooped frame radiating tension, but she didn't say anything.

As her fingers brushed the lid of the box, out of the corner of her eye she saw her grandmother flinch, but it didn't stop her from prising the lid upwards. It reached that point of no return and popped open.

'Oh!'

The folds of skin on Nan's throat quivered.

With the tip of her finger Lisa touched the ring of tiny pearls, interspersed with equally small rubies encircling a pea-sized diamond, well petit pois, perhaps, but still significant.

'Wow, that's pretty.' And valuable, in her humble and not very informed opinion. At the very least, old. The rich navy velvet inside the box had faded around the edges and the elegant script on the inside satin of the lid spoke of a bygone age.

Nan sniffed again. 'Hmm, belonged to his grandmother, apparently.'

'What, my father's?'

'Yes. He gave it to your mother.' She spat the words out with the unwillingness of a miser parting with pennies. 'When they got engaged.'

'So it was...' Confused, Lisa tried to gauge her Nan's expression, but the gimlet eyes were giving nothing away. 'Mum's engagement ring.'

'I suppose.'

'Oh.' Betrayal and hurt splintered at the same time, making her vision a touch blurry. She had no idea what to say. Why hadn't her grandmother given her the ring? Hadn't her mother wanted her to have it?

'Don't look at me like that,' snapped Nan. 'She wanted it to go back to Vittorio. Said it was a family heirloom and should be returned. She didn't feel right keeping it.'

Ah, so that explained Nan's strange reticence. 'Why didn't you do it, then?'

Nan shrugged. 'Never got round to it.'

Lisa couldn't hide the spark of surprise or the quick instinctive censure she felt at Nan's admission.

'Don't look at me like that, Missy. It wasn't like I had time on my hands. I had you to look after, a job and a house to sort out. There was a lot to do. And then, well, life goes on and I forgot all about it.'

Guilt took the edge off Lisa's disapproval. It can't have been easy for Nan after the death of her only child suddenly having to become stand-in mother to a young, bereaved girl.

Lisa looked at the ring as her grandmother let out an exaggerated sigh. 'And who knows where he is now? It's not like he left a forwarding address.'

'But we shouldn't keep it, not... not if Mum wanted it to go back to him.' Saying the words out loud caused a painful pang. Why hadn't Mum wanted her to have the ring?

'Well, you're more than welcome to try and find the bugger if you want. I'll leave it up to you, but you might as well have it. No good to me.

'Now are you going to take me to Morrisons or not?'

Lisa snapped the ring box closed, putting it and the photos back into the envelope. She knew from the set of her Nan's jaw that the discussion was over. She had no idea what she was going to do with them but she tucked the envelope into her handbag.

'I haven't got all day, you know.'

Lisa bit back a smile at the irony of the words. Nan filled her days crocheting squares for blankets for Africa, tending her dahlias, doing the *Daily Mirror* crossword with almost religious fervour, and gossiping and drinking endless cups of tea with her best friend next door, Laura. A trip to Morrisons inevitably took twice as long as it should because she, oblivious to other shoppers trying to reach around her to pick things off the shelves, insisted on checking every price, tapping away on her calculator, to ensure that she was getting her money's worth.

'You can have any of those tablecloths if you want them, otherwise they can go down to the charity shop. You can drop them off for me. And there's a box of biscuits I found you can have. Left over from one of Sir Robert's Christmas hampers. God knows why he keeps turning up.'

Lisa suspected that with a house-bound wife, fading rapidly in recent months, he was probably rather lonely. He was always quick to accept a cup of tea on his annual visit.

Nan waved the pack of shortbread biscuits at her. 'I can't tell him I give half the stuff away. Too fancy by half.'

Nan didn't do fancy when it came to food. Meat and two veg had been her and Lisa's staple diet for ever.

'Your mother's been gone these past twenty years. Sir Robert's been carrying paternalism too far, in my mind.'

Lisa had always thought the hampers were rather generous, although she was equally relieved that Nan didn't expect either of them to eat some of the weird and wonderful contents.

'Thanks. Are they in date?' Lisa peered at the tiny 'best before' information. 'Those chocolates you gave me last time were two years past their date.'

'Nonsense. That doesn't mean anything.'

Lisa gave an inward shudder. She regularly sorted through Nan's fridge on the quiet. Eating here was a bit like playing 'past-the-sell-by-date Russian roulette'.

She waited as Nan pulled on her outsized mohair coat, which made her look like a baby woolly mammoth and was probably from about the same period in history.

'Don't forget to put them boxes in your car.'

By the time they left, heading towards the superstore on the edge of town, Lisa's car looked like a jumble sale on wheels and the envelope in her bag weighed heavily on her mind.

Chapter 2

It had been a simple plan. Clean and effective. In and out. Finish work, drive to the pub, pick Siena up after her shift, not even have to go into the pub, then drive her home, girls' night in, a few glasses of Prosecco and crash in the spare room.

Lisa kicked the flabby tyre of her loyal but flagging-a-bit-these-days Mini.

'Ouch.' Not so flabby after all.

Not wanting to abandon her car on one of the country lanes, it had limped the last quarter of the mile here. Now safe in the pub car park, she didn't feel quite so helpless.

'Need a hand?' asked a languid voice from behind her.

Lisa closed her eyes and curled her fingers tight into her palms, registering the bite of her fingernails. He wasn't supposed to be here at this time. On Tuesdays, he didn't manage the pub until 7.30. She'd planned it so that she wouldn't have to see him.

Quite how she resisted the overwhelming urge to gnash her teeth or growl out loud, she didn't know. Ninety-nine point nine, nine per cent of her would have loved to tell him to get stuffed, but unfortunately there was a stupid niggly, and practical, nought point one per cent that admitted she probably did need help. While she was prepared to have a go at most things, and had got as far as taking out the flimsy-looking jack, which didn't look as if it were capable of lifting a shoe box let alone a car, those slimy black bolts on the wheel looked completely beyond her.

She gave Will's tall, slim frame a quick glance. Big mistake. It reminded her that his slender build belied a sinewy muscled strength and, under his clothes, the tautest, toned stomach she'd ever seen. The man had abs. Words died in her throat and she stood there, looking like a complete idiot.

'Is that a, "Yes, gosh, Will, thanks that would be super", I hear? Or a "Sod off, I've got this?"' His fake falsetto reminded her exactly why she invested so much effort in avoiding him and his supersized ego and vastly inflated superiority complex.

He'd already approached the rear of her Mini. 'Christ, how old is this thing? You still have a spare?'

With a determined grimace, she ignored him and dropped down by the wheel to manoeuvre the jack underneath the car, inserting the winding handle, as if she had the first clue what she was doing, saying with outward cheer, 'No problem, I've got this. I can always call the AA if it's too much trouble.'

As he hoisted the spare out, he muttered something under his breath which sounded distinctly like 'you're always too much trouble'.

Without saying anything else, he nudged her out of the way.

'Thanks,' she muttered as he set to work, kneeling on the

tarmac, its surface wet from a recent shower, his head down as he started cranking up the car. It had been one of those days where the weather couldn't make up its mind.

'You here to see Siena?'

'Yes,' she answered shortly, glaring down at the stubby blonde ponytail brushing the back of his neck. Grown men shouldn't have surfer-boy hair and it shouldn't be sexy. He wasn't sexy. Or even likeable. But a memory surfaced of that long hair brushing her skin when loose, bringing with it a quick flutter of awareness. The long hair helped create a casual look, when Will was anything but casual, except for his dealings with women.

She shifted her weight from foot to foot and pushed her hands into her pockets. The flutter turned into full-scale butterflies and she froze, praying that none of this was obvious. The butterflies could just sodding well back off and behave. She. Did. Not. Have. Feelings for Will.

With studied nonchalance, she looked around at the rolling green hills surrounding the village nestled in the valley, its line of houses following the ribbon of a stream that flowed down to the River Ouzel. She sighed, the sight soothing her. The pub, despite its ownership, was one of her favourite places. Perched on the edge of the wide green, the sturdy brick-and-timber construction had been in situ for several hundred years, standing guard over the inhabitants with imposing presence.

'You can go in, if you like.' Will had raised the car up. 'Siena's nearly finished her shift.'

Despite being here to see Siena, it didn't seem right to abandon Will in the damp car park when he was doing her a favour, even though he was the last person on the planet that she wanted to spend any time with.

'Do you need any help?' she asked, with a barely concealed sigh. It was difficult to overcome a lifetime's training of good manners.

He gave her an amused look.

Then again...

She turned her back on him and surveyed the quiet car park. In less than an hour, the pub would be buzzing. Whatever other faults he had, and there were a gazillion, Will certainly knew how to run a successful business. People came from miles around to eat here.

'I hear you're opening a new restaurant. That'll be nice.'

With one raised eyebrow, he managed to make her regret opening her mouth.

'I'm just making small talk. It feels a bit bad to abandon you when you're being all chivalrous and fixing my car for me.' She shivered, conscious of a light bite to the air. Summer was taking its time to arrive this year.

'I've been waiting for the right location.'

'Location, location, location,' she said, not that she had any idea about suitable locations. The street where her tiny terraced house was located in the nearby town wasn't about to make it onto any television programmes in the des res stakes.

'It's important, but I finally found the sweetest spot. The old post-office building on the High Street.'

'Really? It looks a bit grot.'

'It won't by the time I've finished.' Will's quiet, confident declaration was no idle boast. When they'd lived in the village as teenagers, the pub had been the haunt of elderly men who nursed one pint over endless dominoes marathons. He'd transformed this place.

'Hmm.' She didn't have the imagination for that sort of thing. 'What sort of food are you going to do?'

'Authentic Italian. Want to come and work for me?'

'No thanks...' Although there was no point cutting her nose off; the extra money would come in handy – as a teaching assistant she was only paid for term-time. 'Well, maybe in the holidays, but I'm only half Italian, so probably not authentic enough,' she added.

'I'm not that fussy.' He gave a careless shrug. 'A waitress is a waitress.'

'Don't we know it,' snapped Lisa. With a sniff she flounced off into the pub. He could bloody well get on with it, then.

'Hey, Lisa.' Siena tossed down her tea towel and stepped out from behind the bar to give Lisa a swift hug. 'You look seriously pissed off.'

'Flat tyre.' Lisa rolled her eyes. 'I got it on the way here.' And a run-in with her least-favourite person on the planet.

'Bummer. Do you need to call someone?' Siena shrugged, with her usual Gallic charm. Although English, she'd spent most of her life in France and had been born with a silver spoon in her red-lipped little *bouche*. Lisa smiled. She couldn't imagine Siena even attempting to change a tyre.

'Will's changing it for me.' Lisa flashed her friend a wicked grin.

'Is he now?' Siena raised one of her elegantly arched

eyebrows, managing to combine surprise and feline amusement with a mere shapely lift.

'He might as well make himself useful for a change.' Lisa put down her bag on one of the bar stools and hopped up on the other one. 'We could be here for a while. I could murder a drink. You don't mind staying here for a bit, do you?'

'No, suits me.' Siena wiped her hands on a tea towel. 'Might even get a few on the house, if Will's feeling in a good mood.'

Lisa doubted that even Pollyanna would be hard pressed to maintain a sunny disposition after having changed a tyre.

'Give me five minutes to finish tidying up in the kitchen and I'll join you out here. Marcus will get you a drink, won't you?' Siena called over to the shaggy bear of a barman, busy replenishing the glass racks from the under-counter dishwasher. 'Be a sweetie and pour me my usual.'

'Hey Lisa, babe. How you doing? What's it to be?' Marcus spoke with a lovely Edinburgh burr, which Lisa could never get enough of. His accent brought back a vague memory of her mother, who'd been brought up in Scotland. She had a singular recollection of being very young and visiting there and being very put out that she never saw a single man in a kilt. Wasn't it supposed to be the national costume?

Half-Scottish and half-Italian, she'd barely left Bedfordshire in years. She ought to remedy that one of these days.

'G&T, please.'

'I see Siena's been educating you. What sort of gin do you want? Dorothy Parker, Bombay Sapphire, Hendricks?'

'Hendricks, with cucumber.' Lisa grinned at him. 'I'm getting a taste for it, see, although I'd better stick to one as there'll be Prosecco at Siena's and I'm driving in the morning. Can't overdo it. I've got to take Nan for a hospital appointment.'

'How is the wee battle-axe?'

'Battling. She's so rude to the consultant.'

'At her age, she's allowed to be.'

'No, at her age she should know better. Dr Gupta speaks perfectly good English and Nan insists she can't understand a word he's saying.'

'Is he English?'

'No,' Lisa giggled. 'He's got the strongest Northern Irish accent I've ever heard: born and bred in Belfast. She's being contrary because he's clearly British despite his name and the colour of his skin.'

'She's from a different generation, I guess.'

'My mum married an Italian; you'd have thought she might have got used to it. There's no excuse. She's just being rude.'

Will walked into the pub, wiping his black hands, about half an hour later. 'All done. I've put the spare on. You'll need to take the other one to the garage, see if it can be repaired or buy a new one.'

'Thank you. Very much.' She grimaced. Yeah, she knew about the tyres, but buying a new spare was going to wipe out the pathetic little rainy-day fund she'd scrimped and saved for.

When Siena's lips twitched, Lisa realised how it had looked. 'I am... very grateful. Er... can I buy you a drink?'

Will looked at the bar, again with that amused smirk.

'Okay, you own the place,' she said. 'It was a gesture.'

He grinned at her, unabashed, but then, when was he ever abashed – or whatever the opposite was?

As she turned to look away, he said, 'Do you know what...?' She frowned.

'Changing tyres is thirsty work. I'll have a pint.' Typical, now he was being contrary.

With a wink at Siena, he added. 'Married in May will do nicely.'

Siena smiled, leaning back in her chair with one of her cool, unperturbed Gallic shrugs. 'Tease all you want, it's Jason's best-selling beer.' Her look said it all. She was very proud of her boyfriend, Jason, who'd set up a successful micro-brewery in the barn complex at the back of the pub.

'I can't believe he went and named it that. It was meant to be a joke.' Will nudged Siena. 'That's what falling in love does for you. Rots your brain cells. Head over heels! More like arse about tit.'

Siena sipped her gin. 'Mock all you like. We're very happy and you... I think, are just jealous.'

'Jealous. Yeah, right.' Will sneered, although when he did it to Siena, he did it with a smile. 'You keep believing that, sweet cheeks.'

'I will,' quipped Siena, with her usual insouciance.

Lisa caught Marcus's eye with a nod and ordered Will's drink. 'There you go.'

'Thank you. And make sure you do get a spare sorted.'

'Anyone would think you cared,' said Lisa, raising a deliberately cheeky smile. It wouldn't do to let Will know how much he needled her.

'No, I don't want some poor other sod to spend half an hour getting a wheel off, only to find there's no spare.'

He always had an answer.

Luckily, he took a few sips of his pint and retreated to prop up the bar and chat to Marcus, far enough away that Lisa could talk to Siena without Will butting in, as he was prone to doing.

'You've got that grumpy "I-hate-Will" face on again,' said Siena, with her uncanny white-witch sense.

'No I haven't. See.' Lisa plastered a happy smile on her face. She lifted her drink and took a sip. 'I'm getting a taste for this gin malarkey.'

Siena ignored her attempt to change the subject. 'Yes, you have. Honestly you two, you're like a brother and sister, with all the bickering. You shouldn't let him get to you.' She gave Lisa a stern look. 'He's doing it on purpose, just because he gets a response. Ignore him. He's like one of those silly schoolboys in the playground.'

Lisa massaged the tight muscle in her right shoulder. 'I know. He's an idiot.'

But ignoring him was easier said than done. He did everything he could to wind her up. Regret pinched at her. Once they'd had a bantering, fun friendship, where they'd take the piss out of each other constantly, but after one hideously misjudged night, they'd gone from nought to snide in twenty-four hours. If only it were possible to turn the clock back, she never would have kissed him.

'Lisa, Lisa, Lisa.' Giovanni's sing-song Italian accent rang out across the pub as he loped across the room, a broad smile filling his too-handsome-for-his-own-good face. 'Bellissima. You look bellissima.'

An exaggeration, Lord love him, as she'd come straight from work. Knackered from a day on her feet dealing with a bunch of energy-sapping demons otherwise known as 'early-years children', everything drooped and her get up and go had got up and gone, but Giovanni's blatant, eager charm did good things to her ego, especially with Will in sight.

'Hey, Giovanni, how you doing?' She greeted him with a grin.

He gave her an exuberant hug and kisses on each cheek.

'Glad when your British summer arrives. I have a small little problem with all this rain.'

He lifted his feet to show sodden trouser hems, which had clearly had a bit of a dunking. 'Piddles everywhere.'

'Puddles,' corrected Lisa, stifling a laugh at the disgruntled expression in his dark-brown eyes. 'Hopefully, the summer will arrive soon. You have to remember all this rain is what makes this country a green and pleasant land.' She nodded her head towards the view through the French doors. The hillside rose, coated in a blanket of brilliant green, the trees rounded and full like plump broccoli.

'Hmm,' said Giovanni, not looking the least bit convinced, but then he flashed his model-boy smile at her. 'Can I buy you a drink? Are you staying?' The hopeful look made her pause.

'Sorry, not tonight.'

When his face fell, she added quickly, 'I popped in to pick Siena up. Jason's away. As soon as we finish these, we're heading back to hers.' Lisa winked. 'She's making me dinner.'

'Ah,' Giovanni gave her a mournful puppy-dog look. 'I miss my mother's cooking. Home cooking. And female company.'

Lisa laughed and punched him on the arm. 'Sorry mate, girls' night. And don't give me that. You eat here all the time. Don't let Al hear you say that. He'll try out one of his concoctions on you.' Giovanni lived in the flat above the pub and ate with the rest of the staff, including resident-chef Al, who had moments of gastronomic brilliance interspersed with extraordinary creative flashes of culinary lunacy.

Giovanni shuddered. 'I'm still getting over the beetroot-jelly-and-horseradish-with-beef combination.' He shot a quick look towards the kitchen before leaning down and whispering with a teasing laugh, 'Thank goodness Will is opening a proper restaurant with real food.'

'Yes, he's got great plans,' said Siena, arriving back from the ladies, pushing him out of the way and plonking herself down at the table. 'Although Al is sulking that he doesn't get to play too.'

Giovanni beamed at her, although Siena had that effect on most men. 'And I am very thankful for that. He was suggesting pizza kedgeree.'

'Please don't tell me…' Giovanni nodded gleefully. 'Smoked mackerel and boiled egg.'

'Yuk,' chorused both Siena and Lisa.

'Ah, ladies, I must go.' Giovanni grinned as Will yelled. 'Get your arse over here and stop flirting with the help.'

'The boss is calling.' With that he shot away, waving his hands in a placating manner that simply made Will scowl even more.

'My feet are killing me. You might have to carry me out to the car, Lisa.'

'No chance,' she responded. 'I've been with the tiddlers in reception class today. Have you seen the size of the chairs in there? My thighs are knackered, crouching down all day. Roll on the school hols.'

'Yes, you lucky thing. Six whole weeks off.'

Lisa winced. 'You're kidding. I was hoping Will might give me a few shifts.' With a pained sigh, she glanced quickly over Siena's shoulder. 'Needs must. God he's a bad-tempered sod.'

'Not to me he isn't,' said Siena with a sly, piercing look her way, which Lisa ignored.

'I suppose I'll have to grovel, but some extra cash would be handy. I might have been able afford to go on holiday, except now it looks as if I'll have to go tyre-shopping instead.'

At Siena's amused expression, Lisa poked her in the ribs. 'Don't look like that.'

'You must be desperate,' teased Siena.

'I am, believe me.' She picked at the beer mat on the table. 'Clearly a case of better the job you know. Besides, I like it here.' The pub drew people from miles around with its renowned gastro menu. 'And most of the staff are lovely. No make that all of the staff, with one exception.'

Siena didn't say a word, just smiled serenely and chinked her glass against Lisa's. 'Salut.'

'Cheers.'

'What do you think I should do?'

Lisa sat at Siena's kitchen table, the open ring box in her hand.

'Keep it,' said Siena, taking it out of her hand and dancing across the kitchen, holding the ring up to the light so that the diamond sparkled.

'Really?' Lisa sat up straighter.

'No, not really,' Siena's mouth turned down in sympathy. 'It's gorgeous. That's a lot of carat.'

Of course, Siena would know.

'It's real?'

Siena nodded. 'I'm pretty sure.'

Lisa had explained the whole story to Siena and although she didn't voice the bewilderment that her mother hadn't left the ring to her, Siena had picked up on it and given her hand a quick squeeze. 'Maybe your mum felt because they'd split up it should go back to his family.'

A lump formed in Lisa's throat. She was his family. His daughter. Although he'd clearly forgotten that. Anger flared and she lifted her chin. 'I am family. I'd like to remind him of that.'

He might have forgotten but, she gritted her teeth, when Nan went he would be all the family she had. Goosebumps prickled her skin. Nan had plenty of years left in her. She didn't need to worry about that just yet.

Siena's face softened. 'Who knows? Maybe your mother thought that if he got the ring after she died, he might come for you? Does he know she died?'

'You're too nice, Siena.' Lisa sighed. 'He wasn't interested in having me. He came to the funeral. Nan didn't like him much but she did let him know. He came. And left straight after the ceremony.' She took in a breath, keeping her voice steady and fighting to contain the hurt. Left without her.

'But,' said Siena, handing the ring back with a rueful smile on her face, 'I think you've already answered your own question, *n'est ce pas*?'

Lisa's mouth tightened. It was the right thing to do. She could do the right thing even if her father hadn't been able to. A brief, unhappy smile lit her face at the thought of being able to take the moral high ground. Yes, she should return the ring and tell him exactly what she thought of him. She didn't need him, or anything from him.

She tapped the photograph. 'He can have the ring back. I don't want it. But I need to find him first. This photo is years old. The house might not even be there any more.'

'You could go to Rome and find out.'

Lisa whipped her head around and glared at Siena.

'Yes, why didn't I think of that?' Her voice dripped with sarcasm. 'I'll hop on a plane and go to Rome. Silly me.' Lisa rolled her eyes and shook her head, softening her next words. 'I forgot you were an international jetsetter once upon a time. Unfortunately, it's not that simple for us mere mortals, unless you have a handy jet standing by that I could borrow. And I don't particularly want to meet my father. Just give him the ring back.'

'Okay, not the best idea,' said Siena with her usual understanding shrug. 'But you could check the electoral roll. See if the Vettese family still lives there. That's what I would do.'

Lisa hadn't thought that far ahead. If she were honest with herself, she'd been hoping it would prove impossible to track him down. She had a lot to say to him, if she ever got that far. The chicken side of her hoped she'd never find him.

'That's a great idea.' She lifted her glass of Prosecco and chinked it against Siena's.

'You could ask Giovanni for some help. He can translate for you and explain how to find things like that out.'

'Brilliant.' Siena didn't notice her half-hearted response.

'I know,' said Siena a touch smugly, with a ridiculously happy grin.

'When is Jason back?

'Tomorrow night.' Siena giggled. 'I spoke to him earlier. He's very grumpy.'

'I can imagine. He doesn't strike me as a suit person at the best of times.' Siena's boyfriend, Jason, wore jeans all the time, although, she had to admit, he wore them well. He'd gone north to visit Siena's sister, Laurie, and her boyfriend to have the suit fitting that he'd been ducking out of for several months.

'He has to wear a cravat too.' Siena tried to keep a serious face. 'I don't think any of that occurred to him when Cam asked him to be best man.'

'What about you? All sorted on the bridesmaid front?'

Siena snorted. 'Done and dusted. Although I'm going up to see Laurie next week for a final fitting.' She lifted her shoulders. 'Or that's my excuse. Laurie's organising everything by herself. I want to give her some moral support. I'm the only family around,' she paused, a tinge of sadness in her voice.

Lisa had always thought that Siena's mother must have been a bit of a cold fish, separating the two sisters when she split up from Laurie's dad and taking Siena to live with her in France. They'd been reunited after some beyond-the-grave manipulation from their Uncle Miles, who'd engineered things so that Laurie ended up driving across Europe in a vintage Ferrari in the company of, according to Siena, the 'utterly delicious Cam', who'd subsequently proposed to Laurie. The wedding was due to take place at the end of the summer.

Siena leaned over and laid a hand on Lisa's forearm. 'You should try to find your father, for your own sake. Maybe there's another side to the story.'

Lisa scowled. 'I'm sure there is, but it won't make any difference to me. He left me and my mum. I don't owe him anything but the ring.'

Chapter 3

Lisa eyed the posters in the waiting room. She could probably recite the text on them word for word after the length of time they'd been waiting. Her head ached slightly, which was annoying after she'd turned down the rest of the bottle of Prosecco as she and Siena sat and watched *Bridesmaids*.

Nan fidgeted beside her and sighed loudly, making sure the administrator at the front desk could hear her.

'I could have died by the time I get to see this chappie,' she tutted. 'Waste of time. My dahlias need looking after. I'm dying for a cuppa.'

'Do you want me to go and get one for you? It shouldn't be too much longer.'

'Hmph, you said that an hour ago. If it says the appointment is at half past nine, it should be at half past nine, not half past whenever the flamin' doctor feels like it.' She waved the appointment letter, which hadn't left her hand since they'd arrived, like a matador's cape. All eyes in the packed waiting room turned their way.

Lisa gritted her teeth, fighting the urge to shrink back in her seat.

'The doctor's very busy. I'm sure he'll call you soon.'

'Hmph. He might have all day, but I don't. I'll give him another five minutes and then we're off.'

Lisa counted very slowly to ten in her head before saying, as placidly as she could, 'Do you want me to ask how much longer it will be?'

The secretary at the window opposite had her head down, busy sorting papers, avoiding catching anyone's eye, even though she had to have heard every word of Nan's carrying voice. Sensible woman. Cantankerous patients were probably the norm.

'What's the point? They never tell you the truth,' she grumbled, looking pointedly at the watch on her scrawny wrist.

'Mrs Whitaker.' The Irish accent rang out as Dr Gupta, Nan's favourite nemesis, appeared. Tall and patrician, with a narrow aquiline nose and dark skin, he reminded Lisa of some ancient king, and next to him, Nan, an irritating terrier nipping around his ankles who he always forbore with regal grace.

'About bloody time.' Nan's voice, sharp and shrewish, made the whole waiting room look up.

Dr Gupta smiled, his expression completely bland. Poor sod, no doubt, was used to it.

'Do you want me to come in with you?' offered Lisa. She ought to. She felt increasingly responsible for her gran, even though she knew what the response would be.

'What the flamin' hell would I want that for? I'm old enough to be your grandmother.'

Lisa smiled as serenely as she could manage. 'You are my grandmother.'

'Exactly.' Nan glared at Lisa, picked up her capricious handbag and, like a stately ostrich, head held high, stalked towards the doctor, who, bless him, exchanged a subtle, understanding look with Lisa.

She wilted back into her seat. Another round to Nan. It was all very well for her to be gung ho and have that *I'm made of granite* attitude, but she was getting on a bit and didn't look after herself properly; her blood pressure was sky high, she didn't take her tablets, refused to cut down on her salt and persisted in having regular fry-ups as well as Friday-night fish and chips every week. And the doctor didn't even know about the sneaky pack of Benson and Hedges she kept in the sideboard for high days and holidays.

Lisa had tried, but she'd lost count of the times she'd been accused of being the healthy-living police. Nan's attitude was *when I go, I go,* which was all well and good, but she was putting herself at risk.

Lisa frowned down at the institutional greyed carpet. And when Nan went, what then? She didn't do feeling sorry for herself. Most of the time she refused to think about it, but when Nan went... she would be on her own. There were some second cousins in Glasgow, a generation older, with their own families now and hundreds of miles away. Family by blood, but not much else.

Lisa's chest tightened thinking about it. But Nan had years left... if she followed the doctor's advice.

Dr Gupta's face was stern when he came out and Nan's a pallid white.

Lisa jumped up. 'Is everything alright?'

Dr Gupta started to shake his head, but Nan glared up at him with a basilisk stare. 'I'm fine. Old age and fussing. Just a lot of nonsense.'

'Make sure you get the prescription from the pharmacy and,' his voice hardened, 'take the tablets.' He looked at Lisa, his face softening fractionally, 'She needs to make sure she takes her medication regularly. Not,' he sighed, 'a tablet or two, here and there.'

'She is the cat's mother,' Nan sniffed, her prune mouth wrinkling, 'and I'm not in La La Land yet, y'know.'

'Just take the medication, Mrs Whitaker.' Dr Gupta's thin lips sealed in a terse line.

Lisa could understand his frustration. He could have an armful of medical degrees and boy-scout badges but Nan would still know best.

'Can we go home, Lisa? I don't like the smell. It smells of hospitals. Old people and cat pee.'

Nan marched towards the door and, as Lisa turned to follow, the doctor laid a hand on her arm. 'You need to make sure she takes the tablets. She's at very high risk of a stroke, which might not be fatal but could seriously impair her life. Do you know the signs of a stroke? What to do, if she should have one?'

Lisa shook her head, mute, fear clutching at her heart.

He nodded towards the receptionist. 'Take some leaflets with you.'

'Thank you.'

'Remember, with a stroke, the faster you act the better the outcome.'

Chapter 4

'Lisa, Bellissima,' Giovanni slid his hand across the table and took hers. 'You're very quiet. Is everything okay?'

Resisting the urge to snatch it back, she said, 'Sorry,' dredged up a smile and gave his hand a more business-like squeeze back before pulling away. She should have postponed this evening. 'I'm a bit worried about my nan.'

Not to mention rather worried that Giovanni had got the wrong end of the stick. When she'd arranged to meet him at the pub, she'd hoped to disabuse him of the wrong idea and that being surrounded by people they both knew would rob the occasion of any sense of romance. Unfortunately, he'd insisted on coming to eat at a restaurant instead.

Coming here after Nan's hospital visit this morning probably hadn't been the best idea. Bloody Google had provided her with more information than she wanted to know, which now buzzed around her head, along with a threatening dark-grey halo of depression and indecision.

She gave him a wan smile. 'Sorry, I'm not the best company tonight.'

Leaning over the table, he took her chin and lifted it, his

solemn, dark eyes staring down with great tenderness. In another mood, Lisa might have giggled. Giovanni was lovely but he did tend to take himself rather seriously. He saw himself as arch protector and had a great sense of chivalry, which was damn nice in this day and age and she should give him a break. It made a pleasant change.

'You're always good company, Bellissima. Your smile makes up a room.'

Lisa's lips twitched. Only the fractured Italian accent allowed him to get away with the outrageous compliments.

'I wanted some help with something, but I'm worried about Nan.' Despite the doctor's advice, Lisa had left her tucking into her battered cod and chips, along with her bosom buddy, Laura. The two of them had been cackling like a pair of old witches, planning a marathon soap-opera session. Since discovering Netflix, the two of them had become Friday-night binge-watchers and Lisa had yet to fathom their obsession with Season Two of *Breaking Bad*. When Nan had wondered aloud about the feasibility of planting marijuana in among her dahlias, Lisa prayed that it had been her warped sense of humour rather than a serious pension-booster.

Giovanni gave a wary nod. Nan hadn't hesitated to show her disapproval where he was concerned. Luckily he had a healthy Italian respect for all things 'family' and didn't let it bother him, unlike Will who seemed to hold Nan in mutual dislike. Nan disliked most men on principle, Giovanni double lucked out because he was Italian.

'Is she ill?'

'No, but she will be if she doesn't take doctor's orders.'

Giovanni smiled. 'My Nonna is the same. That generation... they lived through the war. They think they're indestructible. They're made of strong stone. Marble.'

Lisa hoped so.

She straightened up, the menu in her hand. 'What are you going to have?'

Giovanni sighed and looked mournful. 'I don't know. It's too hard to choose.'

Who knew that an Italian could have such a passion for Chinese food? It amused Lisa no end.

'Duck? You like that with the pancakes and the hoisin sauce.'

His face brightened and then his mouth drooped, 'Yes, but they never bring enough pancakes.'

Lisa let out a peal of laughter. 'You can always ask for more.'

'Yes, I can, can't I?' He smiled back, happy again now.

She took a sip of wine and decided the way to do this was to dive right in, otherwise she'd been fending off Giovanni's flirtatious overtures all evening.

'I wanted to ask you to help me.'

'Yes. I will help you.'

Lisa shook her head, amused by his enthusiasm. 'But you don't even know what it is yet?'

'For a beautiful lady, anything.'

'I... need to find my father.'

'Ah, yes, Signore Vettese.' Giovanni had claimed kinship as soon as he'd heard her Italian surname.

'I think he's in Rome.'

'You don't know?'

She shook her head, trying to pretend nonchalance. She never talked about this stuff. 'He was a jockey. When I was two, he left my mum – I don't know why – and went to work at a racing stables in the north of England. After my mother died, my Nan contacted him. He came to the funeral.' She swallowed hard. That was the bit that hurt. He didn't stay or take her with him. 'After the funeral he went back to Italy and Nan never heard from him again.'

Giovanni pulled a sympathetic face but didn't say anything.

'I need to... to try and track him down.' For the second time in as many days, she relayed the story of the sketchy clue of the old photograph as to his whereabouts, but for some reason she omitted mention of the ring.

'I've done some research on Google, but I can only find out so much. I think it's because I'm not in Italy. I think the searches would bring up more if I were in the country and I don't speak Italian.'

'You would like to go to Italy?' He straightened, his eyes gleaming with sudden interest.

'No,' she laughed at the boyish enthusiasm. 'Can't afford it. But you're going back soon and I wondered if you might help me. Do some research on the internet for me, while you're there.'

Giovanni looked disappointed, then with a shrug he replied. 'For me this would be no problem. But I think it would be better for you to come to Italy yourself.'

His face stilled and then he beamed. 'You will be on the school holidays soon. You could come then, to Rome, with me.'

'That's very kind of you but...'

'No.' He sat up straighter, as if blindsided by a thunderbolt. 'But you must come!' With sudden fervour, he said, 'I have friends there who work in the local government in Rome. They will know someone at the *Commissione Elettorale Comunale.* That is the Municipal Electoral Commission.'

'I...' Lisa forced herself to appear positive. Quite frankly, she'd give her right arm to go to Rome. Anywhere. But, seriously, daydreams apart, she couldn't afford to go to Rome.

'Yes.' Giovanni looked as if he'd made a monumental discovery. 'You must come to Rome. We can find your papa and I can show you the Eternal City.'

'I can't.' Lisa wished she could.

'Why not? You must come. This is the very good reason.'

'It might be, but I don't have a very good bank balance.'

Giovanni looked blank.

'I can't afford it.'

But she had a credit card. She could book the flights on that and blow the car fund on a budget hotel. If worst came to worst, she could always buy a bicycle.

He frowned and then broke into a broad grin. 'Bellissima. My parents have a big apartment in Rome. With lots of room.' He grabbed her hand across the table. 'I can show you all the sites, the Colosseo, Fontana di Trevi, San Pietro, Piazza Di Spagna.'

Lisa flinched. 'Stop!' The temptation rose in her mind. She'd love to see all those places.

'Lisa, Lisa.' Giovanni smiled broadly, drawing himself up straight. Lisa could almost imagine him clasping the hilt of a sword. 'I would do this thing for you. Family is important. Together we will find your papa. Besides, I will be in Italy for the month anyway.'

'That's kind of you, but...' She didn't dare tell him she had no intention of reconnecting with her father. All she wanted was to give him the ring back. And tell him that he was welcome to it. She'd really like that. Make it clear that she'd done just fine without him.

And see Rome for a week. That would be wonderful.

'Tell me when you want to come. I can meet you at the airport.'

Lisa hesitated. 'What about your parents? Would they be okay having a complete stranger staying with them in their apartment?'

Giovanni let out a bark of amused laughter. 'No proper Roman stays in the capital for the summer. My parents leave to visit my Nonna. She has a house a long way north of the city. Rome is too hot and too full of tourists.' Giovanni's face darkened as he said the latter part.

'But I would be a tourist,' she teased.

'A beautiful one.'

It was very tempting. 'I could look into flights.' They'd probably be far too expensive.

Chapter 5

Will's footsteps echoed in the empty room, dust rising in small puffs from the wooden floorboards. He wheeled around suddenly, tipping his head to one side. Yes, the pizza oven would go in that corner, with a curved serving area in front of it, open to the restaurant, allowing customers to see the flames as the pizzas were slid in and out of the oven on a big wooden paddle. Not that it was going to be all pizza. There would be a mix of authentic Italian food.

With a nod to himself, he paced to the opposite wall and reached out to touch the old crumbling plaster, the only clues to its history the darker squares where pictures once hung. As his fingers touched the wall, a cascade of rubble tumbled down. He winced. Shit, this place was going to need some serious work.

Was he mad? Taking this on when the pub was doing so well. This was a new challenge and, once it took off, perhaps his father would at last accept that Will might not be in banking or insurance but he was a successful businessman in his own right.

Ignoring the trickle of plaster dust, he pointed. 'This wall will be shelved, floor to ceiling, and filled with recipe books.' The ideas had been in his head for so long, it was easy to picture them. 'I've already got Siena scouring second-hand bookshops and charity shops for Italian recipe books.' And it would be somewhere to offload his own collection, which numbered in the hundreds.

'Right,' said Giovanni, squinting at the bare wall and nodding. 'There will be much work.'

Will ignored the comment. Like he didn't know that. And how much it would cost. Most of the time these days he dreamed in spreadsheets and project plans.

'And here,' he pointed, 'there will be curved booths and tables for groups of six to eight. At the back we'll build a conservatory area and have smaller, more intimate, tables for couples.'

'It's going to be great,' said Giovanni, nodding enthusiastically. Will sighed, almost feeling envious at the younger man's naivety. He bloody hoped it would be, otherwise his father really would have something to crow about. Just once, he'd like his dad to say, *Well done* rather than, *Why leave a proper job to be arsing about behind a bar?* or *When are you going to give up playing at being landlord?*

Giovanni had no idea what was resting on this. He was far too naïve and unworldly. He came from a privileged background where everything had been hard-fought.

For Will, opening a second restaurant was a gamble. A question of speculating to accumulate, when he could easily have kept on with the pub without overstretching himself.

It was a bonus that Giovanni wasn't that astute. Will had

the vision and plans, whereas Giovanni provided a healthy dose of passion and authenticity as well as his consummate customer-service skills. Initially Will took him on as a favour to his father, who knew Giovanni's father, who was desperate for a placement for his son to learn better English.

It turned out the arrangement suited everyone as Giovanni, rather less spoilt than Will had supposed, was keen to do anything that gave him a reprieve from the family's watchful gaze. He turned out to be a surprisingly good worker.

'This is going to be a real Italian trattoria, with everything sourced from authentic suppliers. I've got a contact at the Italian Trade Delegation, who I've been talking to about some suppliers and importers. It would be great if I could go over there. He could set me up with a few meetings.' Will paused. 'I may have a few in Rome. Don't suppose I could bum a bed?'

Giovanni's face fell as a range of emotions crossed his face.

'Problem?' Will felt the sweat pooling on his palms at his outrageous fibs.

'No, no.' Giovanni swallowed, a brave tilt to his chin as he said, manfully, 'No problem, boss.'

Will nodded, not feeling the least bit guilty. Okay, he might have overheard Giovanni telling Siena that Lisa was coming to stay and which flights Lisa had booked. It just so happened that those flights suited him too. But that didn't mean anything. She'd booked the cheapest flights. So had he.

'Don't worry.' Will gave him a perfunctory smile. 'I'm not about to rain on your parade.'

Giovanni looked uncertain, but he clearly understood enough as his brow darkened with a touch of petulant schoolboy about his expression. 'Lisa and I are friends. I am helping her.'

'Yeah, right.' Will had seen Giovanni watching her at the pub. Definitely a case of puppy love. Poor bastard didn't stand a chance. A lifetime of living with Nan's strident views on the opposite sex was bound to put anyone off. Lisa was as into commitment as Will was.

Once he thought he knew her better than anyone. They'd virtually grown up together until he'd gone away to uni and work. When he came back he realised something was different. For months, they'd skirted around each other, keeping their distance, until that one stupid night. Now she hated him and that suited him just fine.

'I'll stay out of your way.' Well out of the way. He didn't want his face slapped. 'All I want is a bed for a couple of nights. I'll be out with suppliers all the time. That's why I'm asking. Every cent I save on not paying for hotels can be invested in here.' He pointed to the sagging electrical cables hanging from a hole in the ceiling. 'The sofa will do. You won't even know I'm there. I promise you.'

Will held his nerve, trying to ignore the disappointment on the other man's face. Okay, he was being a prize shit. Taking advantage of being the boss. Lisa would be furious. But needs must. To make this place a success it needed every last drop of capital he could lay his hands on, every penny he saved elsewhere could be spent here.

It was one hell of a surprise when he'd heard that she was going to stay with the Italian. He couldn't care less who Lisa went out with, but he didn't think Giovanni was... good enough was perhaps a bit strong. Giovanni seemed a bit of a mama's boy or was that a convenient stereotype? Lisa needed someone with a bit more oomph.

'I've found a place outside Rome that produces guanciale. It will make the perfect amatriciana. Then there's a couple of farming co-operatives producing olive oil and pecorino I want to check out. And of course, pasta. I want bucatini and paccheri instead of your bog-standard spaghetti and penne.'

'Si, si,' nodded Giovanni. 'English people think they know pasta. They don't.' His hands waved enthusiastically. 'Yes. You can come stay.'

They locked up the derelict building and piled into Will's Golf to take the short drive back to the pub, which was closing as he parked, and said goodnight to Giovanni.

The courtyard behind the pub had fallen silent, the last few punters gently persuaded on their way home. He liked this time of night. Running a pub meant that you couldn't be too picky about the company you kept, but when everyone had left, he relished the solitude and the privacy of his flat, away from the staff quarters above the pub. As he unlocked his front door, he couldn't throw off the slight twinge of guilt remembering Giovanni's earlier chagrined expression. He quashed any incipient sense of remorse firmly. Once in Italy he would do what he always did; keep a healthy distance from Lisa. Even if he had any interest there, he'd been well and truly warned off. And it had been just as well. He, they, neither of them did relationships. He didn't have the time or the inclination. Too much aggravation and hassle.

So why couldn't he stop poking her like a bear with a stick?

He couldn't help trying to get a reaction out of her all the time. There were plenty of other women. Plenty. But for some reason she niggled; a constant itch plaguing him.

He shouldered the door closed and headed into the open-plan kitchen, lounge and diner, immediately consumed with an image of Lisa dodging behind his dining table, a bacon butty in her hand, laughing up at him.

One night. One best forgotten.

Chapter 6

Her ankle ached by the time the car finally pulled into the manically busy car park, the long snail's pace up the hill had had her foot tapping non-stop in between anxious looks at her watch. Passport, phone. She opened her bag. Yup, still there, like they had been when the taxi lurched up the slip road off the M1 towards Luton. Zipped into the pocket. The messenger bag looped over her head across her body. She patted it. Safe and secure.

Hurling herself out of the cab, Lisa waited, her foot going into action again, as the taxi driver took forever to open the boot. With hurried thanks, she grabbed the handle of her case, grateful for the swell of people all headed in the same direction. Pulling the case along, she stepped into the slip-stream of two girls who clearly knew what they were doing and followed them towards the terminal.

Thank goodness for Giovanni's heads-up that she should check in online. The queues snaking round and round and back on themselves, as people filed up to the check-in desks, looked horrendous. She clutched her phone tightly, unconvinced that flashing a phone app at someone was going to be enough to get her on a plane. What if she'd lost it or the battery died, which it was prone to do?

Riffling through her bag she produced the little plastic bag of toiletries ready for the x-ray machines, and as she glanced up, on the other side of the cavernous hall, out of the corner of her eye, she spotted the back of a blonde head with a stubby ponytail rather like Will's. The man was tall enough to be him and had that same confident stride.

She pinched her lips. A trip like this was for Will, Mr Sophisticated, no more stressful than popping out to the shops. He wouldn't be checking he had his phone or passport with him once, let alone on the half hour, every half hour.

'Everything in the tray, Miss,' snapped an excessively grumpy security man. Why were they always so cross? Seriously? With her flushed red cheeks, two-year-old phone and sad collection of make-up, she looked like a major security threat? Flustered, she dumped everything into the grey plastic tray and when she looked up the Will lookalike had gone.

The departure lounge she could cope with, as for once there were plenty of signs with details of all the flights leaving, meaning there was absolutely no danger of her missing her flight, and, more importantly, it looked more like a shopping centre. Boots, Monsoon, WH Smiths, the familiar names and layouts made her breathing ease up. Despite being much later than she'd planned, there was half an hour before the plane left and the gate number for boarding still hadn't been announced. Bags of time to pick up a guide book to read on the plane and check out the duty-free perfume. She could do this. She would be fine on a plane on her own. All she needed to do was keep breathing. Focus on one minute at a time.

How bloody stupid. Why were there two flights to Rome within twenty minutes of each other? And why had she been looking at the wrong one? They'd announced the gate number for her flight ten minutes ago! Duh! The horrible pull-along case, which had seemed so brilliant earlier, suddenly had a life of its own and did not want to partake in the hurried slalom through other travellers all heading down the same wide corridor. The damn thing kept twisting over. She could feel the patches of sweat pooling under her arms. Stupid bloody airline rules, the security people had deemed her deodorant too big and confiscated it. She'd have to sit, all hot and smelly, next to someone for the next few hours. How embarrassing.

When she finally got to the gate, it was a relief to see that although she was the last to arrive, there were still a couple of people ahead of her.

Thankfully the bright, shiny lady with perfect glossy lipstick at the desk had received some sort of ninja training because she caught Lisa's phone before it dropped to the floor and smashed into a thousand, useless app-unfriendly pieces.

By the time Lisa arrived at her seat, a window one, there was lots of kerfuffle as the middle-aged woman who had the seat next to hers ponderously rose to her feet to let her get past. She felt hot, bothered, very flustered and totally out of sorts. Not herself at all. There was no room in the overhead locker and a frantic search ensued, trying to find a suitable space for her case, before the air hostess, a fake smile pasted on her face at Lisa's incompetence, came and rescued her, by which time her flight neighbour had huffed and puffed and tutted enough times that Lisa was ready to curl up and die.

If it hadn't been exactly the sort of thing Nan would do, she might have been tempted to shout at the top of her voice, 'Give me an effing break! This is my first time flying on my own.'

Dropping down into the seat, feeling a fine sheen of sweat coating every limb, she grabbed the seat belt and secured it as tightly as it would go. How on earth had she managed to book a window seat? Another rookie mistake. Easy, she wouldn't look out.

Damn! She'd left her book in the overhead locker and now her neighbour, dressed in an unfortunate tweed ensemble that gave off a slight whiff of damp dog, had sat down again. There was no way on earth Lisa would dare ask her to move. She'd have to make do with one of the leaflets the doctor had given her at the hospital, even though she'd read it several times over.

She swallowed hard, feeling heat racing over her skin. This was a nightmare. She. Was. Not. Going. To. Cry. This was supposed to be a holiday as well as a mission. An adventure. A half-smothered laugh escaped at the thought, which sounded more Tolkien than Lisa Vettese. At least she wouldn't have to contend with a horde of Orcs or evil wizards, although her hostile neighbour might give them a run for their money.

It was easy. Giovanni would meet her at the airport. She tried hard to re-ignite the tremor of excitement she'd felt at the thought of seeing all the places she'd only heard of up until now.

It was no good, as the captain announced the fasten seat belts notice, her limbs had turned rigid and her rib cage felt like a stone sarcophagus with every shallow breath.

Out of the corner of her eye, she noticed the stewardess talking to Tweedy-knickers. Breathe. And breathe again. Suddenly her neighbour had gone and someone else slipped into the seat beside her. Then the plane started moving, taxiing away from the gate. She closed her eyes. Breathe. It wasn't even the serious stuff yet.

She opened her eyes. Faded denim-clad thighs next to hers.

'Hey, Lisa, fancy seeing you here. Interesting reading?'

'Will!' She sat up so hard she banged her head on the head rest. 'What the hell! What are you doing here?'

He lifted one eyebrow, in a studied move that immediately had her on the defensive. Why the fuck couldn't she be icily sophisticated and nonplussed around Will? It bugged her that he was always able to raise a reaction from her.

'Would you believe, taking a flight to Rome?'

'Ha, ha very funny. I meant…' What did she mean? Of course, he was flying to Rome, that was where the plane was going.

Lisa frowned suspiciously. 'Why are you going to Rome?'

Will's eyes twinkled with devilment and her stomach fell. No, please no.

'Giovanni invited me.'

Her stomach contracted, like a balloon deflating, and for a minute she thought she might be sick before the longing to punch Will really, really hard in the solar plexus took over, leaving the knuckles of her cramped fists twitching with desire.

She'd been worried enough about spending time with Giovanni and keeping things cool, but tossing Will into the mix gave her palpitations. That was a balancing act she didn't want to be involved with.

'Don't worry, I've got no intention of playing gooseberry. I'll be doing some serious business. Sourcing some suppliers. Giovanni having a spare room was too good an opportunity to miss. The timing was perfect.'

'Perfect?' her voice pitched upwards in disbelief. Surely Will couldn't believe that. Was he that thick-skinned? 'What and you just happened to be on my flight?'

'It made sense. Means Giovanni only needs to make one trip out to the airport.'

'And when did you decide this?' And why hadn't Giovanni mentioned it?

'Was a last-minute thing. I managed to set up a few appointments in Italy. As I said, the opportunity was too good.' Like the slippery toad he was, she noticed he slid out of answering the question.

'Appointments?' Lisa looked at him, innocence and nonchalance written all over his carefully posed face. Ha! She didn't think so. But she wasn't big headed enough to think he'd done it purely to wind her up. Clearly he was so bloody self-centred, it hadn't even occurred to him that he might be intruding.

'Yep, while you two love birds are taking in the city, I'll be out doing business and in the evenings, while you're romantically dining a deux, I'll be wining and dining local restaurateurs, picking their brains.' Why did he have to sound so damn patronising? Like he was her elderly bloody aunt or something.

Superior sod was only two years older than her and she'd known him since she was eight. He ought to remember that she had memories of him as a schoolboy with gangly legs in regulation uniform grey shorts. Nan had worked for his family as their daily, so Lisa had spent many a school holiday in the big farmhouse kitchen at his parents' home. When they were older they used to walk to the bus stop, on their way to school together, although he'd gone to a very different school. And despite the best efforts of the pretty, posh girls from the other school, he still sat with the cleaner's granddaughter. When she was sixteen, he went off to university and not long after that Nan had decided to move out of the village when she stopped driving.

'Yes, I'm looking forward to having a wonderful time.' She deliberately added a touch of huskiness to her voice. Let him think what he liked. She certainly wasn't going to tell him that she and Giovanni were just friends.

The plane turned, a slow, wide swing, and she saw the runway stretching out, before it completed its turn to face the long expanse of tarmac. Her knees turned to jelly and she gripped her armrest, her fingers cramping.

'I'm quite surprised you took Giovanni up on his offer,' said Will, in a conversational tone.

'Why?' she asked sharply, taking a quick breath as she registered the engines revving up.

Will shrugged, an amused look on his face that had her itching to wipe it off. Arrogant git.

'It's quite a commitment, going on holiday with someone. You're not exactly the committing type.'

'Says who?' she asked, her head snapping towards him, half an ear on the increasing roar of the engine and conscious of that horrible sensation of being on the back of racehorse about to charge into action and unable to stop it.

'You, I seem to recall. You told me you weren't on the market for that sort of relationship.'

She pursed her lips, wishing she'd said a lot less to him that night nine months ago. Her words had been fuelled by a healthy dose of self-preservation. If only she'd had the sense to stick to them.

The plane picked up pace. She cast a fleeting glance out of the window at the trees speeding past. She leaned harder into her seat, bracing herself.

'You seemed quite adamant,' added Will, with a perverse grin, his voice filled with teasing challenge. Women chased him all the time, but she wanted to be different. And she didn't want to depend on anyone. She thought that perhaps they'd found common ground, because he didn't do commitment either. Boy, did he not do commitment. She'd lost count of the women he'd seen in the last seven months. No, that was a humungous lie. There'd been Izzie, the vet's assistant, Cordelia, the interior designer, two Charlottes, Eva, Olivia, Thea, Martina, Ella and Dora, short for Isadora, which exactly summed up the sort of well-bred, well-educated and well-connected women Will associated with. She had been an anomaly. Although, to be fair, he'd treated her equally badly.

She shouldn't complain. Everyone knew what he was like. She should have stuck to her guns and not given in to the beguiling undercurrent of chemistry that crackled between them. At fifteen they'd been friends. At twenty, when he came back from university, something had changed, which probably had a lot to do with the fact that he wasn't a boy any more. Luckily he'd gone off to do something in the City, like his dad. Then he came back again.

It was when she started work at the pub that *something* had reared its head. After managing to resist for six months, she'd given in, tired and fed up after a horrendously long week at work, going home to solitary meals. After the late-night shift at the pub, against all her better judgement, when one too many brushes up against him had ignited her hormone levels to combustion, she'd foolishly let them do the talking. She might have even made the first move. She was still furious with herself for letting down her guard.

Memories slid through like tendrils of mist, snaking, damn them, through the barriers she usually managed to keep in place, before building into full-blown images, bringing with them the heat and taste of him. They exploded in her head, sending a rush of adrenaline punching into her system, making her pulse surge with fevered heat.

She clenched her fists tight beneath her legs, but it was no use, she couldn't get him out of her stupid head. Heat gathered between her thighs as she tried to dispel what had become an indelible vision of his body gliding over hers, the remembrance of heated skin to skin and his hands tenderly cupping her face as he kissed her with a passionate thoroughness, as if scouring every other emotion out of her.

No wonder he was such a success with women; he had a brilliant routine. He'd successfully made her feel as if she were the only woman who had ever mattered to him. Or had she fooled herself because she was lonely? Whichever it had been, all the defences she'd so carefully constructed to protect herself from ever falling in love had gone up in smoke.

She should have stuck to her guns. Being independent was the best way to be. That way you couldn't be let down by anyone. And hadn't he shown her the truth of that?

She scowled, scrunching up her face, as if there were a nasty smell in the vicinity, which there might as well have been. Will was bad news. A womaniser, who moved on to the next woman as soon as he'd made a conquest. She'd been a challenge, like an unclimbed mountain to be scaled. And the minute he'd conquered her, he'd moved on to the next.

'Maybe I've found the right person to have a relationship with,' she snapped.

'What, Giovanni?' Will scoffed. 'He's not right for you.'

'Why not?' she asked, unable to keep the outrage at bay. 'Although, what the hell it's got to do with you, I've no idea.' How dare Will presume he knew her or what was right for her?

'I know you.' Much as she wanted to, she couldn't duck his serious contemplation. 'You need someone stronger. More worldly. Someone who will treat you as an equal.'

Lisa deliberately didn't say anything. That counted him out. Will was infinitely superior and he knew it. Although it was doubly annoying that he'd nailed the very reason she was doing her best to discourage Giovanni's determined flirtation, but she was damned if she was going to admit it out loud, especially not now and not to him, of all people.

'Come on. Giovanni's a lovely guy, but so is a Labrador puppy. There's no emotional maturity there. Plus, he's a good Italian mama's boy. He's not looking for an equal; he's looking for someone to replace his mother. Someone who will look after him, tell him he's wonderful and pick up after him. I can't see you putting up with that.'

'And you would know, would you?' challenged Lisa, ignoring the flash of fury that his astute assessment triggered.

'And there we go.' Will smiled and he reached out and touched her hand. 'You okay now?'

'What?' The unexpected contact startled her. It occurred to her that she hadn't touched Will since that weekend or he her. Why now? They'd both been at great pains to avoid each other ever since THAT night.

He nodded his head towards the window and the view of the fields below them.

'We're safely off the ground.' He leaned forward and fished a book out of the seat pocket.

She stared at his bowed head in open-mouthed astonishment, but he gave no sign of acknowledging it. She felt completely wrong-footed. Had his strategy been a deliberate distraction attempt, then? Had she told him over the late-night Cointreau they'd once shared? Could he have squirreled away the fact that she was terrified of take-offs and landings?

Low-level anxiety about the take-off had been bubbling

away ever since she'd woken this morning and here she was, already several thousand feet up, without the usual sensation of sweat-drenched panic. Instead all her focus had been on the feelings Will stirred up.

She squirmed in her seat, not wanting to give him any credit for being kind. Will didn't do 'kind'. He was a bastard. A lying two-faced bastard. Surely he hadn't deliberately wound her up just to help her. Winding her up was standard Will operating procedure.

He turned and caught her studying him.

'What?' he asked, resting a book of Italian recipes against his stomach, one finger lazily tracing the large silver scar on the palm of his left hand. Burns were an occupational hazard in professional kitchens, but he'd had that one a very long time. She'd often wondered how he'd got it.

'What's the deal with this Italian restaurant you're setting up? Won't it be pizza and pasta just like everyone else?' She could needle too if she wanted.

Siena was right. They were as bad as brother and sister.

Will's mouth twisted in a supercilious grimace. And she realised she'd answered the question.

'Okay, why do you need to go to Italy?' What she meant was why now and why Rome.

She nodded at the recipe book. 'Wouldn't desk research have sufficed?'

'I want it to be authentic. Give people a taste of Italy that they've tried on their holidays. I'm going to break down the menu into different regional specialities.'

'What, so you're going to go to all the different parts of

Italy as part of this re…?' her voice died away as her words suddenly conjured up a vivid image: Will talking about his passion for Italian food, tracing a map of Italy on her naked stomach, pointing out Siena, Pisa and Bologna, before being distracted by the possible whereabouts of Sicily. That conversation hadn't ever been finished. Heat flooded her cheeks and her nipples sprang to ridiculously misplaced attention at the memory of his hand dipping lower and lower.

To her surprise he looked away. Most unlike the cocky self-assured Will she was used to.

'Obviously not, but I've been to… Sic… places in recent years and kept notes. But I've not been to Rome for a long time. This was the perfect opportunity.'

Chapter 7

'Welcome to Rome.' Giovanni, planted an enthusiastic kiss on her lips, casting a slightly triumphant glance Will's way. Lisa took a quick, indrawn breath and almost laughed out loud, except it might have hurt his feelings. Really? Giovanni thought he had competition there?

Tucking away her amusement, she focused on the cheerful chaotic family group that had emerged alongside them in the arrivals hall. With vociferous cries of delight, they fell upon a brown-eyed cherubic toddler, indiscriminate in his smiles as he was passed among welcoming aunts and uncles. A strange pang struck Lisa as he was finally hoisted onto his father's shoulders. Waves of love radiated from the family group and for a brief second she wondered what it would feel like to be part of that. Nan loved her, but she was hardly the demonstrative type.

Nan's response to her saying goodbye last night, and imploring her to take her tablets and behave, was a strident huff and a few choice words about Lisa's fussing. Fussing! If only she knew. Reading those bloody leaflets that Dr Gupta had pressed upon her had left Lisa terrified and reinforced her decision to come to Rome. It was now or never. If anything did happen to Nan, she wouldn't be able to leave her and she wanted this business with her father sorted before then. Lisa ignored the cowardly whisper, pointing out it would also be far easier to give him the ring and walk away without a backward glance, while Nan was still alive.

'Come on. The car is this way.' Giovani took her case and expertly wove his way through the busy airport and, when they stepped outside through the doors, even though it was nearly four o'clock in the afternoon, they were hit by a shaft of Italian heat and brilliant sunshine, a gorgeous contrast to the grey dampness of Luton they'd left scant hours ago. Her spirits lifted. She was here, in Rome and it had been kind of Giovanni to invite her. Despite the doubts that Will had planted in her head, she resolved to make the most of the next few days and enjoy herself.

She would cross any romantically inclined bridges with Giovanni as they came. Will's dour predictions were Will being cynical. The young Italian was handsome and full of fun and, more importantly, he liked her. Perhaps she should give him a chance and see what developed and not assume that Giovanni was necessarily stereotypical of Italian men.

They stopped beside a tiny, battered Fiat 500, with one wing mirror missing. It looked as if it had done battle in a demolition derby and lost.

'Seriously?' Will drawled, looking at the car. 'Is it safe?'

'Yes.' Giovanni grinned. 'Perfect for Rome traffic.'

'And what about the luggage?' He indicated his and Lisa's cases, looking at the tiny boot.

'No problem.' Giovanni picked up Lisa's case and manhandled it into the back seat waiting for Will to follow suit.

With both cases wedged in the back there was only room for one passenger to squeeze in next to them.

Giovanni held open the driver's seat and indicated to Will that he should get in the back. Will glanced down at his long legs; Giovanni grinned and held the door wider. Lisa almost giggled.

'You're kidding,' said Will with a scowl.

'It's not far.' Giovanni gave him a cheerful grin.

Lisa bit back a smile as Will climbed into the back, resigned disgust written all over his face.

The traffic was every bit as chaotic as Lisa had been led to believe. Cars zipped in and out of lanes with gay abandon, heedless of blaring horns, leaving eye-wateringly negligible gaps between bumpers. She crossed her fingers tight under her thighs and wondered whether she might have been better in the back. Being back on the plane was almost preferable to this. Giovanni's jerky, rapid-braking style of driving made her feel slightly sick as did his habit of turning to talk to her as he drove. The car didn't have any air conditioning and when Giovanni opened all the windows as they came to a stop in grindingly slow traffic, the car filled with hazy exhaust fumes.

'This is the main road into Rome. It's usually a lot busier than this,' said Giovanni, before changing lanes with startling speed, squeezing the car into a gap in the next lane, which was moving fractionally quicker than theirs. Two seconds later he whipped the car back into the original lane, which had started to edge forwards more quickly. This constant lane-changing, trying to second-guess the traffic queues, interspersed with a running commentary on the other drivers, didn't help the queasiness dancing in her stomach.

'We have a whole week. Are there any places that you would like to visit? We have a wealth of sights. The tourist season is very busy now.' He grinned at Lisa, and she smiled uncertainly. She wished he'd watch the road instead of turning her way like that, but she was grateful he hadn't said anything about looking for her father.

For some reason, she didn't want Will to know the real reason for her visit.

While looking out at the houses beside the road, and the streets beyond, it struck her rather forcefully that this could be a wild goose chase. It had seemed quite simple when she was at home. Now the practicality and the enormity rocked home. Rome was a big city. The photo and address were very old. Anything could have happened in the intervening years.

'I... the usual places, I guess.' She'd fully intended to read her guide book on the plane, but with Will sitting next to her she'd been reluctant. An organised person might have planned and prepared much earlier. In fact, he made her feel like a grubby, unsophisticated schoolgirl on her first trip abroad. Flying by herself, while absolutely terrifying, had also felt grown up and glamorous and ever so slightly daring. Will made it look like hopping on a bloody bus.

With a fixed smile, she focused on the sights around them, which looked rather industrial and run down, although every now and then they'd dip below an ancient viaduct running over the road. As they neared the city, the buildings started to become more interesting, the juxtapositions decidedly odd. There, next to a modern square electrical department store was an ancient bridge, the worn pointing making the bricks look as if they might tumble down at any moment. A huge many-tiered church towered over a square, the white marble making it look like an elaborate wedding cake. The numbers of pedestrians increased, gaily taking their life in their hands as they sauntered through the traffic, which had once again begun to back up.

Despite the touch of a headache from the liberal use of horns and the fumes, Lisa was fascinated by the good-natured chaos. Cars seemed to join the main arteries of roads from every side road, opening like tributaries flooding evermore into a river already threatening to burst its banks. Drivers threw their hands up in the air, tooting with exasperated exuberance, and it seemed like a contest as to who could toot loudest and longest. Giovanni seemed completely unconcerned about the early-evening cacophony around them, with the window open and his arm resting on the opening, he tapped along to the Europop blasting from the car's radio. Most of the songs seemed to be English, to be fair, but the stream of Italian between, spoken at the speed of light, was yet another reminder that she wasn't in Leighton Buzzard any more.

She squirmed in her seat, itching to get out and walk along the streets in the balmy air, along with the early-evening crowd, who all looked as if they had somewhere to be. It was infectious, that sense of a city on the move, heading somewhere important. Were that couple, arm in arm, going home to eat pasta? Was the handsome man with the briefcase heading to a rendezvous with a gorgeous brunette, already waiting with a double espresso in a café? Lisa sighed.

'You okay?' asked Giovanni. 'We're nearly there.'

'I'm fine. Is the traffic always like this?'

He let out an uproarious laugh. 'No, this is good. This is tourist season, remember. No one stays in Rome in the summer unless they have to.'

With a sudden lurch, Giovanni hauled the car into a side street, hurtling along the quiet road, racing through the gears before dropping back down, with equal drama, to throw the car around another corner, before screeching to a halt outside a gate. With a quick toot, it rolled open with slow grace.

After a short drive along a winding foliage-bordered road, Giovanni pulled up with a flourish, throwing his arm out of the open window to indicate the building nestled right between one of the ancient arches of the aqueduct.

'Wow! This is the apartment?' Lisa gasped. It reminded her of some crab or snail which had taken up residence in someone else's shell.

'Very nice. I wasn't expecting this,' murmured Will, as he clambered out of the back of the car, stretching as he did so. Lisa averted her eyes from the flash of stomach and dark-blonde hair above the waistband of his very low-slung jeans, irritated by the rapturous appreciation of her hormones. Since when were they in charge?

'I didn't know they were allowed to do things like this.' Thinking about bricks and mortar was a good distraction.

The planning departments at home wouldn't let someone build within spitting distance of this type of ancient monument, let alone use the walls of it as part of the structure.

Will laughed. 'Welcome to Italy. I think they take their history in their stride because there's so much of it.'

'Si, si.' Giovanni pulled her case out of the back of the car and carried it to the door, before opening up with a large, old-fashioned key.

The entrance led into a high-ceilinged, cool, dark hall, tiled in black-and-white marble stone. To their left, an ornate wrought-iron railing edged a wide staircase, which curved up and around two sides of the room, the stone steps worn in the middle, smoothed away by many years of footsteps treading up and down them.

'We are on the first floor,' Giovanni announced with pride, leading the way upwards.

At the top, directly opposite the last step, was a rather imposing doorway, with highly polished and embellished brass knobs on each of the double doors.

Lisa had visions of the *Lord of the Rings* again, arriving at some Middle Earth palace. Giovanni opened both doors, throwing them wide and stepping back like Sir Walter Raleigh, ushering Lisa in.

After the dark hallway, they were bathed in light, which came flooding in from a series of windows, each dressed with full-length flowing drapes in some gauzy fabric, secured with silken tie-backs like willowy maidens in chiffon dresses belted at the waist.

'It's lovely,' said Lisa, entranced by the beautiful room,

which combined modern elegant comfort with period charm. Stylish plush-velvet sofas in deep plum faced each other across a contemporary glass-and-gilt table on a faded silk rug. Over by the windows, the sumptuous lines of a pale-grey chaise longue practically begged for someone to drop down and recline into its plump upholstery to enjoy the view out over the extensive gardens.

Giving the furniture a very wide berth, in case she succumbed to the urge to lie down and test the chaise, she crossed to one of the three floor-length French windows. Each one opened onto its own balcony, the central one being double the size of the other two and big enough to hold a small bistro table and two chairs.

'Oh, this is gorgeous,' she said, a broad grin taking over her face.

Directly opposite was a mansion-style house, perfectly placed in the centre of landscaped gardens, dotted with unfamiliar shrubs. The very grand entrance to the house had a twin set of staircases with cream balustrades curving up to meet each other at the imposing entrance, like a perfectly trimmed moustache.

'Who lives there?' asked Lisa, turning back to look over her shoulder, but either Giovanni hadn't heard or didn't know because he melted away with her case.

Will came to join on her on the balcony.

'Hmm, very nice.' He leaned on the railing and surveyed the grounds.

She waited for him to make some clever comment, but he seemed to be content to drink in the view.

The scent of pine teased the air and she tipped her face up to the sunshine, a sense of contentment filling her. Maybe it wouldn't be so bad with Will around.

'Guess we'd better find out where we're all sleeping. And what the price of the accommodation will be?' With a barely suppressed smirk, he went back inside.

Who had she been kidding? Having Will around was going to be every bit as bad as she'd first thought.

Lisa unpacked quickly, stowing underwear in the shallow drawers of a French grey-painted dressing table and hanging a couple of dresses and pairs of trousers in the sort of wardrobe with little lace-dressed windows that ought to have some fancy name. Her jeans were sticking to her legs and she relished the cooler linen as she slid into a pair of loose trousers and yanked on a clean rose-pink t-shirt.

Thanks for letting me raid your wardrobe. Yay for linen!

She paused in her text to Siena and added *Did you know Will was coming too??????!!!! He was on my flight. Sat next to me. Invited himself to stay at Giovanni's place too. I could bloody kill him. Angry face, can't find emoticons.*

Crossing to the tiny dressing table, she plugged her ailing phone into charge. The battery was rubbish.

As she did, Siena's response came back.

Nooooo! He said he was going away, but didn't say where! Now I realise why he was being deliberately cagey. Obviously couldn't bear to let you go! xxx

Lisa pulled a face as she read the text.

Ha! Yeah right. He says he's got lots of business meetings, hopefully he'll stay out of our way. Damn cheeky, though. Poor Giovanni could hardly say no. Typical bloody Will.

She pulled out the photograph of her father, touching the glossy front. It felt furtive to hide the picture and she had nothing to hide, but she slid it between the pages of her guide book and into her handbag. Having heard plenty about handbag-snatchers and pickpockets in Rome, she popped the ring box in amongst her underwear.

With that done she glanced around the room, giving the narrow, single, walnut-wood sleigh bed a cautious glance. While there was barely room to swing a hamster, let alone a cat, it was exceptionally pretty, with its pale-blue and white lace-trimmed bedding, matching curtains and ornate plaster-work on the ceiling. Moreover, it was her own room, so Will could stuff his earlier insinuations.

With a quick spritz of perfume, regretting her confiscated deodorant, she was ready to go. Giovanni had suggested they go out to a local bar in ten minutes and having had a brief look at the tiny kitchen and the sparse contents of its fridge, it was clear that any eating to be done wasn't going to be here. There wasn't even any beer in the fridge.

Will met her in the hall, looking annoyingly fresh, his hair damp.

'Have you had a shower?' she asked accusingly, wishing she'd had time to explore the bathroom situation.

'Yup.'

'A record-breaking one. Have you even unpacked?'

Will shrugged with complete unconcern. 'Nope.'

'Boys.' She looked over his shoulder into his room, where

she could see a trail of clothes on his floor leading to a door on the other side – obviously an en-suite bathroom.

'I was hot. And Giovanni said…' Will looked at his watch.

They were bang on time and Giovanni had yet to emerge from his room on the opposite side of the hallway. She looked again at Will's room.

'Nice room,' she commented, unable to keep the acidic tone out of her voice.

'It's okay, how's yours?'

'Fine,' she said tightly. How come he'd got the better room? 'How long are you staying?'

Will smiled. 'Fed up with me, already?'

'I'm always fed up with you.'

His smile deepened, lazy amusement dancing in his eyes, making her want to punch him hard in the washboard stomach and wipe it off his handsome bloody face.

'After tonight you won't see me. I've got my first appointment fixed up in the morning. I'm off to visit a place outside Rome where they make cheese to die for and then I'm seeing a guy who runs a restaurant in Trastevere. I'm here to work.'

That was one thing about Will. He worked hard. It was typical that he'd got everything thoroughly organised, while she had a hazy itinerary and a goal, which as yet, she had no idea how to achieve.

At last, Giovanni emerged from his room, his Hugo Boss aftershave arriving before him.

'Ah, we're all ready. Let's go.'

Chapter 8

It was heaven to be outside in the warm evening, the streets busier now. Her heart lifted, her steps light. This felt like being on holiday. She was in Rome. Unfamiliar cars lined the kerbs, nose to tail, like ants on a mission, and crammed into every available space, making the street look impossibly narrow. A scooter whizzed by, the driver's shirt billowing out as a girl behind, her bag strapped across her, hung on to him, her hands gesticulating as they zipped by, their heads topped by old-fashioned-styled glossy coloured helmets that reminded of her bowling balls. Ahead, blocking their way, an elderly woman, her wiry hair ruthlessly dyed black, paused to let a tiny dog on a lead nose at the gutter.

Giovanni swung by her, chatting in cheerful Italian, and she raised a hand and patted him on the shoulder.

'Do you know her?' asked Lisa, thinking that the gesture was so Italian; even in the big city people knew each other, had a sense of community.

'No.' Giovanni grinned. 'I told her she'd better get a move on or she'd miss the game.'

He looked at his watch and picked up his pace. They turned

into another street, with a few shop fronts. 'Nearly there.'

Lisa bit back the slight sense of disappointment as he ushered them through the doorway of small fairly insignificant-looking bar. Not quite what she'd imagined on her first night in Rome. She looked about her but, then, it was probably one of those places only known to the locals, which had an amazing atmosphere and fantastic food.

It certainly didn't match the image she'd had in her head since she'd set off this morning, which included eating outside on pavement tables as she watched the world go by. This was not that restaurant.

'Giovanni!' called the barman as soon as they walked in, unleashing a torrent of teasing Italian and coming forward to slap Giovanni on the back as he grinned with an approving nod at Lisa. She might not have understood the words but she could get the gist of it. It was a fairly unsubtle thumbs-up and impossible not to smile back.

'They love blondes in Italy,' muttered Will in her ear. Trust him to take the shine out of the moment.

'Lisa, this is Alberto.'

'Ciao,' he nodded, with an immediate flirtatious smile. 'Welcome.'

'Thank you, it's lovely to be here.'

She didn't think she'd ever seen quite so many bottles crammed into such a small space. Tall, slender glass bottles containing liqueurs in a variety of startling colours and shapes alongside shorter, fatter bottles with dark glass masking their contents. Most were coated with a fuzzy layer of dust, which suggested they might have been there since the days of Ancient

Rome. Campari, Galliano, Sambuca, Limoncello, Strega, Grappa, Aperol, Fernet Branca. Half of them she'd never even heard of, let alone tasted.

Unfortunately, no such riches awaited on the food front. The glass-fronted fridge offered an extremely sad selection. She scanned the few pathetic-looking slices of pizza, topped with rubbery-looking mozzarella, alongside a couple of limp sandwiches, pale, drooping lettuce escaping from the sides and a solitary indeterminate pastry, which had left translucent patches of grease on the paper around it.

Alberto caught her eye and shrugged. 'We're closed tomorrow, but we have plenty to drink.' With a proud flick of the wrist he waved behind him.

'You certainly do,' said Lisa, wondering if she should be brave and try something local, except she wouldn't know where to start. Nan had brought her up on plain, sensible fare and she wasn't much of a drinker. The recent conversion to gin was down to Siena's influence.

Will stepped forward. 'I'll have a Peroni. Lisa, what would you like? Giovanni?'

'The same,' she said, relieved, not having a clue what Peroni might be. Leaving Will to sort out the drinks, Giovanni ushered her on to the back of the narrow bar, where their progress was halted by loud shouts.

'Gio!'

'Ciao!'

In the crossfire of Italian, she had no idea what was being said, but it was clear everyone was happy to see Giovanni. There was also a definite festive atmosphere, but she didn't think it was triggered by the return of the prodigal son. Although lots of the insistent young men wanted to be introduced to Lisa, shaking her hand and making teasing comments to Giovanni, their attention was only half on the job of flirting with the blonde newcomer.

She followed as Giovani wove his way through the tight formation of Formica tables. A locals' place, it held all the glamour of a school cafeteria and pretty much the same atmosphere, with its noisy chatter from the predominantly male clientele in the room, all of whom were transfixed by the large TV screen that dominated the corner and the group of excitable on-screen pundits holding court.

Giovanni's head swung towards the screen and he managed to navigate to a table, pull out a chair and sit down.

'It's Derby della Capitale, Roma v Lazio.' His eyes gleamed with amused fervour. 'Life or death! You don't mind, do you? It's the Italian way.'

Lisa shook her head with a good-natured smile, despite the distinct sinking of her heart. This was not how she'd imagined spending her first night in Rome.

But Giovanni was her host. She had free accommodation and it was only one night. Besides, she was good at making the best of a bad job.

She sat down opposite him, amused by his stalwart attempts to chat to her, despite the terrible distraction of the TV screen above her head.

Will brought the drinks, tall glasses of golden lager, with condensation sliding down the outside. Brilliant, just what the doctor ordered. Long and cold.

As with every other man in the place, his head slid like a magnet seeking due North – towards the screen.

'Who's playing?'

'Roma.' Giovanni grinned and reached for his drink. 'And Lazio.'

'Ah.' Will raised his glass in a toast and stared up at the screen.

'Thanks,' said Lisa, making an unnoticed toast too. Boys were boys whatever nationality. It was a wasted gesture as neither of them even noticed.

Her stomach grumbled at the first hit of cold beer, reminding her that she hadn't eaten all day. Her own fault for letting her stupid nerves get the better of her and skipping breakfast before the flight, and then on the plane, deciding to give her bucking bronco of a stomach a break and save her appetite for some delicious authentic Italian pizza or a nice safe pasta dish this evening. The prospect of which was fading with every cheer at the TV. Once the game kicked off, the noise levels ratcheted up.

Watching Giovanni and Will's rapt faces, she contented herself with thoughts of what Nan might have said in this situation. No-holds-barred Nan's tongue. Half of Lisa's life had been spent smoothing the bulldozer tracks of Nan, over-compensating for her rudeness, as if going out of her way not to give offence might balance the cosmic scales. Unfortunately Nan believed that age conferred the absolute right to say whatever she thought, to whomever, whenever. It could be cringingly embarrassing. Like the time she'd informed the lady in the chemist, in front of a queue of people, that she was wasting her money buying Preparation H. According to Nan, the best cure for piles was apple cider vinegar, which she explained at full volume before proceeding to give precise instructions as to how she should soak cotton wool balls in the vinegar and apply them to the area. Despite the poor woman's hunch-shouldered attempt to impersonate a tortoise, Nan went on to ask how big they were before informing everyone that her own were like bunches of grapes.

At this exact moment, Lisa could imagine Nan's view would have run along the lines, *'I haven't flown a thousand flaming miles to watch a bunch of overpaid big girl's blouses chasing a bit of leather around a well-mown lawn.'*

Lisa sighed quietly to herself. She glanced at the little figures dodging and sliding across the screen. Did she mind that much? She hated people who made a fuss about something when they didn't get their own way. This wasn't the end of the world. She had beer. She was in Italy. It was warm. But she was hungry, boy was she hungry. Even the scabby-looking pizza would do.

Will looked up as if he'd heard her sigh and gave her one of his lopsided, cynical smiles. Was it commiseration or amusement? It was hard to tell.

Two goals in, thankfully to Roma, and Will stood up, offering to buy a second round of drinks. Giovanni, unable to peel himself from the action on the screen, held up his glass.

'I'll come with you.' She wanted to check out the pizza. A slice would keep them going until dinner.

'Pants!' Damn. The chiller cabinet was now utterly bare.

Lisa stared at it, hoping that something might miraculously appear.

'Double pants,' said Will, his lips turning downward. 'I'm ruddy starving. I was hoping there might be a bit of that dodgy-looking pizza left.'

Lisa gave him a surprised look. 'You must be desperate.'

He gave her a pitying smile. 'Yes, but not to worry. I can leave lover-boy and bugger off to find somewhere to eat. Whereas you...'

'Thanks. You're all heart.' She looked up at him. 'You wouldn't do that, would you?' Her stomach growled at the very thought.

'Er, hello. Yes, I would. I've come here on a food pilgrimage. I'm here, basically, to eat. Challenge my taste buds and treat them to some authentic Roman specialities. Not to sit in this dump and drink lager that is freely available back home. You, on the other hand,' he said with mocking amusement, 'are a guest. Ever so slightly beholden to your host. See, this is where inviting myself gives me the ultimate get-out clause. I notice you got the spare, spare room.'

'Yes!' She pouted. 'How come? I should have had your room.'

'Lisa, Lisa, Lisa,' Will shook his head at her naivety as it suddenly dawned on her.

'Oh.'

'Oh? Come on. Surely you realise the price of a free holiday? I suspect young Giovanni is assuming you'll move into the master suite at some stage.'

Lisa narrowed a glare at him, looking superior and smug

as always. 'He's not that much younger than you and some men are gentlemen.' She paused with great deliberation. 'Sorry, forgot... not a concept you're familiar with. You don't have a gentlemanly bone in your body.'

Will grinned. 'Do I need one?' He looked down at himself and Lisa couldn't help herself following his gaze. The well-washed t-shirt, featuring some band she'd never heard of, hugged his broad shoulders and skimmed his torso. It had shrunk at some stage and only just touched the top of his low-slung jeans. When he moved it lifted to reveal lean hips, the top of his jersey boxer shorts, which were unaccountably a brilliant turquoise blue and that damned trail of dark-blonde hair that stirred her up every time she caught a glimpse.

'I'm quite happy as I am.'

She forced herself to look back at his face, a hot, unwelcome flush racing through her to meet his pale-blue eyes dancing as if he knew exactly what she was thinking. Lisa closed her mouth tight, fighting against the silly giddy pulse of her heart. Saying what she thought about him would make him think that she gave a toss and she bloody didn't.

'Another beer?' he asked.

'Yes please, although I'm going to need some food to soak it up at some stage.'

'The Italians eat late, I'm afraid.'

And they didn't have a crisp culture either, thought Lisa, scanning the back of the bar for any signs of snacks.

Will ordered three more Peronis and gave her two to carry back, while he settled the bill for a second time. 'Can I get these?' she asked.

'No, you're fine.'

Lisa wound her way back to the table, the noise almost taking off the roof as a unanimous cheer went up. Clearly someone had scored.

Taking a sip of Peroni, she pulled out the pocket guide to Rome, dislodging the small bundle of Euro notes, a begrudging gift from Nan, who'd muttered with her usual tart discontent, '*Ancient history is best left alone. If that man wanted his ring back, he could have got in touch at any time and he'd have done so by now and he'd never have left your mother high and dry the way he did.*'

She tucked the money into her purse and picked up the guide book, fingering the edge of the photo sandwiched between the cover and first page. Something bounced off the cover of the book as Will flicked a packet of pistachio nuts at her.

'All they had, I'm afraid.'

'Thank you.'

He nodded and gave her one of his twisted smiles, which made her stomach go a little squiggly inside. Damn, she didn't want him to do nice things.

After another half hour, Lisa's patience was starting to evaporate. Even poring over the sights of the Trevi Fountain, the Pantheon, the Colosseum, the Vatican and the Sistine Chapel, all of which she planned to visit, weren't consoling her.

She was dying to know if Giovanni had spoken yet to his friend at the electoral register and found out if the address was still valid.

Nausea danced low in her belly as it struck her. If it was, she'd have to go. Really have to go. Knock on a strange door. Speak to someone she couldn't even picture in her head. No excuses. What on earth what would she say? '*Thanks for nothing mate.*' No, that sounded too angry, like she cared.

'*I'm returning this. I don't need it. Rather like you.*'

Unfortunately, she doubted she could frame the haughty, dismissive words as she thrust the ring box at him. Even in rehearsing the words in her head she could feel the give-away nervous croak in her throat.

'*I've done perfectly well without you.*'

Who was she kidding? She'd probably burst into tears rather than manage a cool, detached demeanour. Shifting in her seat, she squirmed. It had seemed so simple at home. That remote fantasy. But the reality didn't seem so appealing now. All the possible images in her head dissolved into a knot of pure terror. Suddenly she wasn't sure this was such a good idea.

Looking up, she realised a) Will was studying her and b) she had chewed one fingernail to near death. She pasted a dismissive expression on her face and buried her head in her guide book with determined fervour, as if the shopping section contained the answer to the meaning of life.

Eventually Will got up and went to the loo and Lisa grabbed Giovanni's elbow.

'Have you spoken to your friend?' she asked quietly, keeping a watchful eye on the door at the back of the restaurant.

Giovanni suddenly looked like a small boy caught out. 'Bellissima. Don't worry. We have all week.'

'I know but...'

'I will call Luca tomorrow.'

'You mean you haven't spoken to him yet?' He'd had two weeks to speak to his friend.

Giovanni shrugged. 'He's… been on the holidays.' His gaze slid back the television. 'He will be back tomorrow. I'm sure and I will speak to him then. And then we go find your father. But tomorrow I show you my city.'

A minute ago, she would have been relieved, only now she felt irritated. Talk about contrary.

Chapter 9

'Coffee?' asked Giovanni, leading the way into the kitchen, bouncing off the doorway.

'Have you got any food?' she asked hopefully.

Giovanni looked blank and opened the fridge and poked at a couple of jars in there.

'No.' He shrugged and closed it again. 'We'll go out for breakfast.'

He put an espresso pot on the stove, filling it clumsily, spilling coffee everywhere, the black grounds trickling across the floor and spreading like iron filings. 'Ooops,' he giggled and staggered as he tried to brush them up with his fingers. Alberto had broken out the Grappa at the end of the game. One fiery sip had been enough for Lisa. Not so for Giovanni, who had downed several.

Will led him to a chair. 'I think you'd better sit down, mate.'

Lisa searched through a few cupboards before finding a dustpan and brush. Will took it from her and swept up the grounds. By the time he'd finished, Giovanni had his head on the table and was already asleep.

'Always was a lightweight,' observed Will, as he tipped the

coffee grounds in the bin. 'Although Grappa is lethal. Sixty per cent proof.' He shook his head. 'Let's see what we can find. My stomach thinks my throat's been slit.'

Will crossed to the fridge and took a look before opening a couple of cupboards and rooting among the sparse shelves.

'Right, you can be my sous chef.'

Lisa wasn't about to argue.

He passed her a couple of jars from the fridge, artichokes, sundried tomatoes and olives.

'Chuck me a handful of each of those and we can start chopping while I get this pasta on to boil.' He pulled out a bag of pasta shapes that Lisa had never seen before. She took one of the small, thin tubes.

'Reginelle,' said Will, chopping the artichokes with skilled speed as she wrestled with the jar of sundried tomatoes. It was always a mystery to her that people were prepared to eat things that looked like half-dead animals.

'You sound as if you're some sort of pasta expert.' And a right know-it-all. She scowled at him to let him know it wasn't a compliment and managed to spill oil down her t-shirt as the lid finally pinged off the jar.

'I'm learning but there are over 180 different types of pasta.'

'Why so many? Surely they all,' she lifted her shoulders, pulling the revolting-looking sundried tomatoes out of the jar and trying hard not to look at them, as she started to slice, 'pretty much taste the same.'

Will looked horrified. 'Hush your mouth; you'll have us deported! All the same!'

Lisa looked away, interested in spite of herself.

'Your food education has been sadly lacking. You have the tiny pasta shapes, like stellette, the little stars, that you put in soups or broths.' He paused and pointed his knife at her chopping. 'Smaller than that.'

She wrinkled her nose; she wasn't even sure she liked touching them.

'And then there are things like tripolini, tiny bow-tie shapes, that you find in soup or salad. Then you have all the different pastas you eat with sauces but the type of pasta depends on the thickness of the sauces. Then you have your stuffed pasta, tortellini, capeletti and ravioli, but again depending on the size of the packets you have ravioletti, raviolei and raviolo.'

Deftly he scooped the chopped tomatoes and tossed them and the artichokes into a sizzling pan. Lisa's stomach let out a loud unladylike rumble, which was punctuated by a gentle snore from behind them. Giovanni was out for the count.

At last Will served up the contents of the large pasta bowls, steaming and aromatic. Despite the bits of slimy tomato, artichokes, which looked beige and unappetising, and olives, which she knew tasted bitter, it smelt quite good. At least she could pick those bits out and just eat the pasta.

Lisa gave a hungry moan. 'This smells amazing.' No faulting Will's prowess in the kitchen. She hadn't realised he could cook. At the pub he employed the rather eccentric Al as chef.

With an exasperated glance at the tiny table in the kitchen, over which Giovanni was currently slumped, she frowned.

'Do you think we should wake him up?'

'No,' said Will emphatically. 'There's a table out on the balcony. I'm eating out there.'

He pulled open a drawer and fished out some cutlery. 'Here, you take these and the plates. I'll bring the rest.'

Carrying two dishes on one arm, she made her way through the salon and out onto the balcony, blinking furiously. It was like being back in the pub, when she used to be a regular waitress, when they used to get on so well.

Quickly he grated the rather pathetic lump of Parmesan he'd found at the back of the fridge and, with a last-minute glance at the sleeping Giovanni, he grabbed a bottle of red wine he'd spotted in the wine rack. A rather good Montepulciano D'Abruzzo. Tough. Hopefully Giovanni's parents hadn't been saving it for a special occasion. It could always be replaced.

A golden glow came from outside, where the balcony overlooked the gardens and the villa opposite. Carefully placed lights highlighted the stone balustrades and urns at the entrance and the stylised topiary shapes and the tall cypresses in the grounds. It was rather romantic, if you went in for that sort of thing.

He paused for a minute before he stepped out on the balcony, looking at Lisa sitting patiently, her face in profile, the signature thick tawny-blonde hair flowing down her back, her head tilting this way and that as she drank in the view like a butterfly trying to capture the best nectar in the garden. Serene and content, she looked at home on the balcony, sitting on one of the bistro chairs. It was almost possible to imagine she was sitting there waiting for him, rather than resigned and resentful that he'd crashed her party.

His next step stalled, unable to move over the threshold as it hit him. A punch of regret seared through him as reality slapped him in the face. What the fuck was he playing at? That stupid dog-in-the-manger impulse had really got the better of him. Bloody stupid.

Why the hell had he decided to stick a spanner in the works and come out here? She was better off with Giovanni. No, fuck that. She wasn't better off with Giovanni, he wasn't right for her. Which begged the question – what was she up to? Will knew Giovanni had been interested in her for months and she'd not shown any sign of reciprocating.

Will prayed she wouldn't look up as his gaze roved over her, steeling himself against the familiar leap of his pulse. She deserved much better; someone who could be there for the long haul. Even though she'd said she didn't want commitment, he knew she needed someone in her life. Someone who would look out for her and be there for her when her Nan had gone.

Not someone who couldn't even measure up to his own damn family.

'Are you going to come out here or lurk in the doorway, because my manners are about to go down the swannee any second.' Lisa's grumpy expression forced him to move.

Since when did she have a problem with manners around him? 'Start. I wouldn't want you to starve.'

She gave him a sour smile, picked up her fork and examined the food, as if she were worried something nasty might jump out and bite her.

'Everything alright?' he asked, amused when he noticed she'd pushed the artichokes to one side already. 'Want a glass?' He put the bottle and glasses down.

'Mmm,' she mumbled through her food, her head down,

hunched over it as if fearful it might be snatched away from her at any second. Not that he blamed her, his stomach felt as if it had been excavated by a bulldozer.

He poured the rich ruby wine into the glasses and took a deep sniff.

She eyed him suspiciously.

'It's a good one.'

'I wouldn't know, you're the gastrodom.'

'Is that even a word?' Will looked thoughtful for a minute and took a long swallow. 'I rather like it – ruler of the known gastroverse.'

She scowled at him again, spurring on the devil inside that took delight in winding her up. It took him back to a more carefree time, when they'd been friends and there'd been no other overtones.

'I rather like the dom element...'

With a toss of her head, swinging her hair down her back, she reached for her glass and took a hefty gulp.

'Ooh,' she paused, as caution set in. It was almost comical, her wavering for a second before she could bring herself to say it. 'This is nice. Really nice.'

'We aim to please.'

'And the food is nice too.' She took a healthy bite of pasta and he noticed she'd accidentally scooped up a piece of sundried tomato. He watched closely. 'I... the tomatoes are actually okay.' She took another mouthful, this time not avoiding the little slivers of red, and munched with thoughtful application before she pronounced, a little more enthusiastically, 'Really good.' Another pause. 'Thank you.'

'It's alright. I needed to eat too.'

'Well, of course.'

'Why the change of heart?' Damn, he hadn't meant to bring it up. Now he sounded like a jealous idiot.

She shrugged and examined the far corner of the garden. 'I don't know what you mean.'

'You and Giovanni? I didn't think you were interested.'

'Maybe a cheap holiday was too good to pass up,' she said evasively.

He narrowed his eyes at her. 'You hate flying. What changed? You suddenly decided Giovanni was the one?'

She scowled at him. 'And it has to do with you, how?'

'I don't see you two together.' Why couldn't he keep his mouth shut? Back off, be indifferent. It was nothing to do with him and he didn't want it to be anything to do with him.

'And what? You're the expert on relationships all of a sudden, Mr Two-dates-and-then-you've-passed-your-sell-by? I hardly think you're qualified to comment.'

'Who knew there's a degree in observation and common sense?'

'I was referring to your track record. Nine different women in the last se... however many months.'

'You've been counting?' His voice acquired a bored drawl to hide the sudden quickening of his pulse at the thought she'd been keeping count. 'I had no idea you were so interested in my well-being.'

'I wasn't. I'm not. It never ceases to amaze me that there are that many gullible women out there, that's all.'

The narrowed-eyed stare she shot his way packed a full punch of icy disdain and it stung. 'Everyone I date knows what they're getting into. I'm not looking for a relationship.'

'Yeah, I think everyone knows what a tart you are,' she jibed.

His stomach clenched, but he shrugged. 'Better than promising something you can't deliver.' It never ceased to amaze him that his parents ever made a contract of marriage. The only promise they could deliver on was leading each other up the garden path.

'True, at least you're honest about it,' she said.

Will tensed, his skin itching as a furious blush burnt the skin of his cheeks. 'Yes, I'm honest. I don't lie to anyone.' He hadn't lied to her. She'd backed off as much as he had. And okay, maybe it had suited him and been a bit of a relief, but they'd both been guilty of total and utter inertia.

It was better this way. He'd seen too often the chaos his parents' parlous relationship left in its wake. Rows, recriminations, hide-piercing sarcasm, withering insults. It was so bloody exhausting.

She eyed him over her wine glass and, being honest herself, her mouth dipped in a moue of acknowledgement. She lifted her glass and toasted him.

'Lovely meal, thank you.'

'My pleasure.' It was like a sea mist lifting, both of them realising that they could stay holed up at the impasse, retreat to their usual entrenched positions or make an attempt to be civilised.

'So, where are you going to drag Giovanni tomorrow?'

A guilty expression, as furtive as a fox skirting the suburban shadows, crossed her face.

'The usual tourist hot spots, I'm afraid.'

'Why are you afraid?' he asked, a teasing challenge in his voice.

She straightened and looked down her nose at him. 'Because I'm sure Mr Well-seasoned, Euro-rail-during-my-gap-year is well beyond all that. Don't tell me, the cheese farm you're visiting tomorrow is one of five on a south-facing slope, where the cows eat organic grass and the cheese is turned daily by peasant stock groomed for generations for this particular task?'

'I'm not that much of a tourist snob. The reason places like the Spanish Steps, the Vatican et al are popular is because they are amazing. There's nowhere quite like Rome in the world. The Eternal City. Antiquities, culture, history. It's got the lot. Go forth, my child and enjoy.' He employed a suitably patronising note in his voice before adding, 'And I must ask them tomorrow who does turn the cheese. That might be a nice detail for the menu.'

Chapter 10

The sunshine streaming through the full-length filmy curtains made Lisa push back the white, crisp, cotton sheets and skip the few steps it took to cross the cool, tiled floor and throw open the French doors. She stepped out onto the balcony, squinting in the brilliant light and drank in the scent of the dew-laden wisteria tracing its way around the railings. Lifting her head and rolling back her shoulders, she stretched, a sudden leap of joy firing through her at the magical warmth of the early-morning rays touching her skin.

Swallows darted and danced, wheeling across the brilliant blue sky, flashy and exuberant, racing across the front of the balcony and up beyond to the eaves, before peeling back out in swift formation. A frisson of excitement danced low in her belly. Rome. Today she could explore worry-free. By tomorrow, Giovanni would have spoken to his friend and she'd have to think about addresses, rings and family.

Across the way, the grand villa slept, the blinds at its many windows pulled like blank stares and no sign of life anywhere. The lights which last night had lit up its glorious façades had been switched off and, with a fanciful thought, she imagined the house like Sleeping Beauty, waiting to be awoken by a prince racing up the stairs, running his hand along the elaborate balustrade alongside.

Her daydreams were interrupted by the sudden whiny buzz of a scooter, which whizzed up the driveway. Bright scarlet with its single headlight and antennae-like mirrors, it reminded her of fierce red ant. As it came closer, she saw that the driver was a woman, wearing navy Capri pants, a white shirt and a natty, colourful scarf, which she recognised as having a definite touch of Missoni about it. Siena had taught her well. The girl on the scooter pulled to a stop below, cut the engine and stepped off before lifting off her helmet. Lisa could have predicted the clichéd fall of glossy brunette hair that came tumbling down. In her big sunglasses and chic clothes, the woman looked like some movie starlet and the scene was straight from some Hollywood film in the sixties.

With practised ease, the woman hung the helmet on the handlebars and then sauntered out of view, her footsteps crunching on the gravel, the sound of which was quickly followed by the peal of a bell somewhere in the flat. Lisa straightened.

Was she a friend of Giovanni's? What sort of state was he going to be in this morning? Checking the time on her phone, she realised it was quite early. Seven-thirty. Should she answer the door? Was anyone else up?

Then she heard the slam of the front door. Muffled voices and the squeaky drag of a chair on the kitchen floor. She looked at the time again, relieved that someone had saved her the indignity of the job of answering the door to the glamorous starlet, wearing her skimpy plain cotton bum-skimming t-shirt and a sleep-worn face. This woman probably wore silk peignoirs in bed, whatever they were.

The smell of coffee, dark, rich and beguiling lured her down the corridor, where she could hear Will in the kitchen, chatting with ease, interspersed with light melodic laughter.

She paused for a second before stepping into the kitchen.

'Morning.' She took in the scene. Will sat at the table, leaning back, his chair tipped on two legs, opposite the woman from the scooter.

'Lisa, you're up early. Coffee?'

Even before she'd nodded her head, he eased himself to his feet, rising with his usual languid grace that never failed to stop her in her tracks. She couldn't even define why. Though he was long, lean and loose-limbed he was also broad in the shoulders and had a dusting of hair on his well-muscled chest. She might have had only the one night with him, but the shape of his body without his clothes on was indelibly etched into her memory.

As he lifted the silver pot from the stove, she stared at the dark-blonde hair on his forearms, the memory of its unexpectedly silky feel bringing an unwelcome burst of... something, she didn't want to think about.

Will poured her what looked like a thimbleful of coffee in a tiny cup, without any milk.

She liked her coffee with plenty of milk. There wasn't even room for a splash in this doll-sized cup.

'This is Gisella.'

The girl rose and put out her hand. 'Buon giorno.'

Lisa shook the proffered hand, 'Buon giorno.' Her first

Italian words. Maybe she should learn Italian. 'Is that the proper way to say it?'

The girl smiled, her wide, pink-painted lips suddenly dominating her face. She was gorgeous, but Lisa winced at her own uncharitable thought, that she did have one hell of a big all-the-better-to-kiss-you-with mouth.

'I'm not sure I'm very proper.' She flashed a charming, confident smile. 'My brother is always complaining about my behaviour, but he is, as you say, a stuffed shirt.'

Lisa hadn't ever used the phrase stuffed shirt in her entire life. This girl's command of English was flawless and virtually accentless.

'Wow, your English is amazing.'

Gisella tossed her hair over her shoulder, sending a waft of definite night-time perfume Lisa's way. 'I spent six years in London.'

'Is that how you know Will?' asked Lisa, glancing to where he sat at the table, sipping from a tiny cup of espresso, frowning down at a list on a sheet of paper in front of him, a pencil held in the other hand.

'No, I never met him before today.' The mouth curved with cat-like satisfaction as she shot a glance at him.

'Her Aunt Dorothea is a friend of my mother,' Will chipped in. 'I needed an Italian-speaking guide.'

Gisella beamed at him. 'We're going to,' she rattled off a name quickly. Lisa didn't catch it but she did spot the appraising once-over the other woman gave her. 'I didn't realise someone else might be coming.' With a rueful smile, she added, 'I only have transport for one.'

Gisella's frank look was a head-on question. Lisa rather liked her honest approach. It was clear they were agreeing territorial rights.

'No worries, we're not together. He's my... boyfriend's boss.'

Will lifted his head and shot a sharp stare at her before going straight back to his list.

Lisa clenched her fist out of sight. How she described Giovanni was nothing to do with him. Besides, Gisella's face had lifted and the big, wide grin was far friendlier suddenly. You didn't need to have Sherlock Holmes's powers of detection to work out why.

Well as far as Lisa was concerned, Gisella was welcome to him. In fact, she seemed just his type. Posh, glamorous bird with bags of self-confidence.

'Right.' Will jumped up. 'Enough of this chatting. We've got work to do.' He tucked his notes into a plastic wallet and waved it at her. 'Have a good day, Lisa. See you later.'

Lisa looked up, pen in hand, literally about to write the first line, when Giovanni finally emerged, his dark hair damp and a cloud of aftershave, like an aura, around him.

'Bellissima. Buon giorno.'

'It's almost buon pomeriggio,' she retorted, waving her guide book at him, with a teasing smile. It had been put to excellent use in the last hour and half. 'I've been waiting ages for you. I bet your head hurts this morning.' She eyed him, but apart from looking a little bleary-eyed, he showed no overt hangover symptoms. In fact, he looked handsome. Very handsome. He was a nice guy. Good boyfriend material. The absolute opposite to bloody Will with his stupid ponytail and tall, lean grace. Giovanni was a lot sturdier – no, not that much sturdier. Muscly. It might run to fat later, but that was it. Broad in the chest. And dressed beautifully. Smart. Neat.

'No, we Italians are brought up on Grappa. No headache.' He shook it. 'See.'

'Hmm, well it's a good job you're up now. I was about to leave you a note and go out without you,' said Lisa, almost bouncing on her tiptoes with anticipation, her bag was all packed with the day's essentials, a hat, sun-cream, a bottle of water, plasters and a book and she'd painstakingly planned her route for the morning. 'Painstaking' being the operative word. She and maps didn't see eye to eye. Top of her list was the Colosseum.

With an apologetic smile, Giovanni took her hand. 'I will make it up to you. But Roma versus Lazio. It was life or death.'

'I didn't see anyone dying last night,' teased Lisa, unable to stay cross with him. He was charming. A genuinely nice guy. 'Sleeping perhaps.'

Giovanni gave her a boyish, slightly chagrined, smile. 'I'm a bad boy. It's football. It's Italy.' His mouth turned down in a pretty good impression of hangdog, which might have worked if Lisa hadn't seen the hopeful twinkle in his eye.

'Yeah, yeah. I've heard it all before.' Lisa shook her head, a smile playing around her lips. How could you get cross with someone who always had a ready smile?

'This morning, I will take you to the best bakery in Roma.' He puffed his chest out slightly like a proud pigeon and announced, 'Pasticceria Regoli.' She almost expected him to sweep down into a courtly bow, brushing a feathery plumed hat across the floor. 'Breakfast Italian style. Pastries and cakes. Not a sausage or a bacon in sight. You will love it.'

'Done, I'm starving.' She headed towards the door, determined not to give him a chance to delay her any longer. 'But you owe me big time. I'm going to need a serious sugar fix and a proper coffee.'

Old-fashioned blue lettering on a white background proclaimed the bakery name, with extravagant curlicues on the P and G, as if promising that bit extra. Old and young stood in a very long queue, heads peering ahead in happy anticipation of the goodies to come.

At last they were inside the narrow brick-walled shop and the sight of the long counter, filled with delectable-looking pastries, made it almost worth the wait.

She let slip a greedy moan as her eye caught the icing-sugar-dusted star-shaped pastries, the puffed layers almost buoyant, filled with a generous filling of cream and strawberries, that filled the bottom level of the glass-fronted cabinet. Rows of glossy fruit tartlets, laden with kiwi fruit and huge strawberry slices, nestled next to cream and raspberry mini tarts as well as familiar choux pastry-style éclairs and horn-and-cream puffs, all of which were arranged in beautiful symmetry.

'I don't know where to start,' said Lisa, amazed at the cornucopia of sweet delights on offer, although slightly concerned by the unfamiliar-looking cakes further along, particularly the alien-looking white creamy pastries that looked as if they were topped with snow and labelled with exotic names, *faggotini di ricotta, maritozzi con la panna, bavarese, cannelloni Sicilian*. Ricotta was cheese, wasn't it? She didn't fancy that in a cake at all.

'What about this one? It's one of my favourites.' Giovanni pointed to a dumpling-shaped choux-pastry puff with a sage-green topping.

'Er... what's the green?' It looked rather bilious to her.

'Pistachio icing.'

'Hmm, I'm not sure.' She looked around. 'What about that one? What's that?' She pointed to a nearby confection, which had all identifiable elements, including puff pastry, cream and glistening strawberries.

'*Tortine fragoline di bosco*. It's very good.'

Will would have loved it in here. No doubt he'd have bought up half the shop and insisted on trying them all and making her try them too, but she was more than happy with a strawberry pastry.

With their cakes tied up in pretty blue-wrapped parcels and a steaming coffee from the bakery's sister shop next door, Giovanni led them down the road to a nearby park, where they perched on a bench.

'My Nonna used to bring me here when I was a small boy and she would always buy me one of these on the way.' He held up a white confection, which she didn't fancy the look of and was rather grateful he didn't offer her a bite.

'Although I was never allowed to eat it in the park, that would have been... *volgare*, I think it's the same as vulgar?'

'Yes. It sounds lovely, though. And Nonna, that's your grandmother? Yes?' Giovanni nodded. Lisa smiled and took a bite of her strawberry pastry, enjoying the juicy sweetness offset by the light, crisp pastry.

'She liked to spoiled me. She brought me here to Regoli and the park every week. We would do two…' Giovanni indicated a circle with his finger, 'around the park and then home to eat cake.'

Lisa had a sudden image of a rather regal woman.

'My nan used to take me to work with her.' Lisa squinted up at the sun, remembering vividly sitting in the kitchen helping peel potatoes along with Will as her Nan whizzed around like a tiny whirling dervish, setting the place to rights. 'And we'd stop off at the Co-op on the way home and get a pack of doughnuts.' She laughed. 'Not quite the same. They probably went down just as well, although Will was always pissed off he didn't get one.'

'I didn't know your grandmother had worked at the pub.'

Lisa laughed. 'You're joking. This was years before. My nan was Will's parents' daily.'

Giovanni frowned.

'A cleaner-come-housekeeper. She went there every day to keep the house tidy. Clean up after them.' Lisa gave in to impish mischief. 'Like a servant.' His Nonna sounded as if she might have had a nan of her own. 'A long time before the pub.'

'Ah.' He frowned harder. 'But I thought the pub was a family business. I thought it had been in Will's family for generations.'

'That's what Will's parents would like everyone to think. They own, or rather owned, a lot of land in the village, including the pub, which was leased to a brewery. Over the years they've had to sell quite a bit.' Lisa paused, feeling slightly disloyal. Will never mentioned his parents. She knew more than most because Nan had worked for the family and was well aware Will's father had run through the family money.

'Will persuaded them to hang on to the leasehold of the pub and let him have a go at running it.' That made it sound quite straightforward, as if they'd done Will a favour, not that he'd had to beg his father. While she had a fairly dim view of Will's dealings with the opposite sex, she couldn't deny that he'd worked his socks off to make the place a huge success. She pulled a face. Although his parents had made him pay for the privilege. He'd never said anything, but she often wondered if it was Will who'd kept the family afloat the last few years and ensured that his much-younger sister stayed at her expensive boarding school.

And why the hell were they talking about bloody Will? It was bad enough that he'd hijacked her holiday.

Lisa turned the map on its side and took another look, tilting her head almost side on to try and get her bearings. Nope, none of it made sense. It was almost as if some kind of dyslexia set in the minute she tried to make sense of the jumble of roads, but she refused to give in.

'You don't need the map. Today I will be guide,' said Giovanni, trying to wrestle it from her.

Lisa flapped his hand away. 'But you don't know where I want to go.'

'I know all the best places in Rome.'

'You might do but I have a list.'

'A list? You can't do Rome by list. You have to live and breathe it. I will show you what you need to see.'

'As long as that includes this lot,' she showed him her guide book marked with yellow sticky notes, 'that's fine.'

'Hmm,' He looked at his watch. 'I want to take you to a nice place for lunch.'

'Sounds nice. Presumably we can see some things on the way. Where are we going? Show me on the map and we can work out a route.'

'I know my way.'

Lisa put her hand on her hip, her eyes sparkling. Typical male – thought he knew better. Well, she wasn't going to get cross with him. Not on her holiday.

'You might know the way, buster, but I want to get my bearings. See where I'm going. It's not the same… without the map and knowing where we are.' Okay, that was a big fat lie as even with the map she would never know where she was going, but she liked to dream.

He nudged her and put an arm around her shoulder and firmly removed the map from her grasp. 'But we look like tourists.' His face filled with mock horror and he looked left and right back over his shoulder.

'We are tourists.' Lisa laughed and snatched the map back and held it up out of reach, dancing forward a few steps. It was heaven to feel so light-hearted and free. Nowhere to be. No one expecting you. No one to look after. Today she could please herself.

'But I am not a tourist.' Giovanni wrinkled his nose, the faintest of pouts touching his lips. 'It's not cool.'

Lisa laughed and poked his arm. 'I'm not cool. I don't want to be cool. I'm on holiday and a tourist.' She linked her arm through his and gave him a squeeze, with a happy grin. 'You'll have to hide behind your sunglasses.'

'Okay, for you, Bellissima.' He gave a deliberately tragic sigh.

Lisa stopped and turned the map again, so that it faced the same direction as they were headed, even though it was now upside down. 'Where are we? Do we go this way?'

'Here,' he pointed and turned the map the right way up.

'Oops. Show me.'

He traced the route with his fingers. 'If we walk along here, it takes us into the heart of the city, where many of the sights are.'

'Brilliant. Look, I can see the Trevi Fountain. We can go there first.' She felt him shift, next to her. 'Don't sigh again.'

'Everyone goes there. It will be very busy. And hot. Very hot. We could go tomorrow. Start early.' He shrugged with a disarming tilt to his mouth. 'Okay?'

'Giovanni, I know it will be busy, but I only have five days left and...' She left the words hanging.

'Okay, okay.' He held up his hands in mock surrender. 'For you, Bellissima, I will face the hordes, battle through the crowds, all for the fair Lisa and the ridiculous fountain.'

'Now, you're being mean,' she swiped her map at him. 'The fountain is famous. It can't be ridiculous if everyone wants to see it. I saw it in a film.'

'*La Dolce Vita*,' said Giovanni, with a world-weary sigh. 'Everyone...'

'No, not that one, it was... I can't remember, but it was a

rom-com and it's top of my tourist list, well after the Colosseum, of course.' She smiled at him. 'I think I'm developing a bit of an obsession about it?' What she'd read in the guide book to date had fascinated her. And then, of course, she had seen *that* film.

'Too much Russell Crowe and *Gladiator*.' It was a shame the bakery had been in the opposite direction this morning, she was dying for her first glimpse of the famous structure.

'Russell Crowe. You think he's better-looking than me?' Giovanni pretended affront.

Lisa tilted her head considering, a smile playing at her lips. 'Hmm close, but you just edge it.'

With a toss of his head that was almost camp, Giovanni glared at her.

'I'm teasing. He doesn't come close. You have better legs.' She looked down at his tanned muscular calves. 'Definitely.'

'I'll forgive you.'

'Enough for us to detour, this way? Then I could see it. Just the outside today.' She traced a route with a wistful finger.

Giovanni shook his head. 'No, it's quicker this way. We can do the Colosseum tomorrow. It will be busy, far too busy by now. Full of tourists. You need to go early as there are long queues for tickets.'

'I don't mind queuing.'

Giovanni shrugged. 'It will be full of too many people. And too hot.'

'You're Italian, you should be used to the heat.'

'No, Romans leave the city at this time of year, remember? Only the stupid tourists stay.' He pouted again.

She nudged him. 'Humour me.'

He grinned with good nature as she took another look at the map before taking it from her again.

'We go down here, along here and then on to the fountain.'

'Okay, I can see it now. Via Sistina, then along the Via del Tritone and on to the Fontana di Trevi.' She savoured the Italian names, rolling the consonants around her tongue like marbles, spreading the vowels out with a dreadful sing-song Italian accent. Giovanni shook his head, putting his hand over his ears and pulled a face of pretend horror before linking his arm through hers.

'Enough, I give in. Today, I will play tourist.'

The bells of a nearby church, out of view, pealed, their musical notes ringing out in bright celebration. Eleven-thirty and already the sweltering heat, sticky and close, made her glad she'd plumped for a loose linen dress, pinched from Siena, and not the practical denim shorts she would normally have worn. As usual Giovanni was immaculately turned out; no wonder he hadn't emerged until well after nine. She suspected he spent more time and money on personal grooming than she did. Was that an Italian-man thing?

He wore crisp, navy chino shorts, bare feet with American-style loafers and a button-down collar Ralph Lauren shirt along with Ray-Ban sunglasses. Despite his earlier protestations, he looked impervious to the heat, with knife-edge creases on his shorts and shirt sleeves. Quite a few of the sultry women, always in pairs, it seemed, gave him a second glance over the top of their sunglasses as they sashayed past, hips swinging with confident provocation. Subtle they were not. Lisa straightened up, wishing she fancied him a little bit.

Everyone, it seemed, strolled in Rome. It was too hot to do anything else. The leisurely pace made a pleasant change, or at least she thought it did. There was still that slight itch, of needing to get things done quickly. Usually she had a million and one things to do: work, checking up, subtly mind you, on Nan, seeing friends and keeping up with dull household stuff, which, to be honest, always came bottom of the list, as well as picking up extra shifts at the pub restaurant when she could, although those had been far fewer as she'd been avoiding Will as much as possible.

There always seemed to be too much to do and too little time. It felt rather decadent to be ambling along. She needed to take a breath, savour each moment, take her time and enjoy this.

Walking along the crowded cobbled streets as part of the holiday throng certainly helped slow the pace – you couldn't hurry. And she was going to take today. Be a tourist. Not think about finding her dad. That was for another day. Today was about being on holiday.

With a sigh, she pushed the unwelcome thoughts to the very back of her head and tilted her face up to the sun. Siena had made a good call insisting she bought these big Calvin Klein sunglasses in TK Maxx.

'Wow.' Lisa stared. 'It's...'

Noise and movement struck her. The constant crashing rush of water, rising above the chatter of the crowd as the torrents spilled down, tumbling with fierce energy over the rocks of the Trevi Fountain.

'Come,' Giovanni led the way down steps towards the fountain. The cool mist drifting from the water was a welcome relief, as was the shady semi-circular seating area, currently packed with tourists.

He wound his way through the crowded rows, intent on finding a gap on one of the stone benches before spotting a family gathering up their belongings and lurking with detached politeness.

'Signorina,' he ushered her into the seat.

Lisa sat down, enjoying the cool dampness as she watched the fine droplets of water dancing in the air. She watched the constant motion, as the water pulsed with life and energy, sunlight dancing and twinkling on the choppy surface. The water looked so clear and clean, it was tempting to throw yourself in. She dug in the bag slung across her front to find her phone, relieved that for once it had enough charge left to take a few pictures.

Snapping away, she captured several tourists as they tossed in coins, throwing them over their shoulders. With their serious screwed-up expressions, did they believe that they'd come back? It was a rather lovely tradition. Lisa smiled. When had the tradition, which apparently ensured you returned to Rome, begun? Or was it some enterprising city councillor from bygone days who had dreamed up the plan as a money-making exercise.

'If you throw a second coin, you will find love,' said Giovanni, following her gaze. 'A third, marriage.' He leaned back on his elbows just out of her eye-line.

'I wonder what they do with all those coins,' mused Lisa, looking at them dotted about the floor of the main pool.

'They're collected by a local charity, Caritas, which provides people in need in the city with food.'

She turned in surprise. 'I'm...'

He waved his mobile at her, with an irrepressible grin. 'This is a good website. Nine facts about the Trevi Fountain on my phone.'

'You,' she shoved at him, before propping her chin on her hands to people-watch. 'That's cheating.'

Suddenly Giovanni nudged her. 'Watch. Those two young girls over to the left.'

Lisa turned to look at them. Small and slight, the pair looked like careworn teenagers, arms folded as if bored. They didn't look particularly interesting, but then one of them moved, as quick as a lizard slipping through a crack. Lisa almost thought she'd imagined the girl's hands slipping towards the bag of the woman in front of her. Luckily the woman, a larger middle-aged lady dressed in white jeans that must have had some serious seams, turned at exactly the right moment, denying the girl her prey.

'Pickpockets everywhere. You need to keep an eye out and be careful at all times. Keep your bag zipped up and your phone in your bag. Don't put anything in your pockets or on your back.'

'Shouldn't we do something?'

Giovanni shrugged. 'There are policemen around. The minute you approach them, they slide away, like cockroaches into the sewers, but then pop up again later. They work in gangs. You challenge them, they will surround you, letting the others get away.'

Lisa watched as the two girls scoped out another potential victim and then one of them gave the other a lightning-fingered signal as two policemen moved into view. The girls melted away into the crowd in opposite directions. She tugged her handbag tighter to her. She'd be seriously pissed off if anyone pinched her purse or phone. And even though her phone could do with an upgrade, as it was constantly running out of battery, it had all her contact numbers in it and it took pictures.

It was fun people-watching, although when she glanced at Giovanni he was absorbed in his phone. Peeping over his shoulder, she found him checking his Facebook newsfeed.

'Stand up; we need a selfie. You can post it.'

Giovanni jumped up, ready as always to pose for the camera, although he refused to remove his sunglasses and it took five attempts before he let her keep the picture.

'You can post that one, delete the others.'

'Honestly, you're so vain.' She shook her head, unable to see anything wrong with the pictures, but he'd retreated back to his phone. While he was engrossed, she moved down to the front, to the very edge of the water to take more pictures. Twisting, she tried to take a selfie getting most of the fountain in, but it wasn't easy.

'Do you want me to take one of you, honey? In front of the fountain?'

'That would be great,' said Lisa to the smiley American lady with her teenage daughter, and handed over her phone.

'Say cheese,' called the woman cheerfully. 'There you go. You're English.'

'Yes, and you're American.'

'We certainly are, from Wisconsin. Me and my daughter, Jessie. Doing a tour of Italy. Here for two days and then onto Tuscany, Venice, the lakes.' She gave Lisa a shrewd, assessing look. 'I wish I'd been as brave as you when I was your age. Travelling solo.'

'Oh, I'm not... I'm with my... friend.' She looked towards Giovanni but all she could see was the top of his head as he peered down at his phone. Travelling solo did not appeal to her. She'd hate to be here on her own. Talking, sharing and pointing out the little details with someone else, no matter how blasé they were, was so much more fun.

'Aw, well, y'all have a good holiday.'

Lisa gave her a smile and turned back to the fountain, people-watching again. Teenage couples intertwined as if their lives depended on it, probably French, two older couples laden with sensible hats, rucksacks and sturdy shoes, definitely German, and a small boy with dark hair and big brown eyes, leaning over the wall dropping handfuls of coins from chubby fingers was Italian. His mother scooped him, laughing as she held up her purse. She spotted Lisa watching and lifted her shoulders in an amused what-can-you-do gesture as she indicated the empty coin compartment, although there was a definite twinkle in her eye. Lisa gave her a smile, thoroughly amused by the scene and warmed by the mother's reaction. Would her mother have been that indulgent? Found it funny?

Dad obviously did, as he arrived chuckling and threw his

arms around them both, encircling them in a warm hug that made Lisa's eyes suddenly blur and her heart miss a beat.

Turning her back on the fountain and the little family unit, she started back to Giovanni, who only looked up from his blasted phone when her shadow fell across him.

'You've finished?' He sprang to his feet.

'Yes. It's wonderful. It makes you wonder about the people who built it, the craftsmen, the people who commissioned it and all the people who visit.'

Her thoughts went back to the young family. Would the little boy remember this day? A memory, faded by time, drifted into her head. Stepping stones on a river. Her father jumping her from one to the next with supreme confidence, as if to make up for the fact that her legs were far too short. With the fragment came the sense of being happy. She'd been giggling.

Giovanni was still fiddling with his phone. 'Are you hungry? I know a place for lunch. Very nice. Come on.' He tugged at her hand and started guiding her away.

She glanced back to take one last look at the fountain. She hadn't even thrown in a coin.

'Wait,' she said, but Giovanni hadn't heard and was already ploughing ahead, as if he couldn't wait to leave the place. She sighed and followed. Maybe, it was a bit boring revisiting places you'd probably been to a million times before. How would she feel if Giovanni insisted they visit Covent Garden or Buckingham Palace in London? Perhaps they were a bad comparison, as she loved going to the busy piazza and no matter how many times she'd visited Buckingham Palace, she always spent ages wondering what went on behind the scenes. Neither ever grew old.

She looked at him fondly. He had a very short attention span. But she couldn't help feeling a tiny bit aggrieved that she'd not tossed a coin into the fountain.

The streets around the fountain brimmed with shops and restaurants, noise, colour and atmosphere. Giovanni threaded his way down the street, confidently winding around the throngs of people, tutting when he had to stop behind huddles of people who had decided to pause in the most inappropriate places.

Lisa took her time admiring the Murano-glass necklaces and wine-stoppers in shop windows and the goods in the leather shops. There were some gorgeous handbags.

Further down the street a bright-pink one caught her eye in a shop window. Probably some designer copy. Siena would know. She toyed with taking a picture and sending it to her for an opinion. Giovanni, now at the corner of the street, had stopped to wait for her. She signalled with a hand, pointing that she was going into the shop. Giovanni beckoned her and rolled his eyes.

With a laugh she shook her head. Blatantly ignoring him and his crossed arms, she ducked into the doorway of the shop, around which a selection of messenger bags in bright primary colours hung, vivid yellow, royal blue, emerald green and the pretty fuchsia pink that had caught her eye.

Siena would love it in here. There was a brilliant selection, and to her surprise the price tags fell within her price range – well – on a day she might be treating herself. Picking up the pink bag, she opened it up. With all those inside pockets, her nan would love it too, as it was both practical and pretty.

'Lisa!' Giovanni appeared at her elbow, exasperation flashing in his narrow-eyed expression. 'What are you doing?'

'Just browsing.

'Here?' He looked around. 'I can take you somewhere much better. Proper shops, with real Italian designs. This is tourist tat. It's a rip-off.' He flipped the tag on the pink bag. 'Knock-offs and not real leather.'

'Which is probably why I can afford them,' replied Lisa with a good-natured smile, holding the bag. Even Siena, designer fashionista extraordinaire, lowered herself to buy cheap and cheerful.

'Come on.' He took it from her and put it back on the shelf. 'We haven't got time. If we don't go to the restaurant soon, we won't get a good table. It's one of the best in Rome and very popular. You're going to love it.'

'Okay, then,' she said. It was day one; she might see lots of other things she'd like to buy. It wouldn't do to spend all her money on the first day.

As they walked past the window, she gave the pink bag a last wistful look. Giovanni took her hand. 'I will buy you a much nicer handbag.'

'You can't do that,' she said, before adding quickly, 'but it is a kind thought.'

Once out of the shop, Giovanni caught her arm in his and was happy to saunter along. It seemed he didn't like to be stationary for too long. Now Lisa thought of it, he was always on the move at the restaurant.

They strolled on. Rome buzzed with lively scenes, the cramped shops, selling everything from pizza, coffee cups and pictures, restaurants with pavement tables, every one full and people inspecting a huge array of fridge magnets on every corner stall. She could hear a dozen different languages as people jostled by in the narrow streets, carefully watching the cobbled stones and uneven flags of the pavements. Gaggles of children from some language school propped up a wall on the corner, sitting on the floor, their logoed rucksacks dumped by their legs, oblivious of people trying to walk by. A small gang of Japanese tourists marched resolutely by, following their tour guide, who held a red flag aloft to ensure they couldn't get lost.

Once they came to a main road, the pavements cleared and their pace picked up.

As they drew up to a glass-fronted hotel, Giovanni took her hand and led her through a pair of beaten-metal doors with golden lions sporting flowing manes for door handles. As Lisa stood basically gawking at the opulence, a concierge, in the sort of designer suit Siena could have named in two seconds flat, opened the door and two supermodel brunette types stepped out on matching spaghetti legs, loping like predatory cats in spiked heels. Lisa had an impression of big glossy hair, big sunglasses and big handbags as they clattered past in a cloud of perfume.

She looked down at her Primark knock-off converse pumps.

'Are you sure I'm dressed for this place?'

'Si, you're beautiful.'

Not quite what she'd asked, but she shrugged.

Icy-cold air hit them as they stepped inside the stylish reception area. Sod the dress code, she prayed no one would mistake her nipples for coat hooks.

Chilly in temperature and chilly in style. It was certainly rather chic, although not the most welcoming reception area she'd ever seen, at least she thought it was a reception area, it was hard to tell. There was a long, glass, curved bench and a desk affair housing a white iMac on each end, but nothing else. Behind it was a marble wall, down which cascaded a solid flow of water, which Lisa swore glittered. A discreet Swarovski crystal logo on the side of the water feature suggested it might be full of crystals. Or, then again, it could be ice.

Giovanni steered her towards the opposite wall.

'We're going up to the top floor to the restaurant. This hotel, Midas, opened last year.'

'It's... um, very nice.'

'It is, isn't it?' Giovanni beamed, as a glass box slid down to halt before them.

Lisa had never been in a lift where you could see through the floor. Smoothly it started to slide upwards, leaving her stomach a floor behind. Blindly she felt for something to hold on to, but there was nothing but cool, flat glass. Panic nudged her as the ground floor fell away beneath them. She edged into the corner, a hand on either wall, and held her breath. It was almost as bad as flying.

'No! Lisa, you're not scared of heights.' Giovanni peeled one of her hands from the wall. 'There's nothing to be afraid of. We're perfectly safe.'

Her teeth were gritted so firmly she couldn't speak, but she held the tension in her neck, her limbs rigid and managed a half-nod.

'Oh Belissima. Poor you. It's okay. This isn't high. Really. Look,' he pointed downwards.

She squeezed her eyes tightly shut.

'It's not like New York. This is the tallest building in this part of Rome. No building is permitted to be taller than St Peter's Basilica. You can't be frightened.'

Rooted to the spot, she looked at him.

'Don't worry. I'll look after you. Look, we're here now.'

The lift did that floaty up-and-down thing as it came to a halt, which didn't reassure her at all. It made her stomach clench, but at least it signified they'd arrived.

'See. Nothing to be frightened of.'

Sure, nothing, except falling, dying or a heart attack. Over the years every rational argument had been played through her head, but when it came to it, something else took over and she couldn't fight the irrational fear that flooded her body, leaving her stiff with terror.

Like an old lady, finding her way into her slippers, she shuffled out of the lift, barely able to take in the swish bar in front of them.

'I think I'll find the ladies.'

'Okay.' Giovanni hailed the maître d'.

Lisa sank onto the loo seat, her legs now feeling like jelly. She was such a noodle but she couldn't help it, she bloody hated heights. At least on a plane you couldn't see down unless you chose to look out the window. She had no idea how many floors up they were: twenty, a hundred, she didn't care. She would be taking the stairs when they left.

She leaned against the cubicle wall, grateful for the cool tiles against her cheek, suddenly exhausted by the rush of adrenaline that had spiked through her system.

The table offered a bird's-eye view of the city, which she could cope with because it wasn't looking directly down. Even so she sat with her back to the view, much to Giovanni's amusement.

'Poor Lisa. Here, have a glass of Prosecco.' He lifted the bottle from a glossy, black wine cooler. Nothing in here had been left to chance. Every item had clearly been designer-sourced. The wine cooler, in the centre of the table, no exception.

Lisa shifted in the Perspex Philippe Starck chair, her thighs sticking to the hard surface. She only knew it was because she'd seen this very chair in a Sunday supplement once.

'Salut,' he said, lifting his glass. 'To Rome and family.'

'To Rome and family,' she responded, taking a cautious sip of the sparkling wine. Bubbles frothed in her mouth and slipped down her throat. Family. She ought to cut Giovanni some slack. He did understand about family and, left to her own devices, with her map-reading skills she might end up in Sicily. He was on home turf, which was alien to her, any cultural differences were bound to come up. It was natural.

'Better?'

'Much better.' She took a deep breath and rolled her neck, all the tension had gone. 'Sorry, I'm not very good with heights.'

Giovanni looked despondent. 'This is one of the best places in Rome to see the view.'

She peeked over her shoulder at the panorama of the city spread out all around.

'It is wonderful.' As long as she kept her eyes on the skyline. Domes and church towers predominated, terracotta roofs, crosses and statues. 'I'm okay if I look at the horizon and don't look directly down.'

Suddenly Giovanni was all smiles again. He came to stand at her shoulder.

'Look, there's St Peter's,' he pointed. There it was, the huge dome, topped by a golden ball and an ornate cross. From here you could see the statues atop the balustrades around the roof area. A definite must-visit on her list. You couldn't come to Rome and not go to the Vatican.

'What's that?' She kept her head up, focusing on the panorama. 'The green horses and winged creature.' The brilliant white wedding cake of a building dominated the horizon.

'That's the Altare della Patria, something to do with the first king of Italy. Unified the country or something. What do you think of the Prosecco? Good, eh? Now, the food here is very good. Asian fusion.'

She wanted to know more about the building, but clearly Giovanni wasn't interested in such things. 'Not Italian food?' She couldn't resist teasing him as she took another sip of wine. Lunchtime wine, not a good idea; she could already feel it going to her head.

'No, the chef here is very famous in Italy for opening the first Japanese restaurant.'

Did she dare admit she'd never tried Sushi? It all looked too fiddly and slimy and revolting. Raw fish? Seriously? Just the thought of it had the potential to make her gag. Urgh. Nope, she was not going there. Ever.

On the positive side, the menu, with its beaten-metal cover, which she realised was a copy of the fancy doors downstairs, featured a variety of Asian flavours, some of which were cooked. On the down side, it was staunchly written in Italian; no tourists here. Lisa had to rely on Giovanni's translation.

Once done with the menu, Giovanni nodded, with a discreet head jerk towards a couple on the far side of the room.

'Don't turn around but that's the minster for the interior and that's not his wife.' He lowered his voice to a whisper, 'She's a game-show host on AGR. And the man over there in the glasses, he's a DJ on the radio.'

Lisa smoothed the linen skirt of her dress and tucked her shoes under the table.

'And at the far side, in that corner, that's Sophia Jensen. A very famous star – lives here and in Sweden. She once lived with... now was it Henry Mancini or Franco Zeffirelli? I can't remember.'

Oh God, what was she doing here? The girl who couldn't be trusted not to spill her soup down her front.

When it arrived, thankfully the spicy prawn dish was a lot less complicated and fancy than she'd feared, although nothing like she'd expected. Two butterfly prawns, sprinkled with what Giovanni had translated as 'dust', but looked to her like ground-up spices and accompanied by a sweet-basil foam, the less said about which the better.

She pointed her fork at Giovanni as she ate the last mouthful of prawn, one of six in total. Luckily she'd managed to scrape off the green-cuckoo-spit-looking stuff. 'You do realise I've been in Italy for twenty-four hours now and I haven't had a proper Italian meal.' Good as it had been, she didn't count Will's amazing pasta dish last night. 'You owe me pizza.'

'Sh,' Giovanni held his finger up to his lips, 'Don't say the pizza word in here.' He winked at her.

Disappointingly, even the dessert menu stuck to the Asian theme. Dessert should contain chocolate or ice cream. You'd have thought in Italy it was statutory. Mango and sticky rice were not pudding foods. She kept glancing at her watch, the day was slipping away and this seat seemed to be getting harder by the minute. Her backside bones ached.

Her goosebumps retreated in graceful defeat, when they finally stepped back out in the Italian sunshine, the skin on her legs returning to their normal colour instead of mottled blue. Her shoulders relaxed and she immediately felt brighter.

She pulled out her map.

'Show me where we are?'

'Is it going to help?' He asked, smoothing out the creases and opening it up.

'Probably not.' She gave him an impish smile.

'Are you sure you don't want to go shopping?' asked Giovanni, a hopeful look on his face. 'If we go this way,' he pointed to the opposite direction from which they'd originally come, 'there are some wonderful shops.'

'No,' she linked her arm through his. 'We can go shopping anywhere.'

'But Italian fashion... Prada, Dolce & Gabbana, Armani.' He opened his arms in expansive enthusiasm.

'Aren't in my price range,' she said with a cheerful grin, putting her arms on his forearms and shuffling him around in the opposite direction. 'Come on, you. Let's wander. According to the map there's loads to see on the way... I think.'

Giovanni sighed, his good-natured face reminding her of a mournful spaniel.

'Okay, Bellissima. I will show you something truly beyond compare in Rome.' He clapped his hands together, suddenly full of enthusiasm again. The chivalrous knight escorting his lady. 'The Pantheon. That is one of the prima sights in Rome.'

They spent the rest of the afternoon meandering through quieter shady streets, stumbling across church after church, often tucked between buildings like determined cuckoos surviving ongoing development.

When they rounded a corner, coming face to face with the huge columns of the Pantheon, Lisa couldn't help letting out a gasp and putting her hand to her stomach, where a little squiggle of surprise jumped about inside her belly.

This had been here for hundreds of years. It seemed too enormous to take in.

They crossed through huge bronze doors inside, where its hushed and rather gloomy atmosphere amazed and intrigued her. The windowless building felt slightly oppressive, although very cool on the hot summer day.

She stared up at the vast dome above, craning her neck as

she turned in a full circle, trying to absorb the full majesty of the building.

'I guess it doesn't rain very often,' she said to Giovanni, pointing up to the perfect circular hole in the roof of the domed structure.

'Look at the floor.'

Lisa looked down and saw several drains in the marble floor.

They wandered around the edge of the Pantheon, stopping to read the different information boards.

'I'll go and wait outside for you,' said Giovanni when Lisa stopped again to read the words beneath a painting and stepped back to admire the picture in greater depth.

'Okay,' said Lisa and patted his arm. 'You've done well. You can take a culture break.'

When she joined him outside she glanced at her watch. 'Have you seen the time?' Lisa couldn't believe it was nearly five-thirty.

'It's early by Italian standards. We don't go out to eat until late. Shall we stop for a drink on the way home? There's a nice bar near San Giovanni in Laterno.'

'Whatever you say.' Lisa's head swam with history. Should she know what San Giovanni was? Around every corner there was always something to see, another statue, a fountain or a church.

'San Giovanni in Laterno is the Roman Cathedral, the official church of the Pope, not St Peter's, as everyone thinks.'

'I feel woefully ignorant, you know. There's so much history here and I haven't a clue about any of it.'

'Don't worry.' He picked up his pace. 'Come on, I'm ready for a Peroni.'

'Now, that does sound lovely. I feel positively hot and sticky.' Part of her wondered if she lived in a city like Rome, whether she would know more about its history and the places they'd visited. She guessed it was like anything; you took your own history for granted, but she wished they could have done more today. Maybe in future, she'd be a bit more assertive. While she didn't want to upset him, she wanted to make the most of being here.

As she came back from the toilets in the cool marble-clad interior of the bar, and outside onto the pavement terrace, she found Giovanni sitting at a table on the phone, again, this time having a conversation with someone. He was worse than a teenager. When she sat down he didn't look up. Happy to sit and watch the world go by, she stared out across the road alongside them and took a long grateful slug of the ice-cold beer before holding the glass dripping with condensation against her cheek. She felt pink inside and out. Hotter than she'd ever been in her life.

Giovanni's face had darkened, his frown now a full-scale scowl. His voice rose as he rained urgent questions down the line to whoever was on the other end. His hand jigged up and down on his crossed knee, which was also bouncing up and down.

Lisa deliberately looked away. Even though she couldn't understand a word he said, she felt that she was intruding on something very private.

Finally, he put down his phone on the table, his hand

resting on top of it, his shoulders sagging in mournful defeat as he stared sightlessly away to Lisa's left.

She paused a minute, giving him time to get the sheen of tears under control and placed a gentle hand on top of his. He looked up, as if just noticing her.

Her mouth lifted in a soft sympathetic smile. It was pointless asking if everything was okay because clearly something was wrong.

Giovanni looked up at the sky, his throat convulsing, as if he was trying to round up the words.

'Nonna. Mia nonna… That was my mother, she says Nonna is ill.'

Lisa's heart missed a beat and she squeezed his hand as she breathed a heartfelt, 'Oh, I'm sorry.'

'My parents want me to go. Back to Montefiascone. I…' he looked around. 'This evening. Nonna's in the hospital. They think she's had a stroke.' His face crumpled. 'She's seventy-nine.'

Cold washed over her. Six years younger than Nan. What would she do if Nan had a stroke? She'd always seemed indomitable, but the consultant had been quite clear. She'd better be taking her tablets while Lisa was away. It was tempting to text her a reminder, except it would probably make her dig her heels in even more.

Digging into her bag to find her purse, her fingers brushed one of the leaflets she'd been given by the doctor. She wasn't sure that he'd find it helpful. Instead she pulled out some money and thrust a ten-euro note at a passing waiter, praying it was enough, and scooped a hand under Giovanni's elbow.

'Come on, let's get out of here and get you on the road... are you sure you'll be alright to drive? Can you get a train or something?'

'My father is sending a car. It's on the way.'

Lisa nodded. Of course, it was.

Oh, shit, he hadn't phoned his friend about the information on her father. She looked at his bleak face. Now was not the time to ask him.

Chapter 11

Day one couldn't have been better. Will swung his leg off the scooter and stretched, looking at the long stone-built farmhouse shaded by leafy laurels running along the ridge of the hill. Fun as the Vespa was, it was made for the city streets, not careering along long roads out to a hillside hamlet. The little red scooter had whined in protest as it valiantly climbed the steep incline to the hilltop not far outside Rome. But they were here, safe and sound. A small miracle. Gisella gave as good as she got on the road. It was true what they said about Italian drivers.

Gisella had been an excellent guide, happy to humour him as he'd examined bar after bar and restaurant after restaurant this morning. They were almost awash with coffee, as he'd needed to check out the menus in a variety of different places. Good job they only drank the small ferocious doses of espresso. He knew better than to ask for a cappuccino after ten o'clock in the morning. Italian coffee culture had its own rituals, which you flouted at your peril.

Gisella pulled off her helmet, letting her hair spill out with studied nonchalance and paused for a fraction of a second, which told him it was no idle pose. Glorious – and she knew it. Tempting as she was, business came first. Today at any rate.

'I do hope Signor Fancini is expecting you,' she said with a slight pout.

He smiled. 'If not, I shall have to take you out to dinner instead,' he smiled at her. The pout was replaced with an expansive feline smile.

'We eat late in Italy, there's plenty of time.'

The sign with an arrow that read 'ricezione' seemed close enough to English to gamble that this was the correct way to reception.

'You're so excited.' Gisella shook her head. 'About coffee. About pasta. About cheese. Are you sure you're a proper Englishman?'

'Was last time I looked.'

'Since you tried the cheese in the Salumeria in Travastere this morning you've been jumping up and down all day, do you realise?'

Will gave her a sheepish smile. He couldn't deny it. That taste of the Fancini pecorino this morning had stayed with him all day, in a good way. Sharp and salty, he knew exactly how he'd incorporate it into the menus at the new trattoria. It would make a fabulous addition to a simple rocket and radish salad with a lemon dressing or in a courgette and squash salad, the vegetables thinly sliced with a mandolin.

There was also a great story behind the cheese, which always went down well with customers. Signor Fancini had turned a failing family business into a thriving concern, with growing demand for their boutique cheeses.

Will hadn't met him yet, but could relate to turning the family fortunes around.

'This must be him, now.' A tall man, with a thick, dark moustache so cartoonish it didn't look real, came striding towards them.

'Signor William. Welcome. Welcome.'

'Signor Fancini.'

'Please call me Mario.'

Will held onto bubbling laughter by sheer willpower and deliberately avoided looking at the luxuriant moustache. A red hat and a pair of dungarees were all that was required to complete the Super Mario look.

'And please call me Will. Only my mother ever calls me *William*.' He emphasised the name with a strident falsetto, which made Mario grin and shake his hand that bit harder.

'It's the same with Mama.' He inclined his head towards the main farmhouse. 'When I hear *Mario Guiseppe Fancini,* I know it's trouble.'

He and Will exchanged a long-suffering, sympathetic nod at which point Gisella insinuated herself between the two men.

'And I'm Gisella, chauffeur and guide.' Her wide, winsome smile encompassed the two of them and for a minute Will had visions of her linking arms with both men like Dorothy with the Tin Man and the scarecrow in *The Wizard of Oz*.

Mario inclined his head and his moustache twitched, as if hiding a smile under there.

'Welcome. Let me show you around.'

Will had fixed up the meeting weeks ago, having done his

research through the Italian Trade Delegation in London and had planned his itinerary accordingly. Realistically he couldn't deal directly with more than a couple of suppliers, but he wanted to find signature products that he could talk about at length on the menu and sell within the delicatessen area of the restaurant. Part of this trip was to hunt those products down as well as to seek inspiration for authentic recipes.

Despite the homespun feel of the place and the artisan look of the product, this was no amateur outfit.

Mario led them into the long, dark stone-built bar complex, where they had to don blue hairnets, white coats and blue slip covers over their shoes before they could set foot onto the production line.

The cool, dark room had several huge silver bowl-shaped dishes, which Mario led them straight over to.

'These are our kettles, where we heat the milk. Ewes' milk from our own herd.' His eyes gleamed with sudden passion. 'My grandfather established this herd of Sarda sheep, brought all the way from Sardinia. They make the best milk. Which makes the best cheese.' The moustache had taken on a life of its own as Mario warmed to his subject, his hands talking in tandem. 'Our secret is our location. This location has a microclimate with some rain, which means the pasture is... how you say it... lush.'

For the next hour, Will plied Mario with enthusiastic questions about cheese production, which were answered in detail and with endless patience. Will learned that the entire enterprise was family-run, involving Mario's wife, brother, sister-in-law and mother.

They'd reached the end of the tour, finishing up in the drying room, where row upon row of cheeses were lined on shelves, the pungent smell filling the air, before he even noticed that Gisella had melted away at some point.

'Here, you must take some.' Mario pressed several of the small, round cheeses into his hands. 'And stay for dinner. Meet the Fancini family. My mama is a great cook.'

When they emerged into the early evening, Gisella was perched on the Vespa, absorbed in her mobile phone. She looked up and slithered off towards them.

'Ready?'

'Mario's invited us to stay for dinner. Apparently, his mother is a fabulous cook.'

Gisella lips formed the ghost of a pout, and he smiled at her. It was quite amusing. She hadn't quite yet worked out his measure and how far she could push him. Mario had also offered him a lift home later.

'That would have been lovely, but I want to get back to Rome this evening.' Gisella offered an apologetic smile.

'That's a great shame,' said Will, feeling a touch guilty.

'Yes, but perhaps another time.' She looked at her watch with a wistful twist to her lips. 'Enough business for one day, we ought to be starting back. The traffic in Rome will be rather busy now.'

Will felt a spurt of annoyance at her presumption. This was his trip and he wanted to get as much out of each day as humanly possible. This was a one-shot visit.

'Don't worry. Mario has kindly offered me a lift back to Rome after dinner.'

'Oh, right.' Gisella's obvious dismay pricked at him. He hadn't meant to abandon her, and Mario had invited them both, but she'd rather jumped the gun in refusing.

'Sure you can't stay?'

She hesitated and he could see she was torn.

'I don't want to hold you up. You are more than welcome to stay,' he offered her a smile, with a hint of future promise. It wouldn't do to piss her off and she was very attractive and charming. It hadn't been a hardship spending time with her today.

'But I want to discuss a few things with Mario and he's going to set up a cheese-tasting. We're going to talk business.'

A sulky pout replaced her previous eagerness. 'I'd best get back, then.'

Will kissed her on both cheeks. 'Thanks for today. You've been brilliant.'

Just before she pulled on her helmet, she gave him a winning smile. 'Let me know where you'd like to go next.'

She revved the Vespa and drove off with a spit of gravel as she did a showy swerve shooting off down the drive.

Will watched her depart with a rueful smile. Another time, another place, he might have taken her up on her tacit offer. Attractive, but wanted too much too quickly.

'Bit of a she-wolf that one,' said Mario. 'Wants to be in charge too much.'

'I think you might be right. I did invite her to stay for dinner.'

Mario smiled his quiet, contemplative smile. 'I think she had other things in mind for you. And they didn't involve dinner, Signor.'

'I think you might be right.'

Signora Fancini, Mario's mother, was nothing like the lazy stereotype of black-garbed wrinkled old Italian mama Will had imagined. Dressed in a pale-blue shift dress, which showed off a trim waist and broad shoulders, and the chicest flowery apron he'd ever seen, she had the same poise and elegance as his own mother, although that was where the similarity ended. He doubted his mother had ever owned an apron, the kitchen in their house being another room that happened to contain a rather handy storage facility for olives, cheese, lemons, tonic, and Champagne and very occasionally the odd ready-meal.

'Mama, si chiamo Will. Will this my mother, Auzelia.' Mario threw a casual arm around his mother and the two of them exchanged a quick hug that had Will shifting from foot to foot trying to look nonchalant.

'Benvenuto.' She welcomed him with an easy smile and launched into a torrent of Italian, her face lighting up with enthusiasm. He grinned back like an idiot, unaccountably shy in the face of her unconditional warmth, and lifted his shoulders with an apologetic grimace. 'Non parla Italiano.'

Not that it made a blind bit of difference. She trotted over, nimble and neat in sensible polished court shoes, which made her look like a highly efficient PA and that she should be in a shiny office block rather than standing here in this rather idyllic vine-covered pergola, with the sensational view out over the distant domes of the city, and took his hand in a double-handed shake.

Mario offered a quick translation. 'I told her you were

opening a restaurant in England and that you were looking to use our cheese and make Italian food. She's going to show you proper Italian cooking,' his teeth gleamed against the moustache as he smiled at his mother, 'not the tourist nonsense you get in Roma.'

'Great,' said Will, suddenly aware of being nervous. Entirely self-taught, he wasn't a chef or anything close. Dinner with the family was one thing, but this was a bit too up close and personal.

With another burst of Italian, she called to her son, who said, 'I must do a few things. I'll see you in a while. I'll leave you with Auzelia.'

Like a collie herding sheep, before he had chance to protest, she bustled him into a surprisingly modern, bright kitchen with every mod con going, including a huge range stove and an American-style fridge.

'Veni, veni,' Auzelia prodded him and brought him to the quintessentially different feature of the kitchen, a large, flat marble-topped central island, atop which sat a volcano-shaped pile of flour.

'Pasta,' she announced following his gaze. 'Come, I show you.' She rolled up her sleeves and in quick succession cracked open several eggs, depositing them one after another into the centre of the well.

She pointed to her face and to the pasta, making it clear that Will needed to watch closely. Her business-like approach eased his nerves. This he could cope with.

It was fascinating to see the way she worked the eggs into the flour and, in no time at all, had an even dough. After kneading, she indicated that he should take over and pointed to the sink where he should wash his hands.

It had been a while, but once his hands touched the smooth, slightly warm, dough, he soon got into a gentle, well-remembered rhythm. Kneading the dough in the repetitive rolling motion made him relax for the first time in days, freeing up spaces in his head that had been given over to list after list, things that needed to be done, the itinerary for this trip, the products he wanted to source, the fire extinguishers that he mustn't forget to order, checking the building regs had finally been signed off.

All that flowed away as he took in the simple pleasure of rolling the dough this way and that, reflecting on the science at his fingertips, as the kneading tidied up the gluten proteins, giving the finished dough a necessary strength and structure.

Ignoring the dull ache in his biceps and triceps he carried on, a sense of satisfaction settling upon him. It was amazing how a simple pile of flour and eggs could be turned into something completely different. There was something inordinately pleasing about being able to feed people and meet that most basic of needs, even if they weren't necessarily that grateful.

Will's jaw tightened at the memory and he gave the pasta another punishing knead.

'Delicamente. Delicamente,' said Auzelia, combining her gentle scolding with an amused expression. She touched his hands, shaking her head.

With a chagrined nod, he treated the dough more gently, smiling ironically to himself. There was one occasion when his father had pronounced that Will's roast chicken was 'passable'.

His parents had some cock-eyed view that cooking was menial, spending time in the kitchen should be kept to a minimum, and were slightly embarrassed by his ability to knock up a tasty meal.

Auzelia came to stand in front of him, nodding approvingly. 'Bene, bene.'

She took the dough, pulled out a huge knife, second cousin to a machete, and with quick ferocious slices, the blade pinging resoundingly on the marble top, severed the dough into four equal portions.

Will stepped back to watch as she scooped one of the quarters up and began to feed it into a rolling-machine. Deftly she worked the dough through the machine several times until seconds later a foot-long sheet of smooth pasta hung over the back of a wooden chair and she beckoned Will over and thrust a piece of dough into his hand, indicating it was his turn.

Another woman came into the kitchen, a basket on her hip and with a cheerful *Ciao*, encompassing both Will and Auzelia, began to assemble a salad, chatting cheerfully as she sliced peppers at lightning speed, pulling freshly picked rocket from the basket and selecting tomatoes from a triffid of a plant sprawling through the tiled doorway, its branches drooping with the weight of the lush red fruit.

She waved her knife at Will and then at herself. 'Carla, Mario. Marito.' From which Will gathered she was married to his host and could slice and chop quicker than any chef he'd ever worked with.

Leaving him on pasta duty, Auzelia began pulling brown-paper parcels from the fridge and arranging the contents on a large platter, constantly darting back to check on his progress, throwing comments at the other woman.

Will continued to feed the pasta machine, somehow reassured by the constant squeak of the handle on the machine, which made him feel part of action of the vibrant kitchen. Even though he couldn't understand a word the other two women said, they included him with constant smiles and gestures, Auzelia bringing over titbits of meat from the antipasti platter she'd prepared for him to try and Carla offering him slices of tomatoes.

This was a tight-knit family that understood food and the joy of sharing food, and despite the language barrier, he suddenly felt at home in a way he'd never done in his own home.

Once all the pasta was rolled, the sheets hanging from several wooden chair backs, Auzelia changed the rollers and showed Will how to feed the sheets through, to be cut into ribbons of tagliatelle. As they poured out of the machine, with a twist of her wrist she wound the resulting yellow ribbons into what looked like a nest and popped them on the side by the range, where a pan, almost big enough to bath a baby, bubbled with water.

When the last sheet of pasta was done, Auzelia gave his bicep an approving squeeze and rattled off, what he hoped were a whole load of compliments about his athletic prowess with a pasta machine. His arm ached like a bitch, but her warming approval quickly made him forget how much he was feeling it.

Suddenly there was a flurry of activity and Will, caught in the noisy thick of it, found himself squeezing lemons and shaving Pecorino, while Carla rubbed garlic into bread and Auzelia strained the huge vat of pasta. Two younger teenagers appeared and began carrying bowls, plates and cutlery out to the table on the terrace.

Auzelia shooed him out of the kitchen, giving him an enormous bowl of the cooked pasta, which had somehow been drizzled with lemon and oil, tossed with walnuts and rocket and topped with a scattering of curls of cheese. His stomach contracted in sharp hunger; the food looked and smelled delicious.

From the quiet of the farm, which seemed uninhabited and still, suddenly people of all ages teemed out of the woodwork, swarming from every corner like a family of earwigs recently disturbed.

Mario appeared and urged Will to sit down, making swift introductions as the rest of the family sat down. Aside from Carla and Auzelia, there was Mario's brother and wife, Benito and Licia, their children, the two teenagers, his cousins, aunt and uncle and his own son and daughter, who were in their early twenties. Most of the names passed Will by.

The terrace soon rang with laughter and disjointed English.

Dinner with the Fancinis was a noisy, lively affair but Will enjoyed every last minute and morsel of food, from Carla's sweet-tomato bruschetta, which exploded with flavour in his mouth, to the salty salami of the antipasti and finally the simple pasta dish that tasted even better. As he spooned a forkful into his mouth, Auzelia made a comment to Mario, her face alight with amusement. Mario spluttered out a laugh.

'Apparently, you make a very good assistant. She says you can come back any time. Usually she gets the children to take it in turns with the roller. She's very impressed with your stamina.'

Will rubbed at his aching arm and grinned, suddenly feeling very light-hearted. He raised his glass in toast to Auzelia. 'She didn't give me much choice.'

'No, I can believe it.' Mario tapped his glass against Will's.

As they sat outside, the sun began to dip towards the horizon and the lights of Rome blinked into life. The song of cicadas intensified and Carla lit lemon-scented candles to ward off the evening bugs, before bringing out tiny glasses of ice-cold Limoncello.

Will sipped, letting the smooth liquid slip down his throat, enjoying the clean, fresh flavour, the warm evening air and ignored the tiny pang of envy as he listened to the happy chatter and family teasing around him.

Chapter 12

When the sleek, black car sped away, purring out of sight, Lisa let out a long pent-up breath. Thank goodness he'd gone. It was a relief to let go of all that stress. Giovanni's litany, over the last hour, of all the worst things that could possibly happen before he arrived at his Nonna's bedside, made her feel quite sick.

To give herself something to do, she'd started transferring her things from her room to Giovanni's, as he'd suggested she take advantage of the air conditioning and en-suite shower room in his absence. She almost regretted it. It was far too warm to be dashing about. The evening air, hot and heavy, seemed to have pooled in the apartment. She'd leave the rest of her clothes until morning and make herself some food.

In the kitchen, she looked down at the rather limp pizza, already semi-defrosted from its packaging, which had been literally grabbed from a little corner store on the way back from the bar. A few sorry dabs of Mozzarella made up the topping, along with some cardboard discs that might have been pepperoni. A pathetic-looking specimen. A bit like her right now, and Nan would be the last person to thank her for worrying, that was for sure.

After a quick spell in the oven, the pizza gained a little colour and several small puddles of brilliant-orange oil floating about on the surface. After hesitating momentarily, she poured herself a glass of the red wine from the bottle Will had opened last night. It wasn't as if he'd miss it. Probably already at some little bistro wining and dining his new friend.

Shoving, most likely, the worst pizza she'd ever eat in her life onto a plate, she grabbed her little guide book, tucked it under her arm and went back out to the balcony.

Mmm, nice wine. At least, she thought it was. But then, Will knew his stuff and he'd said it was a good one. She tilted her head and gazed out at the rooftops, shimmering in the early-evening haze. Rome, alone. The villa opposite still and silent, mocked her. As if to say, you're on your own now.

She bit her lip. Okay, it was a different country, but she'd cope. She was used to being on her own. Picking up the guide book, she slid the grainy photo from between the pages and looked at the blurred face of the father she'd never known. And didn't need to know. She and Nan had managed thus far perfectly well and once Nan was gone... she swallowed hard. She'd be just fine.

But she did want to get rid of the ring. Sever that last link with Vittorio. Stake her independence. She turned over the picture, tracing the faded writing on the back. It was a shame she no longer had Giovanni's useful contact at the electoral place. She was on her own with this one. Even if it was twenty years old, she had an address. She had a phone app and if she could perhaps borrow Will's laptop on some pretext she could get some idea of which part of Rome the street was in. She looked at her watch. When he got back, she'd ask him then.

Feeling positive, if not completely confident, she turned back to the guide book. In between time, she had another five whole days to fill.

Eventually, when the bats took flight in the garden, wheeling with balletic grace across the skyline, she forced herself to move. Still no sign of Will. Not that she'd been waiting up for him.

Only one-thirty, but it felt like the middle of the night. Air conditioning, she decided, was not her thing. It made too much noise and the chill of the air was too icy. But without it the room was too hot. She was as bad as Goldilocks. Switching it off, she lay on top of the covers, her ears attuning to the unfamiliar creaks of the ancient building. Had Will come home?

Lisa sighed and turned over, trying to find a cool patch on the sheets and escape from the orange lights of the bedside clock-radio. It was as if she were being cooked from the inside out and despite it being of no use at all, she flapped her cotton t-shirt from her body.

For a while, she tossed and turned, aware each time she moved of the baleful glare of the orange light impressing on her that a bare ten minutes had elapsed since her last turn. Two-twenty now.

The silver light of a near-full moon streamed in through the tall windows. She listened hard, but there were too many unfamiliar night sounds. Was that a door, a slight squeak of hinges? She listened hard but heard nothing else.

Maybe he was already back. Would she have heard him through her fitful sleep? Even though he didn't deserve it, she'd left a light on for him, as if to persuade herself she wasn't completely alone. A sad indictment. So much for being independent.

Was he still out with the lovely Gisella? He'd probably taken her out for dinner. She bet they'd had a good Italian meal. Her stomach grumbled at the thought. Short-changed by the hideous pizza. She patted it. Tomorrow, she would treat herself to a proper slap-up lunch. Outdoors. She didn't care how touristy it was.

It was no good. She was now wide awake. And she wasn't worried about Will. That would be plain crazy and he'd laugh his socks off if he thought she was. She knew exactly what he was like. Gisella looked the type who knew precisely what she was letting herself in for with Will and could cope more than admirably. Only idiots like Lisa made stupid mistakes, caught out by a moment of weakness, when fear of the future and loneliness had persuaded her into giving friendship and sexual chemistry a chance.

With sudden resolve, banishing the wash of emotion that threatened to rise up and swamp her, she swung her legs out of the bed and padded to the door. The hinges squeaked with spooky old-house authenticity as she opened it, and she smiled sadly at the image of her tiptoeing through the moon glow in her white top. There was no one else here, so why the hell was she creeping along?

The light in the hall had stayed on. Will hadn't come back. In her chest, her heart twisted. Running true to form, but seriously, she pulled herself up short. What else did you expect from Will?

The air in the kitchen almost felt heavy, it was so close and still. Sweat pooled and ran down between her breasts.

She opened the fridge and grabbed herself a bottle of cold water, holding it to her chest, letting the cold condensation cool her skin. Taking a sip, she misjudged the bottle in the dark and missed her mouth, spilling half of the bottle down her front, but the chill of the water was a blessed relief.

Lured by the moonlight, she padded through the shadowy salon and went out onto the balcony. The lights around the house had been switched off for the night. Leaning against the railings, she looked out over the garden, dappled by the silver glow, a black-and-white tableau, making shadows longer, the dark hollows darker and the contrasts secretive. She welcomed the slight cool breeze, which disturbed the heavy, hot air.

'Waiting for Romeo?' drawled a familiar voice.

Lisa whipped around to face Will, tucked in the shadow of the balcony, her heart startled into a gallop by his unexpected presence.

'What the hell!' her voice squeaked, giving her away. She clapped one hand to her damp chest, where her heart pounded like a sledgehammer, and the other dropped to the hem of her t-shirt, tugging it down, hopefully to cover her dignity. She didn't dare look down to check, but instead she held his gaze, as if it would prevent him from looking down.

'Sorry… didn't mean to frighten you.' Will rose in one fluid move, with his usual grace. For a tall man, he moved extremely well.

'What did you mean to do?' She glared at him, hanging on to the hem of her t-shirt and was pleased to see that he, at least, had the conscience to look apologetic. 'Do you have to jump out at unsuspecting females? I'd have thought you had enough of them at your beck and call already.'

Will's chin lifted and, for a second, his face lit by moonlight, she thought she saw some different expression flash in his eyes.

'I wasn't expecting you to be flitting about like some gothic heroine in the middle of the night. Your new chambers not up to par?' His lip curled slightly.

'They're fine, thank you.' She scowled at him, backing up against the railings, bending her knees slightly. He'd obviously come in and seen her original bedroom door open and the room unoccupied. 'I wasn't expecting anyone to be out here now. Just got back?'

'I've been back a while. I thought I'd take in the night air. Didn't mean to startle you. I thought you might have seen me and then when you hadn't, it was a bit late. The last thing I expected was you wafting about doing your Juliet thing.' He cast a brief glance towards her chest and a wicked grin lit up his face.

'I wasn't wafting about. I'm hot and I couldn't sleep.' She sounded grumpy and irritable.

'It's Italy. It's the summer. What did you expect?'

'I wasn't complaining. It was an observation.' She pulled at the hem of her t-shirt again, the damp fabric stretching taut... oh shit, wet t-shirt alert. The bloody fabric had gone completely transparent.

No wonder he was grinning like an idiot. She flushed and turned away to look back at the garden, surreptitiously stretching her t-shirt down. Now she was stuck.

They lapsed into an awkward silence. Why didn't he leave? Was he doing this deliberately? If she left now, she'd have to do that awkward shuffle to avoid flashing her bottom at him.

If he was any kind of gentleman, he'd have seen her predicament and buggered off, but oh no, not Will. He was milking the situation for maximum embarrassment.

Well, she was going to pretend everything was fine and brazen it out until he left.

'How was...'

'Did you...'

Their simultaneous questions hung in the air.

'You, first,' said Lisa, turning to look at him over her shoulder. She glanced at the chair. If she sat down and crossed her arms, she might regain a little dignity.

'How was your day? See everything you wanted to? Was Giovanni a good little tour guide?'

Her mouth tightened as she weighed up her answer. 'Yes.' With determined enthusiasm she added, 'We went to a fabulous restaurant.' She named it.

Will whistled. 'Very nice. Michelin star. Giovanni went all out to impress, then.'

'It was lovely.' And her nose would surely start growing soon.

'If you like that premier-dining-experience crap. Personally, when I'm eating I want proper food, not an experience.'

'The food was exquisite,' she lied. It had been far too pretentious for her taste. 'Asian fusion. I'd have thought it was right up your street.'

Will let out a mocking laugh. 'Anything with "fusion" in it shouts bollocks to me. Why muck about with food traditions that have been long-established? There's a reason places have regional specialities. Access to fresh, local ingredients, recipes that have been handed down through the generations, yada, yada.'

Lisa pressed her lips firmly together, refusing to admit that she actually agreed with him.

'How was the lovely Gisella?' Annoyingly, her voice held a tart, sharp tone.

'Gisella was fine, thank you very much. Now she was a good tour guide. Really exerted herself on my behalf.' Will grinned, clearly very pleased with himself and the night's results.

'Giovanni took me to an amazing bakery place for breakfast. Not far from here. You should check it out.'

'Yeah?' Will cocked his head, as if waiting for more.

She clenched her palms by her sides. 'The real deal. A family-run place. Popular with the locals, the queue was down the street.'

'Always a good sign. Near here?'

'Yes, not far at all. Pasticceria Regoli.' She was pleased she could remember the name.

Will sat up. 'I've heard of it.' Of course he had.

'It's five minutes' walk. You should check it out.'

'I will.'

The awkwardness was back.

'I ought to go back to bed.'

'Yes, I don't want Giovanni coming out looking for you and dragging you, caveman-style, back to bed.'

'Giovanni?' She stalled for a minute, realising that Will didn't know he'd left. 'I think he's a little more civilised than that. He knows how to treat a woman.' She tilted her chin and looked down her nose at him and then at her translucent t-shirt. 'Unlike some, he's a gentleman. Good night, Will.'

With that she marched off, uncaring about the view she gave him.

Chapter 13

Stupid, stupid. Lisa banged her head on the pillows. All very well making big middle-of-the-night statements, but now, with bright morning sunshine burning through the curtains, Giovanni's absence was going to come back and bite her in the bottom. A bottom she had well and truly flashed at Will last night. And then he'd wonder why she hadn't immediately disabused him of the idea she was sleeping with Giovanni.

Idiot. Idiot. She. Did. Not. Care. Will could think what he liked. She did not like Will. Will did not like her. End of story.

Hopefully he'd be off with the glamorous Gisella this morning and he'd have already gone, but taking no chances, she slipped on a bra and knickers with the t-shirt.

No such luck.

Will lounged at the kitchen table, his laptop open and a demi-tasse of thick, dark coffee in his other hand.

'Morning.'

'Morning.' Without realising it, she tugged at the hem of her t-shirt, wishing she'd brought some sort of robe with her to Italy.

She gazed longingly at the coffee.

'Help yourself, there's another cup in there.'

'Thanks.' She busied herself at the stove, pouring the coffee, stiffening when Will asked.

'Where are you and Giovanni off to today, then?'

Darn it. She'd hoped he might disappear before she had to admit anything.

For a minute she stood with her back to him, feeling like an absolute lemon and then, with sudden bravery, whirled round and caught Will... looking at her legs?

Although now he'd shifted the direction of his gaze back to his laptop, he'd definitely been looking at her legs.

She stared at him, noting that he'd subtly straightened up, as if he'd not been aware of what he was doing before.

'He's not here. His grandmother's ill and he's gone back to...' Shit, where was it he'd gone? 'To the country. She's had a stroke or something.' She blurted the words out.

Will chuckled. Yes, he had the bare-faced bloody effrontery to chuckle.

'So he dashed off to the rescue, leaving you alone in Rome. Not very gentlemanly.' He emphasised the word and looked down the t-shirt skimming her thighs, bringing a vivid blush to her cheeks. This deliberate perusal, very different from the thoughtful consideration he'd been giving them ten seconds before.

'His grandmother might be dying.' Lisa was shocked at Will's attitude.

'His grandmother has been dying for at least the last six months. Giovanni gets a call once a month, demanding he returns home because they're about to call the priest in for last rites.'

'Really,' Lisa sat down with a thunk, almost sending her coffee slopping over the side of the cup as she cradled it in her hands.

'Italian blackmail of the maternal kind. A quick yank of the chain. The family has other plans for him.'

'That's very cynical.' She eyed him over the rim of her cup, inhaling the delicious aroma. Whatever Will's faults, he certainly knew how to make a good cup of coffee. 'What if she's genuinely ill this time?'

Will shrugged. 'Then she's cried wolf once too often. But I bet your bottom dollar that Giovanni's told Mama all about the beautiful blonde who's come to stay with him in Rome. The English beautiful blonde, who possibly doesn't fit in with their plans for him.'

'What do you mean?' Lisa bristled, crossing her legs under the table.

'Look around you. This place is pretty palatial. This is the dower house. Who do you think owns the large villa opposite?'

Lisa's heart did an uncomfortable somersault. 'I... don't know.'

'This place is Giovanni's apartment. That place is Ma and Pa's.'

Lisa bit her lip. 'How do you know?'

'Gisella told me. Places like this in Rome are few and far between. This much land in the city centre. She was very impressed and quite keen to meet Prince Giovanni.'

Lisa's eye's widened. 'Prince!'

'They abolished the nobility in 1948, or at least stopped recognising the nobility. Still, I reckon Giovanni could trace his family tree back to at least a Conte and a Contessa. He's not royalty but pretty well connected. I would imagine Ma and Pa aren't going to leave the next generation to chance.'

Lisa drew herself up in her seat and threw him a snooty glare. 'I wasn't planning on providing the next generation.' And if they were like that, she didn't want to know them. She'd had enough of that attitude from Will's new school friends on the bus once they'd discovered her nan cleaned for his parents. Was that why he'd pulled back from her once before? 'Giovanni and I are just good friends.' She winced at the cliché.

'You keep believing that.'

He moved to pour himself a second cup of coffee and then, ignoring her, began leafing through the thick folder in front of him, humming slightly to himself as he tapped occasionally at his open laptop.

She stole a look across the table at him and then wished she hadn't. His blonde hair, loose this morning and slightly damp, hung over his face and she could smell the slight woodsy scent of the shower gel she knew he used. It brought back a memory so sharp and acute it almost felled her.

Breakfast together, laughing as he dished up bacon butties, and chasing her around the table trying to get her to take a bite of his, dabbed with his special mustard after she'd admitted she'd never tried the stuff because she didn't like the colour. Her tentative bite and shocked gasp at the sudden heat on her tongue, eliciting a grin of delighted approval when she'd acknowledged that, actually, it was bloody lovely and snatched the bun from him and finished the lot.

There'd been no awkwardness that morning in the surprisingly spotless kitchen of his flat in the converted outbuilding behind the pub. Waking up, groggy with tiredness, he'd brought her a cup of coffee while she'd sneaked second admiring looks at his broad chest and muscled legs.

She closed her eyes, trying to shut out the images, but her heart pinched painfully in her chest. Any fool would have realised it was easier to promise to call later that day than see the brief interlude for what it was. Hormones and a lapse in her defences.

He never did call and the next time she'd seen him, he treated her with cool distance, making her go over and over the night in her head, examining every nuance to try and work out where she'd got it so wrong.

Swallowing down the lump in her throat, she glanced up at Will, knowing he had one gorgeous body under his clothes. Thank God, despite the absolute temptation, they hadn't had sex, even though his kisses had turned her inside out and every which way up. With tender strokes of her face, he'd looked into her eyes, suggesting they took it slowly, making sharing the same bed and being held all night seem far more intimate.

'Earth to Lisa.'

She snapped her head up, a blush suffusing her cheeks. Had he caught her staring at his chest?

She stiffened her spine, rather proud of the fact that ever since that night she'd successfully managed to act as if nothing had happened and pleased she'd never succumbed to asking why he'd never called her.

The prompt arrival of Cordelia on the scene had been a statutory reminder. Charming girls was Will's speciality and she'd been bamboozled by the sizzling chemistry between them into thinking that this time might be different.

'What are you up today, without young Giovanni to hold your hand?'

She started guiltily, almost hiding the guide book and photo behind her back.

'I thought I'd see the Colosseum today.' And then do some map-reading.

'What, getting your gladiator fix in?'

She shrugged. 'Why not? It's top of my list.'

'Surprised you didn't go there yesterday instead of fannying about in some poncey restaurant.'

'I've got plenty of time.'

'When's Giovanni coming back?'

'I don't know. He said he'd text me.' Her phone had remained resolutely silent, though.

'You need to be careful out there. Rome's unfortunately renowned for its pickpockets and bag-snatchers preying on unwary tourists.'

'Anyone would think you care,' she snapped, irritated by his know-it-all attitude and then more irritated with herself because she'd said that phrase to him before. What if he thought it was a Freudian slip? That she wanted him to care. She didn't. She knew darn well he was incapable of caring about anyone but himself.

'Just don't want to have to come to your rescue... oh bugger.' He glanced down at his phone.

'Something wrong?' she asked, pleased that whatever message he'd received had wiped the superior smile from his face and then felt bad about the petty thought. He brought the worst out in her and she didn't like it. Petty point-scoring. It was mean and not her at all. He had this effect on her.

'Supplier I was hoping to visit today has bloody well cancelled.'

'Isn't the lovely Gisella around to entertain you instead?' As soon as the words left her mouth, she wished she could take them back.

He stretched, pushing his hair from his face, the movement emphasising the toned chest and broad shoulders. She looked away quickly and picked up her coffee, taking a healthy swig.

'Alas, she's working today. I was planning to visit a tasting of aged and flavoured balsamic vinegars. Oh well. They're running it tomorrow.' He grinned. 'Maybe I'll take in some culture instead. I've never been to the Colosseum.' He shot her a challenging look, which made her mouth go dry. 'We could call a truce for the day.'

What?

Some crazy part of her brain decided to make itself known and started shouting yes, yes in her head. It had taken her pulse with it, which had careered off at a vein-popping rate.

Trying to reintroduce a touch of sanity, she took a breath, suddenly longing to feel nice again. Be herself and not the horrid sniping virago she turned into around him. It would be much better to have some company. Who knew when

Giovanni would return? Several days on her own in a strange city would be quite a long haul. Will was better than no one.

'We could, I suppose.'

'Don't sound too enthusiastic.' If she didn't know better, she might have said Will looked a tiny bit (and she was talking infinitesimally) disappointed.

Enough. She put her coffee cup down with resolve. They were two adults in a strange city; they could be civilised with each other for once. Before *that* night, she'd always teased him, treating him with deliberate amusement. While officially he was the boss, they'd known each other for so long she couldn't take him too seriously and never missed an opportunity to take the piss out of him. Which had been handy camouflage against the inconvenient sizzle of attraction that he'd sparked in her ever since he came back to the village to run the pub. This hideous, suspicious, dancing around each other like boxers waiting to get in the next jab didn't sit well with her.

'Okay,' she said with resolve. She was an adult. Crikey, if she could put up with Nan, a few hours with Will should be a piece of cake.

'It's a truce not root-canal work.' Will's disgruntled expression prodded her conscience. 'I could promise to be on my best behaviour.'

It would take two to make this work and he was holding out the olive branch.

'You have best behaviour?' She asked with a sudden smile. It did take two. 'I thought there was only one setting.'

'I can be utterly charming.' His eyes flashed at her, twinkling with mischief. 'In fact, most women think I am.'

'That's the problem.' She grinned at him. 'They're all gullible idiots.'

She shut down the image of him feathering the softest kisses across her face and said more soberly, 'Luckily for you, I'm not most women.'

He smiled, with a hint of wariness, as if already regretting suggesting they team up. 'No, you're not.'

With a long and loud sigh, she said. 'But as you're the only man I know right now, you'll have to do.' She held out her hand. 'Truce.'

Surprise flickered on his face and then his lips quirked in his crooked smile, which never failed to make her pulse trip. 'It's a deal.' He took her hand and shook it, the firm, capable grasp nice and business-like. She ignored the wayward internal shiver his touch elicited. Her stupid body could just behave itself. Idiotic muscle memory asserting itself. They could do this.

'When do you want to leave?' asked Will

'Give me fifteen minutes?'

'I'd better get my skates on, then,' he said, pushing his hand through still-damp hair, looking down at his scruffy Bermudas and faded t-shirt.

'Is that long enough?' drawled Lisa. 'I can give you longer if you need it.'

He rose and picked up her empty coffee cup along with his and crossed to rinse them both in the sink.

'That will be plenty.' He winked, and then gave her a hammed-up sultry look, 'it doesn't take long to improve on perfection.' Hammed up or not, he packed a punch that sent her disobedient hormones on full-speed spin.

As soon as she walked out the door, he rubbed at his forehead. Shit, he was playing with fire. Whatever had possessed him? She was like an itch, one that wouldn't go away, no matter how hard he tried to put her out of his mind. Yet even so, he couldn't help smiling.

All he had to do was keep her at a distance, not remember the silky feel of all that gorgeous tawny hair. The power of her smile when something pleased her. For some reason it hit him straight in the gut every time. She didn't expect anything from anyone, and it should have made her perfect girlfriend material, except as he'd been told quite forcibly by her pocket pitbull of a grandmother, she didn't need the likes of him in her life.

In fifteen minutes, Lisa being Lisa managed to do enough to make her look even better. She arrived at the front door, her gorgeous hazel eyes brimming with happiness, wearing a big pink sun hat. He did his best, but even a monk would have a hard time not looking at the very short denim shorts she wore, which showed off endless, long, slim legs and the ridiculous scrap of t-shirt material, a halter neck, he thought, that revealed a lot of smooth back and the swell of high, pert breasts.

They hadn't left the apartment yet and he was already thinking about taking a cold shower.

He was pretty sure she didn't have a scrap of make-up on and her fair skin held a hint of roses and a faint glow from yesterday's sun, which had brought out a dusting of freckles dotting her nose and cheekbones. Something turned over in the pit of his belly.

'Got your sun cream and some water?' he asked, taking the cream tote bag from her hands and slinging it over his shoulder, putting his own water bottle into it. The Italian sun in July could be pretty fierce, even at this time of the day.

'Yes.' She looked uncertain and eyed the bag on his shoulder as if reluctant to let it go.

'Right, let's go.'

'Okay.' A smile of mischief lit her face. 'After you.' The sudden sight of her twinkling up at him felt like the sunshine after a storm. His heart did some weird miss-a-beat thing. Probably just shock. It had been a long time since she'd looked at him without wary reserve.

The leafy shade of the lane as they walked down to the main gate created a cool arbour disguising the heat of the sun, which hit them as soon as they got out onto the main street and when he stepped aside to let Lisa move ahead of him, he did his best not to analyse too hard what it was about her bottom that filled those shorts so nicely.

Rome buzzed, the streets thronged with people, the roads busy with traffic and the air pungent with fumes and the tang of food as they walked past restaurants already occupied with people dawdling over small cups of coffee. He paused outside one particularly busy place, trying to store up the details. Anything to distract himself from the slim, lithe figure next to him. What made this place, with every table full, different from the barely filled one next door?

Besides him Lisa stopped, and he caught her light, floral scent, bringing back a memory of her in the pub, dancing out of his way when she'd pushed her flirty teasing to its limits and he'd threatened retaliation of a certain kind. They both knew it was a near-miss kiss.

Will turned his head away, focusing hard on the restaurant, trying not to imagine stealing a kiss from the soft, parted lips next to him. Was it the dark-green foliage climbing up around the stone-arched entrance, the quality of the coffee that people drank from tiny white cups or the pavement location right in the shadow of an ancient church? This was what he wanted to recreate. Give people that feeling of holidays, the taste of Italy and the laid-back sense of having all the time in the world to enjoy the intense flavour of sunshine and tradition.

'Mm, something smells good.' Lisa inhaled deeply, her bare shoulder brushing his arm, and immediately the image of his restaurant included her, seated at a table, with a white dish of pasta in front of her, lights sparkling on the glasses as she lifted one to pink lips, laughing with her typical big, open expression of happiness.

Will tensed and looked at her, her head lifted, her throat in profile and a serene smile on her face.

For good reason the Italians enjoyed their food; all those robust flavours, tomato, garlic and oregano. He eyed the wooden pepper mills, dark, rich olive oil and raffia-coated bottles of red wine on the tables, topped with deep-red tablecloths and ultra-white napkins folded with crisp edges.

'Hungry?' asked Lisa, following his gaze.

Hungry. That didn't begin to describe the way he felt. Why the hell had he thought this was a good idea?

'Did you want to stop?' He could see her nibbling at her lip, looking down the street.

He almost laughed out loud at the contrast between her body language and her face. People-pleaser patience etched into her polite smile while she bounced lightly on her toes belying barely contained frustration at wanting to keep moving.

'I wouldn't dare. You might throw me to the lions. You have that woman-on-a-mission-to-see-the-sights look about you.'

'And what sort of look is that?' She tossed her hair over her shoulders, the brim of her hat skimming his shoulder.

'The one that says if I stop for coffee and a pastry you would slap me.'

'You'd better believe it. Now are you going to keep wasting time?'

'The Colosseum has been there for several thousand years. I don't think another five minutes is going to make a difference.' He couldn't resist teasing her. He nodded towards the restaurant. 'How about a coffee?' A range of emotions flitted across her face as she tried to make up her mind if he was serious or not.

'Shame the lions aren't still there.'

He threw his hand over his heart. 'You wound me.'

She smiled, those sunny dimples suddenly appearing in her cheeks. 'Not as much as a lion would.' It looked as if the thought appealed to her.

'Come on, then, you bloodthirsty wench. My caffeine fix can wait a while.'

'Yes, it can. I had enough of that delaying malarkey yest...' her voice trailed off and she ducked under the brim of her hat, ensuring he couldn't see her expression.

He smiled to himself. So the day out with Giovanni hadn't been quite the success she'd claimed after all. No chance of worrying about Lisa being polite where he was concerned. She'd always gone out of her way to look after everyone else, make them happy and fall in with the consensus, but sometimes he got the impression she didn't always do what she wanted.

He consulted the map again and looked up at the street name. 'We're nearly there.'

They carried on walking along the street and at the bottom of it turned right and – there it was, looming up ahead of them, the stone tiers rising and sunshine slanting through the arches.

Lisa let out a tiny squeak and then blushed, pink spreading to her ears, visible beneath the floppy hat. The two colours toned rather nicely.

'Sorry, it's just...' She held up her hands as if surrendering any further words.

He had to agree it was just...

In silence, almost isolated in their joint awe from the buzz of the world around them, they stood in the middle of the pavement, gazing at the building, stark golden stone against the brilliance of the cloudless blue sky. The world seemed to have stopped, leaving the two of them lost in the moment.

'Wow,' breathed Lisa. 'It's even more amazing than I thought it would be.' She tugged at the tote bag on his shoulder. 'I need my phone.'

Taking several pictures of the imposing structure, they walked closer.

'Can you believe that all this has survived? And right next to this busy road. I can't imagine another city like it.'

After queuing in the dark shady outer area of the building, listening to the click, click of the turnstiles as they waited their turn, they finally emerged, stepping out into the central oval into glaring sun, blinking. He could imagine what it had been like for those entering the ring here, coming up from the dark tunnels below into the searing sun. Conditions for a severe case of stage fright if you were a gladiator and bloody heart failure if you were some poor Christian sod about to face an angry lion.

'Oh my goodness,' said Lisa, turning a full circle as she gazed up at the towering walls and the levels. 'Can you imagine walking out here with all those people cheering and shouting?' She shuddered. 'Those poor people. I'm glad I wasn't born then. I bet I wouldn't have been in the posh seats. More likely down there. The Hypogeum.' She pointed to the lower level and then looked back up quickly.

The floor was long gone, but the remaining lichen-covered walls provided a good impression of the warren of tunnels and small rooms that would have been down there.

'The hypo what?' he asked, amused by the constant changes of expression on her face from serious narrow-eyed study of her guide book to wide-eyed interest.

'Greek for underground, from *hypo* meaning "under" and *gaia* meaning "earth",' she said, looking snootily at him. 'I bet it was pretty grim down there. Whereas you, no doubt,' she wrinkled her nose, 'would have been with the posh nobs. Probably up there,' she swivelled, shading her eyes against the fierce sun, and turning the opposite way, 'in the special boxes, along with the emperors and vestal virgins.'

'I quite fancied myself as a gladiator.' He gave her a wink. 'Striding out to the cheering crowd.' He paused, 'With my big sword.'

She scrunched up her face and peered at his shorts. 'Hmm, yes possibly. I could see you in a skirt.' Then she added with a naughty raise of her eyebrows, 'And you know what they say about men with big swords.'

He laughed. Lisa never gave him an inch.

'Biggus Diccus?'

Lisa let out a peal of laughter and nudged him with her shoulder.

'Hunkus Maximus?'

'No!' And then her mouth firmed, although with a definite hint of a smile and she added, 'Idiot.'

He could almost imagine they were back in the days when she first started working at the pub.

'Makes you feel rather small,' said Lisa, as she took in the view, turning around slowly.

Her reverence made him stop and look at the view again. Inside the oval, the building was far more intricate than the classical arched façade suggested. There were different levels, some of the walls and structure in rustic pebbledash and others in intricate brickwork. The scale of the building was vast, easily holding a similar capacity to that of a modern sporting venue. He guessed it was the ancient equivalent of Wembley Stadium.

Before this morning, he'd had no intention of coming here.

In fact he wasn't quite sure why he'd made the offer. And now he couldn't imagine why on earth you wouldn't come. It was amazing. It struck him that this was the first time in a long time that he'd taken some time out, done something completely unrelated to work. Even going out for a drink or a meal, like at the bar the other night, he was constantly looking at the way they did things, the lighting, the service, the menu. He never switched off.

On his own, he wouldn't have bothered. He might have walked around the outside, admired the building and moved on. He'd have missed out on the atmosphere, the lingering sense of history and the indefinable echo of long-gone crowds.

'It's like the Tardis. Bigger on the inside than the outside.' She gave him a whimsical smile. 'Okay, I know that's not right, but it feels like it, doesn't it?'

But he knew exactly what she meant. The ramped levels, where there was once seating, made the building seem much bigger as did seeing the smaller specks of people on the upper levels.

'Come on, then, let's explore.' Without thinking, he reached out to take her hand and lead her to the nearest set of steps, but luckily she turned and missed the near faux pas.

What the hell was he thinking? Or not thinking? A subconscious desire that needed containing. They'd called a truce, not full-out surrender.

They made their way up to the next level, wandering along stone walkways smoothed by thousands of feet before them. He noticed that Lisa kept well away from the edge, confining her gaze to looking across the amphitheatre rather than down.

'Are you okay?' he asked, 'With the height thing?'

'Not too bad, as long as I don't look directly down.'

Even though there were plenty of modern-day visitors, it was peaceful and quiet, but that didn't stop the overriding sense of atmosphere. Nearly two thousand years of people coming and going. He wondered what it would have been like with the tiers ringing with the noise of all those spectators.

They meandered along the upper level, in and out of the shaded tunnels, which offered respite from the merciless sun, intensified by the ancient stones radiating the heat back at them.

After a while Lisa stopped a good distance in front of a parapet, her nose buried again in her little red guide book.

'Did you know 9,000 animals were killed in the inaugural games held in AD 80?' She took a very quick peep down, as if trying to imagine them and he smiled. Scared and enthusiastic, a cute combination. 'There were 80 entrances, 76 were for spectators. It could hold 50,000 people. And,' she drew herself up, as if saving the best bit for last. He bit back a smile at her serious expression. 'Did you know people had tickets for their seats?' Her voice rose, as if she couldn't contain her excitement. 'Numbered pottery shards! How cool is that?' Her face suddenly lit up with impish amusement, a dimple appearing in one cheek. 'And they got to their seats through passageways called *vomitaria*, which is the Latin for a rapid discharge. Which is where the word "vomit" comes from! Bet you didn't know that, did you?'

'No, I didn't Tour Guide Barbie.'

She spluttered with laughter and batted him on the arm with the book.

'There's more if you want.' She opened it up and stuck her nose back in, like a determined librarian. 'I'm not boring you, am I?'

He pretended to stifle a yawn and in response she lifted the guide book again.

'Not at all.' He tried to lift the book from her fingers, but she danced out of reach, holding it aloft.

'Did you know that they brought all sorts of wild animals here, rhinos, tigers, cheetahs, elephants?'

'No, I didn't.' This time his swipe at the book was successful and he held it high above his head, out of reach.

With a lofty smile, she pulled away and folded her arms.

'And they had zebras and ostriches to pull the chariots.'

'Did you memorise that bloody book?'

'Just the good bits. There's more about naval battles and loads of emperors and what-nots... I'm not that good on the proper history stuff.' He wanted to wipe away the sudden self-deprecatory dip to her mouth.

'You don't need to know whether Claudius Caesar added an East Wing in AD 95 or whether Pope Benedict the 95th built a new stage to appreciate this place and the human history that went on here.'

As he went to tuck the book into her tote bag, something fluttered out of its pages. With a panicked shriek she tried to snatch it out of the air, but the movement wafted what he realised was a photo, out of reach and it sailed over the parapet.

'No!' She threw herself at the wall and leaned over, arms

hopelessly outstretched. 'No, no, no.' Her fingers made tiny, futile grabbing movements.

He leaned over the wall and together they watched the photo twirl and flutter with agonising precision downwards.

'Shit, shit, shit,' muttered Lisa and stepped back hurriedly from the wall, snatching her hat from her head.

'It might land on...' but even as he said the words, the picture drifted to the left and then dropped out of sight, destined for the floor of the hypogeum.

'Please tell me it didn't go over the edge,' her horrified expression held desperation.

'I'm...'

She groaned. 'Oh, no!'

'Oh God, I'm sorry. Was it...'

Her shoulders slumped as she sagged against the wall.

Of course, it bloody was.

She stared down at her feet, her lip clamped between her teeth as she swallowed hard, fighting back tears. Tears? Lisa never cried. Something flipped in his chest and he touched her shoulder. She flinched, as if she'd forgotten he was there.

'Shit, I'm—'

'Don't.' Her words, low and emotionless, were harder to bear than if she'd ranted at him for being an absolute bloody idiot. She looked utterly bereft.

'We might get it back. We can ask...'

Fuck. Fuck. Fuck. There was a buzzing in her ears and all she could think was that she wished she could turn the clock back. Why hadn't she put the photo somewhere safe? Why hadn't she copied the address down. Stupid. Stupid.

Will was saying something to her but she couldn't focus on the words. Tears burned and she tried hard not to blink so they wouldn't spill out, but it was no good, she felt them slip down her cheeks and when she took in a sharp breath to try and stall the sob fighting its way out, like a wave crashing over the breakers, it burst out.

'Hey, hey.' Will slipped his arm around her. 'We'll get it back. They do tours down there. I'm sure we can ask someone to look for it.' He pulled her towards him and put his arms around her, holding her tight.

With her face tucked in between his neck and shoulder, she let the tears run freely, crying quietly, unsure why this well of emotion had risen up.

'It doesn't,' she hiccoughed, 'm-matter.' She tried to tell herself her mother wouldn't know if she didn't return the ring, but it didn't help.

'I think it does.' Will pulled her to his chest as she cried, his hand caressing her hair, stroking it and holding her close, as if trying to absorb her pain. He didn't say anything, just let her cry, for which she was grateful because she was having a hard time trying not sink into his hold, slip her arms around him and cling to him.

Finally, feeling limp and embarrassed, she pulled away, frightened by the sudden realisation that she could happily stay there for ever. When he was nice, there was something dependable about him. With an unladylike sniff, she blinked up at him, wiping at the streaks down her cheeks with the back of her hands. He was already digging in the tote bag and pulled out her handy pack of tissues. She took it, fumbling with the opening.

'Here, let me.' He pulled a tissue out and gently dabbed away at her tears, his fingers brushing her face as he wiped each eye, a frown of concentration on his face as he focused his whole attention on her.

Her heart flipped in her chest, a fizz of something expanding like a firework at the tender caress. With a shuddery breath, she stared up at him, suddenly feeling light-headed and breathless. Her stomach was a mass of swirly knots.

Get a grip, she told herself. This was Will, International Womaniser, number-one playboy and charmer extraordinaire. He was good with women.

He was good with Italian officialdom too. When they returned to the box office, he took charge, managing to make himself understood well enough for them to send for one of the English guides who took the tours around the underground area.

The bright young Italian with his bushy, glossy beard looked mournful when they explained their predicament.

'It is not possible for you to join a tour.' He directed his sympathetic smile to Lisa. 'I am very sorry, Signorina. This is high season in Roma. This area is restricted because of its extreme archaeological value. We have to be very strict about numbers to preserve the site. You must enter on a tour. All the tours are full for the next two weeks.'

Lisa exchanged a resigned look with Will; she hadn't expected anything else.

'Couldn't you squeeze an extra person in, to look for the photograph?'

The young man looked horrified. 'This is an ancient site. It is not permissible. A few areas are accessible to archaeological staff. It is impossible.'

'Okay, but there must be something you can do.'

'I'm afraid there is nothing.' He shook his head with the surety of officialdom.

But Will wasn't going to let it go.

'You could look for the photograph when you are on your tours, couldn't you?' Will insisted. 'We could show you where it went over.'

'I will look and ask the other guides to look too.' The young Italian looked from Lisa to Will, his face grave, 'However, I'm not sure, even with your directions, that we will ever be able to find this picture. From above, the area looks smaller than it is. Below the surface it is very big.'

'We would be grateful if you and your colleagues would do your best. The picture is very important to the signorina.' Will pulled out his wallet. 'There could be a reward.'

'Will,' she said dully, closing her hand over his wallet. 'Honestly, it's... it's not...'

'I can make the request to look for this photograph, but I cannot make a promise.'

'You okay?'

'Yes, I'm fine.' They wandered back into the sunshine. 'Thank you for doing your best. It's not the end of the world if I don't get it back.' But now suddenly it was.

'But it's important to you,' he squeezed her arm.

When had Will turned into such a bloody knight in shining

armour? It was kind of him, super-kind, but she didn't want to dwell on it. Not now. And how come he was being super-sensitive and not even asking her about what was in the photo?

'I'll live,' she said shortly.

He gave her a quick look, but nodded immediately. Contrarily she was irritated by his immediate acquiescence. 'Shall we go for a coffee? I could murder a cappuccino.'

Will looked at his watch and put his fingers to his lips. 'Shush. Not at this time of day. You'll be lynched.'

'What's wrong with cappuccino? It doesn't get more Italian than that?'

'What's wrong?' He put his hands on his hips with mock horror – that crooked smile back in place. 'It's sacrilege. You can't drink cappuccino now.'

'Can't you? Why not?'

'No, you most certainly can't. No milk in your coffee after lunchtime. Didn't Giovanni teach you anything yesterday?'

'Ah, he did keep on about hurrying up because he wanted one. Now I get it. Anything else I need to know, Mr Coffee-Expert.'

'Don't ask for an espresso and absolutely not a double espresso. Coffee here is espresso. And never with anything in it. No hazelnut frappuccino here. The Italians are horrified that Starbucks are planning to invade.'

'I'll try to remember.' Lisa's mouth twitched. 'What about tea? Is that allowed?'

'Not if you're with me. When in Rome and all that.'

'Well, we're most definitely in Rome.'

One of the things you had to admire about Will, one of a growing list, all of a sudden, was his ability to get things done. None of this wandering aimlessly hoping to stumble on a suitable coffee bar. No, he'd got an app, identified a target and they were headed to not just any old coffee bar but one of the best ones in the district.

They sat down at a marble-topped table. 'What am I allowed to order?' asked Lisa, with a teasing lift of her eyebrows, hoping she wouldn't have to try one of the small, dark shots of espresso – they looked too strong and bitter for her.

She looked over to where two baristas operated a huge Gaggia chrome machine with the finesse of organ players in a church, darting back and forth, seizing the handles of the machine with sharp twists and bashing out old coffee grounds in a steady tattoo.

'The coffee here is renowned. What sort of coffee do you like?'

'Coffee, coffee. Preferably with plenty of milk.'

'Yes, but do you like a South American blend with robust flavours or an African roast?'

'Why do you have to go and make it complicated?' Lisa's amusement evaporated. 'Any old coffee will do.' She held up a finger. 'And don't say it… I know you won't agree.' She sighed crossly and then, maybe because Will had been nice to her, she relented. 'You *know* I haven't a clue and that I'm completely stupid when it comes to coffee, food or wine.' She paused, looking away across the room, avoiding his careful gaze. 'Nan never did *fancy foreign malarkey*.'

He didn't say anything until she'd turned uncertainly back to him. 'Lisa, I've never thought you were stupid.' With a gentle smile, he turned the menu her way. 'The only thing you need to know is what you like.'

Lisa looked down at her hands. Will being nice unnerved her. He didn't do nice where she was concerned.

'I know I get a bit carried away sometimes, wanting to share, I guess, but most people tell me to shut up.' A rueful smile touched his mouth, softening his face. 'So what do you like, strong or weak coffee?'

She paused, taking a quick glance at the constant flow of people around them – solitary Italian businessmen, in sharp suits, pairs of immaculately turned-out women, teenagers with backpacks and baseball caps, all of whom queued patiently for their drinks before moving to a tiny bar area, where they knocked back the miniscule cups of coffee in two quick swigs. Coffee in Italy appeared to be a quick and serious business.

'See, even that's too hard for me. I like it medium.'

'Then you should try an Arabica. Nice and smooth, without too much of a caffeine hit socking you with a sucker punch.'

'And there you go, spoiling it with the fancy bit at the end.'

'Sorry.' Will's grin was unrepentant. 'But if you like it, that's one little step in your food knowledge. Nothing complicated about it at all.'

'You make it sound so simple,' she grumbled. 'How did you get to be such a food expert.'

Will looked up, his eyes sharpening. 'I...' Then his mouth firmed with lines of resignation. 'Truth is, I didn't have much choice. It was that or... well, me and Alice wouldn't have starved, but rickets or malnutrition were a strong possibility. There are only so many M&S ready-meals you can eat. And if your kid sister takes out the microwave, you're really stuffed.'

'What?'

'Alice put a metal dish in the microwave while Mum and Dad were away, Cheltenham Gold Cup that weekend, I think, or it might have been Wimbledon. Can't remember, now. She was nine.' A shadow crossed his face. 'Frightened the life out of her. The thing went up so quickly. Stupid thing to do, but I grabbed it and chucked it out of the back door into the garden. Singed half my hair off.' He rubbed at the silver-white scar that took up most of the palm of his hand.

Lisa sat up with a sudden jolt and grabbed it.

'Is that how you did this?' She remembered the dodgy haircut with the slightly frizzled bits at the front and now it came back, the bandaged hand. He can't have been more than fourteen then. He pulled it back sharply. 'It was fine.'

It didn't look fine to her, but his mouth had clamped shut in a mutinous line.

'What did your parents say?'

Will shrugged. 'Not sure they even noticed at first, but they didn't get around to replacing it, so I kind of had to learn to cook pretty quickly. Pissed your nan off a lot. I made quite a lot of mess in the early days. Although, to be fair, she was good about stocking the fridge with fresh veg.'

Lisa stared at him, confused. 'But what about your mum and dad?' Eloise and Richard had been quite the most glamorous people she'd ever seen at that age, always beautifully dressed and on their way to dinner or a party. When Nan took her to the house when she cleaned, Lisa would help put away the discarded costume jewellery that Eloise seemed to scatter liberally about the house.

'What about them?' Will opened the coffee menu and nodded at a waiter.

His sudden shut-down made her pause, not quite sure what to say.

'Well, where were they?'

'Around.' He tried to catch the eye of the waiter again, clearly uncomfortable with the subject. 'We were fine. Alice survived my cooking, although,' his laugh sounded forced, 'she's never let me forget my first spaghetti Bolognese, when I boiled the pasta for too long and it turned into mush or the steak-and-ale pie I attempted to make that was more like beer soup topped with raw pastry. But I got better and started to enjoy it and then I got more ambitious and started trying out new things. And,' he gave her a sparkly I'm-just-fine grin, which said anything but, 'it was handy at uni for getting the girls. "Come back for dinner" is a great line. Never failed. I got quite a reputation, if you know what I mean.'

Normally Lisa would have rolled her eyes and jumped in with some comment, but beneath the bravado she sensed that he was very uncomfortable. His relief when the waiter finally appeared and took their order was almost palpable.

'So you became Leighton Buzzard's answer to Jamie Oliver,' she said jokily. 'Bet your parents were thrilled.'

Will stilled, sudden wariness emanating from him like a cat with its fur standing on end. He toyed with the salt cellar on the table, rolling its base around on one edge. 'Not so you'd notice. In fact, they're quite embarrassed by it. My dad thinks I ought to be something in the City and I'm wasting my time playing at being the landlord.'

'But that's so unfair!' Lisa burst out. 'Everyone knows...'

He raised a frigid eyebrow. 'Knows what?'

Lisa shifted in her seat. 'Everyone knows that you've bailed them out. That the pub is incredibly successful.'

'The joys of village life.' Will scowled.

'I'd suck it up. They all think you're some kind of hero.'

'Which, of course, you know I'm not.'

Lisa bit her lip. 'I wasn't talking about me.'

A calculating smile came over his face. 'Maybe we should.'

'Ha, ha. There's nothing to talk about.' Her heart thudded uncomfortably.

'This photo? You seemed pretty upset when it flew away.'

She thought she didn't, but suddenly the words popped out. 'It was a picture of my father.'

'I know he's never been around. Is he dead? I've never heard you mention him before.'

Her eyes widened. 'Oh shit. I hadn't even thought about that.' The words came out before she could stop them. 'But he's not that old.'

A bemused expression sat on Will's face.

'No one's heard from him in years.' Without realising it, she'd picked up the salt cellar and had unconsciously mimicked Will's earlier moves. Caught out, she grimaced and firmly pushed it away from her. 'His last address was in Rome. It was written on the back of the photo. And I can't remember it exactly.'

'Oh, bugger.' She flinched at the sudden warmth of his hand over hers. 'That's…' he sat up and knocked back his coffee, putting his cup down with a decisive clatter. 'We'll go back, now. There must be a way of us getting it.'

We? Us? Had Will had a personality bypass? This was her problem. His earnest look had her shifting in her seat.

'It doesn't matter.'

'Ah, I've suddenly realised. Hence the trip to Rome. You were going to try and find him.'

Lisa wrinkled her nose in what she hoped was a non-committal way. 'It was a possibility. But a bit of a long shot. Like you said, he could be dead, moved away, anything. And, to be honest, it's not like it's a problem. I've lived this long without knowing him or why he left.' Her back ached as she sat upright, stiff and awkward, suddenly not wanting to talk about this at all, but bloody Will had other ideas.

'Do you remember him?'

An unfamiliar hollowness in her stomach stalled her words. Trying to remember him was like groping in the dark, trying to capture an elusive cloud always out of reach, her hands slipping through the insubstantial mist.

'No, not really.' Saying it out loud made it feel like a failure. Ironic that she felt bad not remembering him, when he was the one who had left.

'The photo was the first time I'd ever seen him.' She shrugged. 'In fact, I'd never thought that much about him for years.' And now it seemed she couldn't stop talking. Or being totally honest. 'I've been brought up by Nan; she's all I know. It never really bothered me until… well, I found the photo and then I started thinking. I had this idea I might track him down, tell him what I thought of him and that I'd been fine without him.' The bloody words kept spilling out and now her voice caught in her throat, her spine stiffening as she realised. It wasn't about returning the damn ring – that had only been a smokescreen. She lifted her chin and looked away to the far side of the bar, focusing on a picture, the Eiffel Tower, for some unfathomable reason.

Will laid a hand over hers. 'Except that's not true, is it? No matter how many times I tell myself I don't care that my dad isn't proud of what I do, even though he's happy to take the benefits, I can't stop hoping. Can't stop trying to impress him.'

She put her hands on the table, almost in surrender. 'I'm not sure what I want.'

'You'll regret it if you don't try to contact him. Always thinking of the "what ifs".'

'How come you're saying that... when, your dad is like that?'

'Because it rubs at part of me inside, always wondering what it is that I can't get right.' Will's sad admission made her heart ache. Super-confident, sometimes arrogant and always cocky Will? It was a side to him she could never have imagined. Her fingers curled around her legs as he added, his voice so quiet that she had to strain to hear it in the noisy coffee shop, 'I'd like nothing better than to have a relationship with him – and I keep trying. And you have to try too.'

'I guess I'm scared of being rejected to my face.'

'But he left your mum, not you.'

'Yes, but he could have come back for me. Especially after Mum had died.'

'Ah, yes.'

'That's the bit that hurts.'

'Maybe...' Will pulled a face, 'he thought you'd be better off with your nan.'

With a reluctant smile, she batted his arm. 'She looked after me well. I know she can be outspoken and difficult, but she loves me.'

'Hmm, I'll take your word for that.' He jumped to his feet. 'Right, well, we'd better get back to the Colosseum. We have to get that photo back.' Will's man-of-action tone brought a grin to her face and a slight flutter in her chest.

'Hold your fire, hot pants. Don't go calling the Batmobile just yet. I didn't write the address down but I've looked at it enough times. I'd know the name of the street if I saw it, something like Via del My tomato, except it's tonata.'

Will sat down again with a thump. 'Well, that narrows it down a bit. He pulled out his phone.

'Yes,' she nodded. 'I did try and look it up on a map, but couldn't find it... but then mine only covers the city centre.'

'Don't suppose you remember the postcode?' Will tapped at his phone screen.

Lisa felt slightly sick. 'I think it might have begun with a 001.'

Will's cheek dimpled and his mouth dropped in a downward curve with a rueful smile.

'What?'

'All Rome postcodes start with 001.'

'And you would know that, wouldn't you?'

'Because Gisella explained it to me.'

Of course she had.

'When we were driving around the city yesterday.'

No doubt she'd whispered it in his ear while they were whizzing around on her Vespa.

'At least you know it is in Rome.'

'Yes, Sherlock,' she said, her words loaded with sarcasm, grateful for the pertinent reminder of who she was dealing with. 'I did get that much. He came from Rome. He was Roman.'

He looked up from the phone. 'Okay, how about this Via del Mattonato?' He showed her the screen.

'That's it! Exactly it.'

'We could just go.' He turned the phone around and held it up with a triumphant flourish.

There it was on the maps app, a little red pin throbbing with portent.

In one fell swoop, Will had swept aside all the procrastination and excuses she'd been surviving on since she'd arrived.

With her index finger, she traced one of the darker veins striping the marble table.

When she finally looked up at him, the silence being too much to ignore, he met her gaze, the blue eyes direct and clear, steadily looking at her and holding the connection between them full on, as if he could see right inside her.

Bugger, now there was nowhere to hide.

He continued to stare at her, using that brilliant interrogator's technique of not saying anything. He made it sound reasonable and sensible. Didn't he realise it was such a long shot after all these years?

'Seems a bit dumb now. I mean it's years ago. He might not be there any more.'

Forcing herself to look away, she glanced over his shoulder to watch one of the female baristas manhandling a sack of coffee beans behind the service desk. Quickly and efficiently, the girl in her apron poured coffee beans into a large glass jar, the beans cascading in with a rush and a rattle. No matter how hard Lisa concentrated on the scene, her peripheral vision couldn't ignore Will's unblinking gaze, intent and utterly serious.

He ought to work for the CIA or something; he was like some bloody truth serum.

Only when she finally turned back to him, exasperated and about to crack, did he speak.

'And he might be.'

'Okay, he might be.'

'People in Italy are more traditional. I suspect property tends to stay in the family.'

He looked around at the building, as if to make his point. On the bricked arches and walls were lots of black-and-white photos, testament to the generations that had run the bar.

'It might be a waste of time. He might not be there,' she insisted again.

Once again, Will, the bastard, didn't say a word. He looked at her.

She blinked. 'Stop that.'

'Stop what?'

'That mind-melding thing you have going on.'

He held up his hands. 'No tricks.'

'Well, stop looking at me like that.'

'I'm not looking at you in any particular way.' He looked amused now.

She glared at him.

'I can't do it.'

'Can't do what?'

Her fingers clenched in her lap.

'I can't bowl up to his front door and just ring the doorbell.'

Will looked at her. 'Yes, you can.'

He made it sound so bloody simple. She shook her head, her hand shaking slightly. 'No, I can't.' And then felt slightly ashamed. Will took his father's rejection on the chin regularly and kept trying.

'I'll come with you.'

The quiet, softly spoken words almost undid her. It felt as if the floor had fallen through, her stomach dropping along with it.

He looked completely serious, his face expressionless.

The minute he offered, all the clouds of doubt parted.

'Are you sure?' She peered at him

'I said I would.' The matter-of-fact words reminded her that Will was nothing if not totally practical.

He lifted his empty coffee cup and toasted her, his mouth twisting in his usual amused smile. 'With your map-reading skills, you'd probably end up in Lazio.'

Chapter 14

As they walked along, after leaving the café, Lisa realised that ever since she'd arrived in Rome, indecision had dogged her like a little black shadow, making her feel a slight sense of shame at her lack of spirit. Even her feet felt lighter on the pavement. They'd decided to go to the address later in the day, when people were more likely to be home after work.

'Which way?' Lisa peered down at the map as they stopped on a street corner. They'd agreed that it was far too late to attempt to visit the Vatican City and were headed towards the Spanish Steps.

'I think it's that way.' Will pointed up the street.

'Are you sure?' Lisa looked back at the map, her brain not able to compute how they could possibly be turning right when the map showed they should be heading left.

'Am I sure?' She could see the amusement, crinkling in the fine lines around his mouth. 'Here,' he turned the map upside down and suddenly it made complete sense.

'Thanks.'

He didn't say a word but she saw his mouth clamp shut. 'Okay, I'm not good with maps.'

'I didn't say a word,' he protested.

'Hmm, you thought it. I'll have you know it's to do with evolution and male/female hunter-gatherer roles. It's why you can't find things, even when you look for them.'

'Really?' With a sceptical, knowing look he guided her down the street in the right direction. 'I've never had a problem.'

'Well, you're the exception, then.'

'Sounds like one of those pop psychology things based on a survey of a handful of people. It's a bit like saying all women love shopping.'

'The women you go out with probably do,' said Lisa, without thinking.

'As long as they don't drag me along, I don't mind,' said Will equably.

Very true. She couldn't imagine Will ever doing anything he didn't want to do.

'You like them to do all the running. Dance to your tune.'

'Why are you having a pop at me?'

Lisa looked up, surprised by the irritation in his voice.

'I work unsociable hours, so they have to fit around me. I always make it clear from the outset. I run a pub. Saturdays and Sundays are my busiest days.'

They walked along the narrow cobbled street, shaded by the high walls of buildings on either side.

'Doesn't seem to put them off,' said Lisa, some imp pushing her on. 'I don't know how you keep track of them all. Do you have to write their names down?'

She almost thought Will looked angry, but he said, with

his usual charming smile and a self-deprecating lift of his shoulders, 'No, I call everyone Babe.'

Shame washed over her. He didn't deserve her carping. He'd shown another side to himself today that made her think that he hid a lot away. Even though she'd seen his parents at first hand, she hadn't appreciated just how self-centred they were or how little care they'd put into looking after their children.

Even as he winked at her, she thought she could see through him. This was Will overcompensating and not taking things seriously, which was fine until he lowered his voice, adding, with a sultry edge, that caused that annoying flutter in her chest again. 'No one's complained yet.'

'Oh my, look at that.' Lisa pointed to a car wedged in between two other cars, bumper to bumper. 'It's true what they say, the parking here is mad.' Her palms had suddenly become very clammy. It had to be the heat.

As Will made desultory comments about the haphazard parking, Lisa lapsed into silence, wondering how often he played to the crowd and avoided letting anyone see his real feelings.

The street market burst upon them, as lively as a circus as they rounded the next corner and almost as if inflamed by the carnival atmosphere, Will grabbed her hand and, like a tug boat, pulled her along in a determined trajectory to a gaily decorated stall that looked more like a fairground attraction.

The hand-grabbing unnerved her at first. Holding hands was, well, it wasn't them, whatever it was, but if she yanked her hand away, it would make a thing of it and it was rather nice in a feeling-looked-after sort of way. She left it there as Will homed in on one particular stall.

Pasta in every guise festooned the tented stall, cellophane bags in rustling rows bulging in baskets on the front, egg-yellow spaghetti bundled in loose loops and long trails of tagliatelle hanging in strips over wooden ladders, as well as candy-striped shapes in black, pink, orange and green.

To her relief, Will let go of her hand to pick up a bag of what looked like faded black liquorice laces.

'What on earth is that?' asked Lisa, fascinated but repelled at the same time. Pasta was cream-coloured, golden-yellow at a push, but not this greyish black colour. 'Surely not pasta?'

'Yes, but it's made with squid ink to give it flavour and colour.'

'Oh.' Sounded revolting to her. 'And what about those?' She pointed to some festive-looking bags of Neapolitan-striped bow-tie shapes.

'They make the green by adding spinach water or sometimes broccoli. The orange is from tomato paste and the pink, beetroot juice.'

'They'd be fabulous…' she deliberately paused, almost laughing out loud at Will's expectant face, 'for the nursery. The children could stick them on collages, like little butterflies. I wonder how well they'd stick with PVC glue.'

She giggled as he swatted at her, saying, 'They'd be fabulous served with a light creamy sauce, you philistine.'

'Mm, I'm not sure.' She wrinkled her nose.

Despite the language barrier, Will managed to start an

enthusiastic conversation with the stall owner. The two of them, one dark head and one light bobbing up and down, talking in pidgin English, pointing and gesticulating around the stall.

By the time Will had purchased a bag of the black squid-ink spaghetti and a normal tagliatelle, as well as having had another two bags of pasta pressed upon him free of charge, he and the stall owner seemed to be best friends.

'Well, that was a result.' Will flashed a business card before tucking it into his wallet. 'Signor Gordano has given me the details of his pasta supplier.'

Lisa hoped the black squid-ink pasta wouldn't top his shopping list and that he wouldn't be cooking it for dinner.

They wandered on through stalls, where the fruit and vegetables looked glossy and bursting with goodness, everything that bit plumper and bigger than she'd seen at home. Dried chillies, like witches' gnarled fingers, were strung up in bunches, and huge bowls of herb-covered chubby olives and bottles of olive oil in varying shades of green were displayed, alongside samples in little white dishes with rustic bread.

He stopped at the oil stall and picked up a bottle, examining the label and holding it up to the light. The owner nodded approvingly and indicated the samples. Will needed no second invitation – like a terrier down a rat hole he was straight in there.

'Go on, try some.' He turned to Lisa. 'Here, this one first. It's fruity and rich.'

Lisa wrinkled her nose. 'What, on its own? No thank you.'

'With the bread.' He pointed to the basket of bread chunks

and then indicated a dark-green oil that had a distinct seaweedy hue.

She watched as he dipped the bread into the bowl, pretty sure that anything that shade of green was bound to taste fairly disgusting. 'Mmm.' Will inhaled deeply and sniffed. 'That's good. Lovely grassy flavour.'

Seriously?

'Go on, try some.'

'No thanks.'

'It's a first-pressing olive oil from Lucca.' Will's face was alight with enthusiasm, watching her as if her opinion mattered. It could be a first-pressing chip-fat oil from Aberdeen for all she knew.

The tourist couple next to Will, who'd been avidly watching, each grabbed a chunk of bread and started dipping and tastings oils.

'That is good,' said the woman to her husband, both of them sporting matching baseball caps with maple leaves decorating the brims, as she nodded her appreciation towards Will.

He was like the Pied Piper. 'Now try that one.' He pointed to a paler one and dipped in his bread, the other couple following suit.

'Come on, Lisa.'

Did she have to? Tentatively, she dipped her bread in the palest oil.

Luckily Will had turned his attention back to Mr and Mrs Baseball Cap from Toronto, who might have been talking basic English but it was a language she didn't know.

The words 'grassy, fruity, floral, eucalyptus, buttery and green', were all murmured with reverent tones. It was oil, for God's sake. It tasted oily.

Will turned his attention back to her as the other couple moved on to another stall. What? Was she supposed to shout 'eureka' and jump up and down?

'It's a bit... er...' She moved her mouth a lot, more to get rid of the slightly claggy feeling. 'You know.'

'Go on,' he said, his voice suddenly husky and his attention dropping to her lips.

A sudden flush raced up her body.

For flip's sake, it was oil and would he quit staring at her lips like that. She licked them and immediately realised it was the wrong thing to do. 'It's got a slight... slight,' Oh Lord, she felt too hot. 'Washing-up-liquidy flavour.'

'Washing-up-liquidy... that's not even a—'

'Yes, definite tones of washing-up liquid,' she said, with a wicked smile, as she warmed to her theme, delighted with the expression on Will's face, 'combined with a waxy finish and hints of river water'.

'Do you really have Italian blood in your veins, Vettese?' Will shook his head in mock despair.

'It's oil, Will. It tastes like oil. Sorry but...' she shrugged her shoulders, grinning up at him.

'Hmph – at least you're honest about it. Come on.' He took her hand again. Why did he keep doing that? And turned his attention to a row of balsamic vinegars.

'Fig, almond, aged.' He murmured, as he perused the line. 'You might like these a bit more.'

'Will, I think you're going to have to accept I'm a complete food philistine.'

'Never.'

As far as Lisa was concerned good old malt vinegar was just fine, preferably on fish and chips, and was about to say so when she caught the expression on Will's face. His lips curved in an unconscious smile, anticipation shining from his eyes. He looked down the row, his hand reaching out towards one bottle and then another, as if he couldn't decide which to try first, and she could feel the suppressed energy held in restraint by the ever-so-slight bounce of his movement, as if he had to force the heels of his feet to stay in touch with the floor.

From somewhere, a flood of affection bloomed in her chest as his passion for food positively glowed. The lines of his body seemed sharper, as if he'd abandoned his usual laid-back, surfer-dude attitude and the cynicism, in the twist of his lips she'd so often spotted, had gone. This was a Will he kept hidden, a side that few other people ever got to see. Even with Jason, though they were business partners, they had that jokey-bloke piss-taking relationship. Who did Will reveal this side of himself to?

She watched as he dipped a piece of bread into a molasses-dark dish of balsamic. He moaned, his eyes closed in bliss. 'Wow, that is amazing.'

With a beatific smile, he grinned at her, 'Try.'

'Is it more amazing than washing-up liquid?'

'Just try it, woman.'

She pulled a face. 'Have you ever seen a fig?'

They looked nasty, reminiscent of shrivelled dead organs of small animals, like ferret hearts or dog kidneys.

Snagging a second piece of bread, he dipped it and held it towards her. Damn, but he was impossible to resist. Her breath caught in her throat when his fingers grazed her lips as he pushed the bread towards her mouth, the brief touch sparking a sudden tingle that almost had her jumping out of her skin. Narrowly avoiding choking, she concentrated hard on the bread, manfully chewing the rustic crust and avoiding Will's intent assessment.

Sweet intensity broke on her tongue; a hit of acidity balanced by a long, sweet flavour she hadn't been expecting at all, which she guessed was the fig.

'Oh my, that's…' and it was, 'gorgeous.' She took another nibble, not quite ready to believe that something that didn't look that great could taste so nice.

'See.'

'Okay, on this occasion, I agree. You can have this one but I stand by what I said about the olive oil.'

'I'll take a bottle,' said Will to the bemused man behind the table. 'The lady approves.' He picked up the bottle and studied the label before handing it back to the stall holder, who wrapped it up in rustic tissue paper, rounding the top off with a sharp twist.

They walked, crossing to take advantage of the shade wherever they could, through quiet streets with hidden churches, towards the Spanish Steps. The heat had built and Lisa could feel it rising from the stone pavements, beating down between the buildings. Will looked cool and unruffled in a loose pale-blue linen shirt over navy, baggy Bermuda shorts. He could have stepped off a beach in Cornwall, but despite not looking anywhere near as smart as Giovanni had done yesterday, he received plenty of attention.

'That bloke couldn't take his eyes off you,' said Lisa, as a preppie Italian peered over his shoulder, almost walking into one of the parked scooters haphazardly abandoned by the kerb. She giggled to herself, eyeing the words on her tote bag, which he carried over his left shoulder. Perhaps she should have pointed the wicked gingerbread man motif on the bag out to him earlier.

'What can I say? Irresistible to both sexes. It's a gift.'

'And with a bucket-load of modesty. You are blessed.'

'And blonde. Remember Italians love blondes.'

'I thought that was blonde women.'

'Isn't that a tad sexist?' Will pouted in a camp way, hand on hip, foot out, before grinning at her, his blue eyes dancing with mischief.

'I guess, if some women find you,' she paused deliberately and then sighed, as if to suggest those women were all deranged, 'gorgeous, why not men as well?' She shot him a deliberately sweet smile. No point making him any more big-headed.

'Amazing isn't it? Some women's taste.' He gave her a measured look. 'Although, obviously, you don't find me gorgeous.'

'Sorry, it's the long hair. Doesn't do it for me.' She lied. Normally it didn't. His thick hair, white-blonde in places, brushed his shoulders, it wasn't that long but... it suited him and reminded her of film star Chris Hemsworth playing the part of James Hunt, the racing driver.

'Takes all sorts.' He lapsed into silence, but she was fairly certain she hadn't hurt his feelings. Will had never been short of admirers his entire life. From day one on the school bus there'd been a bevy of them. Although she was the one he insisted on tickling whenever they got a seat together. He'd worked out exactly the spot to make her double over with gasping giggles every time and seemed to take great delight in tormenting her.

With a smug smile, she glanced at the wording on her tote bag again.

Chapter 15

The Spanish Steps were heaving, quite literally. With the hordes of people sitting on the steps themselves, it was almost impossible to walk up them and tantamount to working your way through an intricate puzzle.

'So, Tour Guide Barbie, do you know how many steps are there?' asked Will when they stopped to pause and look at the view behind them halfway up the flight.

'No,' said Lisa breathing heavily. 'Lots and you've got the book in my bag.' It was hard work climbing the stairs.

'Do you want me to take a picture of you from up there, with the street leading away in the background?' He paused and then added, 'then you can have a rest.'

Cheeky sod.

'Yes please.' She'd taken plenty of pictures, but hardly any with her in them, to prove she'd been here.

Nimble as a goat, he took off, wending his way through the scores of people lining the steps. It wasn't a hardship watching him. Long legs, firm calves stretching and flexing as he went. It also helped to get her breath back. A trickle of sweat found its way down her waistband and she pushed her shoulders back, reaching around to touch the hot skin on her back. It felt a bit tight. In hindsight, the halter neck probably hadn't been such a great idea.

With the sun shining full on it, she worried she might be burning. The brim of her hat gave her some shade, but now that the sun was at its highest point, it wasn't doing such a great job. She glanced up at Will steadily nearing the upper balcony. As soon as he'd taken the picture, she'd head up and join him to retrieve the sun cream from her bag.

In the meantime, she turned away from the sun to look at the street scene below. The fountain at the bottom of the steps was perfectly sandwiched between Dior and Prada, each of the shops on opposite corners of a long street stretching out in the distance, where cars tooted trying to get along the street as people spilled onto the road from the narrow pavements.

When she turned, Will had reached the top and was waving at her over the white balustrade. She stopped to pose, narrowly missing tripping on a Japanese tourist's camera strap. Phew, it was hot. She took the steps slowly, conscious of the sweat beading her forehead under the brim of her hat. In this heat, it was too warm to hurry anywhere.

She finally reached the top, to find Will looking rather disgruntled.

'You took your time,' he said, as she joined him at the stone balustrade to look out over the incredible view. To her surprise, he immediately slung a casual arm along her shoulders, pulling her to lean against the low barrier and pointing to the dome on the skyline. 'San Carlo del Orso,' he said.

'Wow, I'm impressed. Have you been here before?'

He gave her winsome smile, sliding a quick look over her shoulder.

'I overheard the tour guide.'

'You okay? You looked a bit…'

'Some bloke pinched my bum.'

Lisa let out a peal of laughter at his discomforted expression.

'It's not funny. That's never happened to me before.'

She tried to bite back a fresh gale of laughter, which came out rather like a snort. 'S-sorry. It's not funny… it's j-just your expression.' Her shoulders shook with suppressed laughter.

He pulled her closer to him in a pretend neck-lock. 'That's not very kind.'

'S-sorry.' She giggled. 'You should take it as a compliment.'

'What? You'd take having your bottom pinched as a compliment?' asked Will in disgust. 'Thanks for the sympathy.'

She sobered for a second. 'No, sorry. But it's been happening to women for generations. Now you know what it's like.'

'I bloody do. And the guy didn't even look embarrassed. He gave me a wink. His gaydar must be seriously off.'

'Good job I came along to rescue you.'

'Yes.' He looked discomfited and moved his arm. 'Your shoulders feel very hot.'

'Yeah, I need some sun cream on my back.'

Will slipped the tote bag off his shoulders and handed it to her.

As she delved into it she stopped and bit her lip. Perhaps she should confess. Pulling out the sun cream, she looked up at Will. Explain why he might be attracting a bit of unwanted male attention.

'You want me to put that on your back?'

She nodded, wondering whether she should tell him now or after he'd applied the sun cream.

Before she could make the decision, he took the bottle from her.

'Turn around. Oh Lord, he's back again.'

'Who?'

'Man with pink shorts—' Will shuffled her around so that he had his back to the gentleman.

'Oooh, they're a tad tight aren't they?' Lisa had never seen such well-tailored shorts.

'Yes.' Will's response was terse.

'I think he's ogling you,' she said and then gasped as he sprayed sun cream on her back.

'Is that cold?' asked Will, taking his revenge, as he sprayed the lotion across the top of her shoulders and down her back.

'No,' she squeaked, 'it's fine. Oh, you've made a hit.' She watched the handsome Italian in his tortoiseshell sunglasses who seemed mesmerised by Will's bottom.

Will removed her hat, tucking it under one arm as he moved closer. 'I need to make sure you're properly protected,' he whispered, his lips almost touching her ear, making her knees suddenly wobble. Then he whispered again, and this time his lips did touch, 'And this is what you get for laughing. You can be my human shield.' A thousand volts shot through her as his mouth brushed the sensitive skin on her neck.

It wasn't real. He was acting, but her body ignored that superfluous fact, taking charge in response to the seductive touch. Her neck arched involuntarily in flagrant invitation. What was she thinking? Except she wasn't. She closed her eyes as his lips trailed down, sparking an electric zing across her skin.

Damn, he might be making it look good for Young Pink Shorts, but it also felt good. Far too good.

When his fingers touched her, she almost moaned as he gently smoothed the sun cream out across the tops of her shoulders, rolling forwards and backwards in slow, firm caresses that set her nerve endings dancing in delight. Putting on a great show, he went to town on the seductive strokes, taking his sweet time.

Standing in the hot sun, slightly dazed by the gentle rhythm of his hands, she could feel the heat gathering between her legs. This was not good, but at the same time her limbs seemed far too lethargic to move. Lost in his touch, she almost willed him on, feeling her knees softening, wanting to lean back against him. Desire flooded her and her mouth went dry. She didn't want this to stop and it didn't feel as if he planned to any time soon.

Taking his time, he moved downwards across her shoulder blades, with a firm touch up and down, with thorough massaging strokes, before letting his hands glide outwards to cup her ribs, his fingers skimming her sides. The feather-light touch made her gulp and she closed her eyes tighter, suddenly wide awake as her pulse kicked up a notch, her hormones shouting danger, danger. The delicious lethargy now sparked into something hot and desperate, and with a jolt she was suddenly very conscious of the scant distance between the pads of his fingers and the underside of her breasts and the sharp thrill of the tantalising almost-there touch.

Damn. She ached, a dull, desperate sensation radiating over her breasts, her nipples tingling with tarty invitation, desperate for his touch. Oh God, what the hell was she doing?

They'd been here once before and she'd spent the last nine months getting over it. She'd be mad to mistake sexual attraction for something more.

Getting a grip on her emotions, which were tumbling and chasing about like surf on a shore, she straightened, feigning a nonchalance she did not feel. Jittery. Anxious. Hot. Her whole body wanted more. A lot more.

She took a long, shallow breath, relieved she could at least blame the Rome sunshine for the heated flush that ran down her cheekbones, neck and chest and pulled forward away from his touch.

'I think I'm probably done now, thank you.'

She turned to face him, her heart dancing about with gay abandon, having given up on the usual beat pattern.

When she looked up at him, the hint of laughter faded from his eyes and, for a minute, there was a loaded silence between them, the sounds of Rome receding into the background.

He nodded, as if in silent acknowledgement.

Lisa's stomach clenched. She couldn't do this. Not again. She snatched her hat back from him and rammed it on her head.

'I think that did the trick. Pink Shorts is crying into his hanky.'

Will took his cue perfectly. 'Excellent. What does the pesky guide book say about the Spanish Steps?' He paused for a minute and then took up a pose. 'No, wait, let me guess? They're steps. They've been here a long time. Some Pope bloke had them built. There are lot of them. Nice view.'

He dug into the tote bag, awkward as he tried to keep his elbows to himself in the crowd around them, to unearth her book, and handed it over.

With the number of people jostling for a viewing position it was difficult to open it to find the right page.

'Wow, exactly that.' She shifted, pushed along by a Japanese family desperate to have their turn to take photos, and moved out of the way, relinquishing her place at the stone balustrade. 'How did you know?' They strolled away from the throng at the front of the landing area and headed up the final flight of stairs towards the obelisk and church at the top.

'It's a gift.' They exchanged smiles as they plodded up the blinding-white stairs. Lisa's calf muscles protested and she could feel a fine sheen of sweat on her forehead. It probably wasn't the best idea climbing all these stairs in the hottest part of the day.

'What does it say? Give me your five facts,' he ordered.

'They were built to connect the church with the Piazza Spagna, Spanish Square, so-called because the Spanish Embassy was here in the 17th Century.'

'And?'

'They're the widest steps in Europe. 135 of them. Keats, the poet, lived in a house over there on the right and died listening to the fountain. The obelisk is a copy of an ancient Roman obelisk.'

'Okay, and where is the nearest bar selling cold Peroni and gelato?' he teased.

'That's your department, not mine, but it sounds like a plan.'

As they turned onto a quieter street, both of them lapsed into silence, as if lost in their own thoughts. Lisa couldn't help the memories of the first time Will had kissed her filling her head.

They'd finished for the night in the pub, with all the tables laid ready for the next day and everything put to rights when the phone rang. Marcus picked it up as he was on his way upstairs, following Al up to the staff quarters. Will had just poured boiling water into a one-cup cafetière next to where Lisa leaned against the bar, enjoying a well-deserved cuppa.

Funny how she could still picture it so clearly.

'It's Eloise for you.' Marcus handed over the phone and bid them goodnight.

'Hi Mum... yes, sure. No, I can't do without it for the next couple of days.' The weary slump of his shoulders and the resigned tone of his voice had Lisa looking up. She hadn't noticed until then how grey and tired he looked. 'I'll dig out the insurance policy and let you know.'

With a careful, deliberate move, he put down the phone as if resisting the urge to throw it across the room.

'Everything okay?' asked Lisa.

'Yeah.' He sighed. 'The usual madness of my family. Expecting me to pick up the pieces.' His mouth turned down at each corner, lines of tension etched into his forehead. It was a rare admission of the burdens his family placed on him.

Maybe because she was so utterly knackered and had had another run-in with Nan about her health, she could empathise. She wanted to give him a hug. It took her less than three seconds to make up her mind to lay a hand on his arm.

'Anything I can help with?'

His mouth twisted in wry self-deprecation. 'Not unless you've got an untapped skill in car mechanics and bodywork. Mum's pranged the car and wants to borrow mine for a couple of days. She wants me to check my insurance to see if she's covered. Now.' He gave a longing look at the coffee pot.

'Why don't I finish up here while you go and look for the paperwork and I'll bring your coffee over?'

At first he shook his head. 'No, it's...'

Something made her stroke his arm, maybe because he looked so alone and lately she'd come to know that feeling a bit too well. He looked wearily into her face, 'Do you know what? That would be... great.'

He'd left the light on in the lounge and she could hear the bang as a drawer shut coming from the little study through the door off to her left.

'I brought your coffee,' she called, looking around quickly. Will's sanctum always surprised her by being so homely, although it had blokey touches like the huge TV screen in the corner, but then the deep-red sofa was sprinkled with cushions and there were lamps dotted about that cast a gentle ambient light.

She hesitated when Will didn't answer, wondering if her

instinct that he needed company had more to do with her own desire not to go home to an empty house. She put the two mugs down and listened. She couldn't hear anything.

Something drove her to look for him.

He had his back to her, dejection apparent in the defeated droop of his body. In a few quiet steps she went over to him and reached out to touch his shoulder, wanting to let him know he wasn't alone. He stiffened briefly and then turned. As he moved, her hand drifted across his chest and, without thinking, she stepped closer. She could see lines of worry on his face and longed to stroke them away, sympathising with the sense of responsibility he felt for his family and the painful loneliness of needing to be so self-reliant.

His hand snaked around her waist and rested there as his head dropped to touch her forehead. The misery on his face made her ache to comfort him. For a second they stood like that. She wasn't sure who moved first, but their lips touched in a kiss, slow and sweet, and her instinctive hug, offering comfort and understanding, turned into something else, a flash of fire and need, that seemed utterly right in the darkness of the night.

Her memories of how they'd ended up virtually naked, lying full-length on the sofa, entwined, face to face, were lost in the heart-warming sensation let loose by the deepening kisses as his mouth explored hers. Nor could she remember what they'd talked about in between kisses and conversation, until the first streaks of dawn crept across the sky.

What she did remember was the sense of ease between them, the happy glow of being with him and the touch of another body. When the yawn she'd been trying to hold on to, escaped, he quietly suggested they move to his bedroom. Although desire shimmered between them, he'd held back, taking her face in his hands.

'I'm not a good bet, Lisa. Is this a good idea? I can't make any promises. Not when I feel like I'm never going to escape. My parents are so hopeless. I've got enough commitment on my plate. I can't take on anything more.'

She'd touched his face in return, wanting to reassure him. 'And I'm not looking for commitment. I don't want to rely on other people. Nan won't be around for ever. When she goes, I'll have no one. I can't afford to be reliant on anyone.' She'd been on her own for so long. She knew people didn't stick around. Her mother had died. Her father had run off. She'd built up her independence and she was proud of it.

'Maybe we're well-suited then. I know one thing, I've been wanting to kiss you for a very long time and I'm not sure I want to stop.' The look he gave her made her shiver. 'I want you.' His body shifted, backing up his words.

'I want you too, but I'm not asking for anything.'

'Perhaps we can take it one day at a time, see what happens.' Despite the eagerness of their bodies, somehow they'd agreed to take it slowly and she'd fallen asleep in his bed, wrapped in his arms.

Lisa glanced at Will, wondering once again if he remembered that night with such crystal clarity and why, despite saying he would, he'd not called her the very next day or for the three days following.

She'd been too proud and too angry at herself for giving

in to her fledgling feelings and that sharp ache of loneliness. Instead she'd held her head up high, turned up for her next shift the following week and kept a cool distance, pretending that night had never happened. To her relief he'd followed suit and never mentioned it either.

Chapter 16

They flopped into wooden chairs under a large cream umbrella, relieved to get out of the sun for a while. The bar, tucked away down a side street, had an outdoor terrace at the back and it would have been easy to walk on by, but Will seemed to have unerring talent for finding the right place and snagging the last table.

He'd spotted it as soon as they arrived and homed in on it with determined assurance.

'Have you been here before?' asked Lisa.

'No, but it's great, isn't it?' He was already perusing the menu, looking like a sniffer dog on a mission.

'It is, but it looks nothing outside. How did you know?'

He looked up, serious for once. Will with his businessman head on. 'I didn't.'

'So what? Are you like some kind of restaurant-diviner? Or is there a secret code, like a sign in the window to tell other people who own restaurants that this one's okay?'

Will laughed. 'No, that's a Trip Advisor certificate. This place looked busy, nowhere else around here did, so I figured it was a good bet.

'What would you like to drink?'

She caught him giving the room a quick sweep to see what everyone else was drinking.

'How about an Aperol spritz?' He nodded towards the table across the way where two middle-age couples sipped at balloon glasses of an orange-hued drink.

With a thoughtful frown, he started rummaging in one of the pockets of his shorts before producing a stub of a pencil and a battered notebook. 'It's an Italian favourite. I'd forgotten about it. Definitely needs to go on the menu.'

She watched as he hastily scribbled notes with the quick, jerky strokes she associated with him. Decisive and determined that was Will. When he made his mind up, he acted quickly and made things happen. A smile crossed her face as he looked up.

'What?'

'Nothing?' He would be horrified if he knew who she'd compared him to. Like him, Nan didn't dwell on things, made her mind up quickly and didn't regret or admit she'd made a wrong decision. As an approach to life it had both pros and cons.

He tucked the notebook away with a pleased flourish. He was nothing if not single-minded when it came to business.

'Have you got your menu all worked out?' she asked.

'A rough idea. I know the sorts of dishes I want to serve and the feeling I want to create, but coming here cements things. And sourcing some local ingredients will give me a bit of a marketing edge, as well as that touch of authenticity.'

'I never asked, how was the artisan cheese?'

'Perfect, in fact Mario has also put me in touch with a guy who makes Nduja salami.' He picked up his phone and checked the screen, as he'd been doing periodically, rather than obsessively, throughout the day. 'I'm hoping to go and visit him tomorrow. Just trying to make some arrangements.' With a lift of his head he acknowledged the waitress on the other side of the room.

'I'm going to try one of those.' He nodded to the Lucozade look-a-like at the next table.

'What's in it?' asked Lisa, regretting the touch of suspicion that tinged her words. She should take a leaf out of Will's book and embrace all this different stuff. It was a drink, not life or death.

'Two parts Aperol, three parts Prosecco and one part soda.' And before she asked, he explained that Aperol was an aperitif made with bitter oranges and herbs.

'Okay, I'll try one,' she said, feeling positively cosmopolitan as Will ordered their drinks with the calm confidence of a native. None of that dithering that tourists often did, pointing to the menu or making a halting request.

They sat in companionable silence, reading the menus and soaking up the atmosphere. The terrace held about twelve tables, each one full and a low-level hum of chatter buzzed in the air, a pleasant change from the loud, jostling crowds on the Spanish Steps.

The menu was in English and had plenty of familiar dishes listed and although they sounded delicious, her stomach protested.

'I don't know that I'm that hungry,' she said regretfully,

putting down her menu. 'It's a bit hot to eat a big meal. I had all these lovely visions of a proper Italian trattoria with proper pizza or lovely pasta, sitting outside drinking red wine. I think I'm destined not to eat a real Italian meal out while I'm here.'

'Really? And what were you looking forward to? Fish fingers and beans don't feature on many Italian menus.'

'Pizza,' she said defensively. 'I eat pizza and pasta... just not anything too fancy.'

'What sort of pizza? Let me guess, Margherita?' he asked, with a teasing grin.

'It's my favourite and I like spaghetti Bolognese, but,' she ticked off her fingers with her other hand, 'last night I had a frozen flipping pizza and the first night we went to that bar and you cooked pasta, which lovely as it was, even with those brown things in it—'

'Artichokes.'

'Is that what they were? They looked like manky onions.'

'Tasted good, though.'

Lisa shrugged.

'You didn't try them, did you?' Will shook his head, smiling at her, which robbed his words of their accusing tone.

'I don't like them,' said Lisa firmly, crossing her arms over her chest.

Will eyed her for a moment, considering. She met his gaze head-on, tilting her chin up a fraction.

'Have you ever tried one?'

'I know I wouldn't like it.'

Will lifted his brow and stared at her, a smile playing at his lips as she realised how stupid she sounded. 'How?'

Heat flooded her face. This conversation sounded horribly reminiscent of a previous one she'd had, except that time it had been with a four-year-old.

Will continued to watch her, as if wanting an answer.

'Okay, I've never tried one. Darn it.' She looked up at the sky. 'I sound worse than the kids at school.'

Will put down his menu. 'It's a free country, no one has the right to force you to eat anything you don't want to... but,' his face gentled, 'I feel bad for all the things you might miss out on.'

She thought of the sweet, intense bite of the sundried tomato in his pasta dish and honesty compelled her to say, 'I did like the sundried tomatoes, even though they seriously look like a mad professor's embryonic science experiment gone wrong.' She lifted her hands in a what-the-hell-type shrug. 'Don't they?'

'Anything does if you're not used to it.'

'Until the age of ten I thought chips were a foodstuff in their own right, hatched right there in the second drawer down of the freezer. It was a shocker when I discovered they were made from potatoes and even more of a bummer to discover that despite "officially" being a vegetable, they don't count as one of your five a day.'

'That is a bummer,' agreed Will gravely.

'I bet you're shocked, aren't you Mr Foodie?'

'No.'

'Fibber.'

'Okay, a bit surprised.'

'I told you, Nan doesn't hold with any of this foreign muck.

I think it might have been a bit of a protest after my dad did his runner. *See, I told you this foreign stuff is unreliable. Don't touch it with a barge pole.*'

'Or she's from a generation who were brought up only eating meat and two veg.'

'Yes, half a cow and vegetables from the allotment.'

'I've heard far worse. It was quite a good diet, but there is a whole world out there. No wonder your food education is sadly lacking.'

She sighed. 'I am rubbish at trying things. I know I should but... it's like the sundried tomatoes. They look so horrible, I can't bring myself to.' She pulled a face. 'But when I had one in your pasta it was quite nice.'

'It's a question of taste,' Will laughed. 'Tell you what, why don't we have a plate of antipasti to share now and then when,' he paused, 'we've been to your father's, we'll go out for a proper meal. There's a restaurant in that area that was recommended and does a Roman dish I'd like to try. And they do very good pizza.'

'Sounds perfect.' Lisa's hands shook slightly as she picked up the menu. He'd said it. They were going to do it. Find her father.

As if he'd read her mind. Will laid a hand on hers, pushing the menu to one side.

'It will be okay.'

She nodded, conscious of the weight of his hand on hers, anchoring her like some kind of safety rope. Several times today he'd managed to make her feel better, almost as if they were a team. Not a couple, not that, but two together. Somehow it made her feel different, stronger somehow, which didn't make sense. You were strong on your own, leaning on someone else made you weaker, didn't it?

Lisa picked up her menu, wanting to know exactly what was in the antipasti before she committed, but Will took it from her hands with a mischievous challenge, as if he knew exactly what she was doing.

'You look worried,' he observed.

She tilted her chin in the air. 'No,' and made her mind up that she was not going to ask him what the dish comprised of. She could easily avoid anything she didn't like the look of. Antipasti usually included mozzarella, salamis. She liked those things. And there'd be bread.

She fiddled with the cutlery on the white napkin and then hurriedly put her hands in her lap when she realised what she was doing.

Will tipped his head to one side, assessing, as if he could tell exactly what was going on in her head. He had an uncanny way of doing that. 'Tell you what, let's try a little experiment?'

'I'm not sure I like the sound of that.'

The waiter brought their wooden platter, weaving through the tables, the platter held aloft like some championship trophy. Will stood and greeted him before he got to the table.

While they'd been sipping their Aperol spritzers, which Lisa had to admit slipped down a treat with its fragrant zing of orange and refreshing burst of bubbles, Will had rearranged the centre of the table. When the waitress had taken their order, he'd insisted on retaining their menus and set them up like a barricade in the middle of the table.

Lisa caught a quick glimpse of milky-white slices of mozzarella, shavings of pale-pink prosciutto, golden focaccia bread glistening with salt crystals and a blur of other items she couldn't identify before the waiter deftly deposited the board behind the barrier of the menus.

'No looking,' said Will possessively, tucking the menus tightly around the board.

'Okaaay,' she said, unnerved by the sudden concentration on his face.

'I want you to close your eyes.'

'What, here? Now?'

'Yes.'

She shifted in her seat, crossing her legs and wrapping a foot around her calf.

'I'm going to feed you.' His voice lowered and she swallowed, her pulse tripping lightly.

'Feed me?' she squeaked. 'You can't do that!' She looked around at the other busy tables.

'No one's going to know.'

'I'll know. It'll be... weird.'

'It will be an education.'

She folded her arms and glared at him, goosebumps suddenly sweeping along her skin. 'Who says I wanted to be educated?'

'You work in a school.'

'That's below the belt,' she muttered. 'Besides, I'm on holiday.'

'Don't teachers have to take some Hippocratic oath, like doctors? I vow to educate all things that need educating.'

'I'm a teaching assistant.'

Will gave her a sceptical look. 'Okay, what about all the things you might be missing out on?'

'Which I don't know I'm missing. Ignorance is bliss, remember.'

'Education enables you to discover your ignorance.' Will's touché wink robbed the statement of any pomposity.

'Exactly, which means I'll lose the bliss.' She scowled at him 'I'd forgotten about your private-school education.'

Will gave her a bitter smile. 'Thank God it had some benefits. It certainly cost enough. I've just finished paying off the fees.' He looked away over her shoulder, as if embarrassed that he'd let that slip.

He needn't have been, everyone suspected that it was Will who had bailed the family out.

'Oh, okay,' she said, pretending to be cross, nerves rippling, making her stomach churn slightly. 'But if I end up with a terrible addiction to sundried tomatoes, you'll be the one I blame.'

With an approving nod, he shot her his twisted smile. 'I can think of worse things.'

'Be gentle with me. Nothing with tentacles, or fish-eggy things, or raw food that should be cooked. Nothing like oysters.' She shuddered. 'I couldn't...'

Will held up a hand to halt her ridiculous flow.

'Sorry. I'll shut up.' She shook her head. 'It's silly. I'm nervous. How crazy is that?'

'Don't be.' Will's earnest entreaty, spoken in a low voice, hit her hard, creating a low-level yearning for goodness knew what in her chest. It suddenly seemed a rather intimate thing to do in public, making her vulnerable. And food? Wasn't that a bit *9½ Weeks*?

'Trust me.' He laid a hand on hers and gave it a quick squeeze, making her heart flip over with the brief touch before he added with a wicked grin, 'I'll be gentle.'

That was what she was worried about.

'Close your eyes.'

The noise around her intensified. She could hear the rolling rhythm of Italian spoken at the next table by two men in business suits, the rattle of a coffee cup being paired with its saucer, the chink of cutlery on plates, the scrape of chairs on stone and a sudden burst of laughter. Warm air teased her skin, the very slight breeze lifting the damp tendrils of hair that clung around her face. So many aromas swirled around her, and she inhaled, her taste buds tingling, suddenly aware of the true sense of the words mouth-watering.

She swallowed as she heard Will pick up his cutlery and the clink of metal against a china plate.

'Okay, first up.' Did she imagine it or had his voice taken on a sultry tone?

Hesitantly, she opened her mouth, licking her lips, not quite knowing what to expect.

'It's not a bush-tucker trial, Lisa.'

'Easy for you to say that.'

She heard him sigh and could picture his crooked smile of exasperation. Concentrate on the food, you fool, she told herself firmly, but her heart contracted at the easily conjured image.

The first forkful was easy. The cool touch of mozzarella, its texture soft and creamy. A known quantity. Then a spicy sliver of salami, the pungent flavours bursting with garlic and saltiness.

'Now for the next one.' His voice had dropped again and she almost opened her eyes. Was he doing it on purpose?

The tines of the fork touched her mouth. This was new. Firm texture, almost chewy, with leafy, fishy, salty and herby flavours. At first she wasn't sure, but as she chewed the combinations seemed to blend with each other to create one overall perfect taste.

She opened her eyes surprised.

'Describe it for me. Without too much thought. First things that come to mind.'

'Green. Fishiness. Almost sweet.'

'Excellent.'

Lisa beamed. 'Do I get a gold star?'

'Not yet.' He looked down at the platter, his forehead scrunched, as if deciding what next.

'What was it?'

'Acciughe in salsa verde.'

'And what's that when it's at home? Doesn't mean anything to me.'

'Anchovy fillets in green sauce.'

Lisa pulled a face, framing her mouth into a bleurgh shape. 'I hate anchovies!'

He laughed again. 'You mean you've tried them.'

Lisa giggled. 'By accident.'

'But did you like it?'

'Yes,' she nodded, surprised. 'They didn't taste like the ones I've had before. Those were dry, salty and hairy, and sort of caught in your throat.'

'These were fresh anchovy. Quite different. Salty but almost fruity. What about olives?'

'Not wild about them. I have tried them.'

'You might not have tried these ones, Castleveltrano.'

He held a large vibrant-green olive out towards her. Hastily she took it from him before he popped it right into her mouth.

Fleshy and fragrant, they were completely different from the dark, bitter ones she'd tried before. 'Hmm, better than most but... no.'

'Okay, how about this?' Before she could demur, Will popped a sliver of smooth, cured meat in her mouth. Thankfully he seemed absorbed in peeling back a second piece, so she was able to concentrate on the flavour rather than the sudden flutter of intimacy that came with someone feeding her. She glanced around the restaurant, hoping no one was watching them. Richer and stronger than prosciutto and with a slightly firmer texture, she had to work at it with her teeth. Its smooth surface felt almost polished. She chewed it, enjoying the salty beef flavour.

'Nice.'

'Bresaola. Look.' She opened her eyes and he lifted a slice of dark-red meat on his fork to show her.

'You could argue that it's raw; it's not been cooked in an oven, although it has been cured for several months.'

He popped it into his mouth and chewed with obvious enjoyment. With the sunlight slanting down on his blonde hair, graceful as ever, he sat back in his seat, and it hit her again how damn good-looking he was. She hadn't missed the sly glances from the two ladies on the table across the way.

'Right, eyes shut, another one coming up.' With a start, she realised he was giving her an odd look. She prayed he couldn't read her thoughts.

This next taster offered a healthy mouthful of big flavours, with a fleeting combination of textures, some of which she could identify – the slight bite of onion, the long fibres of tomato, something else, a touch smooth, slightly slimy, but tasty and the odd crunch of a soft nut with a subtle flavour. And then Will's finger skimmed her lips as he scooped up a bit she'd missed, taking his sweet bloody time, almost caressing the skin. Her eyes flicked open. Will looked guileless. She faltered a second and closed her eyes again, focusing on the food, analysing it for all she was worth. Flavour, sweet and intense. The sharpness of balsamic, the sweetness of tomatoes and the woody overtones of herbs and the nut thing. She nodded. All in all, it packed an explosive punch in her mouth. Not to mention the sizzle of his touch burning on her lips, which was obviously the result of a far too overactive imagination. He seemed completely unaware of what he was doing to her.

Ever since they'd left the Spanish Steps, there'd been a low-level hum to her body, as if the nerve endings in certain parts of her had woken up from hibernation and were suddenly taking an intense interest in everything.

'Wow,' she said, her eyelids flicking open again, talking about the mouth-watering aftermath of the intense hit of flavours and not the jittery sensation in her stomach. 'What was that?'

'Did you like it?'

'Yes,' she said warily, checking his face. This was Will, he always knew what he was doing, but he looked the picture of innocence.

'It was,' she smacked her lips, 'strong, with interesting flavours. You couldn't eat much of it, though.'

'Caponata. It's a Sicilian vegetable stew made with aubergines, celery and capers.'

'I don't like aubergines.' Lisa frowned. 'But that was delicious.'

'Okay, one last one.'

Reluctantly she shut her eyes, wary this time and ready for any inadvertent touch.

'That was easy.' Thank goodness and she didn't mean identifying the food he'd just given her. The chunk of bread had grazed her mouth rather than his fingers. 'Focaccia bread.'

'That was to cleanse your palate a bit, after the Caponata. Here,' he forked up another chunk of mozzarella and popped it into her mouth, watching her expression all the time.

'You need to eat too.' She picked up her drink, grateful to look away. Will obviously had absolutely no idea what he was doing to her. 'I think I'll be okay from here.' She moved the menus, placing them flat on the table.

He picked up his glass and raised it in a toast to her.

With the bill paid, which Will had insisted on taking care of, and a last mouthful of the rather delicious Aperol spritzer to slurp, Lisa stretched with catlike, if not ladylike, satisfaction.

'That was delicious, thank you.'

'That wasn't so bad, was it?' asked Will, rising from the table.

'No, I didn't spit anything out at you,' she said sweetly, picking up her hat.

'Come on, you liked everything.' He ushered her in front of them as they wove their way through the tables.

'Not the olive.' She threw over her shoulder.

'Apart from the olive and I'll let you off that one because lots of people don't like olives. Not until their palate matures,' he added with a sly wink.

She waited until he caught up with her at the door.

'Yours is obviously ancient, then.'

Will's lips twitched as they stepped out into the sunshine. 'Direct hit. You can have that one, but?'

'Okay, I liked the bresaola and the caponata, and I admit I would never have tried them if I'd known what they were.'

'I'll have you on squid before you know it.'

'No way. Remember, no tentacles and no suckers.'

'What do you want to do for the rest of the afternoon?' He looked down the street. 'We could head back for a siesta before we go out to find your father, or carry on sight-seeing.'

She looked down at the halter-neck top and shorts with a slight wrinkling of her nose.

'I'm not sure I want to meet... anyone looking like this.'

'Then I suggest we amble back to the apartment and freshen up before we go out.'

She nodded.

'Okay, but when we do go, I think I ought to carry this.' She lifted the tote bag from his shoulder, turning it round to show him the front, which featured a big gingerbread man with a large slogan reading, 'I like my men hot and spicy.'

With a long-suffering sigh, he took back the bag. 'I should be grateful it doesn't say "If you're in pink short shorts, come and get me."'

Chapter 17

Will shook his head. Lisa wasn't supposed to forgive him or forget that they'd been sworn enemies. Okay, that was probably a touch dramatic, but she was supposed to keep her distance and treat him as warily as a big bad wolf. Not pick up where they'd left off and treat him like... like what? Typical Lisa, she'd taken everything in her stride, going with the flow, easy-going and cheerful. If he hadn't messed things up with her, they might still be friends. Messed up, shouted his conscience, you shouldn't have been thinking with the wrong part of your anatomy!

Will threw himself moodily on the bed, his skin damp from a very long cold shower and put his hands behind his head, staring up at the ceiling.

It was bloody difficult being friends with someone when you want to kiss the living daylights out of them, hold them close and, now this was sappy, look after them.

He'd had enough of looking after people all his life. It was his turn to look after himself, which is exactly why he'd kept things simple with every girlfriend he'd had. Not that many wanted to stick around once they realised what his working hours were like. Girls tended to want to go out for a Friday and Saturday night. Go away for dirty weekends. Take you to meet their parents. At least he always had a cast-iron excuse to get out of that one.

Not that he needed that excuse with Lisa. Her daunting grandmother would put anyone off. The old battle-axe had pulled no punches when she came to see Will, the day after Lisa had stayed the night. If Lisa hadn't been so fond of her, he might have told her nan where to go.

He remembered the cab pulling up in the cobbled courtyard at the back of the pub at nine o'clock on the Monday morning. Only Jason and Ben were about and at that time of day they were hard at work in the brewery in the far barn.

'Good morning, Mrs Whitaker. What brings you out here?'

'Don't you Mrs Whitaker me, Will Ryan, and you can turn off the charm, I've known you since you were eight-years-old and putting frogs in the cornflakes before your sister's breakfast. And then playing the same trick on Lisa when I brought her to work with me.' Her mouth had wrinkled with displeasure. 'You weren't a gentleman then.'

Despite wanting to remind her he'd been eight and had received a sound thrashing as a result of that particular misdemeanour, an abject reminder he was a constant disappointment to his father, he didn't dare interrupt.

Nan Whitaker in full flow was like a scrappy little tug boat more than ready to take on anything three times her size. 'You're not a gentleman now either, from what I hear.' For a lady of exceedingly small stature, she managed to draw herself up with considerable aplomb, which might have tickled Will if he'd not known that his balls would probably be toast if he so much as let one hair on his eyebrow twitch.

'But I'm hoping I can appeal to your better nature today. And that deep down you might be an honourable man.' The tart look she gave him suggested it was a tall order.

What did you say to that when you had a diminutive virago on your doorstep?

'Would you like to come in?'

Will grinned to himself now, remembering the scene.

Nan had cast a quick look at the cab idling behind her and then peered suspiciously over his shoulder, which prompted the ill-advised quip, 'The den of iniquity is quite clean this morning.'

She'd done that harrumph thing that older people seemed to favour.

'I didn't doubt that. It's one good thing about you, you were always quite tidy, I,' she emphasised the I, 'taught you well.' She sneered and added, 'It's more the dancing girls I'm worried about.'

'No dancing girls this morning. A couple of strippers, but they're long gone.'

'You know what I meant.'

Will had sighed as it hit him, followed by utter disbelief

'Don't tell me you're here about Lisa!'

'Well, who else do you think I'm ruddy here about?'

Will had been struck dumb, speechless and flabbergasted. When he'd said goodbye to Lisa, late afternoon yesterday, it had never occurred to him that her grandmother would come banging on his door to protect her granddaughter's honour.

Oh God, she wasn't going to insist he marry her, was she?

'Ah, nothing to say for yourself.'

'I'm not quite sure what to say, to be honest. I don't know why you're here.'

'Really, your memory is that short? Or have you moved on to the next one already, in which case I've had a wasted journey.'

Will tried to compute what she was saying and had a horrible feeling he looked like some bovine idiot as he tried to find the right words. It had been different with Lisa. She wasn't... she was... okay, he wasn't sure what she was to him. He'd been fighting the attraction to her for months, knowing that once he made a move it would be different and it scared the hell out of him. But this weekend, they'd been like a pair of magnets and he'd been too low to resist.

'Lisa is a grown woman, whatever happened between us this weekend is nobody's business but ours.' Will remembered feeling a flash of fury, hot and tight. How dare her grandmother suggest... what she was suggesting. Taking a leaf out of her book, he drew himself up and with an icy drawl said, 'And I don't like what you're insinuating.'

He meant about Lisa, but Nan missed that. 'You're the love-'em-and-abandon-'em type that gets through women quicker than I get through feather dusters and I don't want Lisa to be another one of your cast-offs. She's a good girl. She's not had it easy, as you well know. She needs... she needs,' Nan suddenly turned white as a sheet and clutched her chest, her mouth opening as she gasped for breath.

Will grabbed the nearest chair and guided her into it.

'Sit down. Are you okay?'

She waved her hand at him. 'I'm... I'm fine.'

She sat there for a minute, clutching her chest as her breathing gradually returned to normal and the scary white pallor left her face.

He'd gone and brought her a glass of water, which she'd drunk without a peep – a fair indication that she wasn't herself.

He pulled up a chair and sat next to her until her colour returned.

'Problem with my blood pressure.' She fixed bird-bright eyes on him. 'I could go at any time. You're not right for her.'

'Don't you think I should be the judge of that, Mrs Whitaker,' he'd said gently.

'You forget, I know your father and your mother, for that matter. Constancy doesn't exactly run in your blood and to date you've been running true to form. Please would you leave my Lisa alone?' Her solemn stare held him like a full beam. 'I want to see her settled before I'm gone. She needs someone. A man of her own. You can see I'm not a well woman. Leave her be.'

Will sat up, suddenly exasperated by the memory. Bloody Nan. He sighed, but when the old woman was clearly ill and could go at any time, how could he have ignored her? Lisa and he probably wouldn't have lasted. Like Nan had pointed out, his track record was shit. And the last thing he needed was another person relying on him. Nan was right, despite what Lisa said, she did need a constant in her life. He wasn't right for her. She deserved a hell of a lot better.

Coming back to the present with a start, he heard Lisa

moving about in the room next door and for a second wondered if she was fresh out of the shower. What was she wearing? Had she put on that subtle perfume that scented the delicate skin on her neck? He was such a bloody idiot. He still fancied her and he couldn't do a damn thing about it. He'd made a promise to her Nan. He'd seen the damage his parents did to one another, and although his father might not approve of him, at least he could do the right thing by Lisa.

He grabbed his phone from the bedside table and re-read the text he'd received earlier. With quick fingers he tapped out a response.

Lisa hovered at the door. She'd decided to dress up as they were going out to dinner. Her stomach had tied itself in the type of knots that were almost impossible to undo and sat inside her like heavyweight dumplings. At the moment, she didn't think she could eat a thing. Bloody typical, would this be another duck? Three dinners out of three uneaten.

Will emerged from his room, whistling cheerfully. She wanted to slap him.

He stopped dead at the expression on her face.

'My whistling that bad?' he asked.

'Inappropriate,' she snapped, immediately feeling guilty.

'Inappropriate whistling, that's a new one. Don't think I've been accused of that one before.' He looked up at the ceiling, as if he were pondering the matter properly.

'Are you winding me up again?'

'Is it working?'

'Yes.'

'Then I am.'

'And I can see through you, Will Ryan.' She tutted. 'You're doing it to take my mind off things.'

'Who, me? Why would I do that?'

'Because,' she poked him in the arm. 'You're a nice man.'

'Nice. Me? No you've definitely got the wrong man.'

'I said nice. We are talking the dog's arse end on the scale of compliments.'

'Ah, that's okay, then. I wouldn't want to be stupendous or anything.'

'No, nowhere close.'

'Not fantastic? Handsome? Sex god, even?'

'Don't get carried away. Just nice.'

He wiped a limp hand across his forehead and sighed pathetically. 'I suppose I can live with nice. Are you set, then? You look lovely, by the way.'

'Thanks.' she blushed. 'Showtime?'

'Yes, and stop worrying. What will be, will be.'

'Che sera, sera.'

'That's the one. This is out of your hands. Just take it as it comes,' he paused 'and other varying platitudes, as you choose. We've no idea what's going to happen, but,' he turned and his blue eyes burned with intensity, 'you're not on your own.'

Her heart lurched in her chest and her mouth dried. She stood on tip toe, putting one hand on his shoulder, and kissed him on his smoothly shaven cheek.

'Like I said, you're a very nice man.'

As she withdrew, he caught her wrist as if he might pull her back towards him. Face to face, she could see a tiny fleck of shaving foam he'd missed, as his gaze held hers and her breath caught in her throat.

'Li…' Her face warmed and then, whatever he was about to say, he changed his mind.

'Come on, we'd better go.' He took her arm and guided her out of the flat, although she could swear she heard him mutter something under his breath.

Platitudes or not, Will's comments had all sounded eminently sensible. Except Lisa wasn't feeling the least bit sensible about this. She was torn, half of her feeling schoolgirl terror and ready to back off and bolt back down into her rabbit hole and forget that her father ever existed, the other half of her excited, with butterflies careering around her stomach, urging her to join in their headlong flight of debauched irresponsibility. What the hell? What have you got to lose? Come on, let's go.

And suddenly it was simple. They were in the back of a cab, Will talking enthusiastically about the merits of Uber, having ordered the cab on the app on his phone. From that he moved seamlessly on to the subjects of Airbnb and a new coffee app he'd found, and before she knew it, the roads narrowed like arteries, getting smaller and smaller, the cobbles bumpier and bumpier and then they were there, disgorged from the safety of the back of the cab and Will was talking soothing bollocks out on the street. The street where her dad might or might not live. The street where at least she knew he had once lived and her mother had once visited.

The sun, now lower in the sky, shed plenty of warmth and although its brightness had faded, Lisa pushed her sunglasses firmly onto her nose. Children's calls rang out, their distant laughter echoing as it bounced from the four-storey buildings on either side of the street, where doors opened straight onto it. There wasn't room for a pavement and a couple of scooters hugged the doorways, as if they might squeeze inside should a car decide to chance its luck down the narrow street, risking wing mirrors. Pots of geraniums clung to deep windowsills on all floors. The old stone buildings looked blank, elderly sun-bleached wooden shutters framing upper windows and their recessed doorways outlined with stone coping. A washing line hung with workmen's overalls was strung across the street. Lisa had the feeling that behind the windows and doors life bustled at odds with its quiet deserted stillness.

Amongst the rest of the tourists in Rome, Lisa didn't feel out of place, but here, suddenly, she was very conscious of being an intruder. There were so many what-ifs, she thought her head might explode with them.

If his family or he lived here, what would she say? What would she do?

It would almost be a relief if he wasn't there. It would stop this wild-goose chase in its tracks. The unanswered questions would stay unanswered, but at least she would have tried.

She took in a shuddery breath, which sounded loud in the silent street. Will took her hand and gave it a squeeze. 'You'll be fine.'

'Fine but bloody terrified.'

He squeezed her hand again, rubbing his thumb over hers.

'I'm glad you're here. Thanks for coming with me.'

Will shrugged and tugged her closer to him, their forearms touching as they walked. She liked that now, when it came to it, he didn't try to say anything clever or funny. His touch was enough of a reassurance.

'It's not exactly obvious what the house numbers are,' he said, pausing in front of one of the dark doorways.

'Maybe the postman knows everyone?'

'No, look.' Next to the door were tiny tiles with the numbers 16 on.

The address was thirty-two. They were half a street away.

Their footsteps tapped on the uneven cobbles.

At last they came to the house. Lisa took in a deep breath and stood looking up at the building. Like all of them along the street, it was impossible to tell if they were occupied or not.

She knocked on the door, the iron shutter across the door rattling slightly in its fixings. They waited, her fingers crossed behind her back. She glanced at Will and sighed.

She knocked again, harder and louder this time. There was every chance that no one was in. It was half past seven. People might not be back from work yet. After knocking for a fourth time, Lisa stepped back and looked up at the building.

'I don't think anyone's home,' she said.

'Doesn't look like it.'

'Damn.' Ironically, having been slow to make up her mind to come, now she was here, she was reluctant to walk away or give up.

'We could go and get a drink and come back in an hour.

Or we could knock on the neighbour's door. See if anyone is home and find out who does live here.'

Lisa looked around at the street. 'It's like the Marie Celeste. I feel like people are watching from the windows, but no one's going to come out, like some creepy film.'

'You've got far too much imagination. We heard children's voices. There are probably plenty of Italian mamas behind the closed doors busy preparing tea for their children.'

They stepped back to look at the houses on either side. One had a tiny tricycle in the doorway and a coloured ribbon flycatcher.

'That one looks as if there'll be someone home.'

'Just have to hope they speak English.'

The knock at the door was answered immediately by a solid solemn-looking boy of about four, who stood there looking at them, sucking his thumb.

'How's your Italian?'

'Not up to this.'

'Buon giorno,' said Lisa and crouched down to his level. 'Mama?'

The little boy peered quizzically at her for a minute, jammed his thumb harder into his mouth and then turned to walk away as a young woman came rushing along the dark hallway, scolding as she came. Lisa imagined he was getting told off for opening the door to strangers.

The woman scuttled the child behind her and came to the front door, suspicion written all over her face.

'Ciao.'

'Ciao, parli Inglese?'

'No,' she shook her head vigorously.

Erm... Signor Vettese?' Lisa pointed to the house next door. 'Ici?'

Why she thought speaking French would make her any more understood she didn't know.

The woman's forehead crumpled into a frown as she leaned slightly forward.

'Signor Vettese?' Lisa tried.

The woman nodded. 'Si. Signor Vettese.'

'He does live here?'

The woman let loose a stream of Italian, her hands gesticulating.

Lisa turned to Will. 'What do you reckon?'

'Hard to say. He could have lived there and done a runner with her best friend, for all we know. He lived there and moved out? He's at work? On holiday? Clearly she knows the name.'

'Un momento.' The woman held up her hand and began calling to the back of the house

'One moment,' translated Will.

'I think I might have got that one.'

Lisa's heart leapt about like a bucking bronco.

'Just checking,' said Will, with an irrepressible grin, and then he caught sight of her face.

'You okay?'

'Yes,' she whispered, her chest suddenly so tight it was hard to breathe. She hadn't expected him to be here and now there was the chance he might be, she felt rather peculiar. Light-headed. Jittery. Sick.

A slouchy teenage girl came to her mother's call, her shoulder hugging the wall as if it were doubtful she had the energy to walk without its support.

She held a mobile phone, both ears wired for sound with a huge pair of white earphones. Lisa could hear the bass from the front door.

'Greta, Greta.' Her mother let loose a torrent of Italian.

With a surly scowl the girl pulled off her earphones. There was a quick exchange before the woman pushed the girl towards Will and Lisa.

'Mi... I parl... speak English.' Her almost unintelligible accent and hesitant delivery suggested her command might be sketchy, but at least it was better than nothing. Her mother beamed, nodding with as much pride as if the girl had snagged an Olympic medal.

'We,' Will gestured between himself and Lisa, giving the girl his super-kilo-watt smile 'are looking for Signor Vettese.'

The sulky face on the young girl's expression transformed. The 'Will effect' had struck again.

'Si, si Signor Vettese.' The girl nodded, clearly anxious to please the handsome Adonis in front of her, her now pretty, young face lighting up.

'Does he live here?' Will pointed to the house next door, his voice gentle and coaxing.

Lisa managed to refrain from nudging him.

The girl creased up her face, deep in thought. 'Signor Vettese.' She nodded again and then shook her head.

'He lives here?' asked Will, again with admirable patience and without resorting to that sort of sing-song voice that

English people often reserved for the hard of hearing and foreigners.

'Si.'

And then she shook her head again.

'He has moved?'

She frowned again. 'Signor Vettese?' She nodded and pointed to the house.

'I don't think she understands,' muttered Lisa, her emotions see-sawing up and down.

The girl shot her a filthy look, before bestowing Will with a sympathetic grimace.

Lisa smiled. She didn't blame her at all; far more experienced women had succumbed to that charm, including herself.

The girl held up one finger. 'Aspetta.' Following the white wire of the headphones, she delved into the back pocket of the tightest jeans Lisa had ever seen. With considerable manoeuvring, no mean feat, the girl inched her phone out and with that lightning dexterity teenagers have with their phones, flashed her fingers over the screen before offering it to Will, giving Lisa the sort of look that said, bet you couldn't do that.

Will beamed at her and then showed Lisa. 'Brilliant. Clever girl. Translation App.'

As he spoke, words flowed on the screen, which brought a delighted smile to the girl's face.

'Does Signor Vettese live next door?

'Si.' She nodded firmly and took the phone from Will to tap the screen before speaking slowly and distinctly in Italian into the phone and handing it back.

But he is away on a business trip for a few days.

She took the phone again. There was obviously some button you had to press to change the translation.

'Do you know when he will be back?'

Lisa waited for the girl to respond and hand the phone back. It was a rather tortuous process, but that might have been because her nervous system had put itself on high alert.

She held her breath.

'Non. Di solito tre o quattro giorni. A volte piu.'

Lisa read the translation. *Usually three or four days. Sometimes more.*

Sometimes more. Did it matter? Three or four days. It had been twenty years or more since she'd seen him.

They'd found him. He was here. That had to be good. Yes, that was good.

Inside it didn't feel particularly good.

She didn't dare look at Will. Instead she stood still, her feet rooted to the floor, her chin held high, swallowing hard.

Her flight home was in four days.

A tight band encircled her ribs. She couldn't look at Will. Just couldn't. It would unleash the tears threatening. Bloody, bloody sod's law. To come this flipping far. And after everything, all her previous doubts dissolved. She did want to meet her father. And now she might not be able to. Like a light switch, now that the possibility had become a potential reality, she wanted it with a hunger she hadn't realised she was capable of.

Will's hand touched the centre of her back. He didn't stroke or soothe her, as if knowing it would open the floodgates.

Instead it was a firm touch, pressing her skin, letting her know he was there.

Her heart hitched.

His hand stayed there, warm and constant.

Something bloomed, sending a gentle rush of heat through her system. Will. Solid. Dependable. For all his playboy reputation, this was the real Will. The Will she remembered from their childhood.

Her hand crept behind her back and she touched his. His fingers lifted to encompass hers, linking them together as they stood shoulder to shoulder.

Suddenly finding her father, an insubstantial figure she didn't even remember, seemed unimportant.

Will spoke and she raised a dazed head to him, his eyes gently smiling down at her.

'What do you want to do?'

Unable to help herself, she drank in every feature, a pulse racing in her throat. A fierce blush raced over her skin as she realised she was staring at his mouth.

Will's mouth twitched and, bloody devil that he was, he leaned into her ear and whispered, 'Apart from that.'

The stern glare she shot him didn't stop the devilment dancing in his eyes and his fingers locked with hers behind them, gave her hand a quick squeeze.

Even the young teenager was giving her strange looks now. She needed to pull herself together.

'If I leave a note, would you give it to him when he gets back?'

Even before the translation app had done its work, Will

delved into the pocket of what were obviously his smart Bermuda shorts and pulled out his pen and little notebook, tearing a sheet of paper out.

'No, no.' The mother darted forward, looking shocked. Throughout the exchange she'd been studying them and had obviously drawn her own conclusions. 'Aspetta. Aspetta.' She darted off and returned with a proper notelet and envelope, which she thrust at Will, patting him on the hand.

These Italian women did have it bad, but Lisa could hardly blame them.

He passed the notelet to her.

Lisa bit her lip, her hand shaking slightly as she took the pen.

What on earth was she going to write? Hi Dad. Dear Father. Signor Vettese. Hello I'm your long, lost daughter. Do you want to be found? If you do, here's my number. No, that sounded far too melodramatic. He'd think she was a right drama queen.

The pen left several dots on the blank card where she'd chickened out each time.

'This is hard.'

'You can do it.' Will's low, firm voice and nudge against her back made her address the card again.

She screwed up her face, trying to think what to write. Keep it simple. She didn't want to sound needy, or desperate to see him, and she didn't want to frighten him off. She just wanted to let him know she was grown up, independent. It was difficult. She could have written a lot more, but in the end, she kept it bald, factual and boring.

Hi, I'm in Rome for the next few days, I would like to meet you if it's convenient.

Lisa Vettese.

Will nudged her. 'Telephone number?'

She slapped her hand over her mouth. What an idiot! She hastily scribbled it on the note, before folding it and slipping it into the envelope and scrawling his name on the front, Vittorio Vettese.

The mother, obvious tears threatening, stepped forward and took the envelope, pressing it fervently to her chest, talking nineteen to the dozen, but clearly promising to guard it with her life and make sure it was delivered.

Her daughter, teenage contempt written all over her face, shook her head before speaking into the phone one last time.

In halting English, she read out the translation, 'You look like him.'

Chapter 18

'I'll have the bucatini amatriciana.'

'And I'll have the Pizza Margherita,' said Lisa, closing her menu with a happy snap and handing it to the waiter.

'Back to playing safe,' teased Will.

'Too right. I think after today, I deserve it. Besides, I've been looking forward to this since I landed at Rome airport, matey.' She looked around the lively restaurant and took a sip of red wine, her face nearly disappearing into the huge balloon glass. 'This is delicious, by the way.'

'It is a good one.' He sniffed at his glass appreciatively. 'A local grape variety. Cesanese. One I wanted to try. As well as the bucatini.'

'I've never even heard of it before. What is it?'

'It's like slightly thicker spaghetti, but with a hole running through the middle. It's very common in Rome and I want to put this dish on the menu.'

'When do you think you'll open?'

'I was hoping to open the weekend after Cam and Laurie's wedding in the first week of September. I could do without the wedding, to be honest. Although after this week I should be able to finalise the menu. Tomorrow morning I've wangled an invitation to a tasting at a local wholesaler, Virginnies. I'm hoping they'll supply all my condiments. I'd like to find a good olive oil and some balsamic vinegars like the ones we tried today. And later in the afternoon, I'm planning,' he glanced at his phone, 'if Charles gets back to me, to visit an estate that produces a wine from this grape variety.'

Lisa wilted slightly. Tomorrow. What was she going to do tomorrow? Time was going to drag while she was on tenterhooks waiting to see if her father called.

Will caught her expression. 'You can come with me, if you like.' He flashed her a grin. 'Another lesson in your food education. I've been invited out to Charles and Dorothea's place, old mates of Mum and Dad's. I'm hoping to do a tasting at the vineyard next to their estate. That should take an hour, and it will be a drive out of Rome, but we could do a bit of exploring as I'll have to hire a car. We could get away from the crowds for a while. See some scenery.'

'That sounds good.'

When her pizza arrived, despite Will teasing her about her unadventurous choice, she enjoyed every last mouthful.

The wood-fired pizza, with its crisp base and tangy tomato topping, ticked every box on her list and was as delicious as it looked.

'Oh,' she moaned after the first mouthful, 'That was worth waiting for. How's yours?'

Will, with a mouthful of food, gave her a big thumb's-up.

She eyed his dish.

'Hmm, I think I might have food envy. What's in it?'

'Not telling you, you have to try it first.' He pushed his dish towards her and laughed at her dismal attempt to fork up the pasta.

'Here, like this.' With some magical flair, he managed to swirl the pasta onto his fork and once again popped it into her mouth.

She sucked in a breath. 'That's spicy.' She took a big glug of water as he smiled lazily at her fanning her face. 'Now will you tell me what's in it?'

'You tell me.'

She leaned back. 'Some kind of meat. Bacon?'

'Pancetta, but close enough.'

'Chillies and tomato.'

'We'll make a foodie of you yet.'

Conversation flowed easily between them over the small table as the restaurant around them buzzed with low-level chatter. It was amusing to watch Will keeping an interested eye on the dishes served up at the nearby tables, his neck craning like an overeager Labrador, although he managed to be an attentive dining companion, stealing bites of her pizza, offering her more pasta and keeping her glass topped up.

Lisa couldn't remember when she'd last enjoyed a meal as much. It wasn't just the food and the wine, but Will's appreciation and determination that she enjoy every last mouthful.

'Here, put a drop of balsamic on the mozzarella. Taste.'

He taught her to swirl the wine around her mouth, to get mouthfeel and examine the resultant burst of flavour.

He didn't lecture or make her feel stupid, he simply couldn't help his enthusiasm. She realised that normally he didn't get to enjoy food in this relaxed and leisurely way. At the pub there were always 101 jobs to do – dealing with suppliers, ordering food, laundering the tablecloths, paying the staff. Will was constantly on the go.

She was laughing at an anecdote he was telling her about his chef, Al, who had a penchant for bizarre combinations, when her phone buzzed. She glanced down and frowned. Nan.

She rarely called and when she did she was always oblivious to the fact that Lisa might be in the middle of something. But she wouldn't call her in Italy if it wasn't important, would she?

'Sorry, it's Nan. Do you mind if I get this?'

'No, not at all.'

Lisa answered the phone with a worried frown.

'Hello Nan. Everything alright?'

'Do you know where those seeds are?'

'Which seeds?' Lisa sighed, relaxing immediately. Seeds she could cope with.

'The antirrhinums. We bought them when we went to Morrisons last week.'

'Aren't they in your seed box?' Lisa shook her head slightly at Will, who smiled as he sipped from his glass. 'Sorry,' she mouthed.

'It's okay,' he mouthed back.

'If they were, I wouldn't be ringing you, would I?' At Nan's tart and loud response, Will gave her a sudden grin. He could clearly hear every strident word.

'Well, I'm sorry I don't know. I remember you unpacking

the shopping. You didn't put them in the cupboard with the teabags, did you?'

'And why would I do that? I'm not senile, you know.'

It was more than Lisa's life was worth to tell her that occasionally she was a bit forgetful. There was the small matter of the load of washing Lisa had found in the oven a few weeks ago.

'It's the next cupboard along – you might have done it without thinking.'

She could hear the cupboard doors in Nan's kitchen banging.

'Nan, I'm in Rome. Can't it wait until I get back?'

'Hmph, and we have to dance to your tune, do we? I guess it must if you're busy gallivanting about on a wild-goose chase. Have you found the no-good loser yet?'

'Not exactly. It's—'

'Didn't think you would. Long gone that one. Just as well. And how's that Italian fella of yours?' Will suddenly seemed very interested in a picture on the wall opposite.

'Giovanni. He's fine.'

'Hmph.'

'How are your dahlias?'

'Getting drowned. We've had so much rain.'

'And are you taking your medication?' Lisa knew the question wouldn't go down well, but she had to ask.

'Don't you start! They give me chronic indigestion.'

'Nan! You promised.'

'I did no such thing.'

'Nan, you have to take them. You know what the doctor said.'

'Him. He's a fusspot. Since when did a bit of what you fancy kill you?'

Quite often, thought Lisa, if you ate what you fancied day in and day out.

'If I eat all the stuff he says, I might as well be dead.'

'Don't say things like that.'

'Why not? It's true. I could die any day now.' Lisa wilted in her seat. 'Aha, I've found them. Right next to the teabags. You must have put them away in the wrong cupboard. Right, I'm away planting.' And with that Nan disconnected the call.

Lisa groaned and laid her head on the table. 'Oh lord, I love her, but she drives me insane. She wants to plant seeds at this time of day.'

'Nothing too serious, then?' Will asked.

'No!' Lisa let out an exasperated huff. 'Not as long as she takes her medication. She's a flipping nightmare. Unfortunately, she refuses to listen to the doctor.' Her lips pressed together in frustration.

'But there's nothing... really wrong with her, is there?' Will looked particularly worried.

Lisa sighed and rocked her head back to look at the ceiling. 'She's got high blood pressure.' She faltered, her breath getting stuck in her throat. 'If she doesn't take her pills properly, she's at very high risk of having a stroke. She won't bloody listen to the doctor or... t-to me.' Embarrassed she blinked away a couple of tears. 'A stroke would...' she gave an ironic laugh, 'kill her. Literally. She would hate to be physically infirm or dependent on anyone else. All I can do is make sure she avoids any kind of stress and nag her about taking the tablets.'

Will looked hugely discomfited, playing with the pepper mill on the table and not looking at her.

'I didn't realise she was that ill...'

'Neither does she. Last time I went to the hospital, the doctor made it quite clear, but she won't listen.'

Will frowned, rubbing at a crease on his forehead.

When the waiter cleared their plates, he presented them with the dessert menu.

'Okay, what would you recommend?' asked Lisa, studying the choices. 'I have to warn you now. Pudding has to contain at least three parts to one of chocolate, otherwise I'm not interested.'

Will, clearly miles away, didn't respond.

'Any suggestions?' she prompted.

'Erm, chocolate ice cream.'

Lisa gave a spluttery laugh. 'I thought, at the very least, you'd make me try something different. Chocolate ice cream is playing safe. How about tiramasu? What's that like?'

'No, it's got coffee in it.' He'd swapped the pepper mill to fiddle with the packets of sugar in the centre of the table.

Lisa perused the menu for another minute.

'What are you going to have?'

'I'm not in the mood for pudding... but you go ahead, if you fancy it.'

'I shall have tiramisu.' Lisa sat up, feeling rather proud of herself, although Will didn't seem to have registered. 'Tiramisu. Aren't you impressed? A model student.'

Will nodded, absorbed in the little paper sleeves of sugar. 'Yes. Great progress.'

The waiter arrived to take their order.

Will shook his head. 'Nothing for me, thank you.'

Lisa pursed her mouth. Well, she was going to have a dessert and she was going to have the tiramisu. Wasn't she? Only suddenly she didn't fancy it any more.

'Caffé?' asked the waiter, his mouth a sad little moue of disappointment, as if he'd taken their rejection of pudding rather personally.

'Do you have,' Lisa glanced at Will, but decided to risk his approbation, 'tea?'

'Yes, signorina, we have green tea, English breakfast tea or mint tea.'

'The English breakfast would be lovely.'

'And for you, sir?'

'Nothing, thank you.'

The waiter nodded and melted away before Lisa could cancel her order.

'I'm sorry, I wouldn't have ordered if I'd realised that you weren't—'

'It's fine.' Will's taut jawline suggested that he was anything but fine.

'Is something wrong, Will?' she finally asked.

He at least had the grace to look ashamed.

'Sorry.' The heavy, thoughtful frown reappeared. 'I've got a bit of headache. It's been a long day and I've got a packed schedule tomorrow.'

'I'm sorry, why didn't you say?'

He lifted his shoulders.

'Do you need any paracetamol?'

'No thanks.'

She got halfway through her tea and gave up. Will had lapsed into silence and she felt guilty.

'Come on, I've had enough. Do you want to get the bill?'

Outside an Uber cab waited. Will and his magic apps in action again.

'Wow, it's busy out here now.'

'Mmm,' said Will, scrolling through his phone.

Lisa turned to look out of the window, suddenly feeling very tired.

It had been a long and quite emotional day and Will had been incredibly supportive. No wonder he had a headache. They had been on the go since first thing this morning.

The lights flashed by as the cab made its way through the traffic, which seemed as bad as ever, even at this time of day. The stuffiness inside the taxi made her wind down the window to let in a bit of air. As she did, it brought in the sound of horns and the chug of the diesel engine.

She peered out of the window, it seemed that there were still so many sights to see. At night, the churches were lit up with well-placed spotlights, sending long shadows upwards, silhouetting statues, highlighting the domes and towers brilliantly in the night skyline.

Will seemed oblivious and spent the whole cab journey on his phone, the light of the screen a constant in the dark, drawing her eye and making her aware of his sudden withdrawal.

At last the cab pulled up outside the gateway to the apartment. They walked up the driveway in silence, cicadas chirping in the grass to their left, silencing as their footsteps crunched up the dark pathway and then starting up again as they moved on.

As they reached the apartment door, Lisa bumped into Will as they both scrabbled in the dark for the light switch. Her fingers brushed his and they both stopped. Lisa froze, the brief touch making her heart ache. Nothing had changed, in fact, if anything, it was worse. After today, she probably loved Will more than she had nine months ago.

In the quick flare of light, she caught a quick glimpse of Will's face screwed up in pain.

She went to touch his arm. 'Oh Will, you really are suffering.'

To her surprise, he flinched.

'Are you sure you don't want a painkiller?'

'No,' he growled. 'I just need some peace and quiet.' And with that he went into his bedroom and shut the door.

Chapter 19

'Mornin…' Lisa's voice trailed away.

'Buon giorno.' Gisella gave her a casual wave from her seat at the breakfast table, where she and Will had their heads together, poring over a map.

'Morning,' said Will, a shade too cheerily.

Clearly his headache had gone. She stood, awkward for a second, feeling she'd wandered onto a stage mid-act without a part to play.

Where had Gisella popped up from? Will hadn't mentioned her yesterday. Lisa felt as if she were sifting through lots of different bits of information and nothing was making sense.

Ignoring the sudden hideous pang in her chest, she helped herself to a coffee, deciding she'd take it back to her room.

'How are you enjoying Rome?' Looking perfectly at home sitting next to Will sipping coffee, Gisella crossed her legs, admiring her own expensive leather pumps.

Lisa could hardly be rude to her, even though every part of her urged her to run away and hide. 'It's a lovely city. So much to see,' she said stiffly, hoping she could make a quick escape.

'It is. Even I haven't visited everything.' She lowered her voice, managing to sound daring and sultry at the same time, 'I've never seen the Sistine Chapel.' She tossed her hair over her shoulder. 'Always too busy.'

Her? Or the museum?

'It's full of tourists,' Gisella pursed her mouth and then brightened, 'but you should go.'

'Thanks,' said Lisa, sudden anger firing through her at the casual dismissal.

'Where are you going today?' asked Gisella, but before Lisa could answer the other girl pronounced rather grandly, 'Will and I are going to a tasting. At Virginnies.'

Lisa shot a look at Will. He was studying the contents of his coffee cup as if it held the secrets to the known universe.

'I'm... I'm not sure.' The pang in her chest turned into full-blown pain. It seemed things had changed somewhat since yesterday.

Will looked up sharply, his stern expression softening for a second, before saying, 'You can come too if you want, but I think you'd find it deadly boring.'

Funny, he hadn't thought that yesterday, when he'd urged her to try the fig balsamic and bought a bottle of it. And what about the trip to the wine estate afterwards? Her toes gripped the floor, as if anchoring herself to the spot, despite the fact she wanted to flee. How stupid could she be?

Gisella laughed. 'I'm sure Lina—'

'Lisa,' she said sharply, pushing her shoulders back, icy calm hiding the furious emotions beneath. Will could take whoever he liked, it wasn't as if he was her... well, her anything.

He'd taken pity on her yesterday when he'd helped her with her dad. He had things of his own to do.

The girl waved her hands in a casual *whatever* dismissal. 'I'm sure she doesn't want to come with us.'

And if it were going to be so dull, why was the Italian girl so keen to go? She certainly didn't look dressed for a vinegar-tasting in her white ankle-skimming jeans and scarlet blousey t-shirt that kept slipping off smooth, brown shoulders. For a second Lisa felt like the second scullery maid below-stairs. Bugger it, she didn't want to spend a minute more than she had to with Will, but there was no way she was going to let Gisella make her feel like a second-class citizen.

'Actually.' Lisa tossed her hair, which was longer and thicker and blonder than Gisella's, over her shoulder. 'I think that would be fascinating. Like you say, anyone can go to the Sistine Chapel.'

Gisella frowned. Clearly she'd meant no such thing.

'When will I ever get the chance to do a balsamic-vinegar tasting again?'

Lisa didn't dare look at Will's face as she flounced out of the room.

'You'll have to go in the back seat,' said Gisella primly, not making any move to clear the rubbish strewn across every inch of the seat. 'I wasn't expecting an extra passenger.'

'No, that's absolutely fine,' said Lisa, with a graciousness that wasn't deserved, clearing herself a space.

Will heaved an internal sigh. He should have known this

was a bad idea. Calling Gisella last night had been a knee-jerk reaction and he was an idiot.

As they drove through the chaotic traffic to the outskirts of Rome, Gisella talked non-stop in a low, musical voice, pitched to exclude Lisa in the back.

'Now, the Fabriganzi, they specialise in seafood.' She laid a hand on his knee. 'You would love it. There's a two-week waiting list for a table, but I could get us a table for dinner there.'

He wished she'd stop giving him that sultry look and focus on the road. Her driving, even by local standards, was atrocious.

'Or there's the Odin, awarded two Michelin stars last month. I know the chef, Gino Lorenzini, fabulous cook, dreadful lover. But then, maybe not,' she winced and threw the car around a corner in a last-minute swerve that almost had it up on two wheels, 'seeing as he's not speaking to me after I went out for dinner with his closest rival, Georgio. Now *he* is good at both.'

Michelin stars had obviously taken the places of notches on Gisella's bedpost.

'I'll give Georgio a ring. I'm sure he could fit us in as a special favour.' She gave him an arch look. 'After all, you owe me dinner. How was dinner with the family formaggio? Provincial? Don't worry,' she patted his knee, her hand sliding up his thigh, 'Giorgio's place is very sophisticated.'

Will's jaw tightened and the hairs on the back of his neck stood up. He could sense Lisa in the back listening to every word. For some reason, Gisella's seasoned flirting made him feel a bit embarrassed. God only knew why? That had been the whole point of inviting her today. He could play this game in his sleep. Usually he'd find it easy to flirt back, keep things light and see where they went. Which was why that night with Lisa had been so scary. She made him feel something that he hadn't thought he was capable of.

'I've got more visits lined up. We'll have to see. I might not have time,' he replied stiffly, aware of Lisa's silence behind him.

Gisella didn't do rebuffs. She simply squeezed his leg, her fingers inching up his inside leg. 'You can always make time,' she said in the sort of throaty voice that might be described as a purr and belonged in a very adult film.

It was a blessed relief to get out of the car when they arrived at Virginnies, a series of dark cellars under the arches of a railway bridge.

Lisa uncoiled herself from the back of the car and when he held the door open for her to clamber out of the back, she shot him a look of utter scorn, her nose tilting in the air.

Damn it. He glared at her and stepped back to let her pass, holding his hand out to help steady her. She pointedly ignored the hand, keeping her distance, as if he had some nasty disease, and turned her back on him. The scent of her light perfume mingled with sun lotion brought back an image of her on the Spanish Steps, his hands sliding over her soft skin.

It sparked a flutter low in his belly. Damn. Yesterday had started with low expectations. A truce to get through the day, but at some point in the morning, resigned companionship had passed some indefinable line and moved into that comfortable, flirty comradeship they'd previously enjoyed. When she'd made the revelations about her father, he'd had to help her. He understood that type of rejection and her need to find out why her father had left.

From the moment, she'd realised her father wasn't there his emotions had been pitched into turmoil, self-preservation fighting the need to reassure her, show her she wasn't alone. Or maybe he'd realised how alone he was and that it didn't feel that great.

This morning he felt as if he'd been pitched into a complicated dance without knowing the right moves, but unfortunately he had no one to blame but himself.

The tasting was in full flow when they entered through high arched wooden doors into the cool interior, where the oils and vinegars had been laid out on long trestle tables in labelled and numbered dishes alongside detailed tasting notes.

'Signor Manelli, good to meet you at last.' Will had been exchanging emails with him for the last few days.

'Call me Franco. Good to meet you too. And Gisella, always a pleasure, and who is this young lady?' He pronounced it *younga,* which brought a ready smile from Lisa.

'This is Lisa, my...' he paused, a prickle down his spine as he looked up to see both women watching him – Lisa with a distinct look of challenge on her face, Gisella's expression was cooler but slightly narrow-eyed. 'She was staying with my work colleague, Giovanni, who unfortunately had to attend to a family matter.' And since when had he started to talk like some nineteenth-century nobleman? Lisa's head dipped and she seemed to be making a detailed study of her toes.

'It is a pleasure to meet you, Lisa. I hope that you will enjoy yourself. We have arranged some excellent products for you to try.'

'Oh, don't worry. Will's the expert,' she shot him a chilly ice-maiden smile, 'especially at sampling *lots of things* at once,' she said airily, before adding, 'I'm completely in the dark. I have no idea what is going on.'

Will thought he was probably the only person who detected the hint of acid in her voice. Her choice of words ratcheted up his incipient sense of guilt. She didn't look at him once.

Franco clasped his hands together, his chubby face beaming. 'I would be delighted to show you.'

Franco led them to the first section, expertly leading them through the busy rows, where other people, clipboards in hand, worked their way up and down. Olives, almond and orange scents filled the air. Hands were shaken, bread dipped, samples tried with slow nods of appreciative approval. Will itched to get started. He had a good idea of what he wanted, but every time he started to run through his mental checklist, he would hear Lisa's light laugh bubbling out, her blonde head bobbing alongside Franco's dark, and, Will was pleased to note, slightly thinning, hair.

Gisella threaded her hand through his arm and sidled closer, pressing her chest into him. If he looked down, he'd get an eyeful of magnificent cleavage. 'I think Franco is rather taken with Lisa.'

'Mmm,' said Will, pulling out his battered notebook. He gave Franco's hairline a second glance. Definitely the start of a monk's tonsure there at the crown of his head.

'Shall we go this way? We can catch up with them later.' Her voice laden with unsubtle promise, Gisella steered him down the aisle in the opposite direction.

An hour in, Will found himself next to Lisa in front of a stall of infused balsamic vinegars.

'It can't possibly taste of chocolate and coffee,' Lisa giggled, holding up a piece of bread.

'Si, si. Try,' said the young Italian behind the table.

Tentatively she dipped her bread in and nibbled at the edge.

'Oh!' she said and spotted Will. To his relief, she grinned at him, 'OMG. Will, you've got to try this. It's amazing. It really does taste of chocolate and coffee.'

She thrust the piece of bread his way and, as her fingers touched his mouth, almost in a slow-motion replay, she realised what she'd done. Her hand stalled, staying in contact with his mouth, fingers almost caressing his lips as their eyes met with an instant exchange of sizzling awareness.

The sound around him receded. There was a weird sensation in his chest, as if someone had kicked him square in the sternum.

Then she snatched her hand away.

'You stupid girl. These are Armani,' shrieked Gisella as dark spots of balsamic rained down her thighs, leaving the sort of healthy spatter enthused about in an episode of a crime investigation drama.

Somehow Gisella had tried to elbow her way between them at precisely the wrong moment and Lisa's hand had hit the edge of one of the saucers on the table, sending it catapulting over and over in an elegant arc, descending through the air.

Oh shit. Why did he do this to himself? It was as if Gisella's screech of alarm was a siren call to all his mistakes, which suddenly compounded themselves into one huge explosion of realisation. Inviting himself to Italy at the same time as Lisa had been the first in a growing catalogue of misjudgement.

Spending the day with her yesterday had simply confirmed what he'd known all along. The feelings he'd tried so hard to deny, burst into awareness, longing and desire overloading his system with a flood of adrenaline that made him feel sick with apprehension and hope.

'Do something, Will!' Gisella's voice almost pierced his eardrum.

Like what?

The spilled vinegar bled into the fabric, blooming with determined intent like ink on blotting paper.

'Don't worry, Gisella,' said Lisa, shooting him a look of exasperation, which he thought was a bit unfair. What did she expect him to do?

'I'm sure it will wash out. But here, I have some wipes.' She dug around inside the gingerbread-man tote bag like some modern-day Mary Poppins.

'That will make it worse.'

'No, they're stain-remover wipes.'

'Who carries stain-remover wipes?' asked Will, disbelieving as Lisa did indeed whip out a tiny packet.

'Someone who spends their life crawling around the floor with small children and everything from urine, poo, vomit, paint and glue,' snapped Lisa, tossing her hair over her shoulder, looking so magnificent and gorgeous, he wanted to throw her down on the nearest table and ravish every last inch of her.

Will pushed a shaky hand through his hair. He was in so much trouble.

'They're ruined.' Gisella tossed her own mane of hair about, clearly aware that every head in the room had swivelled her way. 'I hope you're going to buy me a new pair, Will.'

'I'd try washing them first,' he said shortly, pursing his mouth, ashamed of himself, but revolted by her coy theatrics. Served him right for playing games.

Lisa shot him a scorn-laden scowl, which didn't help.

'Come on, Gisella, let's go to the ladies. I'm sure we can do something.'

'Hmph.' Gisella glared at Lisa and then her whole demeanour suddenly brightened as she spotted a man working his way through the interested crowd. 'Gino, tesoro.'

With a flurry of dramatic kisses and a torrent of fervent, passionate Italian, including a spate of what could have been recriminations, Gino of the Michelin two stars and errant knight on the side, thankfully scooped Gisella into his arms, explained he was taking her off to his nearby flat, and departed, leaving Will and Lisa staring wide-eyed after them.

'I feel as if I had a bit part in an opera,' said Lisa, with a disgusted sigh.

'Yes.' Will ran a hand through his hair. 'She does have a flair for the dramatic.'

Lisa's eyes flashed, with a look of pure fury.

'You're such a bastard,' she spat and stormed out.

The worst thing was, she was absolutely right.

She could bloody throttle Will. Her hands tensed on the handles of her tote bag.

Slumping on a bench under a shady tree in the square opposite Virginnies, she glared across at the doorway, hoping he wouldn't appear. If he came near her, she might give herself away and do something stupid like bursting into tears.

She was such a fool, letting herself get carried away yesterday. Underneath it all, he hadn't changed one sodding bit. Yesterday she'd almost believed that he could be nice.

But he was the same old Will.

With an agonised groan of derision at her own stupidity, she dropped her head in her hands. Her fingers grazed a couple of tears that had committed the sneaky injustice of escaping. Yesterday had been perfect. Too bloody perfect. She was kidding herself if she thought they'd re-established that old flirty friendship. A line had been crossed. All the feelings she thought she'd successfully squashed had come roaring back. The minute he touched the dent of her spine while they were standing on the doorstep of the Vitelli family home, her heart had gone thunk. Bloody bastard had made her fall in love with him again.

Another couple of tears slipped out. Bastard traitors.

And, oh fuck!

Will's feet had appeared in front of her.

'Go away,' she said, not looking up.

'Lisa.' The husky timbre of his voice tugged at her, hollowing out her stomach, but she kept her head down.

'Please... leave me alone.' Shit, her voice sounded all jerky and broken. Stiffening her spine, she froze as he sat down next to her.

'Lisa.'

His fingers lifted her chin and turned her head towards him.

She blinked furiously. Shit, shit, shit. He'd see she'd been crying. Although the bastard must be used to women crying over him. He was such a turd. Except he wasn't. He could be lovely. Charming. Caring. Yesterday, she thought he'd cared about her.

He leant forward and wiped away one of her stupid tears with his thumb. And then he leaned in, his arm sliding around her and, to her utter surprise, he kissed her.

The soft, unexpected touch of his lips on hers sent a frisson sizzling through her veins and she parted them in a silent 'o'. Her heart hammered as their mouths brushed in a tender, gentle kiss before he pulled back and rested his forehead against hers, their noses touching.

'I'm sorry. You're right. I am a bastard. But I think I might be a bastard who's in love with you.'

Lisa's heart flopped about in her chest, doing some sort of weird, almost painful, acrobatics and sending her pulse haywire. All she could do was stare at him. Someone seemed to have wiped her brain and nothing seemed to work: her voice, her tongue, even her face had gone numb and there was a rushing in her ears.

The watchful expression on his face didn't falter as she

stared back at him, looking for clues. He didn't look the least bit cocky or self-satisfied, like a real bastard would. Worry filled his handsome face instead.

'You've got a funny way of showing it,' she said softly.

'I know. I'm an idiot.' He touched her face, soothing away the earlier tear tracks. 'I'm sorry. Gisella was a...' he shook his head, his mouth twisting in self-deprecation, 'one of my master-strokes in self-deception. I panicked...'

Lisa raised an incredulous eyebrow and straightened, moving away from him.

They'd been here before. She couldn't do it again.

'Is that what happened last time as well?' Her words tumbled out, quick and accusing.

His mouth opened and closed.

'Er... Um.'

'Lost for words? That's not like you, Will.' Disappointment reared, hard and fast. Will would never change.

'There were reasons.' He pulled at her hand. 'And that sounds crap. I know it does. Even saying it now sounds rubbish, but there was a very good reason.'

A pigeon fluttered near her foot and she jerked it away, grateful for the excuse to look away from Will's sincere expression, which did strange things to her insides, making her forget what he was really like.

'Yeah it does. As crap as you saying you'd call me and you never did.'

Will let out a quiet sigh. 'There was a...' Then he frowned, as if something checked him and instead he said, 'The truth is, I chickened out.'

He slumped on the bench, his elbows resting on his legs. 'With all those other women, I kept it light, which was pretty easy. Working in a pub you pull the unsociable hours' card to head someone off at the pass – if they start getting too close or too interested.'

She'd never thought of his working hours as being an impediment to a relationship. Working part time in the pub at the weekends, it had been easy to stay for a drink with Marcus, Al, Will and the other waitresses. Some of them went on clubbing after that, but she was always too knackered to join them.

'I've never done commitment. I'm not even sure how to.' His voice sounded hollow.

Everything about his slumped posture suggested defeat. 'Most women want that in the end and I'm a pretty bad bet. My parents made a complete mess of their marriage. On the surface it was all glamour and glitz, but neither of them were faithful. Both had a string of affairs they used to taunt each other with.' With a scowl, he pushed his hair from his face, a sudden surge of anger in his voice. 'I've no bloody idea why they are still together. It wouldn't surprise me to find out I've got a dozen half-siblings tucked away somewhere. I don't want to be like that but… I'm… I'm not sure. Bad blood? I've avoided finding out.'

Shocked, she didn't say anything. His childhood sounded hellish. She wanted to tuck her hand into his, give him comfort to ease the sense of pain she heard in his words. This was the Will she'd spent the night with all those months ago. Not the cocky, superior, cynical Will that he presented to the world.

It was a defence mechanism. And suddenly she felt bad for not seeing it before. As a child visiting his house, with her grandmother, his glamorous, sophisticated, sociable, party-going parents, always darting here there and everywhere, had been utterly bewildering, but she'd had no idea about the affairs or the effect of their parenting on him and his sister.

'It's far easier to play a game than take anyone seriously.' He rubbed at a patch on his shorts, his head turned away from her. 'But it was different with you.

'After that night. I was scared.'

'But…' she interrupted. 'I don't understand. Scared of what? Commitment? I thought I'd made it clear that I don't ever want to rely on anyone, or not a man, anyway. My mum, my nan, they'd managed without a man in their lives. I'm not looking for someone to look after me.'

'But what about family?'

'I don't need one.'

His eyebrows drew together, punctuating his expression with a sharp slash of puzzlement. 'What about your father?'

She stiffened at the implication. 'That's about knowing where I come from. I want to know I have family out there, but I don't want to rely on anyone. I know that sounds contrary, but it makes sense to me.'

'And I always thought I didn't want to look after anyone. But you…' He shrugged, 'I want to be with you.'

His confession, along with the intensity of his gaze roving over her face as if memorising each feature, had her heart turning. It unnerved her but also sparked a sense of excitement at the same time.

'Ironic, then, that I don't want family either, well, my parents at any rate. I'd love to escape them. Despite that, I think perhaps we're two of a kind.'

'I think perhaps we are but,' she fixed him with a candid stare, 'I don't want to be just another one of a long line of women.'

'You never were.' He touched her face. 'I was an idiot.' His fingers traced along her jawline and round to the back of her neck, where they remained.

The rush of feeling bursting out at that moment made her positively light-headed.

'You're still an idiot,' she smiled.

'I'm sorry about Gisella.'

'What sorry that you invited her or sorry that she turned out to be a pain in the arse?'

His lips twitched. 'Both. When I got a text from her last night, at the time it seemed like a good idea to invite her along today.'

'Did you sleep with her the other night?' Lisa gave him a hard stare.

'No! I'm not that bloody fickle. Although I suspect she wasn't averse to the idea.'

'You were out very late.' Damn, that made it sound as if she were jealous. That she cared.

Which judging by Will's sudden smug beam was exactly what he thought.

'She left me at the farm. I stayed and had dinner with the family. Grandma, who would probably win Glamorous Granny of the World, taught me to make home-made pasta. And no Gisella.'

'Until this morning.'

'Which I now know was a really, really bad idea.' He picked up her hand and laced his fingers through hers. 'Actually, I knew when I texted her last night it was a bad idea, but I panicked. Yesterday, there were a hundred times I wanted to kiss you.'

Lisa blushed.

'I was worried you might slap me.'

'There have been a couple of times I've been very tempted to do that,' she said firmly and then lowered her voice to add, 'but not yesterday.'

He scooted closer so that they were thigh to thigh.

'So.'

She turned to him. 'So?'

'We've wasted a hell of a lot of time.'

'You've wasted a lot of time.'

'Okay, I'll take that. How about we spend the rest of our time in Rome making up for it? And this time, see where things go properly.' Although his words might have sounded flippant, the look that he gave her was anything but. The import of the words hung between them.

'Okay, then.' Her husky, tentative words brought a gentle satisfied curve to his lips.

'Mind if I kiss you now?'

With a smile that seemed to take on a life of its own, she shook her head. 'Not at all.'

Chapter 20

'Wow. That is one hell of a view.' Will pulled her closer to him as they surveyed the panorama spread out below them, his arm comfortably resting across her shoulders, as if they'd been together for months rather than a few scant hours.

After finishing at Virginnies, where Will had placed a few orders for the restaurant, he'd reissued his invitation for her to come along with him to the winery. It had been a most un-Will like moment when he'd rather shyly asked if she would like to stay the night as well.

With an equally shy yes, she'd agreed and they'd nipped back to the apartment to grab a change of clothes before picking up a hire car – a rather nice sporty little BMW.

'It's such a beautiful city,' said Lisa, drinking it in, taking care not to look directly over the low wall in front of them. 'Coin in the fountain or not, I hope I get to come back one day.' She sighed with pleasure, but that had a lot to do with the rather lovely weight of Will's arm and the squirmy feelings of anticipation and excitement dancing low in her belly.

The spectacular view offered a rainbow of terracotta, umbers, washed-out peaches and distressed golden yellows, along with the faded verdigris of domed roofs and the hazy blue shadows reminiscent of an impressionist painting. They had stopped at Gianicolo Hill, a popular viewing spot on the edge of the city.

'I wonder what that building is?' As he turned, Will dropped a quick kiss in the sensitive dip between her neck and collarbone, which set her skin tingling, before pointing to a prominent building on the skyline with two towers topped by statuesque winged creatures driving chariots, looking as if they might take flight at any moment,

'Ah, that,' said Lisa, a touch of smugness in her voice, which had as much to do with the feminine satisfaction that came from knowing someone couldn't seem to keep their hands off you, as being in the know, 'is the Altare della Patria, completed in 1925 and built in honour of Victor Emmanuel, the first king of Italy to unite the country.'

Will stepped back. 'I'm impressed. And no guide book.'

'You pick these things up,' said Lisa, with a nonchalant lift of her shoulder.

'Really?' asked Will, scepticism written all over his face.

'No.' Lisa burst out laughing. He knew her too well. 'I saw it on the first day with Giovanni and was so intrigued. I looked it up. Those statues are amazing. It's almost as if they might come to life at any minute.'

'What? Like in *Ghostbusters*?' teased Will, as she nudged him, giggling.

'Now who's the philistine?'

'Come on, selfie time before we get back on the road.' He lifted his camera above their heads to take a couple of shots.

She grinned at the camera, unable to contain the happiness jumping out of every last pore and then made him take one with her phone. She wanted to hold onto this moment forever.

As Will peered over the edge, she took her time studying his profile, trying to work out what it was that made him so damn handsome. She'd recognise it anywhere. Strong chin, wide mouth, well-defined cheekbones, perfect eyebrows that looked as if they'd been deliberately shaped that way, except they'd looked like that for as long as she'd known him. Her fingers itched to trace down his dead-straight nose and stroke that definite dip between his lips and chin. With a rueful smile, she wondered what he'd say if she told him it was rather cute.

They stayed a while longer until their prime viewing position was usurped with Germanic efficiency when a coach arrived, spilling its load of octogenarians in shorts and walking boots on a determined mission to capture the best photographs.

The tremor of excited anticipation, which had been sizzling all the way here, burst into an explosion of fireworks as they pulled up outside the Villa Liguria.

Villa? It was more like a palazzo. Built in golden sun-drenched stone, the house, with its dark-green shutters, looked still and cool among the shady cypress trees that surrounded it.

'Are you sure they won't mind me tagging along?' whispered

Lisa, with a touch of awe, studying the gorgeous building.

The villa had a central tower of three storeys, bookended by two square wings on either side. Each had a balcony bursting with colour as pots of geraniums, bougainvillea and other trailing plants filled every available spot, splashes of brilliant pinks, scarlets and verdant greens tumbling through the iron railings.

Naked statues, which Lisa supposed were Venus or some other Roman goddess, marked the boundaries of a gravelled drive. This encircled a raised fountain featuring a stone dolphin balanced mid-leap above a plume of water spurting from a crown of stone flowers around the edge.

'Don't worry.' Will winked. 'I keep telling you, Italians love blondes.'

'They might not love unexpected guests.'

'Don't worry, there's a campsite nearby if need be.' Then he grinned. 'Sorry, I shouldn't tease you. I think I told you already, the owners are very old family friends of my parents. She was at school with my mother and married Visconti Lanzia, but they lived in London for many years. Like my parents, they're big into horse racing. Unlike my parents, they seem to believe in fidelity.'

'Visconti!'

'Allegedly,' whispered Will. 'Visconti Charles Giancarlo Lanzia. Born and bred in London.'

Lisa folded her arms. He'd just told her this couple were old mates of his parents. But this wasn't quite what she thought she'd been signing up for.

'Lisa,' Will nudged her, grinning like an idiot as he pulled two bags out of the boot of the car. 'I rang before we left the apartment. Spoke to Dorothea. Explained I was bringing a guest with me.'

'You toad!' Lisa grinned back at him. 'I was thinking I was going to be some unwanted guest.'

'No, Dorothea was delighted. She's never had kids of her own. She dotes on other people's. And she loves entertaining. Although, maybe I should remind you that Gisella is her niece.'

'Oh great! Let's hope my reputation hasn't arrived before me.'

'Dorothea is nobody's fool. I suspect she's well aware what a man-eater Gisella is.'

'Yoohoo!' A tiny woman ran lightly down the stairs, which was quite some feat because she was very nearly as wide as she was tall.

'You've arrived. How lovely.' Without further preamble she launched herself at Will, giving him a hug and then turned to Lisa, her plump face glowing with delight. 'Welcome, my dear. It's lovely to see you. Aren't you a handsome boy? Although you don't look like your mother.' Conspiratorially she said to Lisa, 'And she's one gorgeous lady, I'll tell you. Have you met her?'

'A long time ago,' admitted Lisa.

'Gosh.' Dorothea widened her eyes, with coy salaciousness. 'There's a story to be had, I'm supposing.' She was so over the top and arch that Lisa burst out laughing, at which point Dorothea linked arms with her and said, 'I'm going to like you, I know it.'

Will groaned and Dorothea chucked him under the chin as if he were no more than ten.

'Come on, boy. Bring those bags in.'

Dorothea, after instructing them to leave their bags at the foot of a rather grand staircase, led them through a light, airy hallway punctuated by wooden doors, to the back of the villa. A wide terrace flanked the building, filled with the sort of expensive garden furniture you only ever see in catalogues and tall urns with neatly trimmed topiary, cut in the shapes of chess pieces. A free-standing hammock swung gently, as if someone had just left it, and then Lisa spotted the Visconti. He was as tall and thin as his wife was short and wide, but had the same joyous bounce in his walk as he strode to greet them, his droopy tracksuit bottoms somewhat at odds with his elegant white linen shirt and Panama hat.

'Will and lovely lady-friend. You've made excellent time.' His flawless English made his accent almost undetectable.

'Charles, nice to see you. This is Lisa Vettese.'

'Welcome, my dear. We were about to open a bottle for lunchtime drinkies. Prosecco, alright? Or would you prefer something more manly, Will? I rather like the fizz myself, but it's not for everyone.'

Before Will could answer, he led them over to a vine-clad wooden arbour tucked out of sight, on a lawn as immaculate as a cricket square. Dorothea brought up the rear, clucking along behind them like a contented mother hen, muttering cheerfully, 'Vettese. Vettese. Why do I know that name?'

Charles waited for her, pulling out a chair before patting

her with great humour on her very ample bottom. 'Dottie, darling. You think you know everyone.'

An ice-bucket wedged with not one, but two, bottles of Prosecco sat on an elegant cream wrought-iron bistro set of four chairs and a table.

Lunch was served at one-thirty, when a smartly dressed Italian woman brought out a huge flat-bottomed basket.

'Salami di Milano, Parma ham, Cacciatore, Capicola,' trilled Dorothea. 'And cheese, we have Provolone, Bel Paese and Caciotta as well as my favourite, Wensleydale. Poor Charles has to import it especially for me, but I couldn't possibly live without.' The rustic platter of salamis, meats and cheeses was placed in the centre of the table, along with a basket with a mountain of bread, sliced in good thick chunks. More dishes of colourful antipasti were unloaded, including tiny gherkins, a red and yellow pepper salad and a tomato and mozzarella salad.

'Just a light lunch. And then this afternoon, you can visit the winery and taste the wines. Unfortunately, this evening Charles and I have a very dull party to go do, which we can't possibly get out of.' With a petulant sigh, she shook her head but then cheered up. 'But no problem. Annunzia, here, cooks like an angel and had already planned dinner for this evening.' She lowered her voice. 'This way I don't upset her for changing our plans. Honestly, she's a wonder and I don't know what I'd do without her, but it's more than my life's worth to mess up the menu plan.'

'Oh, there's no need,' said Lisa. 'We can go out.' It seemed the height of rudeness to expect Dorothea to cater for them when she wasn't even going to be in.

Sitting sipping Prosecco with the Viscount and Viscountess Lanzia, in the grounds of what might as well have been an Italian palace, she wondered what on earth Nan would think. Even though she sat next to Dorothea, across the table from Will, that spark of awareness remained and every time she caught his eye, her pulse tripped.

Will was talking to Charlie about his restaurant plans while Dorothea cross-examined Lisa with such blatant cheerful nosiness she was impossible to resist.

'You'll have to forgive me, dear, I'm not very up on these things, but shall I put you and Will in the same room tonight? It's such a fag preparing two rooms and changing sheets, only for everyone to start playing musical bedrooms and tip-toeing down corridors in the middle of the night, which is what we had to do in my day. Although it is lovely to have your own space.' Then she added with studied innocence. 'Have you and Will been seeing each other long?'

Lisa pressed her lips tight in a desperate attempt not to burst out laughing, knowing full well Will hadn't informed her until this morning he'd be bringing a guest.

Dorothea grinned unrepentantly. 'I'm desperately intrigued. Especially when you said you knew his mother. You know I was at school with her.'

'I've known Will since I was a child.' Lisa lifted her chin as she added. 'My grandmother worked for his mother. As a daily help.'

Dorothea positively sparkled at this news. 'Oh heavens. How delicious! Does Eloise know you and Will are stepping out? She's such a crashing snob.'

The words gave Lisa a brief qualm.

With a hint of mischief, Dorothea added. 'I ought to give her a call. I haven't spoken to her in a while.'

'I shouldn't think so.' Lisa stiffened. 'It's relatively recent.' Lisa couldn't imagine that Will shared much information with his mother. Was Dorothea going to spill the beans?

'But you've been friends for a long time. I can tell. You look at ease with each other.'

Lisa's eyes twinkled. 'Really? We've been more like enemies for the last nine months.'

'Ooh a touch of the Beatrice and Benedick. My favourite sort of romance. What made you change your mind about him? Apart from the obvious, I'll give you that, he's a handsome devil, and good in the sack, no doubt. Don't look shocked, darling.'

Lisa studied Will out of the corner of her eye, hoping he couldn't hear. What had changed? He'd been nice to her, that didn't sound like a good enough reason to fall in love with someone, but then she'd been a little bit in love with Will for a very long time. When Will was on your side, he was on your side. One hundred per cent reliable and supportive. She'd seen him in action at the pub, his employees, a motley bunch of eccentrics, all adored him, especially Siena, who he'd given a job to when on paper she was the last person to make a decent waitress.

Even when he wasn't being nice to her, like on the plane, he was, albeit in a backhanded sort of way.

She liked the fact he didn't stand on ceremony and treated everyone equally, despite the once-privileged background. She liked that he'd worked hard to make the pub such a success.

And, most of all, she liked that he was honest. She particularly liked the line 'I think I might be a bastard who's in love with you.' It said much more than a glib declaration. He was honest that it scared him. It scared the pants off her too.

'Oh lord, I've put my foot in it. You haven't slept with him yet. Pressure. Pressure. Perhaps I should give you the spare spare room.'

Maybe Will could hear the conversation because he suddenly shot her a knicker-stripping-at-fifty-paces look that made knees tremble even though she was sitting down.

'No, it's f-fine.' It took a while for Lisa to drag a breath up and out.

Halfway through lunch Dorothea suddenly jumped up.

'Don't go anywhere. I've just remembered.' And with that she scurried off, despite her bulk, looking like an agile squirrel, as she hopped over the thyme hedges of the herb garden. When she came back, beaming with delight, she flapped something in her right hand.

'I knew I knew that name.' Dorothea held up a photograph.

'Vettese. Vittorio Vettese. I remembered. He knew Will's parents too. Do you know him?

'Yes,' gasped Lisa. 'My father.'

Dorothea's eyes gleamed with triumph and sudden prurient curiosity.

'Really? He was our jockey.'

The photo showed a group of five people, grouped together in front of a horse, on top of which was perched, quite literally, knees almost up to his chin, a figure in a bright-green silk shirt, with a group of four white stars in the centre, a matching riding hat and racing goggles.

'That's me.' Dorothea pointed to a much younger and slimmer version of herself, wearing a cream-and-pink suit topped with a bright-pink hat with several feathery plumes cascading like a waterfall. 'Charles.' He wore a morning suit. 'And your parents, Will. And Sir Robert. He owned the stables.'

Lisa recognised both Will's parents and, of course, Sir Robert, but her father could have been anyone behind those goggles and the brim of his helmet, except for the racing silk covering the helmet. Emerald green with four white stars: north, south, east and west. The silk sat on top of one of the posts of her dressing table. One of the few mementoes left by her mother.

Dorothea pointed to the horse. 'Going Loco.' She shook her head. 'Which is where our money went, I can tell you. The only person who made anything was Sir Robert. We must have been mad, investing in a horse. Never won a damn thing. That's not true, it did win once. But it didn't matter,' she sat up with a bounce, 'it was always oodles of fun. Going to races when you have a runner. More than exciting. And your father, such a charmer.'

'I'm afraid I don't remember him. He left my mother when I was two.' Lisa touched the picture. 'But I did know Sir Robert – my mother worked for him.'

'Oh, I'm sorry, my dear.' Her plump fingers pleated her skirt. 'You can keep the photo, if you like. I have another one.'

'Thank you, that's very kind.' Taking it, she zipped it

securely in the inside pocket of her handbag. Goggles or not, she didn't want to lose this one.

Dorothea sighed forlornly. 'We had no idea how horrendously expensive the stable fees were going to be. The farrier's bills alone were ridiculous and then the race fees. The feed bills.' She perked up. 'Fun while it lasted, though. Lord it was fun. Being an owner. Going into the owners' enclosure. And your father,' Will and Lisa exchanged looks, not quite sure whose father she was referring to. 'He loved all the attention on race day. Handsome devil. Gosh we had some fun in those days.' Her expression suddenly shrewd, focused on Will. 'Before you were born, of course.'

She frowned. 'I always thought...' Lisa saw her take in a sharp breath and her face crumpled slightly but then immediately brightened.

She went to stand behind her husband, her plump hands gripping his shoulder. 'We should let you young things get off to the winery. I'm sure you want to freshen up before you go.'

Chapter 21

'Well, this is rather nice,' said Will, prowling around the bedroom, opening drawers and wardrobe doors, before stopping in front of a TV screen on the wall. 'We can watch TV in bed.'

'Great.' Lisa put her overnight bag on the old-fashioned four-poster bed, noting her hand shook a little. She didn't even know which side of the bed Will slept on.

Not sure what to do with herself, she examined the high-ceilinged room. Two windows faced out over the gardens and she could see Charles' feet poking out from the gazebo. She suspected he'd settled down for an afternoon snooze. A dressing table with three mirrors sat between the windows, reflecting the bed, which she couldn't stop looking at. Twisting her hands, she wondered whether to unpack her overnight bag. Hang up the one dress she'd brought or put her underwear in the rather grand chest of drawers that guarded the entrance to the alcove of a separate dressing room.

'Nice bathroom,' called Will, his voice echoing slightly from the other room.

She couldn't join him in there. Bathrooms were intimate.

Couples shared bathrooms. What was the suitable adjustment time from… whatever they were to a couple? This was uncharted territory. They'd not even had a proper date. Although she supposed today might have been considered a date.

Last time they'd spent the night together, it hadn't been pre-meditated or planned. It just happened. A gradual deepening of intimacy during the course of the evening as the hours got later. It had seemed perfectly natural to finally give in to the tiredness they'd both been fighting because neither could bear to stop talking.

Coming to Rome with Giovanni had been so much easier. She was in the driving seat and despite all his overtures, she knew she'd never intended to sleep with him.

To her sudden horror, she realised Will was watching her in the mirror of the dressing table and had probably read her not-so-poker face.

With a rush he crossed the room, rugby-tackled her to the bed, pulling them both down, and started tickling her.

'Oy!' She tried to push him away, but his fingers kept rippling up and down her ribs. 'S-st-stop.' Of course he didn't.

'As ticklish as ever,' he grinned down at her as she lay gasping, trying to breathe again, her diaphragm aching from giggling.

'Mean,' she hauled in another breath, 'trick.'

'But effective.' His pupils darkened and his head hovered over hers. 'You were looking as terrified as a virgin bride on her wedding night.'

'And now?' Her voice dropped, husky with desire.

They both stilled.

'Something else altogether.' He kissed her throat. 'I think perhaps I should be terrified.'

She swallowed and tilted her head back, breath stalling in her throat.

Surely he could hear her heart pounding so hard in her chest that it almost hurt, as he lowered his lips to hers with slow, inexorable intent, like a deadly assassin with its target in view.

She sank back into the feather duvet, anchored by the welcome weight of Will's body, shifting to allow his leg to slip between hers and wrapped her arm around his neck, pulling him towards her, with a shocking and thrilling desperation.

The kiss ignited an immediate explosion and things went from playful to passionate in seconds. Inhibition and worry vanished. Pure feeling took charge, as all the pent-up longing of the last interminable months reached fever pitch. Incandescent with need, Lisa pushed her hips against him. With a groan, Will shifted again, making her conscious of the whole length of his sinewy body. Tingles ran in ripples, coalescing into little explosions of joy each time they bumped a knee, a thigh, a hip.

'Lisa.' His husky voice at her ear, wound her up even tighter. Dazed, she stared at him, the blue eyes cloudy with desire, and pulled his mouth back to hers, her eyelids fluttering shut because it was too much. An overload of the senses. 'Tell me if this isn't what you want.'

The serious raw note in his voice turned her insides to liquid. She took in a breath, feeling as if she were on the top of the high diving board.

The simple statement made her heart stall. She wavered for a second. What if she took the step and it went wrong again? Could her heart survive?

Then she looked up into his face, gripped by the intensity of his gaze as he waited. Sometimes you just had to dive in and take the fall, but the rush as you did was worth it.

'I want this.' Her words whispered on the air and his hold on her softened. Relief?

It eased those tentative fears, but she added with a punchy glare at him. 'But, if you don't call me this time, I will kill you.'

She expected him to make some jokey response, but something inside her shivered when Will cupped her face with both hands. The solemn expression almost turned her inside out. A silent question hovered there. Do we do this? As if both of them knew there was no turning back.

She kissed him. Not a fervent, fevered kiss but a considered, heartfelt slide of her lips over his, a haunting yes in the touch of her mouth. No question about the answer.

With a pained sigh of regret, he pulled back.

'We have a date at the winery.' He touched her face, tracing her chin and down her neck. 'And then the rest of the night… and the week is ours.' It sounded like a lovely promise and her senses leapt in anticipation.

'It is.'

The tasting room was as cool and shady as a cave and a complete contrast to the burning heat outside. A bell clanged as they closed the door behind them, the glass panes so old and brittle Lisa worried they might shatter. The whitewashed walls were covered in paintings, which were startlingly contemporary in such a medieval setting.

Through one arch she could see oak barrels lined up, plugged with huge corks stained with red wine, like vibrant lipstick. Through a second arch, the scene was a modern contrast, where huge metal cages of dark-green bottles were being clinked and clunked across the tiled floor to a waiting delivery van. Romance and business hard at work together.

A middle-aged couple were already mid-way through a tasting at the high counter to the right of the room, where a series of opened bottles ranged, reds, whites and even a lonely rosé.

The attractive forty-something woman behind the counter poured the other couple a glass of velvety red, holding the glass up to the light and swirling, before indicating something in the glass with long elegant fingers.

Will strolled forward and took a bottle in his hands, examining the front and back labels before perusing the back one with a thoughtful frown and then moving onto the next. She watched him completely at home in the situation. A slight blush stained her cheeks as she thought of those hands recently roving over her body. She gulped. Anticipation hummed at the thought of what might happen later. Even now, after those kisses, parts of her tingled. He was thorough, she gave him that.

When the other couple's noses were buried in their glasses, the woman turned.

'Buon giorno, Signor Ryan?'

'Yes,' said Will.

'Welcome to Casa Felloni.' Her overt gaze suggested she'd like to eat Will up in several slow, seductive bites.

It didn't faze him, he simply grinned back and then snaked out an arm and pulled her forward. 'This is Lisa.'

To her credit, the woman's smile didn't dim by so much as a kilowatt. She welcomed Lisa with the same easy manner and began to explain the wines.

Lisa was happy to listen to the quick melody of her heavily accented English. Most of it flowed over her, with only the odd words and phrases registering.

She poured an inch of pale white wine into a tall tulip glass.

Lisa had no idea what she was supposed to do. Will twisted his glass this way and that, gently circling the contents before holding it up to the light like a pro. Then he came to stand behind her.

He put his arm around her, his hand over hers, guiding her fingers down to hold the stem of the glass. 'Hold it here, then your hands don't heat up the glass and the wine inside.' His chin almost rested on her shoulder and she could feel his breath on her neck as he added. 'When it comes to holding things, technique is very important.'

'What about the swirling?' Lisa turned her head. 'I wouldn't want to get that wrong.'

'Ouch, no.' He gave her a rueful smile, although his eyes danced wickedly. 'Like this.' With very slow moves he tilted the glass, his body leaning in and touching hers, replicating the movement of the wine in the glass.

'I-I think I've got that.' It took a second for her to frame her next words. Her brain had turned to mush, again. 'Why do you do that?'

'Officially, it helps to release the flavours of the wine. You're getting lots of oxygen in there.' He stopped, holding the glass and her hand perfectly still. 'But I think it's all part of the preamble. The build-up, step by step, to something wonderful.'

Lisa swallowed.

'And each step needs to be taken slowly, slowly, to get it exactly right.' His voice deepened, sending a ripple of awareness through her.

'Then you hold it up to the light to see its colour and see if there's any cloudiness or any impurities in it. Also, see the wine sliding down the inside of the glass.'

He pointed to liquid tracings like an aqueduct arcing around the glass, something she wouldn't have paid any attention to.

'They're legs.' He shot a quick wicked glance her way. 'Some are wider apart than others. The distance between them tells you a bit about the alcoholic strength of the wine. These aren't too wide apart, an indication of a lower alcohol content.'

He held the glass high, their arms mirroring each other, his cheek so close to hers she wasn't sure if she was imagining it or could feel the slight touch. Although all his attention appeared to be focused on the wine glass, his body seemed to be perfectly in tune with hers, his thighs touching the backs of her legs and his left arm wrapped around her waist.

'Even before you taste it, you're getting a strong sense of the essence of the wine. Weighing it up.

'Now you take a good deep sniff, put your nose right into the top of the glass.'

He guided the glass towards her. She inhaled through her nose. And couldn't smell anything but wine.

'What do you smell?'

Lisa wrinkled her forehead. 'Wine.'

'Okay,' he leaned in and sniffed at her glass, all the while holding her in the circle of his arm, pulling her body back against his.

'What does the smell make you think of?'

'Grass,' said Lisa immediately. The wine made her think of a day when you stand on the lawn and the grass has been freshly cut.

'Perfect,' Will squeezed her.

'But that's not a real flavour.'

'Yes. You can describe it any way you want. There tend to be recurring descriptions. It's your senses, your description. Wine is to be enjoyed. Shared.'

'Not,' she said with a touch of cynicism, 'this is an exceptional bouquet bursting with fruit flavours typical of this variety.'

'Works for some people, but not for me.' His voice dropped. 'I know what I like and it doesn't have to be dressed up.' And then he added, 'In fact I prefer it naked.'

She shivered.

'Now to the crunch point. The important part. The bit you've been building up to.' He winked, the hand at her waist having found its way under her t-shirt, his thumb making tiny circles on her skin. 'You can dive right in and make it quick and dirty, which is absolutely fine or you can take it slow and easy, savouring the flavour and the moment.'

Lisa shifted her weight slightly.

'I prefer to take it slowly, savouring every minute of that very first mouthful.' He dipped his head and took a good glug of her wine, swilling it around his mouth. 'After all, why hurry a good thing? You've got all the time in the world.' His half-lidded appraisal of her held smoky promise, making her rather hot. She was suddenly very aware of certain parts of her body, which were sitting up and taking a lot of notice.

'Take a good big sip, whirl it around you mouth and suck in a little bit of air. As you do that you feel the texture change, become more oily, silky.'

Doing as she was told, she was amazed to realise he was right. Suddenly the wine changed in her mouth, almost opening up and she could feel the difference on her tongue. She turned to face Will. 'Wow. I see what you mean.'

He tilted the glass towards himself and took another sip, lifting his head. She watched the strong column of his throat working as he swallowed, fighting the sudden urge to run her lips along his jawline and throat.

'Now, what can you taste?'

She thought hard. She knew what she wanted to taste. 'Nope, still wine. Although I'd say it's light and dry, not floral and not fruity.'

'And that's all valid. I'd say it's herbaceous, grassy. Clean.'

She took another sip. 'Well,' she said hesitantly. 'I can see what you mean, but I don't think I'd have got that as a taste without you telling me.'

And then he grinned at her, 'but I do have the advantage of knowing it's a Frascati and they are all distinct characteristics of that type of wine.'

'You! I know nothing about wine. That's not fair. And it's cheating.' She pushed at him.

'It's very rare, unless you're a professional wine-taster or seriously into wine, that you'd ever do a blind wine-tasting. I don't enjoy them at all. Too much like a one-night stand. A burst of pleasure, without any of the seduction.'

Will stared at her over the rim of the glass. 'For me, the real satisfaction is that slow build-up. The anticipation. That moment when you know you're about to sample a wine you'll love and you've wanted to try for ages.'

He tipped the rest of the Frascati away.

'And as you work along the wines, the sense of anticipation builds as each wine gets stronger, more full-bodied and richer in flavours, as you move from white to red.'

By the time they reached the red wine, Lisa's hormones had tied themselves in knots, like eager children tripping over their own feet in haste.

In fact, she was like one of her children in the nursery when they had ants in their pants, couldn't settle to anything but didn't know what had put the wind up them. Except Lisa knew what had stirred her up and that Will knew exactly what he was doing.

Well, he wasn't going to have the upper hand for too long.

Tasting a little of the red wine, she deliberately let a tiny bit slip down her chin and then scooped it up with one finger and poked the very tip of her tongue out to lick it up, stoically ignoring the self-conscious tremor of her hand, hoping to turn the tables and disconcert him for once.

Unfortunately, that plan backfired spectacularly. Before she could taste the wine on her finger, he'd grasped her wrist and pulled her hand to his mouth. With laughing eyes, his tongue touched her skin with a light flick that immediately sent sizzles dancing southwards. A gasp escaped at the electric fizz that set light to her whole body.

Feeling the blush suffuse across her chest, she turned away. Two more wines to get through. She eyed both bottles and caught Will looking at her with fierce intensity. She clenched her jaw.

How would she get through them if Will kept this up?

Weak-kneed and restless, she wanted him to kiss her. To kiss him. Wanted to wrap her arms around his neck, drag his mouth down to hers.

Heat burned between her legs. Longing. Impatience.

Without meaning to, she knocked back the rest of her glass.

'I think I've probably had enough,' she said faintly, putting her glass down.

Will poured the rest of his glass away, his gaze never leaving her face. She could feel her cheeks burning and a flush race up her throat.

'Do you want to leave?' he asked, his voice full of a different question.

'Er... um, No. You finish.' She nodded towards the two final bottles.

That wicked smile ramped up. 'We can share.'

He helped himself to the next glass, the woman behind the counter thankfully having faded into the background. Lord knows what she thought.

Will went through the same ritual. Lisa's breath felt tight in her chest, unable to drag her attention from him.

Long slender fingers circled the glass stem, as he held the ruby-red wine up to the light. She tried hard not to look at them. Tried hard not to remember their touch all those months ago, but it was impossible. With an inward breath, tension gripped her, as she fought hopelessly against the memory. Those lazy circles his fingers had painted on her stomach, the slow stroke down her breast bone, the delicious diversions where he'd traced the underside of her breasts before teasing the tight, puckered desperate-to-be-touched skin around her nipples. Her mouth dried. When Will offered the glass to her she almost grabbed it from him. The warm mouthful of wine with its full body and rich flavours filled her mouth. She savoured every drop. All her senses attuned. Her skin goose-bumped. Her ears picked out the chink of glass and low conversation in the distance, but she could only hear Will's breath, a slight rasp as he inhaled. Heat radiated, spiralling through her body, and she could almost feel it pulsing, vein by vein, down her arms, legs. Her heart bumped loudly. And she could smell wine and the scent of the man standing so close to her that she could feel the hairs on his forearm brushing against her skin.

It took a minute to focus. Disorientated she'd blinked, the room now much brighter. Will, in a blur of movement, grabbed leaflets and then her hand so quickly she almost missed the counter as she put down the wine glass when he pulled her out of the building.

Half running, half walking they made it back to the car, where Will pinned her up against the door, his lips ravaging over hers, with thorough precision.

'Back to the palazzo,' he growled.

All she could do was nod limply.

Chapter 22

They'd bolted out of the winery, seat belts tangled in their haste to get back to the villa and the short car journey did little to sober them. Will's hand took hers between gear changes, his thumb rubbing the sensitive skin on her wrist, keeping her pulse rate at a steady gallop. Both of them were primed like racehorses, reined in by the starting gate. When the car pulled up, the gravel shearing under the wheels as he braked hard, Will shot her such a heated, passion-filled look that it sent a starburst directly south.

Her mouth had gone dry and her hand shook slightly as she tried to open the car door.

As soon as they stepped out of the car, Dorothea came rushing down the stone stairs, looking flustered and almost panicky.

'Darlings. There you are.' She swallowed hard and looked behind her. Lisa tracked her gaze and saw her and Will's overnight bags tucked into the shadow of the olive tree at the bottom of the stairs.

'Terribly bad news, I'm afraid.' Her eyes were bright and kept darting about like swallows in flight, almost as if she couldn't bring herself to look at either one of them. 'The electricity. Gone. Packed up. Power cut. Happens a lot. You know Italy. It could be hours before it's back on. Sometimes days. I'm terribly sorry. Charles and I, we'll stay with friends. But it would be best if you went back to Rome this evening. It would be miserable here. No food. No light. I've sent Anunzia home. You can't possibly stay here. If you leave now, you can be back in Rome in time for dinner.'

There was an embarrassed silence as Dorothea ground to a halt, twisting her plump hands together. Lisa focused on the flashy rings, the metal bands crimping the doughy flesh, her agitated movements making the stones sparkle in the sunlight.

'Don't worry. That's fine. We don't want to put you to any trouble.'

'I'm sorry. It's just... Well, it would be much easier. Yes, better.'

Will patted her on the arm. 'It's not a problem.'

'Right, well.' Dorothea stepped back, sweeping her arm behind her to where their bags sat. 'Obviously, Charles and I are about to go, and we'd like to lock up the house.'

'Right. Of course.' Taking his cue with admirable calm, Will scooped up the two bags. 'Thanks for having... for lunch. Tell Charles thanks also for the introduction at the winery.'

'Yes, I will.' She backed up a few steps. 'Well. Have a safe journey. Lovely to see you. Nice to meet you... erm, Lisa.'

Dorothea backed up a few steps, as if desperate to put some distance between them. It was almost if they'd developed the plague.

They didn't say a word to each other as the car pulled away, with Dorothea waving from the doorway of the villa. Will stopped at the entrance between the two lion-topped pillars and tweaked the angle of his rear-view mirror, giving a narrow-eyed stare into it for a few seconds before readjusting it again.

They drove in silence until they were out of sight of the house.

'Interesting,' he said.

'What was all that about?' Never in her life had she been faced with such a situation. Although Dorothea hadn't been outwardly rude, it had been thoroughly uncomfortable. Doubly so for Lisa as she hadn't been invited in the first place.

'I haven't got a clue. The fountain still works, though.'

'The fountain?'

'Yes. You'd have thought the pump was powered by electricity.'

'I guess.' Lisa felt a little shocked. Shame and humiliation warred for first place. There was indecent haste and indecent haste. Dorothea had clearly been desperate to get rid of them. 'So no power cut.'

'I don't think so. Besides, she couldn't get rid of us quickly enough.'

'What changed?'

Will snorted. 'The only thing I can think of is that she spoke to my mother. Although why that would change anything...'

Lisa thought for a minute. It made sense to her. Of course, it did. As soon as they'd left Dorothea would have got on the phone to her old friend. What could Eloise have said to her?

What had Dorothea mentioned earlier? Eloise was a crashing snob. Had she raised an objection to Will getting together with her ex-cleaner's granddaughter and insisted Dorothea refuse to put them up? It sounded positively archaic and a tad hypocritical, given what she now knew of Will's parents' morals. Neither of them had gold-plated reputations in that department. Without realising it, she'd stuck her nose up in the air. Eloise could think what she liked. Lisa had nothing to be ashamed of.

As if reading her thoughts, Will reached out and took her hand, giving it a squeeze.

'Her problem, not ours. Gives us a day to ourselves tomorrow. What do you fancy doing?'

Determined to follow his lead, Lisa squeezed his hand back. 'Haven't you got any plans?'

'I've got a meeting set up in the afternoon, but not until three. I'm all yours until then.'

'What's on the agenda? You've done wine, cheese, olive oil and vinegar.' She was grateful that her voice didn't give away the churning sensation in her stomach, like a washing machine on half spin.

'I'm seeing a man about meat.'

She couldn't think of anything else to say. The conversation had grown stilted, fenced in with courtesy, as if to keep the undercurrent of unease between them at bay.

'Where would you like to go?'

Her mind had gone blank. Where did she want to go? Home? That seemed horribly cowardly, but the thought of her own little house suddenly seemed very appealing. She wasn't cut out for this. She liked things straightforward. Nan's direct speaking. This horrible sense of half-truth and intrigue made her long for home. A cup of tea. Knowing where she was and who she was.

For some reason, she thought of Gisella. No doubt Eloise would approve of her. She was related to a Viscount, even if he was an Italian one.

'The Sistine Chapel. I'm a tourist after all.'

'Okay. The Sistine Chapel it is. We'll need to get up early, beat the crowds.'

They lapsed into silence, interspersed with the metallic computerised voice of the hire car's GPS, which decided to take them home via the most direct route, taking them along a series of ever-diminishing roads, along tortuous single tracks, running along steep-sided hills.

Even Will's knuckles turned white as they gripped the steering wheel, easing the car with great care around the hairpin bends. It might have been picturesque, with turnings from the road, promising hidden homes and villas down death-defying tracks, so steep it was a miracle a car could get up or down them, and jaw-dropping views of rocky outcrops dotted with trees, but Lisa could barely bring herself to look beyond the dashboard for more than five seconds at a time.

'Are you okay?' asked Will when the road flattened out briefly, a new incline already rearing ahead of them.

'Fine.' A sheen of sweat pooled at the base of her spine but she gritted her teeth. 'You?'

'I could do with a break. Do you mind if we stop? We're not that far from Rome now. And there's a village up ahead.

I've heard of it. Famous for its square. We could stop here for dinner.'

Lisa let out a wobbly sigh. 'Yes please.'

Peeling her hand from where it clutched her knee, she touched the back of his hand on the steering wheel in gratitude. He didn't try to make light of her fears or dismiss them.

'It's not much further.' He shot her his lopsided grin. 'We could talk about Giovanni. Have you heard from him at all? Are you missing him?'

She let out a strangled laugh, remembering him winding her up on the plane at Luton, deliberately taking her mind off things. 'No. And no. Not a word.'

'Told you. Mama's boy.'

'Does it make you happy being right?'

'Yes.' His voice dropped, a husky undertone giving it a world of extra meaning.

It warmed her. Will hadn't done anything wrong. Like he said, whatever had happened back at the villa wasn't their problem.

'Because then he wouldn't have cleared off and left you for me.'

'Oh.'

Will gave a soft laugh. 'It took me a while to admit that I…' he laughed again, 'that I couldn't bear the thought of him taking you to Rome. I don't know how I managed to kid myself that this was purely a convenient time for a business trip.'

'You were jealous?'

'Extremely, except I didn't realise it at the time. Too busy persuading myself that I knew what was right for you.'

'Arrogant.'

'Always.'

'Don't sound so proud of it,' she retorted while basking in the shot of feminine satisfaction at his admission. 'It's not a nice trait.' But an arrogant man wouldn't try so hard to distract her or make her think of something other than the sheer drop on her right.

He shrugged, but she caught the hint of a smile on his face.

'Hallelujah. One kilometre to go. I think we can make it. And then I'll buy you a stiff drink.'

When they pulled into the village, she wanted to fling the car door open and kiss the ground.

'It's a very popular village.' He pointed up the hill to the crumbling remains of some ancient structure. 'Once a medieval hill fort. Tourists come out here in coach parties to see the sunset.'

She took a picture of Will perched on the low stone wall, Rome shimmering in the distance behind him before they walked down a stony track into the centre of the village.

The track opened out to a pretty and surprisingly lively village square, with several restaurants, already rather busy, edging the square with a fountain spurting water out of a lion's head and cobbled paths crossing the central area.

'Gosh, spoilt for choice. Where do you fancy having a drink?' he asked.

'You're the expert.' See, not arrogant at all. An arrogant person would decide without recourse to her.

'No, I want you to choose and then tell me why.'

'Gosh it's a constant market-research project with you.'

'Why not? You're a potential customer.'

'Don't you want posh people with lots of money?'

Will's searching look made her turn away.

'You have quite an inferiority complex, don't you?'

'Not really.' Will's disbelieving frown made her feel defensive. 'I don't come from the same sort of background as you or mix in your sort of circles. Look at Dorothea and Charles. Your mother and father.'

Will's bark of sharp laughter made her start. 'Those two are living out here in faded splendour because it's a damn sight cheaper than living in London and trying to keep up with the hyphen-Joneses. The reason Charles drives a vintage Mercedes is because it's still going.

'And my parents are up to their necks in debt.'

'It's not the money, though, is it. It's that superior,' she shrugged, 'entitled attitude. They expect everything to be a certain way.' She turned her attention to a board outside one of the many restaurants edging the square.

They perused each menu in turn. The prices were comparable, nothing too expensive.

'Which one do you fancy?' asked Will.

'That one.' Lisa pointed.

'Why?'

She laughed. 'Because I like the look of the chairs.'

'Seriously?'

'No. It's closest to the fountain and it's the busiest. And people are drinking, rather than eating.' Lisa's beautiful smile flooded her face and he wanted to capture that moment for ever.

'I've taught you well.' He threaded his arm through hers and they crossed the open square. A rush of something hit him, like a freak wave picking up his heart and tossing it over and over, through the surf, until he could barely breathe.

Damn. He'd been trying to tell himself that the warm, crazy feelings jumping about like jitterbugs were down to pure sexual attraction, but now he wasn't sure. When he'd said he might be in love with her, it had been an honest response, not wanting to lie to her, but in that moment, he knew there was no *might* about it.

Chapter 23

Her phone, charged for once, beeped as they finished giving their order to the waiter. She frowned. 'Damn, I missed a call. How did that happen?'

'Probably no signal until now.'

'Unknown number.' She screwed up her face. 'Plus three nine. That's an odd number.'

'It's a local number. An Italian number…' his voice trailed away.

'Oh!' Lisa fumbled for her phone, snatching it up. 'Oh my God,' she breathed. 'They left a message. Do you think it's him?' Her voice dipped to a bare whisper and she held the phone up.

'Are you going to listen? Or wave the phone at me?' Will eased it from her fingers, putting it down on the table. 'Do you want a moment on your own to listen?'

Her head shot up. 'No!' She placed a hand on the phone. 'No, I don't. You came with me.' She winced. 'I think I'm too scared to listen. What if he tells me to bugger off? That he wants nothing to do with me?'

'Then he's a bloody idiot,' said Will, thinking that he'd

personally beat the guy to pulp if he said anything to upset her.

Her hand stroked the phone, her fingers sliding backwards and forwards.

'Oh God, I feel sick.' She gulped in air. 'This is crazy.' She picked up the phone.

He could hear quite clearly, even though she held the phone to her ear, her face full of trepidation as she listened intently.

'Lisa, this is Vittorio Vettese. How lovely of you to call to see me. I would be delighted to meet with you. I'm back in Rome for two days before I travel again.'

She put the phone down with a thud on the table.

'He called.' She half-laughed. 'I never thought he would. I can't believe it. I spoke to my dad. Well, he spoke to me.' Unshed tears verged on spilling over. 'He only went and bloody called.'

It was as if she'd been lit up from inside, all shiny and brilliant. 'Oh Will. He called.'

He took her hand. 'He certainly did.'

She suddenly bit her lip and looked not... guilty but... up to something.

'I didn't tell you before.' She beamed, triumphant and sparkling with happiness. 'And I didn't tell him. I wanted him to see me, for me and not because he wanted this back.'

Will had absolutely no idea what she was talking about.

She delved into her handbag and pulled out a box – a jewellery box – and placed it on the table between them, flipping open the lid.

He'd never seen a ring quite like it. Probably antique.

Unusual and, judging by the size of the whacking great diamond in the middle of it, very valuable.

'This was my mother's engagement ring.'

Will wasn't sure what he should say. It was one of those awful, expectant moments, when it was obvious to everyone else but him, what needed to be said.

'It's... erm... very nice.'

'She wanted it to go back to my father.'

Will lifted his head, scanning her face and seeing the bewilderment in the lines etched into her forehead and around her mouth.

'She didn't want me to have it.' There was a whole world of misery in the words, despite the bright brittle slash of her lips, which looked like a demonic facsimile of a chirpy smile.

He took her hand. It felt cold. What did you say to that? Lisa wasn't the sort of person to swallow a platitude.

'That sucks.'

At that she did really smile. 'No shit. It hurts.'

'How do you know she didn't want you to have it?'

'She wrote a letter asking for it to be returned to my dad. That's fairly unequivocal, I'm thinking?'

'Maybe it was a way of reaching out to him to remind him you still existed, if he'd left before.'

'Is that supposed to make me feel better?'

Will winced. 'I don't think there's any way of making you feel better about it. He left. That makes him the bad guy. It's crap that it makes you feel bad too.'

Lisa sat back, lost in thought for a minute, her face suddenly brightening. 'I've never thought about it like that before. I always wondered why he'd left. Why he didn't love me and Mum enough to stay?'

'He's missed out.' Will took her hand. 'And look what you've achieved without him.'

'I'm not sure about that.' Lisa began fiddling with the edge of the tablecloth. 'I'm not exactly Wonder Woman.'

'Thank God. I never liked that outfit. Far too many sequins.'

'You know what I mean.' With a shrug. 'You're a budding restaurant entrepreneur. And the pub has been incredibly successful. It's such an amazing achievement. Siena's got big ambitions and Jason. Me, I love what I do, but it's not a big career.'

'But you love what you do. Isn't that important? What do you feel like when you wake up and have to go to work?'

'As long as Ofsted isn't due, I can't wait to get there. There's always too much to do.'

'And does the day drag? Are you watching the clock till home-time?'

'You're kidding. I haven't got time to look at the clock. Half the time I haven't got time to go to the loo.'

'And what's the best part of your day?'

'When the children come tumbling in, in the morning, trying to get their coats off in the cloakroom. It's a complete bunfight, but they're all keen and shiny and clean. Like little stars buzzing about, all fired up and ready to go.' Lisa glowed as she spoke a mile a minute, making Will grin.

'Except Fraser. He's always half asleep, clutching his blanket. And Noah, scruffy as the artful dodger from the minute he arrives. I'm going to miss this year's lot. We've got some funny ones coming through.' She stopped to take a breath and noticed him laughing at her.

'Okay, I really love my job.'

'And not many people can say that. They might enjoy their jobs, but you love yours. And let's face it, you're doing something positive. Your job counts. Much as I love feeding people and giving them a satisfying experience, I'm not exactly contributing to the future of humanity. No one is ever going to say, I remember that Will Ryan, his restaurant changed my life. Whereas I suspect those children will remember Miss Vettese for years to come. I think that counts for a lot more than running a restaurant, writing a fashion blog or brewing beer, quite frankly.'

'Thank you. No one's ever made me feel quite so noble.' As usual Lisa took refuge in self-deprecation. 'But I'll still never be successful like you. I really admire that.'

'I don't think you're noble.' He let a tinge of irritation colour his words. 'You're honest. And genuine. My parents, well they might not be dishonest but they're shallow. Always flitting to the next thing. Dad did something in the City briefly. Made his money but lived beyond his means. He and Mum lived in cloud-cuckoo land. Always chasing the next thing that would make them happy. Almost as if stopping and slowing down would remove the blinkers. It was exhausting to live with. Your Nan was about the only thing that anchored me and Alice. We were gutted when she left.'

'Really?' She looked sceptical. 'But she was only the cleaner.'

'Like that mattered. She was important to us, because even though she wasn't particularly demonstrative she was a constant. And God knows, we needed one.'

Her hand touched his in silent sympathy. She had an innate ability to know when to soothe him.

'We knew where we were with her. Except when she upped and left.'

'She didn't have a choice,' said Lisa with a snort, pulling away. 'You know they didn't pay her for the last three months. She stuck it out for you and Alice, but we had to eat.'

Will was horrified. 'I had no idea!'

'And your Mum refused to give her references.'

Shame washed over him and he let out an angry sigh. 'I'm so sorry.'

'Why? It's not your fault. Why should you be blamed for something your parents did? It's not as if you had any control over what they did.'

'True. Control was in short supply where they were concerned. Self-control. No wonder your Nan didn't want me to have anything to...' He trailed off feebly. No. No. What to say? How to retrieve the sentence? But he couldn't think of a single word say apart from the obvious. 'To do with you.'

Lisa's lifted her head, like a dog scenting a fox.

Damn. Even her nose quivered with terrier-like curiosity.

'Since when?'

'Well...' All the backtracking in the world wasn't going to recover this one but he was going to do his absolute best. 'She's never liked me.'

'That's rubbish.' Lisa smiled as if he were being ridiculous.

'She doesn't approve of me.'

'I'm sure she doesn't but... since when has that bothered you?'

In for a penny. It was that moment standing on a precipice, did he or didn't he jump? Should he finally tell her the truth?

'You know I didn't call you after that night.'

'Yes, I...' Her breath suddenly caught and the words paused in her half-parted lips. It showed a world of hurt and bewilderment, making the shame wash up again. He reached out and laid a gentle finger on her lips.

'Which I regret so much, but there was a reason.'

Everything receded, life around them a dull hush as they stared at each other, each recalling the notes and beats of that night. A night that had stuck in his memory, a fork in the road, where there'd been two choices and he'd taken the wrong one. A night where friendship and more had briefly shimmered with so much promise.

'I meant everything I said that night.' He hoped she could hear the fierce affirmation in his voice.

Lisa frowned.

'But the next day, your nan came to see me.'

The knife at her elbow pinged off the table, landing on the floor with a metallic clatter. 'Nan?' Her voice echoed with disbelief and suspicion.

He wanted to rein back the words, pulling hard on them, halt the horse now but it was too late. 'She didn't want me to mess you about. Said I should leave you alone.'

Lisa stared at him, leaving him to fill the empty space between them, her forehead furrowed with... disbelief, distrust, confusion. He couldn't read it.

'I... I...'

'You didn't call me because my nan told you not to.' She

shook her head. 'I can't decide whether to be furious with you, insulted or amazed.'

'Which would be better?' asked Will, eyeing her nervously.

'None.' She stood up, pushing her chair back.

She was going to walk away.

And he wasn't going to let it happen for a second time.

He stood up and took her in his arms. 'She wanted the best for you. She didn't think I was the best.'

'And neither of you thought that I might have an opinion of my own?' The air crackled around Lisa.

'She was ill.' He'd wanted to keep it from her. Not worry her. 'She almost passed out on me. I thought she was having some sort of attack. She said she didn't want to leave you on your own. Wanted you to find someone more reliable than me. It worried her. Worried me too, what if I couldn't be reliable enough for you?'

Lisa quivered in his arms.

'I had no idea she was so ill.' He recalled the sense of panic when she'd collapsed on him.

Lisa let out a half-sob.

'Hey, it's okay.' He smoothed her hair from her face, where it had fallen.

'No, it's not.' Lisa's face had crumpled and tears glistened on her eyelashes. 'She is such a...' she winced, 'an old... bat.' With a scowl, she gave her eyes a furious wipe.

'Did she do this?'

Stumbling she grabbed his arm and looked up at him, breathless and gasping.

'Something like that, yes.'

'Hmm,' Lisa shook her head, her mouth crimping in a stern line. 'You've been had, my friend. I promise you, if Nan were seriously ill, she would never let it show.'

'Are you sure?'

'I've lived with her all my life. I know her. That is classic Nan: I need a seat in the theatre, on the bus, I need a discount, I need a refund.'

'I need you to leave my granddaughter alone?'

Lisa stopped, her brows drawing together. 'Except, that doesn't really make sense, does it? I've no idea why she would have interfered like that. And she never said a word to me about it.'

It didn't make sense. Lisa stared up at Will's face. Sincerity shone from his face. A touch of guilt danced. She didn't mean to dismiss his motives. Nan had played him, but she had no idea why.

All these months, she'd thought he'd reverted to being playboy Will and, in fact, he'd been trying to do the right thing. Touched, her heart blossomed in her chest and for some stupid reason, tears began to pool again. She leaned forward to kiss him, hoping that no tell-tale drips would give her away. All that time, she'd been thinking dastardly thoughts about him and he'd done the chivalrous thing and listened to her grandmother.

The kiss, at first a brief touch of lips, her trying to ease the way, became more, a gentle apology for the misunderstanding, sweet and tender. When they pulled away, he pulled her hand up to his and touched each knuckle with a soft kiss. A telling moment of silent communion.

'Come on.' Lisa took his hand. 'Let's get out of here.'

Hand in hand, they strolled back to the car, each lost in thought but maintaining the connection between them with squeezes of each other's fingers. Lisa thought words might have spoiled the starlit walk along the cool, narrow straights and it seemed Will agreed.

Will flicked the fob to open the car, but came to her side and put both arms on the doorframe, pinning her against the door.

'I made promises that night. That I would call. I didn't keep them. This time I will.'

Her heart pounded as he bent to kiss her. Deliberate. Sure. Determined.

Firm lips teased hers with absolute intent. His hands sliding down the metal to her shoulders to hold her.

When he pulled back, he growled, 'You bugged the life out of me and I couldn't say anything. The number of times I wanted to kiss you, just to shut you up.'

'That doesn't sound terribly complimentary.'

'It wasn't supposed to be. You've been like a burr up my backside…'

'And not very romantic at all.'

'I don't feel romantic around you. I feel desperate. Urgent.' He gritted his teeth; she could see his jaw flex. 'Crazy.'

And he kissed her again, the flood of emotion bursting as the forceful, heartfelt touch of his lips overwhelmed her. His hold tightened, pulling her into him, as if he could never get enough of her, as if he wanted to pull her inside him.

Chapter 24

'Aargh,' Lisa put down her phone on her lap. 'This is hopeless.'

The lights of Rome, a distant cluster of lights as dense as the Milky Way, grew brighter, a thankful homing beacon as the roads finally flattened out and they joined the heavy traffic on the outskirts of the city.

She'd tried three times to phone Vittorio back and each time her phone cut out before he could pick up.

'Oh hell. This bloody phone.' Lisa shook it as if that might somehow help the woeful battery life. 'I'm going to run out of charge.'

'Here use my phone.'

Lisa quickly tapped in the number but this time, although it rang, Vittorio didn't pick up and then the signal died again, the phone cutting out mid ring.

'Damn. Still no signal.' A tiny part of her was relieved. What on earth was she going to say?

'Why don't you text him?'

'That's a good idea. Except... what do I say?'

'Why don't you suggest meeting him tomorrow? Tell him

where we're staying and ask him to suggest a meeting place and suitable time?'

Will made it sound easy and, as usual, managed to cut through the rubbish and come up with a practical plan.

Texting her father proved a lot more successful and by the time the car finally pulled up outside the apartment, she'd arranged to meet him the following day at a restaurant near the Colosseum.

'Job done. I'm assuming you don't want me tagging along. I've got an appointment at 3.30.'

'No, I think I ought to go on my own the first time I meet him.' Her nerves hummed. 'It would be easy to be a complete chicken and get you to come too, but I feel it's something I should do on my own.'

'Yeah,' Will winked at her. 'It's a bit soon to be meeting the parents.'

'You don't mean that. I've got you sussed, Will Ryan. If I wanted you to come, I think you would.'

Will tried to deny it but Lisa could tell that if she needed his support, he would be there for her. It was such an intrinsic part of who he was. Always there looking out for the people who mattered, no matter how much they irked him the rest of the time.

He looked uncomfortable at her piercing look. 'Yes, Mr I'm-no-hero. You would.'

When they finally pulled up outside the apartment, although it was gone eleven the sultry heat of the city enveloped them as they stepped out of the car. Quite how she'd managed to stay awake on the last leg of the journey, she wasn't sure. It had been hard work forcing herself not to drop off, but it seemed rude to sleep when Will had done all the driving.

As the heat hit her and the relief at finally getting out of the car, she yawned, hardly able to put one foot in front of the other.

'Come on sleepyhead.' Will looped an arm around her shoulder.

The apartment, with its tiled floors and dark entrance, immediately felt cooler.

He kissed her gently on the forehead as they walked through the door of the apartment, switching on the lights and turning towards the kitchen, where his laptop sat on the table.

With a sigh, he pulled her to him, kissing her mouth with a soft brush of his lips. 'Bugger, I need to log on and catch up with a few emails to do with the pub. Marcus has been texting me all evening. There's a problem with a supplier.' He rolled his neck. 'Could bloody do without it, but that's the downside of being self-employed; you never switch off.' He blinked wearily.

She put her arms around him, massaging his shoulders gently in sympathy. 'Do what you need to. Don't worry, I understand.' And she did. He should be so proud of what he'd achieved and the hard work he'd put in.

'I know what I'd rather do.' He looked at his watch. 'But I need to email Marcus. Why don't you go to bed?

Lisa swallowed, wondering what the etiquette here was?

He stroked a finger down her cheek, the tender gesture making her wilt into him.

All her bones seemed too heavy and even turning her head to kiss his fingers seemed an effort.

'Go on.' The corners of his mouth turned down as duty battled with desire. 'I'll join you in a while... if that's okay.'

Will dealt with the emails as quickly as he could but he needed to retrieve a few documents from his Dropbox account and by the time he'd found the right ones and sent them over to Marcus, nearly forty minutes had elapsed. The stressful drive down the mountain had taken it out of him. He hadn't dared let on to Lisa how freaked out he'd been at some of those hairpin bends. She'd been relying on him to get them home safely.

And he was the last person anyone should rely on. Shit, he rubbed at the back of his neck. What if he let her down again? His shoulders ached. All that tension, no doubt, from concentrating so hard on nursing the car down those roads. Nothing to do with that nagging worry about the new restaurant. What if it wasn't a success? His dad's comments he could cope with but what about Lisa? She admired him now, but what if the restaurant went tits-up? With a weary yawn and a stretch, he switched off the lights and followed the glow of the bedside light in Lisa's room as he made his way down the corridor.

His heart lurched at the picture she made, fast asleep, her hair spread out on the pillow, lying on her side with one arm tucked under her head. Could he look after her properly?

The light on his side of the bed had been left on, like a beacon guiding him home, and he was pleased to see she'd remembered to plug her phone in to charge. The familiar white cable snaked across her bedside table.

Quietly and quickly he stripped off to his boxers, tossing his clothes on the wooden chest at the bottom of the bed and slipped under the covers, carefully easing himself in to avoid waking her. She didn't even stir as he adjusted his weight to lie next to her, his head propped on his elbow as his gaze roved over her face. Her eyelids fluttered, the darker lashes flickering against her creamy skin, but her breathing remained slow and steady. Out for the count. He smiled and resisted the urge to trace her lips with his fingers, surprised at the sudden fierce dart of tenderness the sight of her beside him sparked. Reluctantly he turned to switch out the light and slid down the bed, feeling the warmth of her slim body inches from his. He reached out a tentative hand and touched her arm, a barely-there touch, to let her know he was here or maybe it was to reassure himself she was there. All he could do was his best and hope it would be enough.

Chapter 25

Her neck ached. It would have been much easier to lie on the floor, except there was barely room to stand upright and then you were wedged in.

The fabled colours and artistry of Michelangelo's work on the ceiling of the Sistine Chapel was worth the hour of shuffling along corridors filled with incredible artefact after incredible artefact.

According to her trusty guide book, there were nine miles of art to see in the Vatican Museum and it would take at least four hours to try and see everything. She didn't think her brain could cope with that. What she'd seen to date had been, to use a cliché, mind-blowing, but there was a seed of a headache right in the centre of her forehead.

On the wall opposite, the size and scale of the Last Judgement made Lisa feel small and very insignificant. The details of the robes, the shadowed folds, the lines of flesh and muscle of all those figures and the brilliance of the colours dazzled her. It was difficult to believe it had been painted 500 years ago. Even if she didn't know that much about art, she could appreciate the huge fresco.

It was almost worth getting up early this morning, leaving the sizzle of awareness between her and Will on hold. It seemed hard to believe that just a few hours ago she'd woken immediately aware of him next to her. She smiled to herself as she pictured him before he woke, hugging to herself the private moment when she drank in the sight of him lying next to her. The handsome face relaxed for once. She'd been tempted to trace the musculature of his chest and the blonde hair that dusted the golden skin. At some point in the night he'd pushed the covers down, giving an irresistible view of his long, lean figure, and one leg hooked over them, as if trying to escape the close heat.

Even now as she browsed the memory, her lungs tightened, exactly as they'd done as she'd taken complete advantage and conducted a thorough, leisurely inventory of his body, lust making slow curls in her stomach. All that lifting and carrying in the pub must have honed his physique. She could see the muscles in his abs, a trail of hair arrowing down, which set tiny firecrackers off in her system. She hadn't dared move an inch, not wanting to wake him, even though her hand twitched with a craving to smooth her fingers over his skin, skim over his nipples and down, down that taut, carved stomach.

Just the sight of his body turned her inside out, stirring desire and longing.

She almost laughed out loud. That would surprise the people around her in the crowded room buzzing with tourists. None of them had any idea that she'd tensed, clamping her legs together, mirroring what she'd done this morning when the heat pooling between them had become too intense to ignore. But despite the sexual thrum racing through her, she'd also become acutely aware that she wanted more. She wanted to savour him. Take their time.

It would have been easy to dive in, have what she didn't doubt would be wild, unthinking sex, but he'd done that too many times before. Her chest tightened. Could she really trust that she'd be enough for him? Once they returned to normal life, would he change his mind?

'You're thinking far too hard,' he'd said with a lazy drawl, startling her, when he'd finally woken. 'It's giving me a headache.'

'Will!'

His slow, sleepy smile had done funny things to her heart, almost as if it had turned sideways and upside down.

'Not expecting anyone else, were you?'

'Well in lieu of Tom Hiddleston, I guess you'll do.'

'Who?' He'd lunged towards her, pulling her down on top of him, giving her an enthusiastic kiss, which quickly turned into something else altogether. Beneath her his body felt all male and thoroughly intoxicating. Through his cotton boxers she could feel the hard outline of him, primed and ready for action.

For a while she'd revelled in the kiss, before pulling back. With each move he'd asked the question, do we carry this on?

She remembered her mouth trying to shape the words, but even though she couldn't think of the right ones to say, it clearly gave her away. He'd loosened his hold, studying her face.

Even with the hum of foreign accents, layered on the air, surrounding her in the busy chapel she could recall the tone of his voice as he'd said, 'Morning.' The way it gentled, as if he understood every thought torturing her mind.

Heat suffused her face as she remembered her husky reply of 'Morning.'

He'd stroked her arm, saying, 'You know there's no rush. We've plenty of time.'

A rush of gratitude filled her. Lovely Will. He hadn't seemed disappointed or as if he expected anything. At the time, it had made her heart swell with something she couldn't define, although there was still that tiny shadow of uncertainty. She'd spent so long protecting herself, was she doing the right thing, giving him her heart?

With unspoken accord they'd got up, breakfasted, showered and gathered their things together in plenty of time to beat most the crowds at the Vatican Museum.

A Japanese tourist, full of fervent apology, bumped into her, bringing her back to the present and the room full of people.

Will caught her eye and winked. His hand crept up to massage the crick in her neck and she rolled her head back to take full of advantage of the fingers working the tight muscles there.

'It's...' she breathed, trying to concentrate on the painting on the ceiling.

'It certainly is. I'm running out of superlatives.'

'I'm running out of steam,' said Lisa. 'Bit of a culture overload.'

Turning her attention to the huge wall painting in front of her, she tried to pick out familiar elements.

'Apparently, there was a fig-leaf campaign after Michelangelo died, where lots of the figures were covered up.'

'I've missed Tour Guide Barbie.'

She swatted at him with her guide book, which she'd hardly looked at since they'd entered the chapel. There was barely room in the crowd to turn the pages.

'They didn't do a very good job,' observed Will, scanning the figures opposite them.

'This is interesting. A few decades later, a chap who was nicknamed Il Briggatone, Italian for breeches-maker, was employed to paint over a lot of the nudity.'

'Like I said, he missed quite a few.'

'That's because in the eighties and nineties the paintings were restored and a lot of the figures were undressed again.'

'I know someone I'd like to see undressed again,' breathed Will playfully in her ear, his lips barely skimming her skin.

She pinched her lips before whispering, 'Behave.'

'Do I have to? All this naked flesh is giving me ideas.'

'Ssh, you might get struck down.'

Will's attempt at penitence made her giggle. He didn't do sombre particularly well.

Finally cultured-out, they took refuge in the courtyard gardens, managing to snag a bench in the shade.

Lisa looked at her watch. A few hours to go.

'You sure you don't want me to come with you?'

'No, I'll be fine.' Lisa knew that Will could see right through her confident response.

'I can cancel my meeting.'

She linked her arm through his. It meant a lot that he was

prepared to do that for her. His business was important to him. 'Honestly, I'm a bit nervous. No, make that a lot nervous. But I need to do it.'

'Your phone is fully charged, isn't it? Text me if you need rescuing.'

'Thank you.'

'I'll text you when my meeting is over and I can either come and join you or meet you back at the apartment. Unless you want to spend more time with your dad. Either way, let me know.'

'I'm going to play it by ear.' She had absolutely no idea what to expect. Sitting here now, with only a few hours to go, she felt rather sick.

'It's quite spectacular,' said Will, looking back across the garden at the museum. 'But slightly unnerving. I feel as if I don't belong here. I'm too much of a heathen.'

'No, not heathen. You're a good person. You might not be religious, but you have the right values.'

'What on earth gave you that impression?' asked Will, gruff all of a sudden.

'I just know.' She gave him a steady look, ignoring the brief look of panic in his eyes.

'I think you might bring out my better side.'

Lisa smiled. He was much better than he pretended to be.

'Come on, we've got plenty of time to go to St Peter's.'

Chapter 26

Getting lost had made her slightly late and now she was horribly conscious of her flushed cheeks and slightly damp hair clinging to her neck and face. St Peter's had been awe-inspiring, but also overwhelming. Lisa had found the excessive opulence and wealth slightly unsettling, especially after the riches of the museum.

Trying to cool down in the shade of a group of trees across the street from the restaurant, she scanned the people sitting outside. Most of the tables were full. Healthy wariness mixed with skippy excitement as she assessed each group.

Not the family of four generations with a gummy, ice-cream-smeared baby, nor the two middle-aged women in immaculate tailored shift dresses sipping at their matching glasses of Prosecco. She also dismissed the two older men with greying hair and comfortable paunches and a trio of young mothers, seemingly oblivious of their children playing with a cat under the table, which left several men on their own.

There were three potential candidates – a man engrossed in a map, a blonde man reading a newspaper and a very handsome man in a smart business suit, his hair with a touch of sophisticated grey at the temples talking on his mobile. The first one she ruled out as a tourist and the second was too fair to be Italian. She studied the man in the suit more closely, grateful for the dappled shadows of the trees. Despite the grey, he looked in his mid-forties, which was probably the right age; her mother had been quite young when she'd had her.

Lisa bit the inside of her cheek, knowing that all this surmising and theorising amounted to prevarication – big style. The last thing she wanted to do was approach the wrong man and make a complete fool of herself. The man in the business suit put down his phone, his call obviously over.

It came to her – she could phone him. Congratulating herself on the neat solution, she fished out her mobile, grateful for once that she'd charged it properly. Her hand shook slightly as she unlocked the screen and brought up the number. Turning away slightly, but keeping an eye on the scene, she made the call and held her breath, waiting for it to connect.

The call tone in her ear made her stiffen as she waited. Like an echo, she heard a phone ring and her heart almost bolted into her mouth. The man in the suit went to pick up his phone, his hand hovering over it. Adrenaline surged through with a heady rush, but he didn't pick up. Seriously? He wasn't going to pick up? She willed him to answer the call. Disappointment seared. He wasn't going to answer? Had he seen who the call was from? She almost didn't realise that the phone had stopped ringing her end.

'Hello, Lisa.'

What the hell? Had she missed someone? The sound of the Italian-accented voice made her swallow hard, with stupid gulps, as if she were trying to get down a boiled egg whole. Like a Le Carré spy, she subtly shifted her stance, sliding back into the shadows, allowing her gaze to rove over the other patrons.

No? Really?

It had never occurred to her, in a million light years, that her father might be blonde. She'd presumed he'd be dark. Weren't all Italians dark-haired? Fair men came from the frozen North, of Scandinavian origin and dark men from the Latin south. At least, that's what she'd always assumed.

The blonde man had picked up the phone and she could see him talking. Even though she doubted herself for a minute, convinced she'd made a mistake, his mouth moving in time with the words in her ear confirmed everything. He was Vittorio Vettese, her f... He turned, his profile outlined against the white stucco wall of the restaurant.

Her phone slipped from her fingers into her bag. No. Surely not.

A vice clamped around her lungs as she stared. Stared and stared. It couldn't be. But there was no denying the straight nose. Strong chin. The familiar dip between chin and lips. The shape of his forehead, where it met his nose. All horribly, horribly familiar.

It was like looking at Will. An older Will, but unmistakably Will.

The implications splintered into her brain like a mirror

shattering, the shards slipping from its frame into an ugly sharp, jagged mess. Awareness stabbing with physical pain.

Now she realised. Dorothea's face hadn't been full of embarrassment. It had been horror. No wonder Nan didn't want her and Will to get together.

And, of course, her fingers closed over the ring box in her pocket, that's why her mother had wanted the ring to go back to their father. Will was older than her. The first-born. Italians were traditional.

The older son inherited. The older sibling. Her brother. Half-brother. Who said two halves make a whole?

With sickening fascination, she took another look at Vittorio Vettese, despite the evidence in front of her, still hoping she'd got it wrong and had imagined it.

She'd kissed those lips... no, not those ones but, oh so, similar. Bile rose in her throat, burning at the back of her tongue.

Mesmerised, she watched as he put the phone down with a puzzled frown. Thank God he hadn't thought to look around. Instead, he took a sip of his coffee, his attention going back to the newspaper on the table in front of him, completely oblivious to her whole world imploding a few feet away. She envied him his poise and nonchalance. He was so like Will, with his long legs tucked under the table.

Unable to take her eyes from him she took a step back, conscious of the breath in her lungs, so heavy it almost dragged her down. She wanted to sink through the floor, down, down, far away from anyone. She took another step backwards, then another and another, before bumping into someone, who glared at her.

She kept backing up, praying that he wouldn't look up until she was far enough away to turn the corner of the street and break into a run.

Her breath rasped out of her mouth, hauled back equally quickly, as if her body could barely spare it. Bloody bloody bloke. She'd slammed into him, even though he'd had ample time to move out of the way. His hands were a little too all over her as they steadied her after the impact. It gave her the jar she needed to stop and focus. At least focus on where she was.

She bent double, trying to regain her breathing pattern. Running was not normal. She never ran. And now she remembered exactly why! It hurt when you did it, it hurt when you stopped and it really hurt the next day. But nothing could hurt as much as this. The pain of her heart shattering.

She should have known better. Being independent shielded you from this sort of pain. Being on your own meant you didn't have to feel like this.

Will. Her brother. Her half-brother. But there was brother in the sentence whichever way you looked at it.

Brother. Brother. Brother.

How the hell did she tell him? Or face him?

She'd just found him. Numbness settled around her. What on earth did she do now?

The only place she could think to go was home.

She reached for her phone. Not there. It had to be here somewhere. She checked every pocket of her bag, twice.

It had gone. She remembered the man bumping into her, holding onto her a few seconds too long. She'd misconstrued his flirty smile when something far more underhand had been going on.

It summed up her day.

Chapter 27

When he opened the door, he stopped and listened. The apartment was silent and still with that curious, quiet heaviness that settles when no one is at home. He pulled his shirt from his waistband and flapped it, the coolness of the interior very welcome after yet another very hot and sticky day in Rome. The thought of a nice cool shower was so welcoming, he almost stripped off at the front door. Even if Lisa had been in, she probably wouldn't have minded, and he smiled to himself. Perhaps he should wait for her and persuade her to join him.

Lisa had clearly had a great time with her dad. Forgotten the time and him. Will quashed the grumpy thought. It was the first time they'd met. She was bound to lose track of time. She'd have loads of questions to ask him.

Even so, she could have texted. He'd bloody insisted her phone was fully charged this morning. It couldn't have run out of battery again.

When they got back to England, he was going to buy her a new phone.

In search of cold beer, he strolled into the kitchen and

pulled one straight from the fridge and started to head out to the balcony. At this time of day, now in the shade, it was the perfect spot to sit and put your feet up. His meeting had gone well and in the absence of any word from Lisa he'd stayed and chatted to the owner before taking the scenic route back.

Halfway to the balcony, he realised he'd forgotten a bottle opener. When he retraced his steps back, he spotted it straight away.

His heart collided with his ribs at the sight of the box, placed dead centre in the middle of the table.

The careful positioning, like some clue in a macabre murder mystery, triggered an instinctive sense of unease.

Lisa had been back.

He reached out and opened the box. The ring sat cushioned in the faded velvet, its big fat diamond winking innocently at him.

Lisa had left this here for a reason. Her dad must have wanted her to keep it. But the precise placing, for him to see, didn't feel like triumph.

He dropped the ring box on the table.

'Lisa!' he called, even though he knew the apartment was empty. He hurried to the bedroom.

It was exactly as they'd left it this morning, when Lisa had insisted on straightening the bed, making it neat and tidy. He noticed the phone charger from beside the bed had gone.

And then he realised her pull-along cabin case was also missing.

Despite knowing they would all be empty, he checked the

drawers and wardrobe and then the bathroom with stubborn thoroughness, as if there might be a chance that her things were there and there was a reason for her case not being there, but it was no good. Everything had been taken.

Lisa had gone.

Run away? That wasn't her. She was the type to stand up and face things. Like when he'd never called. She still showed up at the pub to do her shifts. Admittedly with her nose in the air and ignoring him as much as she could, but she hadn't run away from it.

What on earth had happened with her father? Surely if he'd greeted her like the prodigal daughter and invited her to go and stay with him, Lisa would have left a note or at least recharged her sodding phone to call him.

Maybe he'd snatched her and sold her into a trafficking ring. Okay, now that was far-fetched but what other reason could there be for her not being here?

As he looked around the bedroom, the image of her lying in the lamp light last night played like a constant reel in his head.

He snatched up the beer and opener to wrench off the lid, took a long swallow, slammed the bottle down and picked up his phone.

'Hello?' It was answered after one ring.

'Hi, is that Vittorio?'

'Yes, who is this?'

'My name's Will Ryan. I'm here in Rome with Lisa. She was meeting you today. I wondered if she was still with you.'

'No. She did not arrive.'

'What?' He sat down with a thump. 'What do you mean?'

'I waited for an hour. She never came. Although she did call but hung up before she said anything.'

'That's odd. She went to meet you. I've got back to our apartment and she's gone. What time did she call?'

'At a few minutes past three.'

Will didn't understand. She should have been there in plenty of time. She'd left him a few streets away. Even with her dire map-reading skills she couldn't have got lost. Had she chickened out? In those fifteen minutes?

There'd been absolutely no sign that she wouldn't turn up. It was totally out of character. Lisa didn't let people down. He didn't understand.

And if she hadn't met Vittorio, what was it that had changed? What had made her suddenly pack up and leave the apartment without a word?

It had to be something to do with her father.

And why didn't he sound more bothered? He almost sounded relieved.

Will realised he was stroking the ring box. The least he could do was go and meet Vittorio and offer him the ring back. Perhaps it might answer a few questions.

As he finished his beer, he heard a noise and leapt to his feet, relief spilling through him. She was back. Delight warred with anger. She had some explaining to do. Forcing himself to stay put and not going racing to greet her, he waited, sitting at the table with feigned nonchalance as footsteps came closer.

'Will.'

The deep voice made him jump.

'Giovanni!'

The young Italian tossed his bag on one of the kitchen chairs. 'What a journey. I'd forgotten how hot it is here.'

Will wilted on the spot.

'You're back.'

Giovanni shook his head. 'Not for long. Nonna is much better, but Mama has been very shaken. I came back for some papers.' He looked around. 'Where's Lisa?'

Will shrugged, hiding his unease. 'I don't know.'

Giovanni beamed. 'Still out sightseeing?'

Will couldn't answer.

'I can't stay. Will you let her know?'

'Know what?'

Giovanni frowned. 'That I was back and that I'm sorry I can't stay.'

'I can do that.' His clipped tones made Giovanni stare at him.

'And Lisa is, well?'

'She's fine.'

'She managed with the maps?' Giovanni was checking through his pockets before pulling out a key. 'I must go over to the house.' Will could see he was mentally elsewhere.

'She managed just fine.' Will snapped, irritated by his complete thoughtlessness.

Will managed to snag the very last table in the crowded restaurant and immediately ordered a Peroni. He didn't know if it was a good or a bad omen to arrange to meet Vittorio in the same place, but it was close to the apartment and apparently convenient for Vittorio's girlfriend's place.

He played with his phone as he waited. Giovanni hadn't hung around, which he was relieved about. What he and Lisa had was too precious and fragile to hold up to the light, to share with or explain to anyone else.

Dismissing Giovanni from his thoughts, he forced himself to put down his phone. He wouldn't check his texts until the waiter had taken his order. He wouldn't check his phone again until the waiter had walked past three times. He wouldn't check either until the family over the way had packed up their baby and two toddlers.

The silly challenges didn't make it easier or make the time pass any quicker. Lisa still hadn't been in touch.

A shadow fell across the table. He looked up into curious blue eyes, the same shade as his own, as his pulse took up an uncomfortable tattoo.

'Vittorio.'

'Will.'

They nodded at each other. The colour drained out his face so suddenly he could almost feel the veins constricting. It was very weird looking at your older self. Someone familiar and yet not.

Vittorio tilted his head to one side. 'Hmm. Let me guess, you are Eloise's son.' Puckish mischief flitted across his face and he broke into a broad smile. The depth of the lines fanning from around his features suggested it was something he did frequently.

He hailed a waiter and with a nod towards Will's drink, he indicated he'd a have beer too.

'So it would appear,' said Will, his voice dry, hiding the surge of fury at the irreverent amusement of the other man. A sense of absolute powerlessness almost felled him.

This morning, as he swam up from sleep with Lisa at his side, that first waking moment had been suffused with utter certainty. His life suddenly complete. No questions, no queries, no perhaps, maybes or what-ifs. Just bone-deep certainty. And with it came calm, the relaxed feeling of knowing that everything was going to be alright.

Now, in one fell swoop, a dizzying death-knell plummet, the bottom had dropped right out of his world.

And this grinning idiot had absolutely no comprehension of the cataclysmic, heart-in-mouth, effect his appearance must have had on Lisa.

Will closed his eyes, almost feeling her pain, but he had to ask.

'Are you Lisa's father?'

Vittorio laughed, well-defined eyebrows, like a pair of horizontal parentheses, dancing with animation. 'Good lord, no. Is that what the little chick thinks? Now I see why she contacted me.'

Will's fingers balled into fists under the table. The flood of relief rushing through him in a red-hot tide was completely at odds with the bone-crushing tension a second before.

'Lisa's mother was already pregnant by another man when I married her, even though she wasn't showing. But I loved her. She was such a beautiful woman. However,' he shrugged, inviting Will's approval, 'it turns out I'm not a marrying man.'

'Or a father?' Will's jibe went straight over Vittorio's head.

'Eloise decided it was easier if everyone thought you were Richard's child. And our affair... it,' he clicked his fingers, 'pfft.'

Will eyed him dispassionately, keeping the burning ball of fury tightly bound. Knowing his parents, he wasn't even sure he was surprised. Had his father known he wasn't his son? It would explain why Will could never please him. What had him clenching his jaw was the thought of Lisa. She must have seen Vittorio, taken one look and drawn the very worst conclusion. Where was she? She'd obviously fled in a panic. Had she gone to a hotel? Their flights weren't until the day after tomorrow. Letting out a breath, he forced himself to relax. He'd send her a text to explain and everything would be alright.

'Why did Lisa decide she wanted to meet me after all this time? Her mother has been dead for a long time.' And then Vittorio nodded. 'Ah, the delightful mother. My mother-in-law. She is dead?' Will wanted to squirm in his chair. Didn't the man have a single compassionate bone in his body?

'No, she's very much alive.' Will wasn't going to give this man the satisfaction of knowing that Lisa had wanted to bolster what little family she had in readiness for her grandmother's death or that this man, or the myth of him, had been important to her. With a sudden fervour he prayed Nan would live well into her nineties and beyond.

'You were around for the first few years of Lisa's life? I guess she thought you might have some interest in her. We were in Rome for a holiday and she thought she'd look you up.'

He pulled the ring box out of his pocket, but kept it out of sight under the table. He hadn't yet decided what to do with it.

'I remember her. We Italians, we love children. She was a very good child. We called her the little chick because she hopped up and down like a chicken. Always happy, that one. Her mother was a very good mother. But you understand, it was a very long time ago. I was working hard as a jockey. There wasn't much family time. And then I got a job at a racing-stable in the north of England, Wetherby. It was a good time to end things.

'And how are your parents? Eloise still as beautiful? Remember me to her. How is she?'

'She's fine.' Will leaned back and put his arm over the chair alongside him, forcing himself to be entertained by Vittorio rather than give in to the urge to punch his lights out. He was exactly the sort of person who would have fitted right in with his parents. Utterly feckless and totally self-centred. He should be used to this. With his parents he'd learned long ago there was no changing them. But, he suddenly realised their behaviour and attitudes didn't have to define him. With a grim smile he thought of everything he'd done. No wonder his father, or not-his-father, had never thought anything was good enough. Will straightened. He was damn proud of what he'd achieved and he didn't need to prove anything to anyone.

'That was a good time. Sir Robert was a good employer and your parents were great fun. We went to some parties. And raced. It was my life. Now I don't race. I work for the racecourse in Rome. You could come and visit? You and Lisa?'

'I don't know where Lisa is.' Will pursed his lips, knowing it would be useless to say anything about Vittorio or Eloise and Richard's thoughtlessness – he couldn't use the word 'parents' any more, but worry burned a hole in his stomach. 'I'm assuming she saw you and... it was a shock.'

Vittorio laughed. 'A very big shock.'

Will leaned over the table and said with icy fury, 'A terrible shock.' Of course, Vittorio couldn't possibly understand, the heartless... Will mentally used a word he never used.

He stood up, grabbing the ring box before it fell to the floor.

'Lisa wanted to return this to you. Her mother had asked.'

Vittorio opened the box and his face sobered. For the first time, Will saw real emotion there, and to his surprise, Vittorio's face crumpled. 'My Nonna's ring.'

Sadness transformed his face, as if a layer of tracing paper had been laid over it, distorting the previous expressive, care-free character. Will watched as his shoulders sagged, his whole attention focused on the ring.

'The truth is, I really loved Lisa's mother, Hattie.' Vittorio spoke so quietly it was as if he were talking to himself. 'I loved her very much. She was a golden girl. Always smiling. Always happy. Always saw the good in everyone, even Lady Mary.'

Lady Mary?

Vittorio tapped the box with a long slender finger, the exact twin of Will's own index finger. It gave him a funny jolt. History was repeating itself. Lisa was his golden girl. Always happy. Always smiling. Even when she wasn't smiling, her mouth had that cheerful upward curve.

'I remember the day I gave her this ring. I knew she loved him more than me, but I gambled that I would be enough. And she said yes. I was very very happy.' Vittorio looked wistful and a far cry from his laughing self a few moments earlier. 'But it wasn't enough. She didn't love me as much. It was always him. I tried to persuade her to move away with me. Start again. When she died, I didn't contact Lisa. I visited the stables a few times in the first couple of years after she died. Lisa looked very much like her mother. It was too painful.'

Will was confused. 'Who did Hattie love?' Who was Lisa's father?

'Her boss.' Vittorio shook his head with a resigned frown. 'My boss. Sir Robert. He'd have divorced Lady Mary and married Hattie if he could, but then Lady Mary had her accident. Hattie broke it off when she realised she was pregnant. Knew it wasn't fair on Lady Mary, who would never have her own kids after her fall. That was the sort of person Hattie was.'

Will didn't like to point out that having an affair with someone else's husband wasn't necessarily a good thing in the first place.

'I think Lady Mary must have known the truth. She made Hattie's life very difficult after that. Occasionally she'd have to pop up to the yard with Lisa but Lady Mary banned children. Said it was a health-and-safety issue, but everyone knew. She couldn't bear the sight of Lisa.' Vittorio's face twisted with sudden grief. 'And neither could I.' His voice broke and he stared away into space.

Will could picture the portly racing-stable owner sitting at the bar in the pub. Without fail he popped in every Thursday, the night that someone went to sit with his wife. Lady Mary had broken her back in a riding accident over thirty years ago. With sudden insight, he understood the veneer of sadness that surrounded the older man. He'd lost a lot – as well as his wife.

Will flinched. Did his mother and Richard know any of this? Did Nan?

And Lisa, where was she now? She needed to know that Vittorio wasn't her father. That he wasn't her brother. He picked up his phone and texted her, leaving Vittorio lost in thought. Why wasn't she answering? At least, wherever she was, she had her phone charger with her and once she'd charged her phone she'd get the message and contact him.

Chapter 28

'A seat has become available on the flight to Leeds/Bradford Airport. That's all I can offer you.'

Lisa had checked at the desk with listless determination through three, then four, then five flights. She was beginning to despair she'd ever get home.

'I'll take it.'

'Lucky, eh? The very last flight tonight.'

Lisa gave her a weak smile. Lucky was the last thing she felt. How unlucky did you have to be to go and fall in love with your own brother?

Handing over her credit card with shaky hands, she couldn't even summon the energy to wince at the outrageous price. She didn't care. She wanted to go home. Back to her own life – away from all this. Run away and keep running. Guilt pinged like a bell on a reception desk, pulling her back. What must Will be thinking? She should have left a note, but there were no words. And she couldn't have faced him.

How could she have looked into his eyes and told him? She felt so fragile, it would have killed her. And how would that scene have played out, the two of them suddenly unable to touch each other, as if a glass screen had come down between them? It seemed impossible to take on board. What they'd shared was so wrong, when it had seemed so right. Cold shame washed over her. He was her brother. She tried to shut out the images of him holding her, kissing, touching. It was wrong. And so unfair.

Thank goodness no one else knew. And never needed to know. It would remain their horrible secret. She wanted to wind a clock back and not know herself. She wished she'd never set eyes on Vittorio Vettese. Was that very wicked?

With another hour and a half to kill before the flight she trailed, head down, one foot in front of the other, to the internet café at the other end of the terminal. Her phone might have been crap but it had been useful. It was going to take forever to collect all the numbers she needed on a new phone.

Lisa had intended to send a message to Siena via Skype, *Just to let you know change of plan, you don't need to pick me up. Have lost phone. Will be in touch soon,* but Siena was on line and responded immediately.

Hey Lisa! That's a pain. Have you got another lift?

Lisa could imagine Siena at home typing away with her usual princess Pollyanna perkiness. She could do with a bit of her perpetual sunshine right now. Her fingers hovered over the keyboard. Her emotions were too raw to even consider telling her the whole story, but suddenly she needed to talk to Siena.

On my way home. At airport now.

Why? Two days early! Did you and Giovanni fall out? The Italian Stallion not so stallion after all???

Lisa managed to summon up a weak smile. If only she knew. Next to Will, Giovanni was more of a show pony.

No. She paused, wanting to share, but not everything. *Not Giovanni. He had to leave. His grandmother was ill. It's a long story.*

I knew it. It was just you and Will?

Lisa's fingers hesitated, honesty fighting with circumspection and a tinge of shame. Will was her brother. Those kisses had to be forgotten. His touch. All buried. She couldn't, and didn't, want to blame Will or make it look as if they'd fallen out. That would be wrong. If she said it was complicated, Siena would want to solve things.

Before she could type anything, Siena had come back, her mind galloping ahead, gathering up the bare facts.

I knew there was something. You two watch each other all the time. That brother-and-sister bickering didn't fool me. I think you two are made for each other.

A sob escaped. The screen blurred. That sick-in-the-stomach feeling hit again.

Will and I are friends, that's all. We spent some time together and came to a truce. It almost killed her to type the next line. *But I realised he's not right for me.*

Could she be friends with him? Oh God, they were family. Her body froze. Could she ever speak to him again? See him without wanting something that she could never have. Longing stabbed into her, blind and unthinking. When Nan died, he and Vittorio would be her entire living family.

No? I might be talking out of turn, but I think the two of you are perfect for each other. Sad face (can't find emoticon thingy). Are you sure? I think he cares, but has been hiding behind all those girls.

Tears seeped down Lisa's face as regret pulled at her.

Will see you when I get back.

You okay? Wish I was there with you. What aren't you telling me? Are you sure you're okay? Let me pick you up. What time does your flight get in?

Flight lands at 11.45… but at Leeds/Bradford Airport. Only flight I could get. Don't worry. Going to get a hotel tonight. Will tell you more when I get home.

Call me… get a phone sorted quick. Missing you. Big hugs. Love xx

Numbness pervaded every last bit of her. Her brain had all but shut down; now she no longer needed to think. Red-eyed, she handed her passport over, wondering if the UK official might refuse her entry. In her current state, she probably looked more vampire than human.

Before she knew it, she was through the nothing to declare and out into the unfamiliar building. Disorientated she looked around for signs to a taxi rank to take her to the nearest hotel.

At this time of night there were a few desultory souls waiting at the railings for arrivals, some with signs. Mr Smith. Good luck with that one. Mr Van Etterlink. Mr George Vassou. Miss Lisa Vettese.

She did a double-take. The large A3 piece of paper had her name written in huge capitals, almost shouting at her, as if someone really didn't want her to miss it.

The woman holding the paper up, scanning people

anxiously, had mid-brown hair cut in stylish layers and wore jeans with a bright lime-green cardigan and coordinating scarf. She looked chic and neat, making Lisa feel rather bedraggled. Who was she? And what was she doing here?

The easy tears that were constantly lying in wait seeped out. Siena must have sent her. No one else knew she was on this flight.

On wobbly colt-like legs, Lisa walked over to the sign.

'Hi, I'm...' she nodded at the sheet of paper.

'Hi.' The woman smiled cautiously at her. 'I'm Laurie, Siena's sister. She called and said you needed picking up.'

Lisa almost crumpled on the spot. Relief and gratitude intermingled with surprise.

'Oh. I... er.' She'd heard a lot about Laurie, but had never met her. She and Siena had been estranged for many years, through no fault of their own, and in the last few years had been working towards being sisters again.

Laurie folded away the paper into neat squares and tucked it into her bag. 'Siena was worried about you landing alone this late and I live in York.'

Lisa's geography was hazy, but she was pretty sure York wasn't exactly next door. This was a big ask. Tears threatened again. Lovely Siena. What a friend.

'That's kind of you,' stammered Lisa. 'I... er.'

Laurie looked serious. 'Siena wouldn't have asked if it wasn't important. She's talked about you a lot.' Her face lifted with a kind smile. 'You helped her when she first came over. The first proper friend she'd ever had. It's the least I can do for my little sister.'

'I didn't do that much. Siena's so positive. She did a lot herself.' They exchanged a look. Siena had arrived with no money and no friends. She'd built a life for herself, making the most of things without ever moaning or complaining.

'You helped. We thought you could come back to Merryview with me tonight and then I can put you on a train tomorrow. Much nicer than a strange hotel.'

'That would be... b-be lovely.' Her voice broke. She was in danger of breaking down completely and sobbing, which wouldn't do at all. She straightened, the muscles in her shoulder so tight they protested. 'Thank you. I... that's kind. I can't tell you how much I appreciate it.'

What had Siena said to her? Laurie seemed much more reserved than her sister, but exuded gentle understanding. The type to wait for information being volunteered rather than asking lots of questions. At this present moment, the perfect companion.

With quiet, calm efficiency she steered Lisa out to the car park and into the car.

'Don't worry if you want to sleep. It'll take us about an hour to get home. I bet you're shattered. I always find travelling takes it out of you, even if you're just sitting on a plane.'

Lisa loved her for not saying the obvious: when you're travelling and having an emotional meltdown.

Being in the car in the dark was rather like being a cocoon, easier to switch off and step back from reality. It had been good of Laurie to come all this way. An hour here and another back, for someone she didn't know. Lisa knew she ought to make the effort to appear normal.

'Siena says you're getting married.'

Laurie nodded vigorously. 'Yes and even though it's a small wedding, there seems a lot to do.' She gave a quick laugh. 'I don't know why I thought the end of the summer would be a good idea. Cam didn't want to wait.' The latter was stated with happy pride. 'Which would have been fine but we never expected to have quite this many guests in our first season. And I'm studying for a qualification in wine. It's manic. Not that I'm complaining.'

'Siena told me you'd opened a boutique hotel. It's going well, then?'

'Yes. It was a big gamble, as neither of us have ever done anything like it before. Bit of a steep learning curve. I inherited the house from my uncle and it's way too big for me and Cam to rattle around in. It also came with a fabulous wine cellar and Uncle Miles's collection of vintage cars. The idea is to offer leisure breaks – that's the official terminology, apparently, to people who are interested in one or the other, or both. Our plan originally was to find a way of sharing the house and the cars, but it's kind of taken over. I run wine-tastings and Cam takes people out in the cars. We had no idea that it would take off the way it has. Word of mouth, mainly.'

'Hard work,' said Lisa, thinking of the pub, which had thrived thanks as much to word of mouth as Will's long hours and dedication.

'Yes. But I'm enjoying it.' Laurie shook her head. 'I used to work in a library, so it's quite different.'

'Noisier, I would image.'

Laurie laughed. 'You're not kidding, although I miss some of the regulars. What do you do?'

'I work in a school, although I also do quite a bit of waitressing in the holidays at the pub where Siena works. I still have three weeks left before school starts again.'

'Is it hard looking after a lot of children?' The question had a wistful note to it. 'I'm not sure I could look after one. I'd be worried I'd get it wrong.'

Lisa shot her a sidelong glance, in time to see Laurie's hand slide over her stomach.

'There is no wrong and right,' she reassured her. 'Children need to feel loved, secure and safe. Do that and you're doing a good job. Follow your instincts. It's not called maternal instinct for nothing. Not that I would know.'

'Hmm,' mused Laurie.

'Ah,' said Lisa, suddenly remembering a conversation with Siena. 'I grew up with my nan and I barely remember my mother.'

'You've heard about Celeste, then,' said Laurie dryly.

'A little,' said Lisa warily. While she thought, from what she'd heard, that Siena and Laurie's mother sounded a rather cold fish, she was still their mother. It did sound callous, though, leaving Laurie's father and taking one of her daughters with her to live in France. The two sisters hadn't met until they were in their twenties.

'I'm dithering about whether I should invite her to the wedding or not.'

Lisa wasn't sure what to say to that. If she were getting married, would she invite Vittorio?

'Cam's no use at all. No, that's not true. He's totally

supportive. He says I should do what I want and not worry about anyone else's feelings, but I'm not sure.' Laurie sighed. 'Sorry, I don't know why I'm bothering you with this.'

'Sometimes it's easier to talk to a stranger,' said Lisa, sitting up straighter, realising she'd slid right down in her seat. 'They can offer a different perspective.'

She twisted her hands in her lap before finally saying, 'Did Siena say anything?' She hated feeling this pathetic, but this helpless, bereft sensation had knocked her off-balance. Even when she and Will had had their near-miss, she hadn't gone into a decline. Sometimes you had to get on with things. This time, it wasn't so easy.

There was a measured pause before Laurie spoke, as if feeling her way diplomatically. 'Not much. She said you were coming home early and something was wrong. She thought Will might have broken your heart. I don't know him that well, although Cam and Jason both think highly of him.'

'So do I,' said Lisa in a small voice, feeling her chest tighten. There was something about Laurie's calm common sense that she could trust. Heart-broken summed it up well, but it would be wrong to blame Will for that or let Laurie think ill of him. He didn't deserve it, especially when he'd been nothing but lovely the whole time they'd been in Rome. 'It's not Will's fault. He hasn't done anything wrong. Neither of us have. The worst thing is, we were good together. Really,' the lump in her throat made it hard to speak, 'really good. I went to Rome to f-find my f-father and I-I…' she tried hard to hold back the sob, 'it's such a m-mess. I don't even know how I'm going to go home after this.'

Like wanting to lance a boil full of poison, she had to get the words out. Far easier to confide in Laurie than Siena.

'Will and me... we h-have the same father.'

Laurie's heartfelt and nonplussed, 'Oh,' summed up the hopelessness of the situation rather well.

Chapter 29

Tiredness her constant companion for the last twelve hours, now upped and sodding well left. No sooner had Laurie left her, after showing her into a pretty single room, she'd stripped and left her clothes where they were. She lay under the comforting weight of duck down, and even though her eyes felt they'd been removed, rolled in sawdust and stuffed back in, she was wide awake, thoughts spinning like a dozen plates. She tried to empty her mind, but like a roller-coaster, every now and then it would regain momentum, a new upsetting thought rushing in and then receding as she forced it away.

Nan. Will. Siena. Vittorio. So many conversations that needed to be had. Her heart hitched with regret at her cowardice. Letting Will down like that.

Poor Will. He didn't know. What must he be thinking? He said he loved her. She prayed for a moment that he hadn't meant it. That he wasn't serious. And that hurt too, because she knew, with sudden certainty that he did. She closed her scratchy eyes and pictured him sitting at the table alone in the Rome apartment. It was probably best that he thought she'd just upped and left. Better for him to hate her. Better than this awful guilt-filled nausea, when she thought of how much she loved him and how wrong, wrong, wrong it was.

She wrapped her arms around her body, as if they might offer some kind of protection and ward off the sense of dislocation, and let the tears have their way, streaming down her face, her body shaking with silent sobs.

Chapter 30

'Morning. I brought you a cup of tea.' Laurie held a tray and then added with a mischievous smile, reminding Lisa of Siena, 'And a coffee, because I didn't know which you'd prefer.'

Lisa scrambled up to sitting position. 'You didn't need to do that. What time is it? Sorry, is it terribly late?'

Laurie put down the tray beside the bed and held up a hand in a halt sign. 'Don't worry. You're fine.'

'Sorry, but you've already been incredibly kind.' It felt like she was in a hotel, which she guessed it was, except she wasn't a paying guest and shouldn't be treated as such. 'I mean... this is one of your rooms.'

'And it was empty. It's not a problem. We didn't have any guests last night.' Laurie's shoulders drooped briefly. 'The new lot arrive today.'

In the morning light, Lisa saw the dark shadows under her eyes.

'It was also easier to bring it to you as you don't know where you are. It's quite rambling downstairs. When we have people here, Cam and I have a private sitting room, where we eat. But as we have no one here today, we'll have breakfast in the dining room. If you feel up to it, it'll be ready in about half an hour. But don't feel you have to or that I'm kicking you out.'

Her face softened. 'How are you feeling?'

'Confused. Sad. Guilty.'

'Guilty? Why? It's hardly your fault.'

'I keep thinking about Will. He doesn't know. He must be wondering why I disappeared. But I can't bear to…' There was a physical ache in her chest, like some huge stone had been lodged firmly behind her breastbone.

'Do you want me to get Siena to contact him?'

Lisa shook her head. 'I don't want anyone else to know. I feel… soiled. It's a horrible feeling. And what will people think? I can't bear the thought of anyone,' she looked at Laurie, 'else, knowing.'

'Don't worry. I haven't told Cam. And I won't tell Siena. That's entirely up to you.'

'I'm so confused. I don't know what I want.'

'Well, have a drink. Are you hungry?'

'Starving.' She gave Laurie a limp smile. 'I'm never going to be one of those lovelorn types who can't eat a thing.' Moping wasn't going to help. She had to get on with it.

'Glad to hear it. See you in a bit.'

Amazing what a shower and the prospect of food could do. There wasn't exactly a spring in her step as she came down the rather amazing wooden staircase, which last night she'd failed to appreciate, but she'd girded her loins and given herself a talking-to. The situation wasn't going to change. It was going to be hard at first, but it would get better. One day, hard as it was to imagine, she and Will would be... no, she couldn't even begin to envision seeing him again. Park that thought for the time being. But in the short term, life went on. She had her job. Friends. Nan. That was as far as she could think now. Like putting books back on the shelf, she mentally tucked Will and Vittorio at the far end of the bookcase and deliberately focused on her surroundings.

Her fingers trailed along the William Morris wallpaper, recognising the famous strawberry thief pattern thanks to an art topic they'd done at school last year. It suited the grand entrance hall, which was probably bigger than the entire square footage of the ground floor of her house. At the bottom, she stopped, her hand resting on the dark, elaborately carved, newel post. The house reminded her of the Cluedo mansion. A long, narrow corridor with stone flags led away and to the right, a heavy wooden door ajar, enough for her to see a bright, light-filled dining room. Confident that she was in the right place, Lisa pushed open the door. Her eyes were immediately drawn to the bay window with its table, laid with breakfast things and the couple silhouetted in the sunshine. Laurie was looking up into the laughing eyes of a tall man, while his hand smoothed down her back as if comforting her. She had an anxious frown on her face and Cam, who else could it be, was talking in a soothing voice.

Lisa could almost feel the connection between the two of them. Worried she was interrupting, she stopped, wondering if she could diplomatically withdraw, but it was too late, Cam looked over.

'Hi. Lisa?'

'Yes,' she said a touch shyly. With green eyes and despite the slightly shaggy, curly hair, he looked like a male model. When his face creased into a quick, ready smile, it packed quite a punch, but there was no doubt, from the way he tucked Laurie into his side, that there was only one woman for him.

'Nice to meet you. Please say you want some breakfast. Laurie's been making me be polite and wait.'

Laurie dug her elbow in his ribs. 'Excuse him, he has no manners.'

He grinned cheerfully and pulled a chair out for Laurie and then a second one for Lisa.

'Gets by on a bucket load of charm,' said Laurie, sinking into her seat, shaking her head, a warm smile belying her words.

Cam dropped a quick kiss on her lips. 'And why not?' He winked at Lisa.

Sitting with the two of them, both of whom were clearly besotted with each other, could have made her envious and long for Will, but instead being in the warmth of their happiness was surprisingly comforting.

'Toast? Croissant? Muffins?' Laurie offered her a plate and Lisa helped herself to a croissant.

'Home-made. Strawberry,' said Cam, pushing across a pretty glass dish of bright-red jam with a silver spoon tucked in.

'This is all lovely,' said Lisa, admiring the white china pattered with delicate sprigs of flowers as she shook out the heavy damask napkin.

'My uncle had great taste and lots of money. There's stacks of stuff. Honestly, we've got jam spoons, honey twizzlers, tortoiseshell mustard spoons, cruets, gravy boats, sugar tongs...'

'You name it, we've got it,' Cam chimed in.

'And it seemed a shame not to use everything,' finished Laurie.

'I bet the guests love it. My room is gorgeous. If they're all like that, no wonder it's been so popular.'

Laurie cleared her throat. A look was exchanged between her and Cam, and then he gave a brief nod of his head.

'We are and it can be hard work. There's no point beating about the bush. We wondered if you might like to stay on for a couple of weeks and work here. You said last night you had three weeks before you go back to school. And that you didn't want to go home. We'd pay you.'

'But...' Lisa was conscious her mouth was open. 'I mean... that would be,' absolutely brilliant, 'wonderful.' She frowned. 'Are you sure?'

'Laurie's pregnant.' Cam said the words with quiet pride. 'It would be great to have another pair of hands, while she's... tired.'

Laurie tried and failed to hide a wry smile. 'What he means is, she's a bit over-emotional just now and can't be trusted not to cry on the guests or run out on them mid-conversation rather than throw up in front of them.'

Now Lisa understood that happy undercurrent she'd sensed between them.

'Congratulations. You must be very excited.'

'Early days at the moment. We're not telling anyone else. But I'm tired all the time. No pressure, but I could really do with some help. Cam was threatening to advertise for someone but we thought it was worth asking you first. I mean you're used to working in the pub. You know how to handle customers. We've got nine bedrooms here for guests.'

'And if you can carry more than two plates at once, you're hired.' Cam grinned at her.

'Obviously, we've sprung it on you,' said Laurie. 'But if you want to stay a couple of days and try it out, that would be fine.'

'Oh God,' Lisa wiped her eyes. 'You've set me off again. That would be... well it would... yes. Yes, please. I'd like that.'

'Excellent,' said Cam. 'And a weight off my mind. Now do you need anything? I,' he shot a firm look at Laurie, 'have to go shopping.'

'I can—'

'No, you're staying here and resting. I can shop.'

Laurie screwed up her face with a comical combination of frustration and crossness that had Cam patting her hand in a patronising, teasing gesture.

'I can do food shopping. Lisa can help if I get stuck.'

Despite her recent education at the hands of Will she wasn't sure she'd be an awful lot of help but decided it probably wouldn't help to volunteer that information. Instead, she nodded and added, 'Course, plus I need to sort out getting another phone. That suits me perfectly.'

Cam drove her in the poshest car she'd even been in in her life, a dark-blue, long and low Aston Martin, with cream-leather seats that seemed to hug her frame in all the right places as he steered with competent dash around the country lanes.

They went into a big Tesco in York, where she picked up a new phone and got it set up and sorted before joining Cam at the checkout, where he was running through Laurie's list, making sure he'd followed it to the letter.

'Green beans, with the bits on either end. Don't bother with the pre-trimmed ones,' he muttered. 'Eggs, free range, large. Not organic. Tonic water, not slim-line. Fever-tree not own brand.'

'Who does the cooking?' asked Lisa. She hadn't thought to ask before.

'Norah, our housekeeper. Literally. She came with the house; we have to keep her. But she wasn't well earlier in the year. We don't want her doing too much, either. Which is why it's great that you've agreed to stay for a couple of weeks.'

'You might not think that if you were expecting me to do any cooking.'

'You're safe on that score.'

'What the...!' Cam squinted at his list. 'Lychees?'

'Tinned fruit aisle, love,' advised the checkout girl.

'Do you want me to go and get them?' asked Lisa, amused by his horrified expression.

'Please. Pregnancy cravings.' He shook his head.

The checkout girl shot a startled look at his stomach.

Without so much as a blink, Cam patted his middle. 'Dreadful they are.'

Lisa fled, a smile on her face for the first time in two days.

She hadn't expected Cam to say anything to her, but when he cleared his throat and looked in the rear-view mirror before they pulled out of the car park, she could almost feel him gathering his courage.

'Laurie told me what happened. I'm sorry.'

'That's okay. Nothing you can do. Nothing anyone can do.' She shrugged and kept her gaze on the white lines running down the middle of the road. It felt as if a large stone had taken up residence in the pit of her stomach.

'You haven't spoken to Will, then?'

'Not much point, really. He's probably relieved. He's not renowned for his staying power with women,' she said bitterly.

'You don't think he might be as upset as you are?' Cam's calm defence of Will made her turn and look at him. Although he kept his eyes on the road, his face was stern.

'I forgot he was a friend of yours.' She swallowed, a fierce blush heating her cheeks, as she waited for him to follow up with a further comment but he kept his counsel. Her stomach contracted, sending pain radiating through her, compounded by a horrible sense of shame. Will deserved better than this.

He hadn't let her down. The situation was beyond their control. But she'd let him down. She'd run away this time. Worse still, she hadn't even had the decency to contact him and let him know the truth about his real father, even after he'd shared his sense of failure about his relationship with the man he thought was his father.

Straightening in her seat, she sneaked another look at Cam and he turned his head and gave her a sad, sympathetic smile.

'I feel sorry for Will too. It's an impossible situation for both of you.'

Tears blurred her vision. She'd never felt quite so devoid of hope as she whispered, 'I know.'

Chapter 31

Lisa collapsed into the sofa, gratefully taking the mug of tea from Laurie. She hadn't stopped all day, from making up twelve beds, collecting up dirty towels, serving welcome tea and cake and clearing up the dining room afterwards. It had been all go, but still not enough to dispel the bleakness that permeated every part of her.

'You will say if we're working you too hard,' said Laurie, sipping delicately at her tea. She looked a little wan and Lisa had had to chase her away when she insisted on helping put the pillowcases on some of the beds. 'You should take breaks. I ought to look up the employment rules and regulations. I'm sure you're supposed to have a proper lunch and coffee breaks. Norah said you haven't eaten anything today.'

Norah reminded her a little of Nan: all bark, a little bite and a touch of grudging kindness lurking somewhere. She doted on Laurie, so Lisa was already quids-in there because she was helping to alleviate Laurie's load.

'I'm fine. Don't forget, I'm used to working in a pub. On a Saturday night, I can tell you there's no time for a break.'

'Well, why don't you take a break now? We serve dinner to the guests tonight at 7.30. Will that be alright?'

'Are you sure? Is there anything else I can do?'

'Eat?'

Lisa sighed. 'I'll try, but it's... Do you want me to clean those windows?' She pointed to the French doors, where a few fingerprints dotted the glass around the handles.

'No! Go phone Siena,' Laurie gave her a candid look, clearly seeing through her delaying tactics. 'She's dying of curiosity, and if she sends me one more text asking about you, I'll accidentally drop my phone down the loo. That girl does not know the meaning of patience.'

'Bless her. I owe her big time.' Lisa hauled herself to her feet. Laurie had already handed Siena's number over on a yellow sticky note, which had been in her back pocket all day.

'You don't have to tell her anything you don't want to. Oh, and I'd be grateful if you didn't mention the bean,' Laurie pointed downwards to her still-flat stomach. 'It's early days and things could go wrong.' She smiled, the dreamy expression lighting up her normally sensible face. 'Cam's taken to calling it the unbaked bean.'

'We could do a deal.'

Laurie raised an eyebrow in question.

Lisa had never played hardball in her life before, but she said firmly, 'I won't tell Siena anything, but I'd rather not let on I'm staying here with you.'

Laurie didn't look happy about it, but she nodded in agreement. 'Okay.'

'Do I need to beat Will up?'

Lisa sat down on the single bed, propped against the

pillows, and looked out of the window, imagining dainty Siena in pugilistic stance, ready to go into battle on her behalf. She owed Siena big time, which was the reason she'd called and now she wished she hadn't. How had she forgotten that Siena could be like a dog with a bone? She wanted everyone to be happy like her.

'No!' She swapped her new mobile phone to the other ear and made herself comfortable. The view out over fields and the wide flat vale of York was rather different to the ones she'd been used to in the last few days, the patchwork of browns and greens a far cry from the terracotta hues of Rome.

'Cut his bits off?'

'Still no!'

'I've been thinking. Why did you come back early? If Giovanni left Rome to visit his family and you were there with Will, he must have done something to upset you.'

Detective Browne-Martin on the case. Typical Siena wanting to solve everyone else's problems.

'Siena, seriously. He hasn't done anything wrong.' If only it were that simple. She clenched the phone hard, praying he didn't feel the way she did. Sick. Bereft. Miserable.

Even though it hurt, she couldn't help picturing his face when he'd kissed her goodbye in the square at St Paul's. Their very last kiss. And neither of them had known.

'Ah! Was it your dad? Did you find him?'

'Yes, I did find him.'

'And?'

'He was away on business. I didn't get to meet him in the end, but we exchanged a few texts and...'

'That's brilliant. When are you going to meet up with him? Are you going to go back to Rome? Is he going to come and visit you?'

Lisa stared out of the window, feeling stiff and awkward, her breath caught in her throat.

'W-we're... in touch.'

'In touch? Aw Lisa. Are you okay?'

Lisa knew she thought the worst, that her father had rejected her.

'I'm fine. It's just, well, all a bit, overwhelming.'

'I know how you feel. It was weird when I first met Laurie. It does get easier.'

'She's lovely. Thanks for getting her to pick me up. I'm grateful you called her.' Lisa seized on the change of tack, glad that Siena had been easily diverted.

'No probs. I'm glad you've met her. She's cool, isn't she? I can't wait for the wedding.'

Lisa smiled to herself, hoping that Laurie's morning sickness improved by then, otherwise she'd have a hard time hiding her pregnancy from anyone.

'So, when are you coming home?'

'Er... I'm going to stay with some friends. Take a few weeks before I go back to work in September.'

'Where? Will you be okay?' Siena's concern echoed in her words.

'I'm fine. Really. I need some time, but please, it isn't Will's fault. I can't tell you why, but he hasn't done anything wrong.'

'Oh, so it is something to do with Will.'

Damn, how had she let that slip?

'No, I just have a lot to think about.'

'Sure?'

'One hundred per cent positive.' Lisa tensed as the familiar ache pulsed in her chest. It hadn't lessened at all. Was it always going to feel this bad?

'You aren't going to tell me anything, are you?'

'No.'

With a heavy sigh, Siena said, 'Okay, I won't ask any more questions, but promise me that if you need me, you'll call.'

'I promise.'

'What do I say to Will when I see him? Won't he ask where you are?'

'Nothing,' Lisa was glad she sounded more resolute than she felt. She kept imagining him coming back to the empty flat, finding her gone. The ring on the table. But she hadn't known what else to do. She winced. She'd been a coward. 'He won't ask.'

'Okay.' Siena's doubt rang across the air waves.

'If he asks, which I highly doubt, you can tell him I've gone away for a few weeks.' Did he feel as bad as she did? She couldn't imagine he'd want to see her after she'd run out on him, however she added as a precaution, 'I'll be in touch soon. But don't give him this number.'

'Okay. I'm going to save it as MI5, then even if he gets hold of my phone he won't know.'

Begrudgingly, Lisa laughed at that. 'One last thing, can you do me a massive favour? Can you pop in and see Nan and explain I've lost my phone, let her know I'm okay and text me her mobile number?'

'Sure. Anything else?'

'I could ask you to check she's taking her medication, but that would be unfair. At the moment she quite likes you. Let's leave it at that.'

Over the next few days, Lisa was kept very busy as several large parties came and went. In her role as chambermaid-come-waitress, she hadn't quite realised how much there was to do. How on earth had Laurie managed on her own over the summer?

'For goodness sake, woman, sit down for a while,' said Cam, pushing her firmly into one of the kitchen chairs on her third day at Merryview, when he caught her carrying an armload of bedsheets after he'd told her they could wait until tomorrow. She'd stripped five double beds and eight twin beds after they'd had a complete change-over, with all eighteen guests checking out on the same day and a further twelve expected that afternoon.

'Yes, lass. Have a cup of tea,' added Norah. 'Honestly, you're making me feel exhaustipated.'

'It's fine,' said Lisa. 'I love it here.' Exhaustion was good. Keeping busy was all that helped her sleep at night.

Cam glowered at her. 'Laurie will worry if you keep up this pace. And I don't want her worried.'

Lisa laughed and held up her hands. 'That's a bit sneaky, playing the Laurie card.'

He shrugged with a deliberate like-I-care lift of his shoulders and a challenging grin.

'Okay. Okay. I'll stop and have a cup of tea.'

But she had every intention of going back and making up

all the beds today, even though some of the rooms wouldn't be occupied for several days.

'You'll burn yourself out,' said Cam, giving her a sharp-eyed once-over, as if reading her mind.

'I would tell you if I wasn't okay.'

'Hmm,' said Cam, disbelieving. Tell you what, why don't you come out with Laurie and me and see the cars? Then you have to take a proper break. Boss's orders.'

'Okay.' She knew nothing about cars but had heard all about them over the last couple of days and had to admit to being quite intrigued. Besides, if Cam was determined she should take a break, she'd rather have something to occupy her.

It was impossible to stop thinking about Will. She'd be stripping a bed and she'd remember him tossing her on the bed at Dorothea's house, or making up the king-size bed in the peacock room and an image of him feeding her would pop into her head. Those few brief days in Rome, it seemed, were indelibly burnt into her brain, never to be eclipsed. No matter how hard she tried shake loose the memories, they clung on like limpets with benign intent.

Chapter 32

Will slammed the door.

'Oh Lord, take cover. His royal pissed-offness is back.' Marcus's not-so *sotte voce* comment made him flex his hand. There were rules about not punching employees. Sadly. Good job Marcus was such an excellent barman and head-waiter. Just now, they were his only redeeming features.

But it was no good. Rounding on Marcus standing behind the bar, he couldn't stop himself from growling, sheer fury burning like a flash down his spine, 'Got something to say, Marcus?' The tight words, hissed through clenched teeth, made the young barman flinch.

To his surprise, the other man threw down his tea towel on the bar and stepped forward, lifting his chin with a slight quiver. 'Do you know what? Yes, I have.'

'Go on,' Will clenched his jaw, his muscles tensing as he bounced on the balls of his feet, reluctantly admiring Marcus's bravery. He was a man who normally went out of his way to avoid confrontation.

'Stop taking it out on us. Whichever bird has got under your skin this time, let it go or go and apologise, but for Pete's sake sort yourself out. I'm sick of having my head bitten off. You might be the boss, but that doesn't mean we have to put up with this shit.'

Will stared at him. Marcus, despite his size, was the most mild-mannered of men.

Al, who was not in the least bit mild, sidled up to stand shoulder to shoulder with Marcus and then Siena slid in next to the two of them. A united front, all three of them looking at him with quiet, determined defiance, although Siena's expression held an undercurrent of sympathy and in the mirror behind the bar, he could see she'd crossed her fingers and Al and Marcus were holding hands.

They were a great team. And they didn't deserve this. Inside something cracked. He felt as if he'd lost his footing and was scrambling in loose scree to get a foothold in life again.

Damn it. Will glared at them.

'Sorry,' he muttered, ducked his head, not able to meet their eyes, and walked out of the pub.

Outside in the courtyard he sat down on one of the metal barrels, the lip digging into his backside, and dropped his head into his hands.

Since when had his life been so out of frigging control? Opening time in less than half an hour and he hadn't changed the barrels or put today's specials on the board. At this rate, there wouldn't be a pub to open. Yesterday, he'd let rip with a rant at a complaining customer and told her to get a life, which was now the first entry in the TripAdvisor review feed, where he'd been likened to Basil Fawlty. This morning he'd sent all the fish delivery back to the supplier because the delivery man had reversed the truck into his car and left an inch-long scratch on the wing. Things that normally he took in his stride on a daily basis, minor irritants, seemed insurmountable at the moment. He was surrounded by idiots.

'Will?'

He raised his head wearily. Siena stood in front of him, her hands twisting.

'Yeah?' he said, his tone distinctly unwelcoming. Nothing Siena could say or do was going to help. Lisa had done a runner and he was furious with her. She'd given up and bolted at the first sign of trouble. Admittedly it looked like insurmountable trouble to her, but if she'd stuck around, she would have realised soon enough that Vittorio wasn't her father. Instead, she'd gone. She hadn't even been prepared to hope or fight. Because Will wasn't worth it.

That was what pissed him off the most. She'd given up on him so damn quickly. Taken the first opportunity to run. Hadn't bothered to wait and check the facts. Hadn't bothered to speak to Vittorio. That hurt, but the fact that she was ignoring the texts he'd sent her had ratcheted up his pissed-offness to a whole new level. He'd bloody phoned, left messages, explained that Vittorio wasn't her father and she still hadn't bothered to respond.

She'd obviously decided that it was better to be on her own. Which said a lot. She hadn't cared about him that much. If you loved someone, surely you respected them enough or cared enough to speak to them face to face? Lisa had just ducked out on him.

Trying to cope with the fury that surged through him on

an hourly basis, along with the dumb, crushing heartache that was a constant in his life now, was just too frigging much. He didn't do that sort of crap.

'Are you okay?'

'What do you think?' Christ, he couldn't even speak without growling now.

'Stupid question.'

'Duh, yeah.' He sighed and looked up at the treeline on the top of the Chiltern Hills rising above the village. Lush and green, the fully leaved trees softened the horizon, a contrast to the earthy tones of Rome.

With a quick, confused frown, Siena spoke, 'She said you hadn't done anything wrong.'

'That was big of her,' said Will, unable to keep the bitterness out of his voice. 'Do you know where she is?' He'd asked several times, but she'd said she didn't.

Siena sighed. He could almost see her battling with her conscience. 'I know where she was, but she wouldn't tell me where she was going.'

'But you're doing that crossing-your-fingers thing again.'

Siena guiltily brought her hand in front of her. 'I truly don't where she is right now, but I do have her new mobile number.'

'New mobile number? What happened to her old one?'

'It was stolen.'

'Stolen? When?'

Siena stepped back, probably alarmed by the mad look in his eyes as he jumped to his feet.

'On her l-last day in Rome, I think.'

Sickness swirled in his stomach. He closed his eyes. All those texts he'd sent. Anxious phone messages. Surely not.

She didn't know. She didn't know. He almost hugged Siena.

'She doesn't know.' The tension that had gripped him for days lifted. 'She still doesn't bloody know.' That explained why she was still hiding from him.

'She doesn't know what?' asked Siena, looking at him with wariness in her eyes.

'It's complicated.'

Siena pouted. 'That's what she said.' She gave an exasperated sigh. 'The pair of you are doing my head in.'

'What's her new number?'

'She didn't want me to give it to you and I'm not going to break my promise.' There was a definite hesitation in her voice.

'But?'

'I think you should go see her nan. She might have Lisa's new number.' With that, Siena fled back into the pub.

'William Ryan. What brings you to my door?' Nan looked him up and down. 'You need a haircut.'

'So I've been told.'

'You'd better come in. I think you've got some explaining to do.'

'I've got some explaining to do?' Will narrowed his eyes at her.

With a sniff, she pulled her diminutive stature to full height. 'Come in.'

She led him through to the kitchen and pointed to an

ancient Formica table. The kitchen didn't look as if it had been touched since the fifties, although everything was spotless.

'Have a seat. I'll make a pot of tea.'

He sat down, for once doing as he was told. It brought back memories of being a child and having her in his family kitchen. She'd been one of the few constants in his life in those days. She might be an old harridan these days, but she was someone who knew right from wrong and, moreover, he trusted her. She'd only ever wanted the best for Lisa.

'Did you know Vittorio was my father?'

Her mouth concertinaed into a series of prune-liked wrinkles. 'I suspected he might be.'

She shook her head. 'You went to Italy with her, didn't you? Couldn't leave well alone. I tried to keep the two of you apart.'

Will shook his head. 'It would have been a lot easier if you'd just told me the truth.'

Nan rolled her eyes. 'Wasn't my place. Telling you things about your mother.'

Will nodded. 'I suppose. Although,' he paused, 'I guess you didn't know he wasn't Lisa's father.'

Nan put the kettle down with a bang, slopping hot water everywhere. She stepped back with a very un-geriatric expletive, shaking her burnt hand, as if that would help. Will jumped up and pulled her towards the cold tap, forcing her hand under it.

'Stop fussing, boy.'

'Basic first aid.' He held her hand under the water, realising, from her brief attempt at resistance, that she was actually quite frail. Her bones under his fingers were twig-thin, easy to snap without a second thought.

'So he wasn't Lisa's father. Well I never. My Hattie played her cards close to her chest with that one. Never said a word that he wasn't.'

'Vittorio said Hattie was already pregnant when they got married.'

'I never knew. Stupid boy. He was so besotted with her. I knew no good would come of it. No surprise when he buggered off. But I couldn't tell Lisa that her Da...Vittorio wasn't interested in her. All he ever thought about was Hattie.'

She paused and Will let her pull her hand out of the stream of cold water. 'Do you know who Lisa's father really is?' Her shrewd eyes fixed on his face.

'Vittorio told me it was Sir Robert.'

'Of course he is. Makes sense now. Wondered why he kept up with the Christmas hampers.' Nan kept nodding, as if all the pieces were falling into place one by one. 'And Lady Mary. She wouldn't have children up at the stables. Not Lisa, any road.'

Will wanted to shake her. Why hadn't she put the pieces together earlier?

'I met up with Vittorio in Rome. He told me that Sir Robert once asked his wife for a divorce. From what Vittorio said, it sounded as if he planned to leave Lady Mary for Hattie. But Lady Mary rode off and had her fall. And then he couldn't leave her, even when Hattie was pregnant with Lisa.'

'Idiots the lot of them. And your mother was no better. Well, all I can say is I'm relieved the two of you aren't brother and sister. I take it from the fact she's gone AWOL that Lisa still thinks otherwise.'

Will couldn't believe that Nan was this cool about the revelations. Although he had to admit that finding out the man he'd always thought of as his father hadn't come as much of a disappointment to him. It made him feel less of a failure, not measuring up to Richard's expectations.

'Do you know where she is?'

Nan looked mutinous for a moment. 'What are you planning?'

'What do you think? I need to speak to her urgently.'

'Don't you think it's best to leave well alone? Lisa's quite happy as she is. And you're not exactly Mr Faithful.'

'On what basis?' snarled Will.

'I watched your parents' shenanigans. And my Hattie's. And never a truer word's been spoken than whoever said, 'the apple doesn't fall far from the tree'. I was determined to keep Lisa away from all that. She deserves a lot better. Needs a bit of stability in her life.'

Will thought he might explode as his face reddened and the pressure in his head at his temples built and built.

'You know that she's terrified you're going to die and leave her alone. So much so she's never taken a chance on happiness herself.'

'Well, of course I'm going to die. Everyone does.' Nan sucked in her cheeks. 'That's daft. Besides, I'm not about to shuffle off any time soon. Fit as a fiddle, I am.'

'Really?' He put his hands on his hips, wanting to square up to her, and then realised it probably looked a bit odd, given she was a good foot smaller than him. He needn't have worried.

'Really, Will Ryan.' She prodded him the chest, which surely looked comical but felt anything but. 'Yes. Got all my marbles.'

'So why's Lisa so worried you might have a stroke at any moment? Why is she constantly worrying about you taking your tablets?'

'Them doctors. Don't know anything. Worryworts.'

'That's not what Lisa thinks. She carries an information leaflet about strokes around with her. She texts you every day to remind you take your pills, but you don't, do you?'

Nan shrugged. 'I forget.'

'Well, you shouldn't. Lisa remembers.'

Nan looked a tad shame-faced. 'She worries too much.'

'No, she doesn't. Lisa is one of the most laid-back, happy-go-lucky people I know. You're the person she worries about constantly.'

'Well, I can't help that, can I?' snapped Nan, turning away from him and starting to dry up the solitary cup and saucer on the draining board.

'Yes, you can.'

'Spare me.' She pitched onto her tiptoes to put the crockery away. 'You're not going to start lecturing me about fish and bloody chips again like Dr Gupta.'

Will leaned against the opposite kitchen bench in the tiny kitchen with his arms folded, pretending nonchalance.

'I couldn't care less what you eat, but I do care that Lisa worries about it. You should at least take the medication properly. Then Lisa could stop worrying as much as she does.'

'And that's all it's going to take.' Nan sniffed and turned her nose up.

'Lisa doesn't want to deprive you of your fish and chips; she wants you to live a full and happy life, but if you have a stroke, it might not be that full or that happy.'

Nan glared at him. 'You're as bad as she is.'

'Yeah, I give a shit. I care that Lisa is worried about you. I care that she's terrified she's going to lose her one remaining family member. I care that she doesn't think there'll be anyone there for her.'

Getting it all off his chest didn't give him an ounce of satisfaction when he saw her wizened frame deflate even further. Her mouth moved but no words came out.

He moved quickly to touch her on her arm, guiding her to one of the chairs in the adjoining dining area.

'I'm fine. Stop fussing,' she patted his hand away.

He did as he was told, but watched her carefully, reminded again how frail she was.

She sat down, holding onto the table, her mouth pinched and white. When her eyes closed for a minute, he reached out to touch her again.

'I'm alright,' she huffed. 'Didn't take my pesky pills this morning.'

She gave him a baleful glare. 'I don't like them. They make me feel funny. Horrible, dizzy. The woman at the newsagent thought I was drunk the last time I took them.'

'Have you told the doctor that? Sometimes they can change them, give you something else that suits you better.'

She huffed again. 'I don't like causing a fuss. There's nothing wrong with me but old age.'

'And high blood pressure, which the right medication can sort out.'

Suddenly she looked old and defeated. 'I don't like going to the doctors. They treat me like I'm an old lady. Bloody hate it, I do. I might be old but I'm not stupid. I was up to no good before they were even born. All the same. Patronising, posh, clever blokes who haven't got the first clue about life.'

He smiled at that, but then she suddenly added, 'I wish Lisa were here.' Her out-of-character tremulous words almost floored him. Sitting in a chair nearly as big as she was, like a child sitting on a throne, she looked rather defenceless and lost.

For someone who'd spent almost his entire life keeping a surreptitious eye out for his wayward parents and younger sister, and swore he'd avoid being responsible for other people in the future, he realised it had become an intrinsic part of his make-up. Family was family. People who needed looking after, needed looking after and it seemed he was pre-disposed to help where he could.

'Come on, get your coat.'

Nan looked at him suspiciously. 'What, have I pulled?'

He saw a little of the old fire spark back up again.

'Don't tell me, you're taking me to the bingo.'

Will laughed, relieved that her fighting spirit had only been taking a brief rest. 'No, but I'm going to take you to the doctors now. Let's get your tablets sorted.'

Nan rolled her eyes, but there was a distinct brightness to

them. 'Alright, but you have to take me to Morrisons afterwards. Lisa always takes me on a Thursday.'

'It's Tuesday.'

'So? You can take me Tuesdays. She can take me Thursdays.'

She pulled on an ancient hairy coat, brushing it down, releasing puffs of dust, or possibly small termites, and grabbed a crocodile handbag.

'Don't think this puts you in my good books, though, young man.'

'I wouldn't dream of it.'

Will opened the front door with a bow and followed her out into the street.

'Good, because if you think I'm telling you that Lisa is staying with that sister of Siena's up in York, you've got another think coming. Now are we going or not?'

Chapter 33

Lisa stifled a yawn, it had been a very long day but she didn't want to appear rude. They were in Cam and Laurie's sitting room, and she was doing her best to fight against the plush worn velvet sofa, which seemed to have designs on eating her up. Her weary body welcomed the soft feather-filled, accommodating cushions, prompting a protest that it had been up since seven helping Norah to serve breakfast to the party who'd arrived to celebrate a sixtieth birthday. Poor Laurie couldn't cope with the smell of bacon at that time of day. In fact, it didn't seem to matter what time of day it was.

Who knew that Cam would be this keen on Scrabble? She gave in to an enormous yawn and shifted slightly from her curled-up position wondering if she might tell him she had to go to bed, but Cam rather studiously ignored her as he looked at his watch.

'Another game?'

He was having a laugh, wasn't he?

Laurie was half asleep leaning against him.

'No, I need to go to bed,' replied Lisa, uncurling and rubbing her tingling left foot, which was about to go numb. Tiredness had finally won over being polite.

'What about a hot chocolate and a nightcap?' Cam bounced to his feet, as if this was the best and most original idea on the planet.

Laurie stirred sleepily. 'That sounds like an excellent...' she slurred her words.

The two of them were mad. It was after eleven. Laurie normally admitted defeat at ten, at which point Cam usually escorted her up for the night.

This evening they were rather like a pair of cats about to have kittens, circling round and round as if trying to find the right spot. And Cam, who normally derided mobile phones, kept checking his. Apparently, there was some auction of a car he was interested in. It had been Cam who had suggested a game of Scrabble, which Laurie had welcomed, but after one game it was clear that Cam didn't have the patience or the interest, although Laurie had enjoyed it before her head started drooping over her collection of letter tiles.

'No brandy in my hot chocolate,' reminded Laurie, 'but I would like some squirty cream and some of those mini marshmallows.'

'Didn't you eat all the mini marshmallows yesterday?' asked Cam.

'Norah bought some more.'

Shaking his head, Cam stalked off to the back of the house to the kitchen, where Norah was still pottering and, no doubt, she would be the one who served up the hot chocolate.

'I love having these cravings,' whispered Laurie. 'It's like a get-out-of-jail-free card all the time.'

By the time Cam brought the mugs back, piled high with cream and sprinkled with pink and white mini marshmallows, Laurie had slid down the sofa and fallen fast asleep.

Cam stood for a minute, a tender smile on his face as he looked down at her. He perched on the edge of the sofa and stroked her face gently. 'Come on you. Bedtime.'

'Sorry,' Laurie's voice slurred and her eyes blinked owlishly. 'Did my best.'

Cam tucked his arms under her and lifted her. 'My hero.' Laurie looped her arms around him and nestled her head into his neck, her eyes fluttering closed.

'I think I'll go up too,' said Lisa.

Cam's resigned expression made her wonder why he'd been so eager for them all to stay up, but she was bushed.

Cam and Laurie's about-to-have-kittens' routine had unsettled her – God knows what they'd be like when Laurie's baby was due. She fell into bed, grateful for Laurie's excellent taste in pure-cotton sheets and blissfully comforting duck-down duvet, but she couldn't sleep and she needed to.

She set her alarm, wishing Cam hadn't been as flipping insistent on playing Scrabble, especially when it clearly wasn't his game. With a sigh, she plumped up the pillows and switched out the light. Her brain sprang into action, like it did every night. What was Will doing at this moment? Rounding up empties in the bar? Locking up the front door after the last regular had been coaxed from their seat at the polished wooden bar. Laughing with Marcus, Al and Siena as they bagged up the money from the till.

Her thoughts seemed to tune in to the same channel constantly. Even when she was stripping beds in the morning, she could picture him opening up for the day. In the kitchen with Marcus and Al, discussing the day's menu. Sorting through the deliveries.

She punched her pillow, which seemed to have developed lumps in the wrong places. Why couldn't they invent a remote to reset your brain and change the channel? Deliberately she focused on tomorrow, knowing that even if she did get to sleep, she'd wake again in time to see the first straggling rays of sunrise clutching at the clouds with pink-and-gold fingers.

The sixtieth-birthday crowd had already declared their intention to be up early and go into York to visit the Minster. They looked like hearty breakfast-eaters, who would want a full English. Like excitable boys, the men were all looking forward to their late-afternoon tour of the hi-tech garage housing the vintage cars and the promised trip to the track to drive some of the collection.

She tried to switch her mind off but it was up and running, thinking of all the things she needed to do tomorrow. She'd promised to help Laurie do some wedding stuff, which was hush, hush as she was keeping the finer detail a secret from Cam. He, in turn, had commandeered her to help with arrangements for the honeymoon, which was also a secret from Laurie. Hopefully she could keep her stories straight and not let anything slip to either one of them.

The arrival of a car crunching to a halt on the gravel outside made her stiffen. A late arrival? She couldn't remember Cam or Laurie mentioning expecting more guests. She listened hard and heard a car door close. Should she get up? Poor Laurie was bushed and if Cam got up he might disturb her. She waited for the jangling peal of the old-fashioned bell. Nothing. She strained to hear and could just make out some slight sounds of movement and low masculine voices. Sounded like Cam had it under control.

With a grateful sigh, she snuggled into the duvet.

The knock at the door had her groaning. Really? She'd finally got comfortable.

'Yes,' she called.

When there was no answer, she threw back the bed covers and padded to the door. Had Laurie forgotten some instruction for the morning? Sent Cam to deliver a message?

The soft knock came again.

Hiding her exasperation and framing a polite smile on her face she opened the door.

Her heart stopped. She stared. White noise rushed in her ears. When she opened her mouth nothing came out.

She registered crumpled clothes and shadowed eyes as he stood, almost swaying on the spot with exhaustion. Her nerve endings buzzed with awareness.

Longing swamped her, followed, like a door slammed, by fear and shame.

She flinched.

He took a step forward and she took a step back, scared that if she touched him, the grief would well up and drown her. Even though it was wrong, she drank in the sight of him. Her throat closed as she tried to speak and his name came out in a strangled croak, 'Will.'

'He's not your father.' Will's hoarse words hung in the air between them as they stared at each other.

She tried to assimilate them, her brain whirling and fuzzy, but her body tuned in immediately, a hot flush of adrenaline coursing through her, making her nerve endings jump and fireworks fizz through every vein.

'Vittorio, he's not your father.'

'But...' she frowned, trying to focus against the wealth of sensation taking her system by storm.

'He's my father, not yours.'

The urgent expression on his face made more impression than his words, but she couldn't manage to frame a single word. Her mouth moved, but everything she thought she might want to say stuck fast in her throat.

'Your mother was already pregnant when he married her. He loved her, even though she was pregnant with another man's baby.' The words came in a rush, like the sea overcoming her, washing in her ears as she tried to make sense of them, her heart lifting in hope and then fighting against the tide. Was it true? Or was it what she wanted to hear?

'He's not your father. We're not related.'

'B-but...'

Will took a step forward, clamping his hands on her arms, his eyes boring into hers. 'We're not... he's not...'

Like a balloon bursting, all the misery of the last few days exploded. Her legs, limp as noodles, barely held her up.

Then his arms slipped around her, pulling her to him so tightly she could barely breathe, but she didn't care. She clung to him, desperate and hopeful, as if she might be absorbed into him, her cheek against the soft, crumpled cotton of his shirt, so fine she could feel warm skin and heartbeats, his and then hers thundering like hooves on the gallops.

Standing in the circle of his solid embrace, feeling his steady breaths, with her head tucked under his chin, inhaling that indefinable Will smell of musky man, washing powder and woodsy soap, she felt as though she'd come home.

A harbour at last. Suddenly she realised in a rush that he'd been the reliable one. She'd run out on him when the odds looked insurmountable. The facts stacked against them. And here he was, holding her as if he'd never let her go again.

She looked up. He smiled, a sweet unWill-like smile edged with tenderness.

'I'm sorry.' With a very shaky hand she reached up and touched his face. 'I'm sorry. When I saw Vittorio, I ran. He looked so like you it completely threw me. But I should have stayed. Should have talked to you.'

He cupped her hand. 'I can understand why you ran. It must have been a hell of a shock. It was a shock when I saw him. Like looking in the mirror in twenty years' time.'

'I didn't know what else to do. I had to get away. When I thought you were my brother, I felt dirty, ashamed, sordid. I couldn't face you. But that's an excuse. I bailed because I was scared… of everything.' Just thinking about it again and remembering that terrible sinking in quicksand sensation, so helpless and out of control, made her suck in a desperate breath, a precursor to an almighty sob. She didn't want to spoil this by crying.

'Hey, it's okay.' He led her over to the bed, where they sat down side by side, thigh to thigh, shoulder to shoulder. He took her hand as she dropped her head on his shoulder.

They sat there for several minutes, peaceable in the shadowed light of the bedside lamp, content to be.

'Lisa.' His voice sounded uncertain.

'Yes.' Trepidation crept into her voice. She hadn't wanted to ask. 'Does he know who my real father is?'

Will turned her to face him and dropped a kiss on her forehead. 'Yes.'

Lisa gulped. 'And did he tell you?'

Will nodded.

'Do I know him?'

Will nodded. 'You do.'

'Oh God.' Lisa's palms turned clammy. 'Not your father. I mean your... other father?'

Will took her hand and squeezed. 'No, thankfully. That would be too weird. It's...' he paused, his eyes roving over her face, as if he were checking she was alright. 'It's... Sir Robert.'

She closed her eyes. Of course, it was. The Christmas hampers. His eagerness to chat in the pub whenever she saw him. The secrecy of her visits to the stables when she was a child. A memory of him weeping at her mother's funeral. He'd always been in the periphery of her life, but she'd never thought anything of it. He was her mother's boss.

'Why didn't I see it? It's so obvious now.'

'You had no reason to question that Vittorio was your

father.'

'True and I don't think Nan ever realised. She assumed Sir Robert was still taking an interest in us because Mum died while she was working for him.'

'No, she didn't. She was convinced Vittorio was your dad. I suspect Sir Robert has had to keep things well hidden because of Lady Mary. She could never have children. I hear she's in a hospice now.'

'Do you think he'll want to... know me?'

Will lifted her chin with his hand and stared into her eyes. 'Why wouldn't he?'

She shrugged uncertainly.

'Lisa, I'm pretty sure he would welcome it.' And then added fiercely. 'And if he doesn't it's his loss.'

Tears filled her eyes. 'I didn't think I wanted family or to need anyone. But I was wrong.'

'Whereas I seem to have got more than my fair share.'

Lisa's eyes widened. 'Oh God, Will I'm sorry. I hadn't even thought about that. Your dad, except he's not. How do you... what do you call him?'

Will's face closed down and he shifted slightly, as if wanting to put distance between them. 'All makes sense now. Why he was always so detached and so quick to disapprove of me. I went to see my mum.' He sighed, his face crumpled and his Adam's apple moved up and down, the tendons in his throat tense. As he turned his head away, suddenly stiff and distant, Lisa reached a hand up to quickly swipe away the lone tear, her heart aching for him. Avoiding her eyes, he kissed the inside of her wrist as he continued, 'She... she thought it was amusing. Laughed, when I asked if my dad knew he wasn't my dad.' He shook his head in silent disbelief. 'Do you know what she said? *"Well, darling, he's never asked for a paternity test, but I'm pretty sure he knows. I think Alice might be his, so that's alright."*'

Lisa gasped and put her arms around him.

He tried to shrug them away. 'I shouldn't have expected anything else.'

Shame washed over her. 'Yes, you should. You deserve better, Will Ryan. You deserve to be loved because you're a wonderful man.' She held his face between her hands and said fiercely because she meant it and it didn't matter if he didn't love her back, 'I love you and don't you ever forget it.'

She felt him go very still, his eyes searching her face as if he didn't dare to believe it.

'I love you, Will.'

To her surprise, a look of relief filled his eyes, which made her heart speed up. It was quickly followed by a more penetrating look of satisfaction and possession. When his mouth curved into a slow, serious smile, it did something strange to her insides, as if a thousand butterflies were beating their way out.

Without breaking their gaze, his lifted his hand and, with his thumb, stroked her cheekbone. 'Thank you.'

'You're welcome,' she smiled back.

'Of course,' his thumb stopped. 'I don't have to tell you because... you should bloody well know by now...' Warmth bloomed, racing through her veins at his oh-so-serious expression.

'I do...' She nodded and her eyes suddenly twinkled up at

him, 'but it would be quite nice to hear.'

With a sudden movement, he scooped her up onto his lap, pulling her close, his mouth touching her cheek, so that she could feel his lips as he punctuated each word with a gentle kiss. 'I. Love. You.'

Then his mouth slid along her cheek to her lips.

The first foray of his tongue touching hers sent a curl of excitement through her, along with a flush of heat. She kissed him back, letting the pent-up hunger take charge. At first they explored each other's mouths, testing and teasing in a slow, all-the-time-in-the-world leisurely dance, becoming accustomed to each other's rhythm. Gradually their steps became more intricate as they gained confidence, the gentle pace upping in tempo, their breathing more fractured.

Will's hand grazed her back, cupping her bottom and pulling her snugly to his body, where she could feel the hard length of him and couldn't resist pressing up against him with a half-swallowed moan.

As the kiss deepened, passion took over and they passed the point of no return, hands on bare skin, touching and stroking. Somehow Will had pushed the fabric of her t-shirt aside, while she'd pulled the shirt from his jeans to run her hands up his warm back. Her hips urged forward in sinuous motion, mirroring her desire. She gasped when his hand slid up one thigh.

'Not fair. You've got too many clothes on,' she whispered.

He grinned. 'Seems fine to me.' He bent and dropped a whisper of a kiss above her breast, before sliding his mouth down, inexorably towards her nipple, which had already puckered in readiness, yelling yes yes here.

'Mm,' she moaned, squirming at the dart of pleasure, as much heaven as torment. His hand at the top of her thigh halted, a calloused thumb circling with hypnotic arousal, which had her shamelessly opening her legs. 'Will,' she pleaded as his hot, wet mouth did delightfully delicious things to her nipple, tugging and teasing, sending shafts of hot white heat southwards.

All of her burned with eager restlessness. With an impatient groan, she rubbed her hand over his jeans, looping her finger around the button and dragging the zip down, touching him through the jersey boxers.

In response, his breathing quickened and his mouth descended again. It enveloped her nipple, his hot tongue and the fierce pulling sensation making her whimper. It was too much; she was on fire. She arched upwards, blindly fumbling for the fastenings of his jeans, desperate to feel his skin on hers.

He lifted his head and stared down at her. 'Need a hand?' he asked, a knowing, smouldering look in his eye that made her shudder.

'Oh God, yes,' she said with heartfelt enthusiasm.

Together they wrestled off his jeans and as he worked his jersey boxers off, she finished unbuttoning his shirt, her hands straying to slide across his toned stomach, skirting the line of dark blonde hair.

Sensation exploded when he touched her, the idling hand that had been caressing her thigh moved back into place, lulling her into a false sense of security, and without warning, one delicious finger slid into that intimate spot, wet and slick in readiness. Hardly able to bear it as he teased the tender nerve endings, she let out a strangled cry, sucking in a harsh breath as he rubbed her hot flesh with slow, firm strokes, relentlessly driving her on, oblivious to her increasingly incoherent murmured moans that punctured the quiet air.

Her hips had a life of their own. Any moment now she was going to burst. She grasped his forearm, trying to slow him down.

He pulled back for a second, eyes glinting wickedly. 'Too much for you.'

Her chest heaved, but she was pleased to see that his was doing the same.

'Mmm.' Her voice came out in a breathy squeak. She shifted position and pushed him back, her hand roving over his body, taking control to give herself a chance to catch up with herself. 'The balance of power is all wrong.'

With a feline smile, she touched her lips to his throat and moved downwards, taking her time exploring his chest and flicking her tongue over his nipples, her insides tightening at his quick flinch and tiny involuntary sigh. Enjoying herself, she took a leisurely inventory, skimming down over the firm pecs and the dips of his abdomen, relishing the feel of his skin.

It was hard to keep her resolve and not throw herself on him and kiss him and beg him to slide into her, the idea of which every part of her body seemed to support, but she wanted him to be as hot, bothered and desperately squirmy and antsy as she was. Her hand worked downwards, teasing him as every now and then she'd take a side trip and glide her fingers over his hips as she took her own sweet time, exploring every dip and dent of his body, although she was getting as turned on hearing his tiny sighs and indrawn breaths.

He let out a throaty groan, calling her name when her hand finally dropped low enough to touch the hard length of him, which stood proud, straining for her touch. With the top of her finger she circled the tip, feeling herself dampen as he bit back a soft groan and she saw his hand fist into the sheet. She dragged one finger down the shaft, slowly, slowly. When she reached the base, where the coarse hair sprang up, she opened up her hand and circled him, pushing up with one smooth motion before sliding down the hard length in measured strokes.

Just as his breathing evened out and he was sighing with pleasure, she upped her pace, deliberately wanting to tease him and bring him to the same half-delirious, desperate state she was in.

'Jesus, Lisa, what...' His head fell back on the pillow, a faint sheen of sweat on his forehead. 'Stop! Ohhh... stop.' His panted pleas turned her inside out and when he grabbed her hand and pushed her onto her back, she opened her legs.

With one smooth, fluid move he slid home and she clenched around him.

The dancing around was over, she urged him on, not that he needed any second invitation. They were so in tune. She'd reached fever pitch and only fast and furious would do.

Chapter 34

'Wow.' It was the third time Will had said the word and he seemed lost for any other vocabulary.

Their feet squeaked on the pristine, shiny floor of the hi-tech garage.

'Which one would you have if you could choose any?' asked Lisa, her hand tucked in his.

'The E-type jag.' Will stopped in front of the racing-green car.

Cam laughed. 'That's Laurie's favourite. I'll take you for a spin later, if you'd like, and you can try her out on the track.'

Will's face brightened with boyish anticipation. 'That would be great.'

'That will keep you quiet while I spend some time with Laurie.' She went up onto tiptoe and whispered in his ear. 'Hush-hush wedding secrets.'

'I heard that,' said Cam. 'I'm starting to get nervous. Don't suppose there's any chance you could be bribed to let me in on what she's planning?'

Lisa's eyes danced. 'Well, I could,' she paused, 'but then she's dying to know what you're planning... and I'm helping you too. It's probably both in your best interests if I don't spill the beans to either of you.'

Cam shook his head in mock disgust. 'Honestly, we've bred a monster. Which reminds me, I've got a couple of calls to make while Laurie's out. Don't worry about locking up, Eddie is around getting everything ready for this afternoon.'

As soon as Cam had gone, Will's arm snaked around her and he pulled her in for a long, hot, scorching kiss, which left her slightly breathless.

'What was that for?'

'Because I haven't kissed you properly for,' he looked at the sturdy watch on his wrist, 'at least one hour and fifteen minutes.'

'You mean improperly,' said Lisa, fanning herself and grinning up at him.

'Not complaining, are you?' asked Will, his mouth crinkling in that familiar crooked smile. 'No,' said Lisa, wary now as he put both hands on her shoulders and drew her slowly towards him before diving straight in and giving in her another thorough kiss, which had her knees almost giving way.

When he lifted his head, he looked a touch dazed too, but managed to ask, 'Improper enough?'

She nodded, her mouth tingling so much she couldn't speak.

They walked towards the door of the garage and out into the courtyard. Lisa couldn't believe she was so lucky, staying in such a lovely place, and now, with Will at her side.

They left the courtyard and rather than go back to the house, they walked out towards the paddock to the side of the house. Leaning on the wooden fence they looked out over the view, down across the flat vale of York, with its patchwork of pale-golden fields bounded by green broccoli floret-like hedges.

Will looked lost in thought as he stared out over the fields. Her eyes roved over his features, gratitude filling her heart. It was hard to believe yesterday that when she'd looked at this same view she'd been so bloody miserable.

'Stop looking at me like that, otherwise I'll drag you back to bed.' Will looked rather pleased with himself. 'Actually, that's probably not a bad idea.'

'I ought to go back soon to do some work. Cam and Laurie have been brilliant. So kind, and I don't want to let them down.' She linked her hand with his. 'You're going to have to wait, buster.'

'I suppose I do owe Cam.' He turned her to face him and moved in front of her, pinning her to the fence with his big, warm body.

'Whereas I have a bone to pick with him. All that Scrabble nonsense.'

Will laughed. 'I never thought it would take me that long to get here. Bloody sod's law there was a major hold-up on the M1. I'd phoned Cam to make sure you were here and told him I was on my way.'

'The sneaky so and so. I wondered what was up. He and Laurie spent hours desperately trying to prolong the evening.' Lisa smiled, leaning into him, laying her head against his shoulder. 'You owe him. He did sterling work. I suspect he hates Scrabble.'

'He said he'd try to make sure you stayed up, but I was

worried you might bolt again.'

'I suppose Siena told you where I was.'

'No,' Will's body shook as if in silent laughter. 'Your Nan did.'

'Nan,' Lisa's head shot up. 'But she hates… I mean she's not your biggest fan.'

'She might have changed her mind, although she did con me into taking her to bloody Morrisons. And then proceeded to ask me at full volume, from the next aisle, whether I'd ever suffered from constipation and what did I think of syrup of figs.'

'Sounds like Nan. Was she okay?'

'Cantankerous. Smart-mouthed. Snappy. I'd say beaming out on normal Nan-channel.'

Lisa shook her head. 'I know I worry about her, but maybe she will go on for ever.'

'I sorted out her medication for her.'

'You did what?' Lisa did a double-take.

When he explained that he'd taken her to the doctors, Lisa stared at him wide-eyed and exceedingly pissed off. 'There are times when I could strangle her. Why couldn't she have told me that her tablets made her feel worse?'

'I suspect it was her way of trying to protect you. Stop you worrying about her.'

'Grrr. Now you're best friends, are you? Do you know what? That bloody irks me! She hasn't had a good word to say about you for years.'

Will grinned. 'I had to do some major sweet-talking and she's no pushover. Problem was, she did think Vittorio was your father. Which is why she was so keen to keep us apart.'

Lisa pinched her lips together. She could imagine all too well how horrified Nan must have been when she'd heard they'd spent the night together. Nan knew plenty of people in the village – it wouldn't have taken long for her to hear about Lisa staying over. She laughed in relief before adding, 'And why Dorothea was so anxious to throw us out.'

'She's going to be mortified when she finds out.'

'Is she likely to find out?' asked Lisa, not imagining for a minute they'd probably ever meet her again.

'I suspect my mother,' he wriggled on the bench, his hand working into the pocket of his hoodie, 'may well spill the beans.'

Lisa rolled her eyes.

'You probably realise why your mum wanted the ring to go back to Vittorio.'

'Yes, it all makes sense now.'

'After you'd left it behind in Rome…'

She flinched. 'Don't… I.'

He shut her up with a kiss. 'Shush. I phoned him. And had a minor heart failure when he said you hadn't turned up.' The mock glare he shot her promised all sorts of retribution of a rather delicious kind. 'I went to meet him.'

'What was he like?' Lisa laced her fingers through his and let them rest on his jean-clad thigh.

'Apart from being my older double, which you spotted before you did a runner, actually quite a nice guy when he stopped being… well, I guess he was trying to protect himself as well. He did love your Mum. Really love her. But sadly for him, it was always Sir Robert and he couldn't bear it, so that's why he left and never took you with him. I felt quite sorry for him in a way. He'd like to meet you.'

'I'd like that too.' She stole a wary look at his face.

'Vittorio said the ring was mine now.'

Lisa nodded. Of course, it was. The rightful heir – and all that.

'But,' he paused, blue eyes suddenly intent, holding her gaze as he brought his hand out of his pocket and held up the velvet box, 'I'd like to give it to you.'

Her eyes widened and it felt as if a thousand currents of fine electricity rushed over her skin.

His throat convulsed. 'Neither of our parents, real or stand-in, are the best adverts for fidelity and happy-ever-after, but... I love you.

'I love you, Lisa Vettese, more than I thought I could ever love anyone. I want you to have the ring. It's a promise from me that I will do everything I can to make you happy and that you are the one and only woman I could ever envisage sharing my life with.' His lopsided smile held a tinge of nerves and hope. 'This is a very badly bungled kind of proposal. I know it's too early, we haven't even... lived together... or had a proper date. You might go off me. You might not want me, but I can't imagine ever wanting to be with anyone else but you. These last few days I've done nothing but think of you. I missed you. Tried to think of every reason why this would be a bad idea. And not one of them would stick. I don't want to make false promises. I've seen too many of those, but do you think you might have me if I asked you to marry me? One day?'

Lisa smiled, loving the way that he'd phrased things. Marriage was too big and scary at this stage, but a promise she could cope with. 'I think it's a very definite possibility. One day.'

His heavy exhale made her touch his lips, charmed to see the slight tremor of his hands as he opened the box.

When he solemnly slipped the ring on her middle finger for now, she thought her heart might burst at the serious expression on his face. 'This is commitment, big time.' And then the sunshine came out in his smile as he added, 'Do you think you'll cope?'

She grinned up at him. 'I can, if you can.'

'It's a deal, then.'

'It most definitely is.'

She held up her hand out in front of them, the brilliant stone twinkling in the sunshine. Will laced his fingers through hers and they stood together hand in hand, with a future that sparkled as brightly as the diamond on her finger. Life was so much better when you had someone to share it with. Thank goodness she'd realised that before it was too late.

Epilogue

It took a few seconds and the first few bars of the explosive notes before Lisa identified the unorthodox music. She turned to Will, frowning in puzzlement. Had the organist got it wrong? He shrugged, equally puzzled.

However, when she saw Cam's shaking shoulders and his lips pressed tight and heard the gale of laughter from the row of pews opposite, where a bevy of very brightly dressed ladies of varying ages sat, she realised that the dramatic rock music, which had now exploded into a fast tempo, was a very deliberate choice. She should have realised super-organised Laurie had planned every last detail.

Cam struggled to hold it together as the music rattled along at a tremendous pace, the most unlikely wedding march ever. He'd ducked his head, almost doubled over. Next to him, Jason elbowed him the ribs, as if to say come on, pull yourself together.

Then the music settled into a more gentle rolling piano melody and everyone shifted and rustled, peering around at the back of the church to look at Laurie framed in the light, on the arm of Eddie, who looked after the cars. With a serene smile on her face, she walked down the aisle. No gliding for Laurie, her purpose was clear in every step, with her eyes fixed on Cam at the front.

Tears sprang to Lisa's eyes and her heart did a funny salmon leap when she saw his face. The previous mirth replaced with guillotine swiftness, with such a solemn tender gaze, steady love beaming out like a beacon to bring her home. There might as well have been no one else in the room.

Will squeezed her hand and out of the corner of her eye, she could see that even he was swallowing hard. With a sudden rush of emotion, she realised that this what she wanted with Will. She'd missed him these last few weeks while she stayed at Merryview, but she hadn't felt she could abandon Cam and Laurie, not when there was so much to do in the house and for the wedding. They'd managed to spend some time together, with Will making regular visits, despite trying to get the restaurant ready for opening, and she'd made a trip to the pub for a very brief weekend, most of which had been spent in his bedroom.

When he looked down at her, those blue eyes boring into hers, warmth bloomed in her chest, making her breath come a little faster and her head swim in dizzy happiness.

As the glowing bride drew level with their pew, the heavy silk of her dress rustled, Lisa smiled, even that was pure Laurie. Classic, simple and beautifully cut. Her hair had been caught up in a chignon, dotted with tiny white flowers and her bouquet was a beautifully bound arrangement of scarlet red roses, which echoed the colour of the groom and best man's cravats, as well as Siena's dress.

A collective sigh whispered through the pretty chapel as Eddie relinquished Laurie's arm and she stepped up to stand beside Cam. Siena took Laurie's bouquet, looking angelically demure, her blonde hair loose down her back, a golden contrast to the scarlet of her dress. The butter-wouldn't-melt expression lasted a few seconds and then she gave Jason a mischievous smile, to which he responded with a quick wink, which lit up his saturnine, dark face.

The rest of the service was considerably more traditional after Meatloaf's 'Bat Out of Hell' musical intro, although Lisa was slightly concerned about what people would think about the buffet that awaited them back at Merryview. Seriously? Sausage rolls and Cornish pasties for a wedding buffet? She'd have expected something rather more sophisticated.

As they left the church, to stand in one happy crowd, the roar of a car engine pierced the cheerful chatter and everyone stopped as a silver Ferrari pulled up. Cam grinned and scooped Laurie up in his arms and carried her over the car. Eddie, who must have sneaked off to bring the car round, opened the passenger door and, with absolutely no regard for the beautiful wedding dress, Cam squished her and the dress into the front seat. As he walked around to the driver's side he mouthed something to Lisa.

She nodded and gave him the thumbs-up and pointed to the boot.

Laurie, who was laughing and shaking her head, whipped her head around to look at her groom and then turned back and waved as Cam revved the engine and the little silver Ferrari disappeared with a dragon's roar.

Siena came rushing over to Lisa's side. 'Are they coming back?'

Lisa shook her head. At Cam's request, she'd packed Laurie's bags for her. 'Nope. They've got a train to catch. Cam wanted to be in Paris in time for dinner.' And tonight, after all the guests had gone, she'd hand the keys over to Norah and return with Will tomorrow morning.

Jason and Will joined them. 'Personally, I think that's the way to do it,' said Jason, straight-faced, as Siena rolled her eyes. 'None of the speeches malarkey and having to mingle with all the relatives.'

Siena pulled a face. 'You have a point there.' And then a horrified expression crossed her face. 'Merde! Typical Laurie! She invited mother and now she's gone.'

Everyone burst out laughing. Jason pulled her to his side. 'So you'll agree to an elopement, then.'

Siena's head shot up, her eyes widening as her hands twisted together, the picture of uncertainty and a contrast to her usual perky confidence. 'Are you asking?'

Lisa didn't hear the answer as he led her away to the cedar-shaded corner to the side of the chapel.

'That's one way of doing it,' said Will. 'But I think we'd better make sure Nan keeps taking her medication.'

Lisa frowned, not quite following.

He kissed her. 'She'd be pretty pissed off if we did that – just eloped. And despite our complicated families, I'd want them all there. Maybe Sir Robert would give you away.'

'I think he'd like that,' she said in a choked voice.

She'd had an emotional meeting with Sir Robert over dinner.

He'd cried, which made her cry too. It was still early days and she couldn't imagine calling him 'Dad' yet, but they had plenty of time to get to know each other better.

With a warm smile, Will took her hand and slid her ring from the middle finger on her right hand before slipping it on to the fourth finger on her left hand. It was a touch loose, but she didn't care.

'Three weeks apart have been too bloody long. I want to marry you sooner rather than later. What do you think?'

Lisa's heart bumped unevenly in her chest, beating with an awkward rhythm not unlike a car with a flat tyre. She held his serious gaze, giving the question careful consideration before answering with a tremulous shake in her voice, 'I think it's a yes.'

'Oy, Ryan.' They both whirled around at Jason's shout, who was grinning and gesticulating with a thumbs-up.

Will groaned, 'Oh hell, I'm never going to hear the last of this.'

Jason mimed drinking a pint. 'Think I'll name my next beer in your honour. I'm thinking of calling it *Head over Heels.*'

Will grinned and pulled Lisa to his side.

'Absolutely fine by me.'

Printed by RR Donnelley at Glasgow, UK